TABLE OF CONTENTS

Writing The Eyeless

Unmade Stories

Contains Spoilers (Fitz's Poem)

INTRODUCTION

Hello, and thanks for reading this book.

As the first volume of *Time, Unincorporated* - a series that will reprint a wide range of *Doctor Who* fanzine writings - this is a collection of various things I've said about *Who* over the years. I love *Doctor Who*, and I've been lucky enough to write original *Doctor Who* novels, audio plays and short stories. I've also written about *Doctor Who* a lot, including a couple of academic articles and work for professional magazines. In the realm of *Doctor Who* non-fiction, though, I'm probably most associated with my timeline of the *Doctor Who* universe. It was first published as *The Doctor Who Chronology* (1994) by Seventh Door Fanzines, then as *A History of the Universe* by Virgin (1996), and it's still available as *AHistory* (2007).

Most of my work about *Doctor Who*, however, has been in fanzines. The first thing that I ever had published was an article about Douglas Adams in *The Pirate Planet* edition of *In-Vision* (1991). The next year, I was lucky enough to meet Mark Jones, then the editor of the fanzine *Matrix*, and wrote some articles for him. My first *Doctor Who* novel, *Just War*, was accepted during this time - and so my later *Matrix* articles were written by a newbie NA author. It was now my job, at least in part, to work out the appeal of *Doctor Who* - and, if possible, to bottle it.

In 2001, I began writing a column (entitled "Beige Planet Lance," a take-off of the Benny novel *Beige Planet Mars* I co-wrote with Mark Clapham) for one of the few remaining old-school, print fanzines: *Enlightenment*. It's published in Canada and backed by a fan club there, the Doctor Who Information Network (www.dwin.org), hence the occasional mention that I'm writing for a Canadian audience. I've really enjoyed writing a page about *Doctor Who* every few months, and if nothing else, my *Enlightenment* columns form a running commentary of a seven-year period (2001-2008) in which *Doctor Who* went from virtually being a cottage industry of books, audios and spin-off projects to returning to the airwaves and becoming the BBC's flagship series.

For *Doctor Who*'s fortieth anniversary in 2003, *Enlightenment* did something more systematic and ambitious - the whole of the November issue (#118) was my year-by-year survey of *Doctor Who*. I used each year to talk about a particular aspect of the series, but it's also a personal account - not something as dreary as a nostalgic look back at the sweets and haircuts and records I had in the seventies, but the first chance I'd had to set down formally what I thought *Doctor Who* was about. It's one person's view, but one, I hope, that celebrates the series, champions its strengths and sheer diversity. (If nothing else, there should be plenty for readers to argue with and get annoyed about.) As this overview is a self-contained entity, I've decided to lead this collection with it. I've also brought it up to date with entries covering the five years since then.

I'm often asked about writing *Doctor Who* novels, and so I kept a running blog while writing my latest book, *The Eyeless*. It's tidied up and also reproduced here, as well as my pitches for *The Infinity Doctors* (1997), *Warlords of Utopia* (2004) and an unmade novel called *To Hold Back Death*. Including them was a "now or almost never" proposition - I've informed Mad Norwegian that, as it took about 15 years for me to amass enough material for this volume, they could be a long time waiting for a second installment.

Historians might wish to know that the text presented here has been compiled from a number of sources. In many cases, digital versions of the published articles no longer exist; we've fallen back on my personal files where possible, but some articles were scanned. The text has been lightly edited, a little for style but mainly for typos (a necessity with the scanned articles, as the process left the text rife with glitches). However, we've resisted the urge to tinker with the content, doing our best to present the text warts and all. I concede that any long-running commentator winds up repeating himself / herself a bit, especially when they write about a series at length and then separately draft a 40-year overview about it - but it's not such a problem that we felt inclined to start cutting text, and have opted for completism.

I should close by saying that *Doctor Who*'s been an important part of my life - it's not the only thing going on in it, but I've met most of my best friends through it, and been given so many amazing opportunities. Above all, I love the attitude *Doctor Who* has, the emphasis on brains and respecting people, the value of diverse viewpoints and science and books and contrarianism, the way it never confuses being nice with weakness, the way that the worst crime in the universe is taking yourself too seriously. I'm nothing like the only person for whom a silly little TV series has been nothing but a positive force, and to see *Doctor Who* as it is here in 2009, at the apex of British cultural life, filling every toyshop and newspaper and at the top of the TV charts... well, part of me looks at that and - quoting the Doctor, naturally - says 'quite right, too'.

A FORTY YEAR ADVENTURE IN TIME AND SPACE

"First, Do No Harm"

an introduction by Lloyd Rose

It's very odd that the idea of the doctor, and of medicine, predates by thousands of years the actually ability of doctors to help anyone in more than small ways. Why should it be? Well, it's because we recognize the presence of evil as being stronger than the promise of a cure. The simple Hippocratic oath, "First, do no harm" is a far more radical sentence in the history of thought than it seems. It recognizes the existence of evil - illness - that is in many ways beyond our control. It is the opposite of magical thinking, witch-doctor think, which promises to make well, to cure. "Do no harm" is the truly radical sentence. "Cultivate your garden" the unforgivable one.

-French intellectual and author Andre Glucksmann

So you abandon your garden, your home planet, and set out to ameliorate suffering wherever you can. Admittedly, this wasn't exactly the idea when *Doctor Who* made its television debut. It conformed to the oldest mythological definition of the hero: someone who fights monsters to save his community. The Doctor saved Earth from Daleks and Cybermen and Krotons and Sontarans and various other invaders / monsters, some of them appealingly dressed in rubber suits with tinfoil accouterments. But a general detestation of all cruelty crept into the show: "All sapient creatures are our kin," the Doctor informed the destruction-bent Sutekh in *Pyramids of Mars*.

Of course, *Pyramids* was the same episode in which the henchmen were mummies, about whom the Doctor, dressed as a mummy himself in order to infiltrate them, reassured his companion, "I shall mingle with the mummies but I shan't linger." Sutekh looked like the spawn of a jackal and a cardboard box. The acting was variable. The sets didn't actually shake, as legend claims so many of them did, but in the inevitable corridor scenes it was a near thing.

In short, the show on one level engenders the perverse delight of a *Godzilla* movie. And the people who created and worked on, though they clearly and unashamedly loved what they were doing, were in on the joke. *Doctor Who* never took itself too seriously - it was light on its feet. The series occasionally descended to embarrassing levels of bad taste but was never rib-nudgingly camp. Unredeemable aesthetically, it had it its own kind of integrity. This combination of shabbiness and fairy-tale truth is what challenges the people behind the new reincarnation of the series. For silly as the Doctor may be, he's also a genuine folk hero. Of the pop variety to be sure, but enduring enough to last for forty years. No fictional character does this by accident.

There's been much debate about what exactly *Doctor Who* is. Science-fiction? Fantasy? Put-on? Comedy? It's not an exact fit with any of these categories. Yet the series isn't just a mishmash either. In an odd way, it harks back to the Grail legends with their monsters, elevation of virtue, and chaste heroes. Without sexual expression until the eighth Doctor actually kissed a girl (and given Paul McGann's looks, this was probably inevitable), the Doctor nonetheless seems not so much asexual as above such petty matters, beyond desire. Sex doesn't tempt him. Money doesn't interest him. Power bores him. He's like some oddball Zen master floating through time and space.

The Grail legends still have artistic and literary validity, but they're long gone as a vital myth, reduced to retellings and literary influences. The modern intellectual prejudice is towards irony, and this deprives the high arts of heroes. To find them you have to go to "disreputable" genre fiction that flies under the radar of irony, such as mysteries, science-fiction, fantasy novels and comic books, or to popular sometimes-art like television and the movies. (Mysteries have so far achieved the highest score: Sherlock Holmes is still going strong at 122 years.) Superman is perhaps the prime example, but *Star Trek* is in there too, not to mention cinema monsters like Dracula and Frankenstein (now cartooned on cereal boxes, but still identifiable).

In this pantheon, the Doctor is the Nerd Triumphant. Almost from the beginning he had the eccentricity and brilliance - and of course the outsider status, not just alienated but genuinely alien. With the entry of Gallifrey into the mythos, he even had a society to ostracise him. Quite often he'd been played by someone way outside the conventional standards of handsomeness. He's more honestly odd than the comic-book heroes, who almost all represent a fantasy of power. The Doctor is too adult a figure for this kind of wish-fulfillment. His closest comic book equivalent isn't Spider-Man or the Watchmen or even the mystical Sandman, but Professor X, the virtuous and id-less grown-up who acts as father-figure and sage to the X-Men. (And if it was an accident, it's still perfect that the fictitious version of the Doctor in the *Whoniverse* is called "Professor X.")

The Doctor stands for bullied outsiders who didn't turn bitter or angry or self-destructive. This is why he's believable as a figure of good. Though he's often presented as near-omnipotent, something about him suggests that it didn't come to him easily. There are shadows in him, traces of melancholy, a suggestion of loneliness. Possibly it comes from the deep knowledge that evil is, finally, beyond his powers.

As the decades passed, the Doctor, along with other icons of pop culture, matured and darkened. He began to show fallibility in his fifth incarnation, approached madness in his sixth, and by his seventh was beginning to abuse his power, manipulating and cheating for "the greater good." Not all of these developments worked - some were pretty embarrassing - but the progression was there. Optimism to uncertainty, confidence to relativism, hope to failure - the moral slide of the 20th century.

The Doctor began as an example of "magical thinking, witch-doctor think, which promises to make well, to cure." He's ended in the world of limitation, faced with how little he, or anyone, can change things. But he keeps fighting, still determined to say "No" to what everyone else accepts as inevitable corruption. He will always try to do no harm.

Lloyd Rose is the author of the acclaimed *Doctor Who* books *The City of the Dead* and *Camera Obscura*. She has written for the TV series *Kingpin* and *Homicide: Life on the Streets*, and for ten years was the theatre critic of *The Washington Post*.

1963

The reason we're here is simple: *Doctor Who* is the perfect format for a long-running series.

If we were to take a time machine and travel back to the spring or summer of 1963 to talk to the creators of *Doctor Who*, what would we say? No-one involved in the drawing up of plans for the new Saturday evening family series would believe us if we told them they were creating something that would endure. People who'd happily go on to create robots powered by static electricity and time machines fuelled by mercury would probably laugh if we told them that the records use lasers for needles in our day. While they could just about have imagined a series of books and records based on the show, how on earth would we explain to them what a 'webcast' was? The idea that *Doctor Who* could survive the end of the television show itself would be inconceivable - it's pretty hard to believe in 2003, after all.

Doctor Who was a weird mix of old and new - the BBC had been chartered in the 1920s, at a time when the prevailing political philosophy was utopian in outlook, and revolved around a meritocratic elite educating and protecting the population. The BBC was an arm of this - it was genuinely believed that television's prime purpose was to better those who watched it. The BBC charter, drawn up by Lord Reith, says they are there to 'entertain and inform', and to this day they are essentially a government-funded organisation whose purpose is - at least in theory - to educate.

In 1963, BBC television was reeling from the success of ITV, the second channel, one that took *commercials*, and which had no mandate except to deliver big audiences to advertisers. *Doctor Who* was commissioned by Sydney Newman, a new broom at the BBC as Head of Drama, brought in specifically to shake up the status quo. Newman was Canadian, but the thing that would really mark him out as 'foreign' at the BBC was that he'd worked in commercial television. He brought new thinking to the BBC, including a sharp awareness of demographics. *Doctor Who* wasn't created out of any love of science fiction or for any artistic reason at all, it was designed to fit a specific 'transitional' spot in the TV schedules - bridging the gap between the sports results and the start of music show *Juke Box Jury*. It was designed to appeal both to dad and to his children. It was family viewing, in other words, and it's no coincidence that the four regular characters provide identification figures for three generations, or that the adults are defined in roles that the younger children would understand - grandfather and two teachers.

Doctor Who was an adventure serial, one there to grab audiences. The

Reithian 'old BBC' attitude was still there, though. These weren't mindless romps - the historical stories would be well-researched and as accurate as the format allowed. The futuristic stories would be morality plays, or would at least try to demonstrate some scientific principle or other.

Two pressures, then - to produce something worthy, but also commercial. Looking at the paths not taken for the show is interesting. The show was always going to be 'science fiction', but the idea of it being either 'literary' science fiction or a more pulpy 'flying saucers' series was dropped. Newman drew the distinction between 'philosophical' stories and 'applied' ones, and *Doctor Who* would be a show in which the hero was practical, in which the regulars had a clear problem to solve.

Lately, *Doctor Who* fans have thought about what the 'comeback' story would be like. How would you introduce *Doctor Who* as a concept to a modern audience? You'd do something very like *An Unearthly Child*. Forty years on, the very first episode of *Doctor Who* still has a good claim to be the best single instalment of the show. It's a story told on such a small scale - only the four regulars have lines and the last half of the episode is a single scene on a single set - but which hints that there's a whole universe just within reach. Unlike the 1996 Paul McGann movie, it never takes the idea of a mysterious man in a time machine for granted. And the first episode ends on a great cliff-hanger.

Doctor Who was very much of its time. But this mix of the old and new would go on to define an era of art. Some scholars trace the beginning of postmodernism to the assassination of JFK. If that's true, *Doctor Who* is the very first art of the postmodern age. *Doctor Who* was something new, something different. And something infinitely larger once you got inside...

1964

There was plenty of *Doctor Who* in 1964 - from the third episode of the first Dalek story, through to the end of *The Dalek Invasion of Earth*. As with a lot of shows, it's interesting to see *Doctor Who* developing before our eyes. The contrast between the first and second Dalek stories is fascinating. Before *Doctor Who* started, there was the sense that it would be entirely worthy. Sydney Newman approached - amongst others - playwright Don Taylor to write for the show, who wondered in his autobiography *Days of Vision* what would have happened:

'the ubiquitous Doctor might have become a trooper in the New Model Army, and a pal of John Lilburne's, or what kind of Orwellian political

futures he might have explored, and how the dramas of European social-
ism and the language of poetry might have impinged upon the voyagers
in the TARDIS.'

Terry Nation had a rather different vision for the show.

Scholars have noted that for the first six weeks, ITV were running an
SF thriller, *Emerald Green*, opposite *Doctor Who*. One of the terrible truths
about television is that your ratings depend far more on what's on the
other side or the weather than anything you're doing. The reason the ratings shot up during the Dalek serial may have more to do with a rival
show ending than anything *Doctor Who* was doing. But perhaps that's
revisionism taken too far. The Daleks were clearly instantly popular.
They, to use the phrase, 'caught the imagination'. Terry Nation's first
scripts may borrow rather heavily from *Dan Dare* and *The Time Machine*,
but they're really clever uses of television. With an average episode
budget of £2300 to play with, he created an alien world in a TV studio
that was barely bigger than the front rooms of the families watching the
show. Each episode is a model of suspense and imagination. You only
need to compare and contrast it with the other contender for the slot, *The
Masters of Luxor*, which is a clever story, but it's slow, it's sedentary and
it seriously outstays its welcome. The Dalek story just races along, and
each individual episode is a nice self-contained piece of drama. The most
dominant characteristic is ambition - this is a story where the writer has
just let rip, where a lesser writer would be consumed with the limits of
the budget and other resources.

It changed the face of the show. Terry Nation had been discussing
doing a historical story set in colonial India. Instead, he ended up writing romps like *The Keys of Marinus* and *The Chase*. The first series tended
to be quite small scale, and a little samey - the regulars would get sepa-
rated from the TARDIS and they'd face a little local difficulty that led
them to a rather desperate battle just to survive and all get back to the
ship. There are some great stories in the first season - the first episode,
the first Dalek story, *Marco Polo* and *The Aztecs*, but the original, serious,
Doctor Who is already wearing a bit thin by the end of the first year.

The second series, though, just cuts loose. Each story experiments with
the form of the show. While there was the odd moment of humour or
dramatic irony in the first set of stories, the second season visibly relax-
es. It's the luxury of success, of course. *Doctor Who* was a hit.

Once again, Terry Nation set the scene. The second Dalek story is just
out and out action adventure, with the only thing you could possibly
gloss as educational being the Doctor's discovery that magnets are magnetic in the cell on the Dalek saucer. The recent DVD release does the

story no favours - the murky old VHS hid some truly horrible production values, and now that it's not a struggle to watch, the script seems
confused in places: did the Daleks firebomb London or not? David
defused the firebomb (using that trusty method of disarming weapons of
mass destruction, pouring acid on it then poking it with a big stick). But
later, there are references to the firebomb going off... and later still, the
Doctor and company get back to the TARDIS, in London. The
Susan/David romance is all there in the script, but Carole Ann Ford and
Peter Fraser seem not to have noticed. The story is also more studio
bound than you remember. But none of this detracts from the fact that
this is a whole new way of telling a *Doctor Who* story - the whole first season only had one short location insert, and not a single alien being menacing the Earth. *Doctor Who* was beginning to evolve - and for the first
time *The Dalek Invasion of Earth* saw the show in the top ten programmes
for the week.

1965

It's odd to think that *Doctor Who* hit its high point thirty-eight years
ago, and has never really recovered that popularity. The only time it
would come close is in the early Tom Baker seasons. The ratings speak
for themselves: the second season was the only time when *Doctor Who*
was regularly in the UK top ten programmes. Twenty episodes in a row
got more than ten million viewers (a feat only matched by Season
Fourteen). It's difficult to imagine *Doctor Who* as being anything other
than 'cult viewing' now, but in 1965 it was mass entertainment, a massive hit for the BBC.

It was also the era of Dalekmania. Sometimes the articles about the
popularity of the Daleks overplay their success. What happened in 1965
was tame by the standards of today's multimedia and franchised TV
shows and films. Far more *Doctor Who* stuff has come out this year, nearly fifteen years after the show went off the air, than did in 1965. While it
wasn't taken for granted that a show would generate spin offs, it wasn't
exactly unprecedented - James Bond, *Dan Dare* and *Thunderbirds* all had
books and toys. But it is extraordinary thing how many toy companies
wanted to make Daleks. There are dozens of basic model Daleks - clockwork, friction driven, with ball bearings, battery operated; small, medium and large. Then there are the kites, skittles, board games, water pis-
tols. Looking at the photos of them, the one thing the toys seem to have
in common is that the people modelling them seem to have done so from
memory, or at times apparently from a vague description.

It's difficult to tell exactly how big the craze was these days - the reports of fans who were there at the time might not be as objective as we might like. But in June, with the Cushing movie coming out during the run of *The Chase*, it must have felt like a phenomenon, and the first generation of *Doctor Who* completists must have already been despairing. Print runs never indicate actual sales, but *The Dalek Pocketbook* and *The Dalek World* had print runs of more than 300,000, and we know that more than a million of the cheapest Dalek toys, the Rolykins, were sold.

The makers of the show always knew the Daleks would be a hit - Terry Nation was commissioned to write a follow up Dalek story before he'd finished the one he was working on. David Whitaker found himself writing or co-writing Dalek books in his spare time. For many years, we had a distorted view of the show in 1965. It was received wisdom that the science fiction stories were both more popular and more interesting than the historical ones, and the Dalek ones were more popular still. In fact, the show prospered throughout the year - *The Web Planet* had another memorable monster in the Zarbi, so its success was perhaps assured, but *The Romans* was watched by more people than ever watched a Dalek story, at least until ITV went on strike in 1979. The second series has a range of styles, and every story has something to recommend it - even *The Chase*, which is confident enough to start mocking the conventions of the series. It's also the story where Ian and Barbara go, and the series becomes the William Hartnell show. It and *The Time Meddler* subtly alter the rules, allowing science fiction to encroach into the stories set in the past.

Nowadays, with every episode that exists out on video, we've had a chance to see these stories for ourselves. It's nearly forty years old, and looks extremely creaky - *The Crusade* is a great script, and has a good cast, but it's particularly cheap-looking. It's perhaps best enjoyed as a novelisation (a book that really bears re-reading, if only to demonstrate that in 1965, there were no qualms about publishing S&M children's books). Over the course of forty years, we've seen a variety of styles, to the point where it's hard to see any common thread or factor that applies to the whole of *Doctor Who*. Fans often say they like the show because the TARDIS can land anywhere, that the Doctor can find himself doing anything. It's perhaps only the 1965 run of episodes where that's actually what happens. The show was confident enough to experiment, it wasn't yet bogged down by expectation or precedent. This genuinely was a time when each story didn't just have a different setting, but a different genre.

1965 wasn't just the high point commercially and in ratings terms, it really has a claim to be the most artistically successful in *Doctor Who*'s long history. After that, though, there was only one way to go...

1966

One of the most baffling unanswered questions about *Doctor Who* is why it wasn't cancelled in 1966. Ratings literally halved - *The Chase* part five got 9 million viewers and was the 11th most watched show that week. *The Savages* part four, exactly a year later, got 4.5 million and was 93rd. That's just to pick a week at random - there are far more marked contrasts: *The Web Planet* 1 (13/02/65) got 13.5 million viewers and was 7th, *The Smugglers* had one episode that got 4.2 million (24/09/66) and the following week's was 109th.

The reason why was simple - *Batman*. The Adam West TV show was scheduled aggressively against *Doctor Who* by most ITV regions, and it was as much an instant sensation as it had been in the USA. The *Doctor Who* craze was replaced by another one, with plenty of new toys and books and games in the shops.

It's obvious, when you look at it, that *Doctor Who* had run its course. The ratings were down, the quality of the stories was down, the companions were pretty unmemorable, the star of the show was that most deadly of combinations: ill and well paid (some reports have William Hartnell as the highest paid actor at the BBC at the time - to put it in perspective, in 1966 we know he was paid more than the combined salaries of the entire regular cast of *Blakes 7* would be during their first season, more than a decade later). The merchandise boom had just vanished - the *Transcendental Toybox* lists 41 Dalek toys issued in 1965, only two in 1966, one of which was simply a red variant of one of the Louis Marks toys from the previous year.

There's never been the slightest hint that the BBC thought of cancelling *Doctor Who* at this point. Did the BBC see *Batman* as a temporary blip? This turned out to be the case - while it would never hit the heights it had in 1965, *Doctor Who*'s ratings would recover and level off. Was it simply that they didn't have anything to replace the show? It looks like *Doctor Who* survived because of some exceptionally lucky timing: new producer Innes Lloyd was already talking to Patrick Troughton in June, just as the ratings started to dip. Rather than seeing him as a man who was presiding over a collapse in the show's fortune, his BBC bosses must have seen Lloyd as the man with the vision to save *Doctor Who*.

Innes Lloyd wasn't making *Doctor Who* like it had been made before - he was taking the 'Doctor Who and the Daleks' of the popular imagination. It was an amalgam of the Cushing movies, the comic strips and the existing show. The emphasis was on the monsters, on fast-moving action. The stories immediately before Lloyd came on board are all quite complex - alliances shift and people double cross and are double crossed in turn. They're all quite intricately plotted. Lloyd stripped that away to simple tales of good versus evil, with strong bad guys doing very straightforward villainy. The Daleks might pretend to be good guys in *The Power of the Daleks*, but no-one believes them, and it's ten minutes before the horrible truth is revealed.

While Lloyd's predecessor, John Wiles, seemed a little overwhelmed by the popularity of the show - and he was lumbered with a vast Dalek story - Lloyd grasped the bull by the horns. In the space of a year, *Doctor Who* became a very different show. The historical stories were dropped - despite still being just as popular as the science fiction ones. The female companion had traditionally been a granddaughter type - a petite young teenager. Polly was the very first 'dollybird' companion, the first who could be called a sex symbol. The Cybermen - the first monsters since the Daleks to rate a second appearance - made their debut. *The War Machines* saw the first story where monsters invaded contemporary Earth. Most radically, of course, not only was the part of the Doctor recast, but so was the character. Gone was the twinkly-eyed grandfather scientist, in came an eccentric middle-aged adventurer. The first Doctor insisted that they mustn't interfere, only observe... the second was there to fight monsters, and said so.

The genius of regenerating the Doctor - not that it was called 'regeneration' until *Planet of the Spiders* - is self-evident, and it's amazing how readily the audience seem to have embraced the idea. But it was simply the most obvious stage of a process that saw *Doctor Who* go from being a surprise hit to a format capable of surviving the departure of the lead actor. Innes Lloyd's contribution to the show isn't often recognised, but he's the man that created *Doctor Who* as we know it.

1967

In 1967, for the first time, *Doctor Who* settled down. It had recovered in the ratings, and was now a fixture at the lower end of the top forty programmes. More importantly, though, Innes Lloyd had transformed the show into, paradoxically, one that was far more like the popular image of *Doctor Who*: a show where lots of monsters invaded Earth (something which had happened in precisely two stories beforehand - one of those being the little-watched *The War Machines*). The historical stories had gone, replaced with yarns about the Abominable Snowmen and Atlantis. The Cybermen appeared twice, the Daleks reappeared, the Yeti and Ice Warriors made their debut. The second season had been marked by experimentation, and the third had flailed around looking for novelty. The fourth and fifth seasons were incredibly formulaic, with almost every story being what fans would later call 'base under siege'. An isolated community of humans - often scientists - is being menaced by monsters who want some device the humans have. Someone in the base is either a willing traitor or is being controlled in some way by the monsters.

Doctor Who got away with it for a very simple reason - every four or six weeks a new story would start, set in an entirely new place, with all but three castmembers changing. It gives the illusion that the Doctor and pals are having a wildly diverse set of adventures.

Nowadays we have an additional problem - only one of the stories from 1967 is complete in the archives: *The Tomb of the Cybermen*, recovered in the early nineties. We're in an odd position with the lost stories. Some of these stories (*The Moonbase, Tomb, The Abominable Snowmen* and *The Ice Warriors*) were among the first to be novelised. Every British fan remembers the scene where the Ice Warrior looms over a screaming Victoria, electricity crackling around its claws. Added to this, older fans in the seventies could fondly remember the monsters. Myths grew up around the stories. Nowadays, we also have the soundtracks and telesnaps to help us try to assess them. There's at least one episode of *most* stories. So they're a weird mix of the utterly familiar and the totally unknown. It's something of a theme with *Doctor Who* fandom - we all think we know these stories, but if the missing episodes were discovered there would be all sorts of pleasant surprises and quiet disappointments. But they aren't really 'lost' at all - we don't consider *Hamlet* a lost play, even though we don't know what the first performance was like. What we have instead - and this is something that we'll come back to later - is *notional Doctor Who*. A *Doctor Who* that we all instinctively know and think of as 'traditional', but which has never actually existed. It's the *Doctor Who* that's in our head, rather than the one that ever found its way to videotape. The Troughton era, more than any other, is more of a feeling than something we've experienced.

Older fans could lord it over the young in the late seventies and eighties - they'd seen *The Evil of the Daleks* and *The Tomb of the Cybermen*, and had been traumatised by the experience. If *Tomb* was ever found, the BBFC would never allow such a 'video nasty' to be released. When *Tomb of the Cybermen* came out, some fans expressed the wish that it had never been found. The horror story they'd grown up *knowing* about turned out to be a very well made piece of sixties children's television, not the ultimate *Doctor Who* experience. Troughton, as ever, wasn't some dark, manipulative figure, but a (far more entertaining) overgrown schoolboy. The Cybermats were, as ever, a bit rubbish. The Cybermen, as ever, had - at best - a vague plan and didn't live up to their premise.

With every surviving episode out on video, now, there's been a complete reassessment of the black and white era. Some fans have flocked to stories like *The Massacre* and *Fury from the Deep* as examples of the *Doctor Who* holy grail. At the time, both were rather forgettable, although the audio tracks suggest that both have surprisingly good scripts. Indeed, ironically, it's the historical stories that now seem to be better written, acted and made than the science fiction ones. Being able to watch, rewind, compare and contrast the Season Six episodes that do exist, it's often a case of a memorable monster and a forgettable story.

1968

The advent of VHS tapes, the Radio Collection CDs, the Missing and Past Doctor adventures and factual books like the excellent *Second Doctor Handbook* means that the eighties fan cliché that Troughton was the 'forgotten Doctor' is now faintly ridiculous. But one of the things that marks out his era is a lack of public profile for the series. Troughton himself was reputedly reluctant to give interviews, but it doesn't exactly look like the magazines or newspapers were falling over themselves to talk to him. Fraser Hines seems to have had a slightly higher profile - indeed, solely on the strength of his *Doctor Who* role, he was felt to be the only 'name' actor in *Emmerdale Farm* when it started in 1972. Famously, Joe Orton, ahem, 'admired' Jamie in his diaries.

One symptom of the show's low profile is the almost total lack of spin-off products. If a *Doctor Who* fan wanted to buy every single piece of official merchandise that came out in 2003, he would spend over £1000. If he added in the various tangential spin-offs, like the Benny audios or the *Faction Paradox* comic, he could spend several hundred pounds more. In 2003, even if you have the money, it's almost impossible to keep track of the various releases, let alone find the time to enjoy them all. This isn't unprecedented - in 1965 and 1966, you'd need a small fortune to buy all the toys, games and books available. Plus you'd have to track them all down yourself, without any *Doctor Who* specialist shops or web pages to helpfully list everything for you. Writing *The Transcendental Toybox* in 2000, David J Howe, the undisputed world expert on *Doctor Who* merchandise, was still unearthing *Doctor Who* stuff from the mid-sixties that he'd previously not known about.

Buying every piece of *Doctor Who* merchandise released in 1968 would cost you about twenty shillings - the price of the Annual (the one with Jamie, the Doctor and the Cybermen on the cover), the Fraser Hines single "Who's Doctor Who" and a year's worth of *TV Comic*. After a boom in *Doctor Who* merchandise in 1965-6, there was a serious lull until Jon

Pertwee's second season, after which the *Doctor Who* industry has never looked back. This lull, of course, encompasses the whole of Patrick Troughton's tenure.

One important reason for this lack of merchandise is that a lot of the stuff released in the Hartnell era - it would be fair to say the vast majority - was related to the Daleks. Terry Nation had withdrawn the rights to the Daleks, with a view to taking a series based around them to America. *The Evil of the Daleks* was the last story to feature them on TV, the *TV Comic* strip abruptly changed from *Doctor Who and the Daleks* to just *Doctor Who* at the same time (the summer of 1967). *The Daleks* strip in *TV Century 21* had ended in January that year.

The Cybermen just didn't catch on in the same way, even though they were heavily-featured on television. In 1968, *The Invasion* was clearly an attempt to do an 'epic' in the same vein of *The Daleks' Master Plan* (and it became practically a pilot episode for the future of the show). The Cybermen are on the cover of the 1968 Annual, and they featured in the comic strip. But the toy companies just didn't bite - there wasn't a single Cyberman toy, jigsaw or even a badge. The reason for this is unclear. The Cybermen change design for every story (except *Tomb*), but each time they have 'handle' ears and boxes on their chests. And, frankly, the accuracy of some of the sixties Daleks toys demonstrates that the toy manufacturers weren't worried too much by faithful reproduction of the monsters from the telly. The Cybermen are more generic a design than the Daleks, but they're more interesting and distinctive than just a simple 'robot man'.

The BBC wouldn't have pushed the Cybermen then in the way they'd push the Teletubbies or Fimbles now, but they would clearly listen to companies who approached them. Why wasn't there more merchandise? Well, the conclusion has to be that - for the only time in *Doctor Who*'s history - the demand just wasn't there.

1969

Terrance Dicks is seen today as perhaps the embodiment of all that's traditional about *Doctor Who*. His recent *Doctor Who* work... by which I mean his work in the last *twenty years*... has tended to plough a familiar furrow, recycling characters and concepts from his previous TV work, like the Death Zone, Rutans, Morbius and vampires, as well as characters created while he was script editor, or which he developed, like the Ogrons, Draconians and Borusa. If it lapses into a self-parodying mass of shocks of hair, blows to the solar plexus and grimaces, then there's never any doubt that the author knows exactly what he's doing. At its worst -

and there's little doubt that's *The Eight Doctors* - it stops being the greatest hits and looks more like a cheap compilation put out to fulfill some contractual obligation. But, while there's certainly evidence that Dicks needs an editor willing to push him, when that happens, books come out that do very well in polls, and his books have always sold more than anyone else's.

Terrance Dicks, then, is Mr Traditional, the man who personifies good old *Doctor Who* like it used to be - the implication being that many of the novels and audios these days take too much pleasure in deviating from that sort of *Doctor Who*. But Terrance Dicks was responsible for overturning what *Doctor Who* was. Each new producer and script editor has stamped their mark on *Doctor Who*. No-one else, not even Innes Lloyd before him, went through the format so systematically with an eye to changing, discarding and adding.

Dicks' first story as script editor was *The Invasion*. While Lethbridge-Stewart had been introduced the previous year, in *The Web of Fear*, *The Invasion* was the first appearance of 'the Brigadier' and of UNIT. *The War Games* finally answered the question implied (if not actually asked) by the series' title. It's an epic ten-parter, but the actual revelations and appearance of the Doctor's home planet are all in a packed final episode. So, for the first time, the Doctor was a Time Lord. The next story, *Spearhead from Space* was as close to a clean break with the past as it's possible to get in a running series - a new Doctor (now with another heart!), a new companion... but most of all, an entirely new premise for the series, one that would soon lead to the Doctor's 'old enemy', the Master, showing up for the first time of many. The TARDIS was all but gone, and the monsters now came to the Doctor rather than vice versa. More than thirty years on, it's tempting to imagine that these things were always part of the *Doctor Who* format. It's tempting to go back and see their roots in the Hartnell era, with 'renegade Time Lord' the Monk, and *The War Machines* seeing the Doctor team up with soldiers to prevent robots overrunning near-contemporary London. It's tempting to imagine that the Silurians, Ogrons, Master and Autons were 'old monsters'. But the truth is that Derrick Sherwin and Terrance Dicks pretty much threw out what had gone before. It would be the third season before the Daleks, then the Ice Warriors, made a return appearance (the big recurring baddies of the Troughton era, the Cyberman, only showed up for two seconds in *Carnival of Monsters*).

The irony was that 1969 was the first time that *Doctor Who* faced cancellation. The ratings weren't particularly bad - they were a little down on the previous year, but one episode was watched by nine million people for the first time since *The Daleks' Master Plan*. Perhaps one clue why the show was under threat can be gleaned by the lack of merchandise. The BBC has never been a commercial operation, it's not that they looked at sales of Dalek toys and decided the show was now unviable. But it is perhaps a symptom that *Doctor Who* was no longer a 'hot' show, one that kids were excited about.

In the event, two things seem to have saved *Doctor Who* at this point. One is that the BBC couldn't find anything to replace it. The proposed series *Snowy Black*, about an Australian fish-out-of-water in London sounds a bit like *Crocodile Dundee* - it also sounds like it wouldn't have lasted very long at all. The other was that the BBC had Jon Pertwee on their books, and couldn't find a suitable vehicle for him that mixed comedy, acting and an appeal to a family audience. Pertwee had become a popular figure on BBC radio, and the Corporation didn't want to lose him to ITV.

So, the changes overseen by Terrance Dicks weren't the reason for *Doctor Who*'s survival. But they would help with the nearest thing the show ever had to a relaunch...

1970

Doctor Who almost didn't make it to the seventies, and then it very nearly didn't make it to 1971. Reports have it that *Inferno* was written with one eye on being the very last *Doctor Who* story. We don't know how closely the BBC management were monitoring the show, but Season Seven looks for all the world like a radical revamp, designed to see if the series deserved a reprieve.

The big change was one that only a minority of the audience would have noticed at the time - the show was now being made in colour. Most British families still had black and white sets. The switch to colour did have one benefit, though - CSO technology, which only worked on colour video, allowed a new range of special effects. *Doctor Who* was at the forefront of experiments with the technique - indeed the next couple of years would see some rather gratuitous uses of CSO. It meant the audience could now see the Doctor being confronted by a dinosaur, the weird interior of an alien spaceship and lava flows. It would be the next season before the writers realised some of the true potential of the technique, though.

Season Seven is perhaps the hardest to fit into the *Doctor Who* canon. After *Spearhead from Space* there are three long stories that feel a bit like hangovers from the sixties, with plotting that meanders from the leisurely to the made-up-as-they-go-along. But they also have a real 'twenty minutes into the future' feel, with the Doctor pitched into a Britain with revolutionary nuclear power stations, drilling experiments and, of course, an extensive space programme. All of these things were exactly what kids of the early 1970s were told the immediate future would be like - even the Mars mission, which seems rather science fictional now. In 1970, flush with the success of the Apollo missions to the Moon, NASA assumed they would land men on Mars in the early eighties... and that 'half the human population' would be working in space by 2050. While the reference books always cite Liz as a 'companion', she's not really playing quite the same subservient role as Zoe, Jo or Sarah, she's more Scully to the Doctor's Mulder.

The most interesting change is that the Doctor doesn't really win in any of the longer stories - he prevents our Earth from being destroyed in *Inferno*, but he's helpless to save the other one; *The Silurians* ends in genocide, literally while the Doctor turns his back; and *The Ambassadors of Death* is more of a no score draw than a victory, with the aliens and humans not wiping each other out (it's an odd ending, as the story just sort of stops). There are monsters in every story, but again - with the possible exception of the Autons - they're not quite as cartoony as the ones Troughton faced. There are no supervillains like Tobias Vaughn - the human traitors and madmen are rather petty, Little Englander types.

The look of the series isn't a radical break - by the sixth season, the once-studio-bound series often had quite lavish location work. But it had never been quite so extensive for quite so many stories in a row. The reduction in the number of episodes seems to have seen at least a modest rise in budgets. Again, if we think the Troughton era was all like *The Krotons* or *The Mind Robber*, then Season Seven looks completely new, but the reality was that The Invasion could fit in there effortlessly. *Doctor Who* had been heading this way, and it's tempting to see The Invasion now as a showcase for how *Doctor Who* was going to look.

Doctor Who, obviously, wasn't cancelled at the end of Season Seven. Ratings were up very slightly, but there wasn't a sudden surge in popularity. It's unclear quite when the production team were told there would be an eighth season, but we do now know that the 'new look' Season Seven had given the show would be heavily modified - toned down, it could be said - when *Doctor Who* returned. So it's clear that there's plenty that wasn't felt to be working. But *Doctor Who* had a new lease of life, and it would very quickly repay the BBC's faith in it...

1971

The eighth season of *Doctor Who* saw Pertwee settle into the role, and under Barry Letts' control, the show became more cuddly and friendly than the previous year. Yates and Jo gave a warmer face to UNIT, which now became rather pally. Unprecedented for *Doctor Who*, there was now a regular cast of six, including the Master. There was now some location filming in places that weren't quarries or refineries, and the cast and crew seemed to have made the most of their away days. When the cast were asked what their favourite story was, they'd always say *The Daemons*. For years, trusting fans assumed that this was because of the script or the story, but the reason they loved it must be obvious: the cast got to stay in a lovely village for a week and got mobbed by adoring fans.

What was most remarkable is how quickly the 'new format' was taken for granted. In part, this is because there was a younger audience, then, and already there were fans too young to remember Patrick Troughton. Just as important, though, there was a mainstream audience and the production team weren't reiterating the past all the time. To all intents and purposes, the show had always starred Jon Pertwee, it was always about a Time Lord exiled to Earth and working for UNIT. MAs and PDAs set during the Pertwee era have incorporated Ian and Barbara, had UNIT remarking on the 'WOTAN incident' and so on. *Doctor Who* in 1971 managed to lose Liz Shaw off-screen, with a single line explaining where she went.

There was a glimmer of the past this season - the Doctor's greatest fear is revealed in *The Mind of Evil*, and it's a parade of old monsters. It's a bit odd to see Koquillon in there - how many of the eight million people watching would have recognised him? - but the rest of the faces are all icons of the show. The year started, of course, with a second Auton story. *Doctor Who* wasn't in denial of its past, but it would create new bits of it as often as it referred to old TV shows - the Doctor's Time Lord friend who showed up at the beginning of the season being just one example. After six years where the Doctor's past was a mystery, now he'd always been a Time Lord, and seemed happy to tell all and sundry... if they didn't already know.

The main development of this season would be the creation of a new villain who would endure: the Master. The Doctor's arch-enemy is now an integral part of the format. Big Finish round off their 'villains' series with him, he's in *Scream of the Shalka*, he's one of the few old baddies to reappear in the EDAs since *The Ancestor Cell*. Significantly, he's the main baddy in both the *Comic Relief* spoof *The Curse of Fatal Death* and was seen as one of the essential elements of the series by Philip Segal - his presence is pretty much the only constant throughout all the various drafts of what would become the 1996 *TVM*.

The odd thing is that the Master's... well... not exactly one of the show's most original creations. *DWM* always used to call him 'The

Doctor's Moriarty', but Moriarty wasn't just Sherlock Holmes with a black deerstalker and evil magnifying glass. The Master's appeal is simple - he's just the Doctor, but nasty. There's very little beyond that. The other thing is that he's a complete rip-off of the Hood from *Thunderbirds*. The 'revamp' of *Doctor Who* that Sherwin and Dicks organised often seemed to be heavily influenced by other things (one of which is Marvel Comics of the time - the Doctor's exile is rather like the Silver Surfer's, and UNIT, particularly early on, are very like SHIELD, even down to the flying HQ in *The Invasion*). But the Hood and the Master could be the same person. The Hood wore rubber masks, hypnotised people and ran an extraordinarily broad evil campaign where the ultimate aim was... rather vague. Like the Hood, the Master wants to steal missiles, start wars, blow people up and so on. But the Master was quickly one of the most popular characters... indeed, during the filming of *The Daemons*, in April 1971, the crowd seemed to like him more than the Doctor himself.

Doctor Who had a confident, successful present. Ratings were up again, the show was regularly back in the top thirty programmes for the first time in years (before *Colony in Space*, the last time two consecutive episodes managed such a feat was *Galaxy Four* in 1965!). *The Daemons* is not the all time classic we were told it was for years, but it's full of energy and confidence.

With the future assured and the present a success, it was time to look to the past.

1972

Let's get one thing straight. *The Three Doctors* isn't the 'tenth anniversary story'. It's the story that marked the start of the tenth season. Splitting hairs, I know, but look - this is the entry for 1972, and I'm talking about *The Three Doctors*. The first episode was broadcast on 30 December 1972, five weeks to the day after the ninth anniversary.

There are a fair few dramas on British TV nowadays that have run for more than ten years - but they're all soaps, however much some of their producers would say they are 'drama serials'. With one exception, they all started after *Doctor Who*. For the record, *Coronation Street* is that exception, the others are *Emmerdale*, *A Touch of Frost*, *EastEnders*, *The Bill*, *Heartbeat*, *Casualty*, *Byker Grove* and *Grange Hill*. Television is pretty ruthless at culling shows even now, and the *Frasiers* and *The Simpsons* of the world are the exception, not a trend. Any show approaching that ten year mark starts to feel the weight of the past. Many, if not all, of the original cast and writers will have moved on, there will - hopefully - be a golden age of the show that the viewers at least dimly remember and prefer to the current run.

Doctor Who got a past on 20 April 1972. That's when the first edition of *The Making of Doctor Who* was published. The day it came out, the cover must have marked it out as very contemporary - it had a Sea Devil on it, a couple of weeks after *The Sea Devils* had been shown on TV. It did what the title said, running through how an episode of television was made, explaining the different departments and stages of the process. Is it any wonder so many *Who* fans have ended up working in TV? It's very tempting to imagine that Mark Gatiss, Russell Davies, Gareth Roberts and Paul Cornell sat reading the book scribbling down notes. Even now, *The Making of Doctor Who* remains one of the very best introductions to how British television is made.

But what this book also did was articulate the history of *Doctor Who* for the first time, right up to the end of *The Sea Devils*. It ran through the fictional history, for a start. It's hard to believe, now that we've all got the stories memorised by rote, but this was the first time that a member of the public could see a list of all the *Doctor Who* stories. Not just that, there was a list of writers, directors and producers... even production codes.

The show was growing up with its audience for the first time. As *The Making of Doctor Who* noted, some of the children who watched the first episode now had children of their own. The show had always been aimed at both adults and children, but it was perhaps now aimed at older children than before. For the first time, we also started to get a sense that the show was getting sent letters. The Blinovitch Limitation Effect scene in *Day of the Daleks* looks for all the world like an answer to letters they'd been sent, and *The Sea Devils* corrects the 'Silurian' stuff, after people wrote in pointing out that the Silurian period was far too early for the reptile men to have lived.

Of the six stories of 1972, only *The Mutants* doesn't feature a returning character. There's a *Doctor Who* universe for the first time. The show had always dropped in little mentions of the recent past, but now the Daleks could return after five years and namedrop a story from the second season. The Ice Warriors returned with the story playing on audience expectations about their motives, which the writer subverted.

It was the start of an inevitable process. *The Making of Doctor Who* gave us a glimpse behind the scenes, but now we know so much that a convention audience can correct an actor on any point of detail. You need a bookcase now, not a book, to store all the information available. Thirty-one years on, it's pretty hard to imagine *Doctor Who* where the writers and audience aren't informed by the history of *Doctor Who*.

1973

Doctor Who is a Time Lord who wanders the universe in his TARDIS with just a pretty female assistant by his side and together they fight monsters like the Daleks.

Or so you'd think.

The first time this actually happens in *Doctor Who* is *Planet of the Daleks*, almost ten years after the series started. Up until *The War Games* he wasn't a Time Lord. He'd not wandered the universe since then, either - barring a couple of excursions in *Colony in Space* and *The Curse of Peladon*. Those two stories were the very first in which the Doctor didn't have a male assistant to help with the fighting (indeed, on telly, counting UNIT regulars but not K9, the Doctor had a man about the place in seventeen of the twenty-six seasons). The Daleks dominated the Hartnell era, but of the others, only Pertwee met them more than twice.

Frontier in Space is a pretty nifty attempt at an anniversary showcase story. While *Carnival of Monsters* is a good, funny story, it's a very odd choice as the Doctor's first excursion into the universe following the end of his exile. *Frontier in Space*, though, gets away from contemporary(ish) Earth and UNIT and into some of the strengths of the era - the Master, a new race of monsters designed by unsung hero of seventies *Doctor Who* John Friedlander, some pretty nifty (for the time) modelwork, a future Earth society that's vaguely plausible for the Apollo generation. Like *The Curse of Peladon*, it feels like it's been informed by *Star Trek* - but there's more than a hint that the Earth of the future is a police state.

There are a few *Doctor Who* stories that, while not the best stories there are, are good, solid examples of the *Doctor Who* format. *Terror of the Zygons* is one of them, so is *The Visitation*. *Frontier in Space* is a good story to show someone who wants to know what *Doctor Who*'s like, especially if they're more used to *Star Trek*. (It's particularly useful, because there are plenty of better stories - the problem with recommending, say, *Genesis of the Daleks*, *City of Death* or *Human Nature* is that whatever you show them next will be a disappointment.)

The faults of the tenth season are only faults now. When *Planet of the Daleks* was repeated about ten years ago, shown at the rate it was meant to be seen, one episode a week, it became a perfectly acceptable story. It's only when you see it all in one go that you realise that episodes 2 - 5 are essentially just the same episode over and over again (if you skip the black and white third episode, you don't actually miss a single important story beat). All the stories suffer from this syndrome a little, but it was hardly a problem at the time, when repeating the same story point several times was a necessary way of reminding your audience what was going on - or just telling them: sometimes over a million people hadn't seen the previous episode.

The Pertwee era now was one of supreme confidence, one where you really feel that everything had come together. Sadly, it was to be something of a culmination - Roger Delgado's death robbed the team of a key regular, and it was already clear that the best the UNIT actors could expect from now on was a couple of stories a year. When Katy Manning left, there was a real sense that things had moved on. Barry Letts, Terrance Dicks and Jon Pertwee would all have gone by the end of the following season. Perhaps that was for the best: it's difficult to see quite what else any of them could say that hadn't already been said in their *Doctor Who* work. While it's possible to picture Pertwee in *The Ark in Space* or *Genesis of the Daleks*, it's hard to imagine his increasingly cosy and familiar performance would be better than what we got.

The Pertwee era has been much-maligned in recent years. Some of that is a half-baked 'political' objection to the Doctor working with the authorities (even though his reluctance and their limitations are constantly pointed out). Some of it is just a case of familiarity breeding contempt. The Pertwee era was a renaissance for *Doctor Who*, and he's the only Doctor to go out with the show healthier than he found it.

1974

The Target novelisations started in January 1974 with *The Auton Invasion* (a logical choice, as it was an adaptation of *Spearhead from Space*, the first Pertwee story and one that was practically a first episode for the current series), and *The Cave Monsters*, based on *The Silurians*.

While the novelisations are fondly remembered, I don't think the impact they made has ever been acknowledged. They've been seen as a useful way of getting a record of the TV show to the fans, or as collectors items with interesting covers. But these books were stalwarts of public libraries in the seventies and early eighties. Some of them sold in the hundreds of thousands. They are a phenomenon in their own right, and the early ones in particular were reprinted and repackaged for a decade.

I should declare an interest. The first book I ever bought with my own money was a copy of *The Cave Monsters*, bought off a market stall on holiday in Wales. I remember it was the first time I even knew there were *Doctor Who* books. My memory is that the stall was overflowing with *Doctor Who* books. There were, at most, twelve titles out at the time. But I think he had all twelve. I remember only buying one, and only later wanting them all. It was, I suspect, one of my more formative experiences. Almost - gulp - thirty years later, I still can't get enough *Doctor*

Who books, despite everyone's best efforts to flood the market for me. I have an infrequent but recurring dream (common to a lot of bibliophiles, I'm told) of finding a bookstall with rows of books I've never heard of by my favourite authors.

Seven books were published in all this year (the three novelisations from the sixties had been republished the previous year). The books weren't, at first, faithful versions of the TV stories - the fact that the first two books had different titles was as good an indication of that as anything else. Neither was every TV story to be adapted - the first book to feature Jo, *The Doomsday Weapon* (*Colony in Space*, in old money), had an introduction scene for her. The changes included expansions and clarifications of things on TV - the superb *Day of the Daleks* adaptation, for example, has much more about the life of the guerillas in the future.

The Cave Monsters took the biscuit, though - it is, at best, loosely based on the TV story. It's much more concise, for one thing. It concentrates on the initial mystery, cuts out a lot of the waiting around caves and all the recap stuff where the same beats are repeated for the benefit of the weekly viewer. The reason it's not called *The Silurians* might be because the monsters aren't called the Silurians - they're the Reptile People. The word 'Silurian' is used once, as a UNIT password.

I'd never seen the TV story, and it was one of the first I got on pirate video. It was crushingly disappointing, a shoddy TV remake of a classic novel from my childhood. The actors hadn't captured the characters (although Pertwee was cool), the dinosaur was even more rubbish than I feared and the cliff-hanger was very badly-staged. The thing that's great about the book is that it's really grounded in reality. I grew up in Derbyshire, where Wenley Moor would be, if it existed (and where they filmed *The League of Gentlemen*, if you want an idea of the landscape). *The Cave Monsters* has lots of ordinary people confronted by monsters who live under the hills there. We see ordinary reactions, monsters living in ordinary airing cupboards, just ordinary life with the most extraordinary intrusion... except we're the intruders, and the monsters have always lived there.

It's a beautifully-crafted science fiction story, a true classic piece of *Doctor Who* - but not on television, where it's padded, ugly and doesn't seem rooted in the ordinary world at all, it's all cyclotrons, government ministers and United Nations troops. It's just not anything like as good.

Until the TV series ended, *Doctor Who* was seen as a television show, with some spin-offs. But perhaps we can appreciate now that, almost as long as there's been *Doctor Who*, it's been short stories, comic strips and novels as much as it's been TV. And those 'spin-offs' are sometimes far more interesting, impressive and enduring than the television shows.

1974, then, was perhaps the year when the Copernican revolution came for *Doctor Who* - the year when *Doctor Who* stopped revolving around the TV series.

1975

There's a *Doctor Who* that only exists in our heads. We know what *Doctor Who* is and isn't, we have a mental picture of it. The problem is that it's a different picture for each of us. There's enough *Doctor Who* that you can take a sample of stories and make a case that it is - or *should be* - challenging, intellectual television, like *Warriors' Gate*, *Kinda* or *Ghost Light*; a romp through history, like *The Visitation*, *Pyramids of Mars* and *The Time Warrior*; satirical, like *The Sun Makers*, *The Curse of Peladon* or *Vengeance on Varos*; a show with great monsters, like *Terror of the Zygons*, *Genesis of the Daleks* or *The Curse of Fenric*; just a silly, fun show, like *The Pirate Planet*, *The Time Meddler* and *Carnival of Monsters*. Some fans have claimed that without Gallifrey and old monsters, the current EDA novels can't be 'real *Doctor Who*', without, apparently, spotting that something like 80% of *Doctor Who* on television didn't have old monsters or Gallifrey either.

There's enough *Doctor Who* to make any sort of consensus among fans impossible. If you love *City of Death*, it doesn't mean you'd like *Earthshock*. Some fans are fans of particular eras, writers or types of stories. Eighties fandom's most frequently used word was 'betrayal'. The direction of the show was felt to have 'betrayed' the show's history. But that was clearly a false premise, and it's been a long time since anyone, or at least anyone you'd want to talk to, has thought like that.

What's often lost in discussions about 'the spirit of *Doctor Who*' or '*Who*ishness' is that there is definitely a 'notional *Doctor Who*'. If you 'think about *Doctor Who*', a fan will have strong thoughts, images and above all feelings. And a whole host of things, from demographics to television ratings to length of tenure to the quality of the product, has usually centred *Doctor Who* in the seventies. *Doctor Who* on television, traditionally, has been seen as a bell curve - the sixties were black and white and mostly of historical interest, the eighties were gaudy and troubled. *Doctor Who* peaked in the mid-seventies with the Doctor going back to Earth's past to fight a parade of classic monsters. *Doctor Who*, in other words, is 'like' *Pyramids of Mars*. A 'typical' story is something like *Genesis of the Daleks*. If you want to show someone a representative story, you could do worse than *Terror of the Zygons*. All stories from 1975. If you ever needed *Doctor Who*'s 'default' year, then go for 1975. Which, pleasingly, is exactly halfway through the television run. It was all downhill from here - slowly, but inevitably.

It's not 'true' in the sense of objectively true: *Doctor Who* was at least as popular in the Hartnell era as Tom Baker's, for example, and there was a new burst of interest with Davison. The incredible thing about the Tom Baker era is that it saw the debut of only one recurring baddy, the Black Guardian. *Doctor Who* just wasn't about old monsters when Tom was Doctor - once past his first season there was, on average, one returning baddy every two seasons. The fourth Doctor visited Earth's past only four times, only once venturing further back than about 1890.

So why is 1975 what the public, the BBC and a vast chunk of fandom have in their heads as 'notional' *Doctor Who*? Well... by 1975 the baby boom generation had settled down and had young kids. Two generations watched it already, and the undergraduates who'd grown up with the show - kids like Douglas Adams and Stephen Fry - were rediscovering the show in university common rooms. Meanwhile, notions of good and evil were being blurred: if a cowboy met an Indian, he was as likely to sympathise with him as shoot him. Post-Vietnam, any conflict had to be abstracted from the real world. And the moon landings were still fresh memory - NASA had launched a mission to Mars and was building a space shuttle. As *Star Wars* would shortly discover, this was box office gold: almost everyone from five to forty five was in the market for family SF you could get your teeth into. *Doctor Who* fitted the bill perfectly, and with more than a quarter of a century of nostalgia, we now view 1975 with an added sheen of nostalgia and can appreciate the seventies kitsch.

As is well known, of course, the fans at the time hated it...

1976

There is a BBC weatherman called Michael Fish. He has been a weatherman for over thirty years. He must have broadcast ten thousand weather forecasts in his time. He's remembered for *one* of them: in 1987, he mocked a viewer who'd phoned in to say they'd heard there was a hurricane about to hit Britain. We're not known for our hurricanes, but... well, you can probably guess what happened that night, if you don't already know.

The review of *The Deadly Assassin* by Jan Vincent Rudzki, DWAS President in 1976, has the same sort of status in *Doctor Who* fandom. He hated the story for numerous reasons, and not exclusively because of the way it contradicted the past, but it's fair to say that was the thing that seemed to irk him most. It ended with the heartfelt, and capitalised, plea:

'WHAT HAS HAPPENED TO THE MAGIC OF DOCTOR WHO?'

The story went on to be the absolute bottom story in the DWAS poll. This isn't the greatest travesty in the history of *Doctor Who* polling (*Kinda* getting almost half the votes of *Time-Flight* and ranking at the bottom of the Season Nineteen poll in *DWM* is a strong contender for that title), but it now seems very odd. Nowadays, of course, the 'doddery old men' version of Gallifrey introduced in *The Deadly Assassin* is the accepted one. When it was destroyed in the novels, the traditionalists were up in arms that such an 'essential part of the mythos' had gone. The fact that Gallifrey barely appears in *Doctor Who* (it had made only one previous appearance in the EDAs, in *The Eight Doctors*) wasn't deemed that important. The paraphernalia established in *The Deadly Assassin* had become cosy, which is part of the reason it was destroyed; Gallifrey had become a checklist rather than an interesting place. There was, in some quarters, a game based on this: Gallifrey Bingo. Each player wrote down five Gallifreyan things and then won when all five had been mentioned: transduction barriers, Eye of Harmony, the Matrix, Rassilon, the Great Key, artron energy, The High Council, blah blah. Watch or read or listen to any Gallifrey story, and you won't be playing long before someone wins.

The thing that's different, of course, is time. Over time, older fans grew to appreciate (or at least accept) that this was Gallifrey. Younger fans didn't know that there had ever been another version of Gallifrey, or had no problem reconciling the glimpses of the Time Lords from before with the current version. *The Deadly Assassin* version was quickly reiterated in *The Invasion of Time*, and by *The Five Doctors*, seven years later, that was just what Gallifrey was like. What's most interesting, though, is the new mentality that the DWAS piece reveals. A new audience was there for the first time: organised fans. There was now a 'consensus'. There was, of course, no such thing. As I've stated elsewhere, put two *Doctor Who* fans in a room together, and the only thing you can be sure of is that there will be three opinions about *Doctor Who*. But the DWAS gave the illusion that 'fans' were opposed to the Hinchcliffe agenda.

There's an obvious point: if you're a fan of something, and that thing changes, then you might not be a fan of it any more. Rudzki's piece says we've 'always' known things about Gallifrey that are overturned in *The Deadly Assassin*. At the time, *The War Games* (the first time the Time Lords were mentioned) was barely six years old. That's the same vintage as the McGann movie, now. Have we 'always' known the Doctor was half-human? The word 'Gallifrey' had first been used less than eighteen stories before (and how many times had it been spoken since then? - I make it two), it wasn't exactly part of the show's ancient heritage.

Graham Williams would later note that there seemed to be a direct correlation between which stories the fans liked and the story's ratings... an inverse correlation (it certainly holds for *The Deadly Assassin*, the first show since *The Chase* with every episode in the top twenty). There was now a new audience, one judging *Doctor Who* by a different standard. Rudzki's criticism spent three lines out of three pages discussing how 'someone who hardly ever watches' would see it.

It was a new phenomenon in 1976, but it was a mentality that would come to dominate *Doctor Who*.

1977

I remember being horrified by *Horror of Fang Rock*.

I was six. The first episode, in fact, was broadcast on my sixth birthday. And they'd ruined it. *Doctor Who* was rubbish, for the first time ever. I'd waited so long for it to come back on TV, but it was poorly-made, so small scale and dingy. It wasn't funny, it wasn't scary, the monster was rubbish, not one person got strangled. And the most horrifying thing of all... I realised why. I saw the end credits, and noticed the producer was different.

One of the most remarkable things about *Doctor Who* is that the show has always encouraged even its youngest viewer to realise that it's just a TV show. I had a copy of the second edition of *The Making of Doctor Who* by then, I knew the producer was called Phillip Hinchcliffe, I knew what a producer did and that he was in charge, so if it had changed, it was because the new producer had said it should. That book starts with a section called 'How It All Began' - it's a history of the production of the show, not of the Doctor, the Daleks and Gallifrey. There's a chapter called 'Tom Baker is Doctor Who'. This in a book that assumes on page one that the reader wasn't old enough to watch the first episode, thirteen years before.

Terrance Dicks was spot on in my case, and I daresay he was spot on in thousands of other cases. *Doctor Who* encourages intelligence in its audience. It is educational, teaching fanboys all about the St Bartholomew's Day Massacre or entropy at an early age. It's perhaps a bit much to say that *Doctor Who* is responsible for my love of learning, for my avid reading, or my interests in science and history. But it fuelled them and I learned. The kids at my school who liked *Doctor Who*, who were really into it, were all smarter than the kids who weren't into it. (Although let's get one thing clear: *everyone* watched it. There was one kid in my class who didn't... and he was bullied for it. Not by me, I hasten to add. But this was the one time when *not* being a *Who* fan marked you out as a social outcast. A golden, enlightened age.)

We all knew it wasn't real. How on earth could it possibly be real? We all knew the Doctor was an actor called Tom Baker, that the monsters were men dressed up, that the horrific scars and burns were cool make up.

There was a reason why there was a new producer of *Doctor Who*. Mary Whitehouse, the anti-violence campaigner, had concentrated her fire on *Doctor Who* and forced the last producer out. It was, she said, full of violence. People being strangled. Some girl, somewhere, had tried to strangle her brother after watching the show. I doubted this. I knew that some kids liked beating people up. The people watching *Doctor Who*, though, knew that the Doctor never used violence. Not only that, he stopped those that used it.

And one other crucial thing: it wasn't real. There was all the difference in the world between a Robot of Death strangling someone on *Doctor Who* and a real person trying to strangle a child.

Mary Whitehouse was *wrong*, in other words.

But people listened to her. The BBC had toned down the scary bits of *Doctor Who*, to protect children like us. Everyone in my class loved *Doctor Who* the way it was. None of us ever strangled anyone. A bunch of us sat in the playground and agreed that what Mary Whitehouse was saying was just plain wrong.

And so, at the age of six, I realised that a lot of kids were smarter than a lot of grown ups. I realised that my classmates could run rings round Mary Whitehouse's blinkered, poisonous, ignorant argument. It taught me that people in authority could be wrong, and that people could set themselves up as figures of authority as a way to spread their lies. And that other grown ups believed them. And those people had to be fought, because they were worse than any Dalek or Cyberman, because Daleks and Cybermen weren't real, they couldn't really hurt people.

If *Doctor Who* has ever taught me anything more valuable than that, I don't know what it was.

The second most important thing I learned that year was that I wanted a robot dog.

1978

There are times when I envy my parents' generation for being the one that first listened to Elvis and the Beatles. To be the one that had "Heartbreak Hotel" or "Yesterday" written for them. I remember singing "Yellow Submarine" in primary school - handily for the format of this essay, it would have been around 1978 - thinking it was some folk song. It's hard to imagine that there was a time when no-one, anywhere had ever heard it and that some people remember where they heard it the first time.

Then I remember... I was born in 1971, so I was the perfect age when *Star Wars* came out, and I wouldn't swap that for the world.

I was a huge *Doctor Who* fan long before *Star Wars*. But, and I'm not exactly unique here, I was swept up and away when I first saw the movie. I collected all the books and toys, I made up stories and drew pictures. I now understand why some people don't like it or think it's a silly kid's film. All I ask is that those people understand that they're *wrong*, and recant.

Can you imagine what it must have been like if you were making *Doctor Who* when *Star Wars* came out? You had a show that was, superficially, the same sort of thing but which was actually almost the opposite sort of thing, and which couldn't possibly compete with the spectacle of a big budget American movie. *Doctor Who*, once again, thrived because someone new showed up at exactly the right moment, and because of a decision made elsewhere in the BBC.

The BBC had just commissioned *Blakes 7*. This would be hugely useful to *Doctor Who*, because the show was - or quickly became - basically *Star Wars* on a BBC budget. The *Blakes* episode *Project Avalon* is just the cheap bits of *Star Wars*: our heroes rescue the princess from the baddies, but there's a tracking device on board and the baddies come after them. Travis was Vader to Servalan's Tarkin. Having a show like *Blakes 7* around kept the BBC from making *Doctor Who* more like *Star Wars*.

The new arrival on the *Doctor Who* production team was, of course, Douglas Adams. A ferociously clever man, a brilliant writer, and a science fiction aficionado, Adams is something of a hero of mine, if for no other reason that - according to MJ Simpson's biography of him - he escorted Lalla Ward to the premiere of *The Empire Strikes Back*. That's my very definition of the perfect night out. Respect to the man who achieved it.

Adams knew that *Doctor Who* couldn't ignore *Star Wars*, and he knew the show couldn't possibly match it. Much of Season Sixteen has little lifts from *Star Wars* - none so blatant as the electric swordfight in *The Androids of Tara*. To Adams the solution must have looked obvious - the show had a tradition of parody and comedy (with Tom Baker and K9 those elements were only being emphasized), and the undergraduates and Americans who were an increasingly important part of the audience loved *Monty Python*. *Blakes 7* took some of the pressure off to be serious - and anyway, they weren't allowed to be too violent. Season Fifteen had

been, mostly, a rather toothless version of Hinchcliffe's *Doctor Who*.
Adams reinvented *Doctor Who* with *The Pirate Planet* - a story that
worked brilliantly on two levels: as *Star Wars* style action-adventure on
one hand, as a skilful and knowledgeable parody of science fiction
clichés on the other. There are cyborgs and guards, aircars and laser gun
battles, robots fighting each other. With *Star Wars* around, these weren't
obscure bits of SF fan lore, every member of the audience would understand what was going on.

Fans, perhaps predictably, hated the Williams era at the time. Ian
Levine would soon describe it as '*Fawlty Towers* in space' - astonishingly
he meant it as an insult, which is a bit like slagging off a play by calling
it 'Shakespearean' or a song by accusing it of being 'worthy of the
Beatles'. The fans liked the dreary and lightweight *The Stones of Blood*,
which was, apparently, 'serious'. But Douglas Adams and Graham
Williams hit upon the formula that would sear itself into the national
consciousness. *Doctor Who* had always been there - from now on, though,
Tom Baker, his scarf and K9 would be the image the mainstream audience had of *Doctor Who*.

Doctor Who didn't dumb down in the face of *Star Wars*. To its eternal
credit, it became smarter and funnier instead.

1979

There's now a race on. Will the Russell Davies revival of *Doctor Who*
make it to screen before November 2005?

Doctor Who ran for twenty-six years and two weeks on television.
Doctor Who Weekly first appeared in October 1979. In other words, we're
close to the point where *DWM* has been going longer than the show that
inspired it, the world's longest running television series (as was, anyway
- *Star Trek* is clearly five or six separate series, so doesn't count, but sure-
ly some other show has been running longer somewhere - Japan? - since).
This will make the *DWM* comic strip the longest continuing version of
Doctor Who. Unless the television show starts running again...

Doctor Who Weekly / Monthly / Magazine is an extraordinary success
story, particularly given that the company that first published it was set
up mainly to bring out cheap cash-in reprints of American superhero
strips that almost invariably lasted less than a year, and the company
that publishes it now are mainly around to sell football stickers. It's
always looked odd - and Marvel's attempts to create titles like it based
around things like *Blakes 7* and Hammer Horror came and went.

Early *DWM*s were extraordinarily fresh and exciting - imagine a time
when every *Doctor Who* photograph in a magazine had never been pub-

lished before. Members of DWAS had already had very detailed plot synopses of old stories (far better than the paragraphs in the *Radio Times* Special or *The Making of Doctor Who*), but now anyone with a newsagent could get hold of the information. Not that those early issues were always right - the write up for *The Time Meddler* quotes the Doctor as saying 'To think that a fellow Gallifreyan would stoop so low', for example. On the whole, though, the magazine gave out reliable information, and avoided getting mired in the sort of arguments and factionalism that tend to ensue in *Doctor Who* fandom.

Doctor Who Weekly was also published at just the right time - the show was on a ratings high, and it was about to be revamped by a producer who was very well aware of the value of publicity and the difficulty of getting it. John Nathan-Turner and *Doctor Who Weekly* quickly began exchanging information, and publicity shots, set visits and other previews were made available to the magazine and its readers.

Doctor Who Magazine has always been officially licenced, and always had a close relationship with the producer of the show. This is always a double-edged sword, and in the mid-eighties (in particular), *DWM* was criticised for ignoring the crisis affecting the show. It's true that a *DWM* reader in 1986 would have only the barest glimmer that all was not well. As a professional magazine, it also has to pay close attention both to legal niceties and general courtesy... something most fanzines don't feel too troubled by. It's tended to take things the BBC says at face value, particularly when talking about the 'new series', and it's rarely named names or pointed fingers when things have gone wrong.

But, as with other *Doctor Who* merchandise, critics should look very carefully at the competition - the other officially-sanctioned tie-in magazines. There are, or have been, plenty of these: *Buffy, Star Trek, Star Wars, Xena, Babylon 5, Alias*. They are usually thin, glossy, and very visually-based: they have posters and the pictures accompanying the articles usually take up twice as much room as the text. Coverage of the series is generally breathless and uncritical, interviews are fawning and superficial, every episode review contains the word 'amazing'. The magazines tend to vanish the moment the show's run ends, if not before. Compared to them, *DWM* is a snake pit for the makers of *Doctor Who*. Yes, there's long been a policy that reviewers should emphasise the positive aspects of a new story, but they've never been afraid to criticise. Interviewers, at their best, have managed to get some genuine insights out of their subjects (although the questions are occasionally rather crass - asking Roy Castle how many tapes of William Russell he watched to nail the part of Ian Chesterton for the movie was something of a nadir).

The rough stuff used to be in the fanzines (it's now online), but *DWM* has been an important part of *Doctor Who* for a very long time. Almost longer than the TV show, now...

1980

As an exercise in throwing the baby out with the bathwater, Season Eighteen has rarely been bettered. Take a smart, funny, successful show and turn it into a dull, pompous failure.

The second episode of *Meglos* got exactly ten million viewers less than the second episode of *City of Death*. Fans are quick to credit the ITV strike for the success of Season Seventeen, and the fact that *Buck Rogers* was networked opposite Season Eighteen. Ratings aren't a scientific method of gauging quality, and it's pointless comparing ratings from 1963 with ratings now, and you never know *why* people watch or don't watch, but week on week, they're a good indication of whether people are keen to come back to watch a show. People just didn't want to watch Season Eighteen.

The redeeming feature was always said to be that the production values of Season Eighteen were so much higher than the previous year. But that's just not true - compare the jungle in *The Creature from the Pit* with the one in *Meglos*, or the modelwork in *City of Death* with that of *State of Decay*. Nearly a quarter of a century on, it's almost impossible to discern any difference between the 'glossy, fast-paced' Leisure Hive and the 'shoddy, unrehearsed' *The Horns of Nimon*.

The conventional fan post mortem is that the mainstream audience preferred the 'high production values' and 'eye candy' and 'realistic look' of *Buck Rogers* to the intellectual fare of *Doctor Who*. It's easy enough to agree that Matthew Waterhouse isn't eye candy. But *Buck Rogers* wasn't exactly a high-budget show. Isn't it obvious that the reason *Buck Rogers* did so well is precisely because it was more camp and more funny than Season Eighteen? If you loved *The Horns of Nimon* (and people did, there's just no two ways about it - more than twice as many people watched the last episode of that than stuck with *The Leisure Hive*), then you'd much prefer to see the robots, monsters and general foolishness of *Buck Rogers*.

The traditional fan reaction has been to blame the audience, but... hang on a moment. It's *Gil Gerard* in *Buck Rogers*, not exactly world-class competition. *Doctor Who* in the Williams era regularly kicked around the *Hulk*, *CHiPS*, *Logan's Run*... all 'glossy' American shows.

Season Eighteen is beloved of the fans. It's a very mixed bag, though. *The Leisure Hive* is glossy, but empty; *Meglos* is the worst-made, least imaginative story for a very long time indeed; *Full Circle* has some strong monster moments, but also some terrible acting; *State of Decay* is fun, but extremely straightforward; *Warriors' Gate* is gorgeous, but you need to tape it and savour it; *The Keeper of Traken* is dull, dull and then dull, and when fans say they like it, they mean they like the skirts; *Logopolis* makes absolutely no sense, but has a genuinely powerful end-of-an-era ending. The stock of all of these stories, with the possible exception of *Warriors' Gate*, has done nothing but plummet over the years.

The problem is that John Nathan-Turner came in with an agenda to get rid of things that weren't working, or weren't serious enough. He's not really replacing them with anything. The original script for *The Leisure Hive* had the Foamasi as comedy Mafia types. That was cut out... and in the final version, they're just colourless bad guys. In previous years, Tom Baker was able to hide the dull bits of scripts with a little bit of performance nonsense or an ad lib. Here, the dull bits are allowed onto screen. *The Leisure Hive* - the whole 'bold, new direction' starts with a two minute tracking shot of some beach huts. It's perhaps fair that the show needed more control, that it needed 'reigning in'. But the revamp completely missed the point, and it looks extremely dated now. Compare and contrast the Season Seventeen and Season Eighteen theme music and opening titles, and see which one sounds and looks the best nowadays.

It's difficult to overstate how much of a disaster Season Eighteen was. It did so badly that the departure of Tom Baker from the role that had made him famous, a departure that had been one of the top items on the news, barely scraped into the top 100 programmes. *Full Circle* scored the lowest ever placing (170th), and the lowest rating up to that point (3.7 million viewers). Once again, *Doctor Who* had gone from a popularity high to an all-time low in the space of a year.

Most significantly, it did so appallingly badly that *Doctor Who* lost its prime Saturday night slot.

1981

Tom Baker's seven-year era doesn't seem that long now - it's seven years since the Paul McGann movie, and while a lot's happened since then, it still feels like the pretty recent past, at least to me.

But in 1981, Tom Baker was synonymous with the show, and even with *Doctor Who Monthly*, novelisations featuring previous incarnations, the shiny new Lofficier *Programme Guide* and a fandom that had finally coalesced into the sort of collective consciousness we know and love now, all of which celebrated the pre-Tom past, anyone playing the fifth Doctor was going to face a hard sell.

Up until now, there had only been 'the Doctor'. 1981 saw a systematic strategy on the production team's part to emphasis that Tom Baker was only the 'current Doctor'. The centre piece of this was the first ever 'out of season' repeats of the show. Repeats had become something of a tradition - every year, a couple of stories from the last season were shown again over the summer. "The Five Faces of Doctor Who" would be different - on BBC2, in weekday slots (testing the water for the big change to come), an example of each Doctor's era was shown.

The restrictions were that they had to be complete in the archives (the full extent of the junkings of old episodes was only now being mapped, and this was before a lot of stuff was returned to the BBC) and four-parters. There also seems to have been a conscious decision to avoid the Daleks and other memorable monsters.

The five stories were *An Unearthly Child*, *The Krotons*, *Carnival of Monsters*, *The Three Doctors* and *Logopolis*. As I've previously noted, it's probably impossible to sum up *Doctor Who* in five stories (and *The Krotons* and *Logopolis* were the only second and fifth Doctor stories that qualified, so they had to be included) but even given that, it looks like a pretty odd bunch for a 'best of' collection. That's because it's not a 'best of', but a set of episodes designed to demonstrate that there's more to *Doctor Who* than Tom Baker.

One oddity is that to start *The Three Doctors* on the anniversary itself, it was shown after *Carnival of Monsters*, despite the fact it ends leading into it.

To *Doctor Who* fans at the time, this glimpse into the past was manna from heaven. The general public seemed to enjoy them too - in fact, more people watched *Logopolis* Part Three on the repeat than had first time round. Black and white repeats rarely got more than a couple of million viewers - these hovered steadily around 4.5 million. The colour repeats gained at least another million. The exercise would be, ahem, repeated the following year, with *The Curse of Peladon*, *Genesis of the Daleks* and *Earthshock*.

There was one consequence of having a 'current Doctor', though. Up until now, once a Doctor regenerated, it was as if he'd always been the Doctor. When the Doctor saw his face carved on a mountainside, it was Tom Baker's, not William Hartnell's. When Drax met the Doctor, he recognised him straight away. There had been *The Three Doctors*, photos of Hartnell and Troughton in *Day of the Daleks* and a couple of oblique mentions. But for the first time, the production team now stressed that their man was merely one in a line of Doctors. There were Doctors before him, there would be Doctors after him. This was inevitable, given that the audience would have strong, long term memory's of the fifth Doctor's predecessor, but the paradox is that by reminding people of the other Doctors, it weakened Davison's position more than just ignoring the problem - the previous strategy - would have done.

It was a fundamental change in the way *Doctor Who* was seen, more than just the Pertwee era's acknowledgement of the show's past. It was the beginning of a trend that would see the show addressing its own past and internal mythology more and more. At the moment that the Doctor got a fresh new face, and a dynamic new look, the show was becoming more insular and self-referential.

1982

Doctor Who Monthly proudly noted that the Season Nineteen TARDIS team of the Doctor, a male assistant and two female companions, mirrored the original TARDIS team. It was a larger regular cast than the show was used to (even during the UNIT era, there was one 'companion', and a large semi-regular cast). It seems to be accident, rather than design, that so many people ended up as regulars, but it was an interesting experiment.

It didn't work, though. During the first two seasons, stories tended to be longer, so the additional companions had more to do in a story. Even then, though, there's barely a story where all the regulars are kept busy - only *The Romans* makes a good stab at it. Usually, one of the regulars disappears for an episode or two, or only appears in a filmed insert, or a subplot involving two companions could just as easily feature one of them. In addition, Ian, Susan and Barbara all had very distinct functions within the plot. Adric, Nyssa and Tegan are more like one of those Venn Diagrams where all three sets intersect. Adric and Nyssa share the 'knowing a bit about made up science' stuff, Adric and Tegan can both be petulant, Nyssa and Tegan can both be caring. The only story that makes a good fist of keeping all the characters involved in the plot all the time, *The Visitation*, looks faintly ridiculous, with the Doctor like a mother duck leading a string of ducklings through the woods. It also, tellingly, has to create a companion figure in Richard Mace.

Season Nineteen is the point where we start to see John Nathan-Turner really making his mark on the series. His first year had been concerned with clearing out the old - not just the cast and K9, but the other touchstones of the series, like the opening titles, the Dudley Simpson music and a lot of the quirky humour. Most people didn't get to the end of *The Unfolding Text* (1983), the first piece of academic criticism of the series, and don't know that the authors concluded that "most of the tertiary educated and science fiction audiences interviewed denied his assertion that he had replaced 'slapstick' with 'wit'." Or, in other words, clever people didn't think *Doctor Who* was as funny as it used to be.

It was certainly *different*, though - in the same book, Douglas Adams suggested that a show could only really change by 15% a year without alienating its audience. He didn't clarify how you quantify that change, but it was clear that *Doctor Who* had changed a lot more than that since his day, only two years before. There was a new set of writers for the year (only Bidmead had written for the show before, once), a completely new cast, a new production team, even... horror of horrors, a new weekday evening timeslot.

The Davison era is one of conflicting demands. Nathan-Turner, Davison and their script editor, Eric Saward all had radically different ideas about what the series should be, and all three make their presence felt. Davison tried to bring warmth and humanity to Saward's darker scripts, Nathan-Turner was looking for ways to bring publicity to the show - mainly by casting famous guest actors. But the other tension was between this new, vulnerable Doctor and his team (both radical departures) and the increasing detailed awareness of the show's past. There was now a large fandom, but more to the point, the general audience was more aware than ever of the noble past - and, perhaps, how far the new Doctor deviated from it. It meant that Davison's era wasn't quite as radical as it could have been.

The short term benefits, though, were obvious and enormous - ratings were pretty much back to where they'd been in the mid-Baker period. There was a new interest in the show, and while many of the old guard continued to complain, there's no doubt that the show got itself a whole new, slightly older, audience. It was the perfect timing to catch the kids who were growing out of *Star Wars* and would soon be packing the cinemas to watch dark SF like *Blade Runner, Terminator, Aliens* and *Robocop*.

However, the huge success of *Earthshock*, its writer becoming script editor and a looming anniversary all conspired to move *Doctor Who* in a different direction...

1983

The twentieth anniversary of the show was a high point for the series, by any standard. In retrospect, it's hard to see what went so wrong, so fast - how a show that looked like a worldbeater in 1983 was given a mortal blow in 1985. But that was the future... in 1983 itself, the Longleat weekend was an extraordinary phenomenon, with many times more people showing up than were expected - more people were there than buy the books or audios these days - enormous traffic jams and people being turned away in droves.

BBC Enterprises were there, trying to gauge whether there would be a demand for *Doctor Who* on videocassette and asking which story should come out first. By the end of the weekend, legend has it, every single story had been requested at least once. Presumably because *Earthshock* had been so popular, and Tom Baker was still the most popular Doctor, the 'perfect storm' title was felt to be *Revenge of the Cybermen*. Perhaps not the title we'd pick in hindsight. It duly came out on 10 October 1983, and it would be twenty years before every existing episode was released on VHS... just in time for the DVD releases to start in earnest. 1984 would see a conscious decision on Target's part to go back and plug the gaps in the novelisation line up.

Doctor Who's past was suddenly big business. The stories of 1983 reflected this, with every single one of them featuring a returning baddy. Some of these, like the Master and the Mara were from the immediate past. Omega wasn't as obscure as might be thought, following *The Three Doctors* repeat. The Brigadier had also featured in that, and was fondly-remembered. The Black Guardian had been a major baddy for a whole season, just a few years before. *The Five Doctors* was an anniversary story, and even if the general audience didn't have the full catalogue of monsters and companions stored away in their memories, Terrance Dicks' deceptively clever script told them everything they needed to know, and kept centre stage for the Time Lords, Master and Cybermen, all of whom had appeared in the last year or so. So there was a lot from the past, but it was relatively accessible.

For the first time, *Doctor Who* was now more than just the current show. Whereas *The Three Doctors* had been a Pertwee story with a cameo from Hartnell and a guest shot from Troughton, *The Five Doctors* was truly an ensemble piece, and Pertwee seemed to get most of the memorable moments.

Further weakening this was the announcement that Davison would be leaving at the end of his third season. The twentieth anniversary *Radio Times* ended with a picture of Colin Baker and Nicola Bryant. It added to the impression that the current Doctor Who was barely being invited to his own birthday party.

Although *Doctor Who* was on a high, Season Twenty is a pretty weak season, all in all. *Snakedance* is fantastic (better than *Kinda*, at the risk of heresy), and *Enlightenment* has its moments, but stories like *Arc of Infinity*, *Mawdryn Undead* and *The King's Demons* are swallowed up by plot holes and story problems, and rely far too much on the audience having good will towards the returning characters. The Master is the ultimate example of this kind of laziness - his plan and methods in *The King's Demons* barely qualify as half-baked, and the audience is expected to fill the gaps themselves. Turlough is a wasted opportunity, again he hasn't quite been thought through enough.

Davison struggles manfully through the year, and never seems to flag, even though he said later that seeing the scripts sped up his decision to leave. Davison is probably the best actor to have played the Doctor, but the scripts rarely rise to his level. The odd thing is that after two seasons where John Nathan-Turner imposed his version onto the series, Season Twenty feels oddly rudderless.

All of this, though, is retrospective. We know now that *Doctor Who* was heading for a fall, and it's tempting to see the seeds of that ever earlier and earlier (more than one fan blames *The Horns of Nimon* [1980] for the death of the TV series [1989]). This, at the time, was a golden age for *Doctor Who*, and if the Davison era's main crime is that it stretches but doesn't reach its full potential, then that's hardly a crime at all.

1984

Q: Where did it all go wrong?
A: *The Twin Dilemma.*

It's that simple.

It's not Colin Baker's fault. As he's spent most of the last twenty years demonstrating, he's committed to the show, he's something of an expert on science fiction, and *Doctor Who* in particular (sharing a flat with Patrick Troughton's son in his formative years probably accounts for that), and he's capable of playing the role.

The traditional view has been to blame John Nathan-Turner. I think there's more than an element of truth in this. Other producers had come in with plans to radically revamp *Doctor Who*. The first three Doctors were all ousted when a new producer came in looking to shake up the show - it's the obvious move to make. John Nathan-Turner enacted his vision of *Doctor Who* as a more grown-up show, one where acting was preferred over ham performance, where big science fiction ideas and human drama could mix. The advent of Eric Saward and the anniversary made the show more populist - playing to the crowds more often, but it was a huge success.

John Nathan-Turner is the only person to cast more than one Doctor - he ended up casting three of them. It's just impossible for one person to mastermind a second radical revamp: Nathan-Turner was reacting against his own agenda. So, instead of a subtle, restrained, sweet Doctor, we got a brash, exuberant, nasty one. Davison was a great choice to play a Doctor reacting against Tom Baker's tenure. But there's a danger of a long-standing producer just swinging the pendulum back the next time he has to rethink.

There's no great sense that the show is building on success. Season Twenty-One is surprisingly violent, with some of the most truly gratuitous horror moments of the whole run of the show - the man with the melted face in *Resurrection*, for example, who appears in one scene and doesn't actually seem to be related to the plot at all.

The decision to make *The Twin Dilemma* the last story of the season was also fatal. It meant there was a story to send to the writers as a showcase for the new Doctor. To a man, they picked up on the performance in the first episode - the strangling and shouting. By the end of the story, the Doctor was already mellowing... but, let's face it, no-one would keep watching *The Twin Dilemma* any longer than they had to. It was a strong, memorable performance, one that a writer could understand and duplicate. If the producer sent you a tape and said 'we want the new Doctor like this', then who were the writers to argue?

The superficial elements of a show are very important - the new Doctor doesn't just look wrong, he's been carefully designed to. One of the favourite JNT convention anecdotes was that he kept sending sketches of the sixth Doctor's costume back because they were too tasteful. It's indicative of a mentality - something good was rejected, something not so good was rejected... and so on, until the horrible end result. It's the first thing anyone who sees even a picture of the Doctor would see. And, at a stroke, three years of careful work to make *Doctor Who* more character-driven and subtle were lost. Technically, the way the cameras worked at the time even meant that everyone else had to wear gaudy colours to maintain a colour balance on screen.

The Twin Dilemma was another in a long line of seminal stories. Unlike *The Invasion* or *The Pirate Planet*, though, it would steer *Doctor Who* down the wrong path. It remains one of the worst, if not *the* worst, *Doctor Who* stories ever made, anywhere. The story makes no sense, the baddy's plan is gibberish, the acting is terrible. The irony is that Colin Baker does immediately stamp his mark on the show.

The show would pay a terrible cost, and it would pay it immediately.

1985

It was all going so well.

Doctor Who was thriving in America. It was packing out conventions, relegating *Star Trek* stars to second billing. All sorts of merchandise was created and repackaged for the US market. The American syndication package concentrated mostly on Tom Baker, but the Marvel US comic reported that there was not only a fifth, but also a sixth Doctor. The old *DWM* strips soon got round to the Davison era.

Any American broadcaster would have thrown their full weight behind it. The conventional reading of *Doctor Who* history has been that the BBC did exactly the opposite. They killed the show at just the moment it was going to become a global mega franchise.

But my theory is just the opposite: I think the BBC went for it, and *Doctor Who* let them down.

The show returned to its Saturday night slot, it was reformatted to a US-friendly forty-five minute episode length. What's more, I think the budgets went up - some of the Season Twenty-Two stories are positively lavish. If *The Mark of the Rani* had been a prestigious ITV historical drama, it would have looked exactly the same as it does. Season Twenty-Two has some of the best ensemble casts - on paper, anyway - in the show's history.

It was all for nothing. Colin Baker met a man from one of the stations showing *Doctor Who* around then, and was asked to 'tell Michael Grade we need more product'. Colin Baker had never met Michael Grade, and Mr Grade had other plans. A third of the nine million people who watched *Attack of the Cybermen* stopped watching *Doctor Who* and never came back. Michael Grade wasn't being particularly mean when he put *Doctor Who* on hiatus, he was doing his job. A big, flagship Saturday night show was being slaughtered in the ratings.

Worse than that: *Doctor Who* just wasn't very good. Sure, there are redeeming features for every story, but trying to find them in Season Twenty-Two already feels like playing Devil's Advocate. The show just doesn't feel comfortable with its new longer episodes - most stories (*Mark of the Rani* being a good example) feel like twenty-five minute two-parters, but stretched beyond the story's ability to cope. Nothing happens in *Mark of the Rani*, the story wends its way until the ninety minutes are up, then stops. It's not about the Master trying to recruit the geniuses of the Industrial Revolution - he muses on the possibility, but doesn't do anything about it. It's not the Rani causing the rioting - it's a side effect of her process she knows nothing about. The baddies aren't doing anything much... and the Doctor simply sabotages the Rani's TARDIS and waits for them to use it. They duly do so at eighty-seven minutes into the story.

Attack of the Cybermen's problem isn't the 'reliance on continuity'. Its problem is simply that the story makes no sense and the baddies have a plan but seem to have no intention of enacting it. The past is used as a talisman, but this time it just rings hollow - how many people would get the Totter's Lane reference or even the references to Mondas or the Tombs? These aren't complicated ideas, but they just aren't used or articulated. Why does the Doctor land in Totter's Lane? Because he did in *An Unearthly Child*, and for no other reason.

The story doesn't have anything approaching wit. More to the point, it's just not the show the American audience was enjoying so much. It's not funny, it's not clever, it's got no obvious new ideas. It feels nasty... and with a nasty Doctor and whiny companion, there's not an ounce of warmth or compassion anywhere.

It's interesting, though: it looks like some more radical solutions were thought of. Grade is said to have talked to all sorts of people about revamping the show: Jeremy Brett and Sydney Newman among them. It was the perfect time for a McGann-style relaunch tailored to the American market. A couple of years later, *Star Trek: The Next Generation* would come along and redefine SF television in the States. The right *Doctor Who* product at this point could have stolen a march on that show. Maybe even usurped its success.

It was too late, though. *Doctor Who* wasn't going to conquer America if it couldn't even persuade the British audience to watch it. Barely two years since Longleat, *The Five Doctors* and a triumphant anniversary, *Doctor Who* was taken off television.

1986

1986 was a great year for *Doctor Who*.

The only slight fly in the ointment was the TV show. It's fair to say that it limped back to television after its eighteen month 'hiatus'. *The Trial of a Time Lord* looked cheap, and - barring barely a handful of nice moments - was uninspired stuff. While the BBC had taken the very unusual step of publicly criticising the production team, they hadn't actually replaced them. John Nathan-Turner and Eric Saward (until he walked out, anyway), were in the unenviable position of being under instruction to revamp a show without any practical guidance how. Nathan-Turner had already revamped the show at least twice. There was always the danger that he'd simply run out of ideas. The fan press, particularly the openly-hostile *DWB*, were keen to remind him that early in his tenure he'd explained why he'd not hiring some of the familiar writers and directors by saying they were '*Who*ed out' - the theory being that *Doctor Who* required energy, enthusiasm and a freshness of approach.

But never mind that. In 1986, there was a merchandising boom, on both sides of the Atlantic. The show was hitting something of a peak of popularity in the States. There were rumours of a movie. The *DWM* comic strip was being drawn by John Ridgway and written by Steve Parkhouse - a combination that was creating a distinctive, visually-rich, always imaginative run of stories. The Audio Visuals, a range of *Doctor Who* stories available on tape, were in full swing. The novelisations were in great shape - they were now almost exclusively written by the original scriptwriters, many returning to *Doctor Who* after decades and bringing a unique insight into the books. They also covered the full range of the series' history (including *Slipback*), and were bringing some of the more obscure stories to light. There were also the very first original novels, based on the further adventures of Harry Sullivan and Turlough. Using our perennial test, how much money a fan would need to buy all the merchandise, 1986 was the most expensive so far, even allowing for inflation.

It was still nascent, but what we had for the first time were a fully-developed strands of *Doctor Who* that had nothing to do with the TV series. More than that, these were writer-driven stories that tried to develop what *Doctor Who* could be, rather than trying to pastiche the series, past or present. More than one novelisation took the opportunity to fix problems with the television version, or to brush aside some of the changes the director, producer or script editor had imposed. *Timelash*, for example, has a completely different ending (it's still not much cop). The spin-off novels had, at best, a tangential relationship with *Doctor Who*. The *DWM* comic strip was absolutely nothing like either Season Twenty-Two or Twenty-Three, operated on a huge scale and played around with both form and the history of the show. The Audio Visuals quickly developed an elaborate internal continuity, recurring bad guys, new companions and with them its own identity. It's hard to see *Sword of Orion* as anything other as a reaction against *Attack of the Cybermen* - a way Cybermen stories 'should' be done.

The fanzine scene was just going up a gear, partly because of cheaper printing, partly because the official magazine was unable or unwilling to criticise the television show at a time when it was clearly in trouble and the fans were practically in full revolt. The 'golden age' fanzines: *In-Vision*, *The Frame*, *Skaro* and *Matrix* were all starting up. For the first time, it became clear that fandom was a really diverse place - all sorts of ages and tastes were out there. A new generation of fans, born around the time the show started and now in their twenties, were starting to make their voices heard: people like David Howe, Gary Russell, Justin Richards, Andy Lane, Bill Baggs and Paul Cornell. They traded video tapes, contributed to fanzines, began to form social networks.

It was a bizarre situation: the television show was, by any definition, failing. The remedial measures seemed to make things worse and it was lurching from crisis to crisis. Meanwhile, the rest of *Doctor Who* was in the healthiest state it had ever been. In hindsight, we can see the foundations of *Doctor Who* in the nineties being laid. *Doctor Who*, increasingly, was something you bought, not something you watched. But for the television series, things were only going to get more bleak...

1987

Colin Baker was not the first Doctor to be sacked. Indeed, depending on how we define terms, he may very well have been the fourth. Hartnell, Pertwee and Tom Baker had all wanted to do more. Had Patrick Troughton decided not to leave, it's certainly possible that the new producer or the BBC management might have pushed him out. Only Peter Davison seems to have freely chosen to go when he did, and even there, he's hinted that he could have been persuaded to stay.

Colin Baker, though, had come into the role promising to beat Tom Baker's seven year tenure. He'd thrown himself into the role (one thing that's not often noted is that there was a barrage of publicity for both of his seasons, with Colin making a lot of public appearances). Fans could have guessed he'd been pushed, even if he hadn't made it public that he had.

Even the fans that had been calling for a complete clearing of the decks were taken aback. Mainly because, once again, the producer survived. The idea that John Nathan-Turner was the only person who could possibly produce the show was always a fatuous one, and it's baffled fans why, if the BBC didn't like his work, he wasn't replaced. There's clearly a missing piece of information there, something we still don't know, more than fifteen years on. The BBC seemed to be looking for a replacement - perhaps it was simply that the ship looked to be sinking, and no-one wanted to jump aboard. That said, it was a plum assignment and a great proving ground. There have been no shortage of people since who've wanted the job, so it seems odd there was no-one around in the eighties. We can discount the darker conspiracy theories - if the BBC just wanted to kill it, they'd have stopped making it in 1985.

Why was it put opposite *Coronation Street*? Because, in 1987, *Coronation Street* was in serious trouble. The long-running soap had lost a lot of established characters, simply through old age - they were retiring or dying. The characters that remained were looking stale, and the ratings were falling. *Doctor Who* was a family show, and the new slot was something of a death slot, but presumably the idea was that it would undermine *Coronation Street* in the process. A strong *Doctor Who* that captured the imagination could start eating away at the soap's fanbase - particularly the younger and smarter members of the audience that advertisers like so much.

So, for the third season in a row, there was a radical revamp of the series, a new Doctor and a new approach. This time, at least, there seemed to be an attempt to do something new, rather than react against something old. Andrew Cartmel was presented with a set of scripts, but insisted that they avoided what had become the clichés - the long TARDIS scene at the beginning, the running around corridors, the constant cycle of being captured and escaping (some stories, like *Vengeance on Varos* seem to consist entirely of those three things). Three new writers contributed to the season - if nothing else, *Doctor Who* could prove its worth to the BBC by developing new writing talent.

The end result are four stories, three of which have a claim to being among the worst ever seen on television, with the fourth being *Delta and the Bannermen* - hardly a classic, but at least *different*. *Time and the Rani* is one of a very few *Doctor Who* television stories written by numbers - an attempt to tell a 'traditional' story which just goes to show that the series is resistant to anything like that. *Paradise Towers* was ruined by the casting - faced with a script about a bunch of sinister little girls fighting a bunch of old fascist caretakers, a bunch of twentysomething women were cast opposite a bunch of twentysomething men. It's a story about a generation gap with no generation gap. *Dragonfire* was also shoddily-made - the script screams that its a pastiche of *Aliens*, but *Aliens* wasn't floodlit.

The season was a mess, but it didn't see the ratings meltdown that was expected. The show was bobbing along the 80s and 90s in the top 100 programmes, but the figures were pretty much where they had been the previous year, against much stiffer opposition. The obvious analysis is that the viewers were down to the bedrock - four million people, who'd always watch *Doctor Who*.

Historical Note: Some of the questions I posed here were later answered in the "Trials and Tribulations" documentary - which I highly recommend - on "The Trial of a Time Lord" DVD set. Jonathan Powell, the head of Series and Serials from 1984 to 1987, says that the BBC higher-ups wanted to cancel Doctor Who in 1985, but reconsidered under threat of a public backlash from the fans (including, it seems, a scheme to picket the House of Commons with Daleks). Powell says that he just couldn't find anyone else to take Nathan-Turner's place, although he also admits that the institutional will needed to reinvent and revitalize Doctor Who just wasn't there.

1988

The twenty-fifth anniversary arrived, and there was no doubt that the show was looking a bit healthier. Andrew Cartmel was able to commission the stories this year, control them from the outset. The Cartmel era was by no means perfect, but each story was somehow more quirky and imaginative than we'd been getting used to. The Saward formula that had seemed so fresh when *Earthshock* was shown had become rather tired.

But perhaps it was too late, perhaps *Doctor Who* had been left too far behind. It was certainly at completely at odds with the science fiction that was around at the time. This was the era of cyberpunk in books, and of dark, violent SF in film. Running against that, *Star Trek: The Next Generation* had made its debut, emphasising character and high concept stories. *Doctor Who*, perhaps for the very first time, seemed oddly divorced from the rest of the world. In science fiction like *Aliens*, *Terminator* and *Robocop*, violence was the solution, not the problem. Humour wasn't just dark, it was pitch black. American superhero comics were reinventing and revamping even the most obscure characters as angst-ridden and 'realistic'.

Cartmel was a comics fan - he suggested that writers for the show read Alan Moore's *The Ballad of Halo Jones* - and some of this was rubbing off on him. But it was always tempered: Ace kind of represented 'youth', but was played by someone old enough to be Ace's mother, and there was twee slang instead of any anger or abrasiveness. The Doctor was, famously, 'more dark', but this consisted of a series of tantalising clues he was keeping secrets and knowing looks, rather than any real meat.

It's fascinating that the three architects of the Cartmel era (Cartmel himself, Marc Platt and Ben Aaronovitch) all took the opportunity of their first New Adventure to tell stories quite unlike the ones on television. *Cat's Cradle: Warhead* and *Transit*, in particular, were drenched in the cyberpunk ethos. More than that, there was sex and violence. Those three books, more than any of the other early ones, were the ones that tried to push *Doctor Who* into a more adult arena. They were also the three that most baffled and alienated sections of fandom (at least two future *Who* novelists appeared in print criticising *Transit*). But it's an indication the writers were at odds with the BBC's (and the producer's) version of *Doctor Who*.

Earlier eras of the show had absorbed things from around them - the Hartnell era was a grab bag of various other shows around; the Pertwee era mixed the spy shows of the late sixties with the seventies interest in the occult; Tom Baker started off in a show that lifted from Hammer

Horror, which became a Python skit on *Star Wars*.

The key thing up until now had been that the show had known which audience it wanted to attract. This had always a broad church, of course, but the Williams era - for example - had successfully appealed to young kids, their parents and university students. There was an acute awareness of the audience. With *Coronation Street* opposite them, there was no hope of attracting many new viewers. The family audience was pretty well obliterated - ultimately, it's the parents that wield the remote control. The kids at university in the late eighties might have dim memories of Tegan and her leather skirts, but there had been little to keep them with the show for the last few years. Who was the Cartmel era made for? Ultimately, the bedrock fans - but even the fans weren't happy. *DWB* was the focal point for a vehement campaign against the current direction of the show, and John Nathan-Turner in particular. Going by the fanzines, half the fans were only watching the show to hate it.

Seedlings were planted in Season Twenty-Five, though. *Remembrance of the Daleks* was the best story in years, and showed a way of using the show's icons to make a form of social commentary. There was something in there for everyone - action, jokes, satire, old monsters. The leap in quality from the last story, *Dragonfire*, to this one is probably the highest in the show's history. The rest of the season was more of a mixed bag, but at least new things were being tried, and there was a distinctive character to the stories.

With only fourteen episodes, all of them scheduled against the toughest competition possible on British television, *Doctor Who* just couldn't make it to the national consciousness, though. The BBC didn't help - the *Radio Times* gave the new season virtually no coverage. It was only a matter of time...

1989

For as long as anyone could remember, the last episode of each season had ended with the announcer telling us '*Doctor Who* will return next year'. The last part of *Survival* ended, and no such announcement was made. The future - if there was to be one - was uncertain.

We'll perhaps never know what the BBC's thinking was at this point - the senior executives who made the decision not to renew the show don't give the sort of interviews we're used to from producers, actors and writers. We can only presume, then, that it was felt that *Doctor Who* was past its best. In 1989, the glory days of the seventies were long behind the show. Colin Baker was perhaps right when he said that the main reason the show went was that there was no-one at the BBC to champion it.

The irony was that Season Twenty-Six was perhaps the strongest series since Davison had left. There was a good mix of stories without the jarring changes in tone between them there had been the previous year. Fans were perhaps too quick to declare *The Curse of Fenric* a 'classic' - it's a good, solid story, and that had become annoyingly rare, but being objective it's hard to place it that high in the list of all time greats. *Ghost Light* falls apart spectacularly in the end, and some of the more important plot points are left a little vague. But it's a contender for the *Doctor Who* story with the best first episode, and it's interesting, clever and atmospheric. *Battlefield* is not a brilliant story. There are hints that a brilliant script has been compromised by the budget, but the end result is, essentially, a load of people nancying around with swords. It doesn't deserve to be the lowest-rating story ever, but neither does it deserve to be the season opener. *Survival* is perhaps a little under-rated - there's some character work in there, memorable monsters and, amazingly, the Master is genuinely sinister again, after far too long as a panto villain.

Not a brilliant season, then, but there are no actively bad stories (for my money, at least, for the first time in over ten years). The most crucial thing, though, was that *Doctor Who* was on the up again. Had seasons Twenty-Five and Twenty-Six been as lacklustre as Twenty-Three and Twenty-Four, then the BBC would have a real case for saying it was past its prime. Here, on a tiny budget and against morale-sapping opposition, the show proved it still had new things to say. Old monsters still showed up, but approached from a new angle. New writers were being discovered and encouraged. A little bit of effort, and the show could improve further.

That said, the show just didn't look like anything else on adult television, now. In the seventies, even prestigious drama like *I, Claudius* was made on videotape. That was less and less common by the end of the eighties - ITV were leading the way with shows like the Jeremy Brett *Sherlock Holmes* and *Inspector Morse* - long, filmed drama that looked more like medium-budget movies. It's a myth to say that no television was 25 minutes long or on videotape - every soap and pretty much every sitcom still is - but *Doctor Who* was looking increasingly odd. In the sixties and seventies, let's not forget that *Doctor Who* - even when it wasn't having one of its peaks of popularity - was a solid, mainstream drama show, appealing to the same sort of audiences as watch *Casualty* or *Heartbeat* now. It held its own against real programmes, it didn't need any excuses made for it. Now, it looked more and more isolated, and the fans were calling for special treatment for it, as though it was some sort of endangered animal.

The fans who spent hours every day agonising about the show, then writing into the BBC perhaps did more harm than good. Those long letters might have started 'Doctor Who isn't as good as it used to be. Here's a fifty-point plan to make it better', but the postroom at the BBC only read the first sentence, then filed it under 'Doctor Who isn't any good'. The BBC were wrong - Doctor Who is a strong format, and the right actor, producer and writers would have made the show the hit of 1990. Never forget, when you watch the Russell Davies version in 2005, that the BBC aren't right to bring it back - they were wrong to neglect the show and then take it off in the first place.

1990

'And then suddenly, one year, there was no spring.'

There had been long gaps in 1981 and 1985/6, but for the first year since it started, there was no new Doctor Who on television in 1990. At first there was talk of an independent production company taking over the show, possibly even Verity Lambert's. Less and less television was being produced 'in house' at the BBC, and it seemed logical that Doctor Who would also have to move with the times.

Even now, fans assumed that Doctor Who would be back sooner rather than later. This was, in part, because that was what the BBC was telling them. But nothing was actually happening, and the various news pages of DWM, DWB and the other fanzines ended up saying very little, except that new novelisations and videos were coming out. It soon became clear that there seemed to be little will on the BBC's part to bring the show back.

1990 was a weird year, then. John Nathan-Turner was gone, so some sections of fandom were very happy... until they realised that nothing else had filled the void. There were rumours of a movie, there were rumours - and even production sketches! - of new bids to make the show. A future where a relaunched Doctor Who would be bigger and better than ever seemed inevitable... except nothing was actually appearing.

The merchandise carried on regardless - the VHS tapes now came with lovely new painted covers and in double box sets - the 1990 crop was particularly good for fans of the black and white show, with (amongst others) the first two Dalek stories and The War Games released. The novelisations, though, were running out of TV stories to adapt. Apart from Battlefield (which came out in July 1991), the Douglas Adams stories and the Saward and Troughton Dalek stories, every TV story was novelised by the end of the year.

Included in that last run, unknown to anyone at the time, was a new pilot for *Doctor Who*. *Remembrance of the Daleks* was a good TV story, if flawed. The novelisation, also by Ben Aaronovitch, didn't just erase the flaws, it added layers of mystery, scale and storytelling to create perhaps the finest *Doctor Who* novelisation of the lot. As the Target range came to an end, it came full circle, with a set of novels that were far more than just a write-up of the TV episodes in question. The novelisations of all the Season Twenty-Five and Twenty-Six stories improve - or at least expand - on the originals, and take the opportunity to clarify plot points and close up some plot holes.

Battlefield, published in 1991, would be the last novelisation published as part of the original run (*The Power of the Daleks*, *The Evil of the Daleks* and the adaptation of the McGann movie would follow). With no new television shows, and with even things like abandoned Season Twenty-Three stories and *The Pestacons* in book form, there was simply nothing left to novelise. The solution was obvious: original novels. Target had actually suggested it several years before, only to have plans vetoed by the production team. In late 1991, they were given the go-ahead.

Behind the scenes, there seems to have been a genuine effort to get a *Doctor Who* movie made, on a number of people's behalf. A few people also tried to interest the BBC in their version of *Doctor Who*.

But the main news of this year was that there was no news. The *Doctor Who* industry carried on as if nothing had happened - as previously noted, *Doctor Who* had been far more than the current show as far back as the twentieth season. As the VHS tapes started to make old stories truly accessible, fans started to look back. The Williams era, reviled for ten years, was reassessed and found favour with a large section of fandom. The Troughton era also received a lot of attention. Fan favourites like *The Web Planet* and *The Daemons* were shown up to be... well, a little dull. For the first time, *Doctor Who* on television wasn't 'The Unfolding Text', it was something with a beginning, middle and an end. Finally, fans could start to write an objective history of the show.

1991

With it now clear there wouldn't be a television series from the BBC, others started to fill the demand for new *Doctor Who* stories.

Bill Baggs' *Stranger* series started with *Summoned by Shadows*, made as a training film for the BBC Film Club, and starring Colin Baker and Nicola Bryant. Restrained performances and a character-driven script made the end result quite unlike Season Twenty-Two, and surprisingly fresh and impressive. Ever since 1986, Colin Baker has been on a mission to prove that it wasn't his fault the show was cancelled. Baggs was by no means the only fan who was being creative - the death of the TV show had seen dozens of talented artists, fan-fiction writers and essayists come out of the woodwork, and this was a golden age for *Doctor Who* fanzines - *The Frame, Matrix, Skaro* and *In-Vision* were all very different, but had high production values and made fascinating reading. *DWB* even went pro, becoming *Dreamwatch*.

A lot of the bitterness and selfishness that had defined eighties fandom was now irrelevant. With no show, ironically, each story could be judged on its merits, without worrying whether it was another nail in the coffin. The stories coming out on VHS were all grist to the mill - and they were also a great leveller: only 'superfans' had all the series on tape in the eighties, now you just needed to go down to Smiths to buy them.

Doctor Who, though, was no longer something that was free. To be an 'active' *Doctor Who* fan, now, you had to buy *DWM* or the VHS tapes. There was a debate at the time in British television about 'pay to view' services. *Doctor Who* fans had long more than paid for *Doctor Who* by buying books, annuals, comics, magazines, toys, records and videos. Some estimates were that *Doctor Who* made five times more than it cost to make - the BBC, though, weren't a commercial organisation. And, of course, they could point to the continued success of the videos as proof that you didn't need a current series to make money from the past.

Someone, though, had a more forward-looking agenda. Peter Darvill-Evans was an editor at Virgin, who now published the novelisations, and realised that the supply was about to dry up. The short term solution was to repackage the old novelisations with new covers, to tie in with video releases (Alistair Pearson's video covers were used, or he did new covers for the books in the same style). This, though, was a limited market, and the future was all-new models.

The New Adventures were born. The most remarkable thing is what they weren't - it would have been all too easy to make them lazy pastiches of the TV show, to use old Doctors and old monsters. At a point when everyone else thinking about *Doctor Who* was looking to the past, Peter Darvill-Evans created a range designed to be as much cutting edge SF as it was *Doctor Who*. The first few books eased the readers into the range. *Timewyrm: Genesys*, the first book, is exactly the sort of 'adult' *Doctor Who* book critics must have feared: the violence is turned up a bit, we see temple prostitutes. It was more adolescent than adult. *Timewyrm: Exodus* and *Timewyrm: Apocalypse* were both solid, but nothing special.

It was Paul Cornell's *Timewyrm: Revelation* that kicked the range into high gear. Currently, it's at exactly the wrong age - like the same year's *Terminator 2*, it's old enough to look dated, but not yet old enough to have any retro chic or nostalgic appeal. It's very 1991. It came out in 1991, though. And to have a *Doctor Who* story that wasn't trying to ape the seventies, recapture the glory years or feebly keep up with 'the kids' was a breath of fresh air. Suddenly, Ace was our age, and listened to our music. The adventure was rich in symbolism and references - everything from Joseph Campbell to the Happy Mondays.

The other impressive thing was that this was a story that just couldn't have worked on television. Not because the action wasn't impressive, or the characters well-drawn. Rather the opposite. This was *Doctor Who* as internal action, as character drama.

I wasn't the only person who read *Timewyrm: Revelation* and who felt like the blinkers had fallen away. *Doctor Who* was bigger, better and had more potential than any of us had realised.

1992

Now the show could be viewed as a whole, and the tapes were there to watch, a whole new generation of analysis came out. Up until now, the Lofficier *Programme Guide*s had been the bible for every fan. Now, *In-Vision*, the Pixley archives in *DWM* and the Howe-Stammers-Walker book series (starting this year, with *The Sixties*) began to cover the series in forensic detail. No other television show has been subjected to so much analysis of what was happening behind-the-scenes. Trying to guess what *Doctor Who*'s legacy will be is always going to be a mug's game, but it's not implausible to imagine that in a hundred years, scholars might be interested in how television was made in the twentieth century. And, if so, there's going to be no richer vein to tap than the work *Doctor Who* historians did in the nineties. The nineties saw some superb work - a combination of a network of contacts, newly available material like the telesnaps and some very talented researchers and writers, all of whom had a genuine love of the show. Virgin's non-fiction output ended up being so comprehensive, in fact, that there's been little new to say since.

Ask most people what they remember about Virgin's *Doctor Who* output, though, and they'll say the New Adventures. 1992 was a seminal year. Ben Aaronovitch, Andrew Cartmel and Marc Platt kicked the series into a high gear, all three of them choosing to tell fast-paced, high concept, grown-up science fiction. It wasn't so much that there was so much sex, drugs and rock and roll in their *Doctor Who* books - it was the fact they didn't seem at all ashamed to put it there. All three are subverting the series (all three doing that, to a greater or larger extent, by taking the Doctor away from the centre of attention). This wasn't just redrawing the boundaries, this was discovering whole new continents and leaping into them without looking back.

Unsurprisingly, a lot of the fanbase was left behind, or scandalised. In retrospect, it's amazing just how tame and straightforward those books are. A glimpse of Ace's nipple, a bit of off-screen sex, a couple of swear words... it would be strictly PG-13 rated stuff. None of the sex and violence seems particularly gratuitous or designed to shock, either. Rather, these books demonstrated just how tame and old-fashioned the TV show was. There was nothing in here that would scandalise a movie-goer, or someone who watched *Brookside* or *Cracker*. *Doctor Who* was out of the bubble it had been in since the mid-eighties, where its only frame of reference had been old *Doctor Who*.

So that's the hypothetical question: had the TV series been like this, what would the reaction have been? The books were very much designed as books, and none of the Aaronovitch-Cartmel-Platt novels would translate easily. All three would need a huge budget, for one thing - this is *Doctor Who* on feature film money, with state of the art special effects. Peter Darvill-Evans seems to have been fond of the SF action films around at the time (it's hard to see 'New Ace', reintroduced in his *Deceit*, as anything other than Sarah Connor from *Terminator 2*). This isn't *Doctor Who* as a TV series, this is *Doctor Who* as a series of movies that sit on the shelf with *Robocop*, *Predator* and *Blade Runner*. There is perhaps something to be said that *Doctor Who* just isn't as dark or cynical as those examples, or as reliant on violence as a solution rather than a problem (while the Doctor's pacifism has been exaggerated by some fans, he's certainly reluctant to resort to violence, even he actually does so rather a lot, and rather ruthlessly). Ultimately, though, the books captured the imagination and fan agenda in a way the last five years on TV had singularly failed to.

The irony of the situation was that this year also saw the debut of Mark Gatiss, writing a much more traditional story, and - in Paul Cornell's second novel, *Love and War* - Benny Summerfield, an extraordinary and popular character. The New Adventures would be characterised by the discovery and development of literally dozens of writers, many of whom have gone on to a successful career, and to a series of spin-offs from spin-offs. But more of that anon...

1993

The thirtieth anniversary was an important moment. There were sections of fandom who still felt that the return to TV was imminent, that the BBC would bring it back for the anniversary. Quite why it was felt that the BBC executives who would make the decision would think this was a milestone worth celebrating was never made clear. But there was a feeling that the only question was whether Bill Baggs or Kevin Davies would direct it.

Behind the scenes, things *were* happening. *The Dark Dimension*, which from the details that have emerged sounds like a pretty dire multi-Doctor story, was certainly at least considered by the BBC. This year, though, saw the end of Green Light's six-year attempt to make a *Doctor Who* movie. Pre-production art and a poster had been produced, and there were several drafts of the script. The thing that both *The Dark Dimension* and *Last of the Time Lords* (the name Green Light gave to their project) had in common was that they were rather episodic stories, mired in Time Lord stuff. As Philip Segal started to work on a *Doctor Who* movie idea of his own, that pattern would continue. This may be coincidence, or it may be evidence that someone at the BBC had something specifically in mind for the series.

Once again, the problem with the story of *Doctor Who* in the nineties is that no-one has interviewed the executives and heads of department who actually wielded the power at the time. The BBC is a big organisation, with many responsibilities. The big questions are exactly how actively did the BBC pursue the return of *Doctor Who* at this time, and who championed it within the BBC? Reports vary wildly - at one extreme nothing was really being done, the press releases were a smokescreen. At the other, the BBC cast around looking to bring it back, but no-one convinced them they had the right way to do it.

The main problem, of course, is that there isn't a 'the BBC'. If BBC Worldwide had their way, *Doctor Who* would never have gone off, because they can sell more DVDs and books off the back of it. Reports indicate that they've often lobbied for the return. BBC Films also seemed keen - it's become a Cannes Film Festival traditional to announce the *Doctor Who* movie. BBC Television, at various times, also seemed keen. The irony could be that having so many people so keen might actually get in the way - there have been plenty of fan rumours over the years that one project has been on the verge of a commission only for another department to veto it because they have something bigger and better planned.

It's entirely possible that there is no one, definitive answer to explain why *Doctor Who* didn't come back quickly to our television screens. The people who've come forward have been closely involved with an individual project, and probably have no idea how close or far they truly were from a commission. Some people, taken at their word, seem to have come very close. Others, taken at their word, were nowhere near as close as they seem to have thought. There may not actually be one person who was in a position to look objectively at the *Doctor Who* situation. If there was, it's highly unlikely he or she spent a vast amount of time looking. And even if there was, he or she's probably not going to be chatting to *DWM* about it at any point soon.

So, in the anniversary year, the only new *Doctor Who* that made it to the screen was a terrible *EastEnders* crossover for Children in Need. Even by the standards of telethon sketches, this was a pretty poor showing. As a celebration of thirty years of *Doctor Who*, after a year in which movies and big budget specials had been rumoured, it looked like a calculated insult more than a celebration. *DWB*, at least, managed to get frothy at the mouth at the return of John Nathan-Turner, and the prospect that, as it had a BBC production code, it was 'canon'.

The novels went monthly at the start of the year. Sections of fandom took out a lot of their resentment on the books, and didn't like the changes at all. Meanwhile, though - seemingly helped by a repeat season - the original novels were enjoying the highest sustained period of sales that they have to date. It was becoming increasingly clear that they were the only continuing adventures of the Doctor that anyone was going to get for a while.

1994

Benny Summerfield was very much of her time - the early to late nineties. She managed to prefigure the two great fictional British women of the decade, Bridget Jones and Lara Croft, while managing to avoid - unlike her more famous sisters - becoming a caricature. As the recession hit, and university goers and sixth formers stayed in higher education to sit it out, the nineties became the decade of the student. Benny, though nominally in her early thirties, was a figure that the readers of the New Adventures could identify with.

She's still going strong, with Big Finish. Her current literary adventures, for those keeping track, are the spin-off from the BF Benny books, which are a spin-off from the BF Benny audios, which are a spin-off from the Benny New Adventures, which are a spin-off from the *Doctor Who* New Adventures, which are a spin-off from a book range spun off from the TV series *Doctor Who*. Over ten years since her debut, she's an established part of the *Doctor Who* canon - a frequent complaint about the early BBC novels was that they couldn't feature her. She's even appeared in the BF Sylvester McCoy adventures. Even just keeping to her Virgin appearances, she's in more *Doctor Who* stories than most incarnations of the Doctor. The writers loved writing for her - perhaps too much, at times, in the *Doctor Who* books. While Fitz has now lasted longer as a companion, it's difficult to imagine him spinning off in the same way, and it's fair to say he's not got the same appeal.

By 1994 (which covers the books from *Conundrum* to *Parasite*), the New Adventures had settled down. Two important developments affected the books this year. The first was the arrival of Rebecca Levene as the Series Editor - she was around from *Deceit*, and given the long gestation periods of novels, it's not always obvious who should be credited with what, but it's generally agreed her first novel as editor was *Tragedy Day*. While she didn't abandon anything Peter Darvill-Evans had done as editor, she now had a stable of established writers to work with, and there were enough books to work out what was working and what wasn't. Rebecca moved the books a little away from the hard SF of books like *Lucifer Rising* and *Deceit* towards a more self-referential, often rather camp, pattern. Old monsters started to appear, but usually radically reinvented or subverted. The books weren't afraid to laugh at themselves, now. It was a case of pendulums swinging: the urge when the books had started was to react against the 'oddball' Cartmel era on TV and produce more serious, grown-up novels. Now, there was room for quirky stories again, like Daniel O'Mahony's *Sapphire and Steel*-as-written-by-Grant-Morrison tale *Falls the Shadow*, or Andy Lane's Sherlock Holmes crossover, *All-Consuming Fire*. The final seal of approval came from Terrance Dicks, whose *Blood Harvest* embraced the New Adventures house style, slipped in some sex, drink and violence, and played around with narrative - all while being a sequel to *State of Decay*.

The other big event was the start of the Missing Adventures. Peter Darvill-Evans had always been resistant to the idea (stating a number of times that the restrictions that would apply to the MAs compared with the NAs would mean it was like owning a house but living in a shed), and under Virgin there was always the impression that the Missing Adventures were second-class citizens. But the books certainly fulfilled a gap in the market.

The books had started with six books a year. Now, already, there were twenty-four. Plus the non-fiction - and Virgin were pretty well publishing one of those every other month, too. It made the books into something of a treadmill. But it also cemented the fact that the books were a success, and removed the biggest objection to them, by creating a range specifically tailored to those who wanted *Doctor Who* 'like it used to be'.

1994 was the first year where most people accepted that there would be no imminent return to TV. It was five years, now, since the TV show had ended. BBV were now established, *DWM* - uniquely among TV tie-in magazines - was thriving without the TV show itself on the air (publishing wisdom was that tie-in magazines suffer even in the gap between seasons, and are doomed when the show ends). The videos were now monthly, and were away from the obvious titles into more 'undiscovered' territory like *Inferno* and *Planet of Evil*.

Doctor Who had adjusted to life without the TV show.

1995

There was, of course, *Doctor Who* fandom on the Internet before 1995. Indeed, looking back over the various archives, by 1995 most of the debates that still rage were already rather well-trodden. So, it's rather arbitrary to pick this year to discuss the Internet and its effect on *Doctor Who* fandom, and I apologise for that.

Doctor Who on the Internet encompasses more than Usenet, mailing lists and message boards. But it's here that people get the full, raw blast of fan discussion. Speech is free on the Internet. There are certainly people who make you feel that it's overpriced, the few who seem to contribute solely to insult or pick at scabby old discussions. That shouldn't diminish from the fact that the Internet is the first forum where fans can give their honest opinions without any distorting of their views. A letters column will always be selective. An editor will strive for balance, they'll avoid inflammatory material. On the Internet, people are free to make their point as many times as they want, using whatever language they want. Some have likened this to a 'bear pit', but the truth is that - barring literally a handful of people - even somewhere like rec.arts.drwho contains enthusiastic, engaged, literate people. The fans pay a lot of money to read the books and buy the audios, and to keep up with all the various lines. If they've paid their money, surely they're entitled to express an opinion? If writers don't like their work being criticised, then the best way to deal with the situation is to write better. A mailing list like Jade Pagoda, dedicated to the *Doctor Who* books, is a writers' dream - a place where passionate, informed people endlessly discuss the books, the range, the writers, the writers' other work. Write a 'serious' novel, even a bestselling one, and you're lucky to get a handful of reviews or any feedback from readers. All the new releases are endlessly discussed and chewed over - and, contrary to the stereotype, the vast majority of what is said is positive, and most criticism is constructive. It's far more common for a release to be heralded as a classic when it's really only just above average than for one to be pounced on and torn to bits by the mob. And, even then, it would be a generous man indeed who said that a few of the releases didn't deserve a good kicking.

The main thing the Internet has done is decentre Britain. *Doctor Who* fandom is enormous and world-spanning. The size of the US market is well known, but Canada and Australia also have a huge number of fans. Nowadays, geography just isn't as relevant as it was - indeed, it's often impossible to say for certain where a fan is writing from. *Doctor Who* fans may be obsessive and pedantic, but we're also international and vaguely organised. There is just no information lag these days - in the mideighties, the American *Doctor Who* comic could pass off information from years before as 'news', but now thanks in large part to the formidable Outpost Gallifrey site (itself American), every *Doctor Who* fan with Internet access has up to the minute news. The magazines that used to provide the service now often seem to plod by comparison, because it takes them a couple of weeks to catch up.

Another boon has been for those marketing *Doctor Who* spin-off products. Internet shopping has made mail order not just acceptable, but perfectly ordinary. Able to sell their products direct to their customers, companies like Big Finish, Telos and Mad Norwegian don't see shops take half the retail price. The irony is that only the BBC have yet to exploit the obvious and existing customer base of *Doctor Who* fans who buy things online. Where are the great deals for customers (British and international) who want to buy the books and DVDs online? Why can't you subscribe to them (most people who buy a *Doctor Who* range seem to buy all or nearly all of them). As it is, the avid American EDA fan buys the books from Amazon instead.

In the end, it's more about weighing your reviews than reading them - the Internet has helped make people aware of all the *Doctor Who* ranges that are out there. It's helped to keep *Doctor Who* fandom a vibrant, active community in a decade where the laws of physics would seem to demand that it should have faded away.

1996

By now, the fans had got used to discounting rumours of a new series, so when Sylvester McCoy mentioned at a convention that his friend Paul McGann was going to play the new Doctor, no-one really believed it. Most of the magazines, if they mentioned it at all, did so in passing.

But, as we've learned since, Phillip Segal had been working for some years with the BBC to bring the show back. The final TV movie perhaps betrays its origin as something that's been cooking for a while. It's a strange piece of work, one that's not quite a series pilot, not quite something that stands on its own. It's also plainly not the story Segal wanted to tell - every previous version started on Gallifrey and featured the Daleks and Master. Those stories are all epics - more to the point, all were series pilots, which would have helped to justify the expense.

The TV Movie is a terrible pilot. I was the first person who had to tell an extended story set afterwards, and pretty soon I'd given up any hope of extrapolating what the Segal series would have been like based on what we saw. Judging from *Regeneration*, the book based on the making of the story, very little of the 'vision' made it to the final product. If *Doctor Who* fans can't work out what would have happened next, pity the poor American TV executives who had to decide whether to follow it up.

Traditionally, reviewers have praised McGann and criticised the script. But I think the it's rather the other way round. Don't get me wrong, the script collapses at the end - as a rule of thumb, if all your characters have no idea what's going on, then neither will the audience. It seems from the script that the original idea was that the Master was going to decay as the story progressed, until - presumably - he was in *The Deadly Assassin* decayed mode by the end, and trying to steal the Doctor's body. Eric Roberts' schedule seemed to rule out the make up job that required. But the rest of the script is up to the job, and successfully introduces the Doctor.

McGann, though, isn't terribly good, and seems a bit lost in places. Hardly his fault - it was apparently filmed very quickly. But watching him in *The TV Movie* after so many years of books featuring him is a bit like watching *Silver Nemesis* after reading *Human Nature* and *The Also People* - it doesn't even seem to be the same sort of thing, let alone the same lead character in the same series. The script does give him some good lines, but the Doctor McGann talks about in the BBV documentary *Bidding Adieu* - a Doctor who was weighted down by centuries of guilt, and who McGann compared with Dracula - is much more interesting. McGann excels at playing rather sinister observer characters - the quiet guy who's far more creepy than he looks. The character "I" in *Withnail and I* (OK, OK - he's named *Marwood*, be like that) is that man, as are his characters in *Nice Town*, *The Rainbow* and *Nature Boy*. He doesn't get any of that to do in *The TV Movie*, with perhaps the exception of the 'walking through glass' scene, which is really rather clever and special - far more interesting than the 'shoes' scene that people took as the cue for the character.

This many years on, *The TV Movie* looks more and more like a footnote. In *Queer as Folk*, Russell Davies himself declared - as a key moment of resolution, no less, god bless you, Mr Davies - 'Paul McGann doesn't count'. Both the EDAs and the McGann audios have been characterised by their lack of any building on *The TV Movie*. The eighth Doctor isn't half-human, he doesn't kiss girls, he doesn't see people's future when he meets them, he doesn't think about Grace.

But there was an opportunity lost here. A funny, self-referential, witty show in which someone runs around fighting monsters in contemporary America. US audiences were ready for that show: *Buffy* started the following year, and it proved to be a cult hit. Now, if it had gone to series, Segal *Who* would have been made by the same people, in the same place, as *Sliders*. It would have looked like *Sliders*. But a slick, American *Doctor Who* done properly could have out Buffied *Buffy*, it could have been there first, and we could have just sat down to the ninth season premiere. Just don't imagine for a minute that it would have been anything like *Reckless Engineering* or *Neverland*.

1997

The reasons the BBC brought the *Doctor Who* books inhouse is unclear (again, while fanboys have interviewed every extra on *The Web Planet* and the costume designer of *Meglos*, the people who actually make the important decisions have proved elusive). By the time they approached authors to contribute, in July 1996, it was already very clear that the McGann movie wasn't going to lead to a new series. The deal they had with Virgin gave them a lot of money for little work and absolutely no risk - taking them inhouse wouldn't make them oodles more money. They didn't seem to have any brilliant international marketing strategy... if they were planning to 'build the brand' in the US on the back of *The TV Movie*, then surely they'd have thought to arrange some form of American distribution. If they'd planned to cash in on a fresh new face as Doctor... well, they'd have put that face on the cover.

It certainly wasn't to punish Virgin for taking *Doctor Who* 'too far', as some fans at the time gleefully speculated. It turned out they weren't so much following in Virgin's footsteps as robbing them for their Nikes. Despite all the rumours that the books would be for kids or that there was to be a range of pure historicals, what we ended up with looked remarkably like they could have been Virgin books (more than one of the early EDAs and PDAs were, in fact, simply rejected Virgin novels dusted off and sent to a different publisher). The writers were, with few exceptions, established writers for Virgin. (Virgin, for their part, kept a lot of us busy on other projects, meaning we couldn't contribute.)

It was while commenting on the late NAs that I coined a phrase that's come to haunt discussion of *Doctor Who*, but one I think is important to understanding the two main sections of fandom: 'the rad/trad divide'. Simply put - and any analysis like this is going to generalise wildly - there are two strains in *Doctor Who* storytelling. The 'traditionalists', or 'trads', want any new novel, audio, webcast or revival of the TV show to be 'just like it was on telly'. The 'radicals', or 'rads', want *Doctor Who* to be more experimental than that, to take their cues from contemporary culture (or to try to anticipate it), and to play around with form and narrative. The only time I think there were actually two rival camps was 1997, with the transition from Virgin to BBC Books.

It's important to stress that neither the trads or rads are 'right', and that both terms are problematic. I don't, for example, know where I fall on the spectrum. I enjoy reading rad books more than trad ones, but is *The Dying Days* really a 'radical' work? Not for my money. When *Alien Bodies*, for example, brings back the Krotons, is it truly radical, or simply traditional with a side order of sarcasm and knowing looks? And, as I've said a few times in this essay, there's no one such thing as '*Doctor Who* like it was on the telly'.

There's also the problem that if *Doctor Who* had continued on television, it would have changed beyond all recognition in the last fifteen years. Take any two stories fifteen years apart, and they could be from different series - *Marco Polo* and *The Invisible Enemy*, for example. *The Monster of Peladon* and *Ghost Light*. There are points of comparison, of course, but they're rather basic ones, like the theme music is the same and there's a character called the Doctor in them. All have different agendas, different narrative techniques.

The books have moved things on. You only need to be a dyed in the wool NA fan who goes back to watch a McCoy story on video to realise that. Or to re-read a 'shocking' early NA like *Cat's Cradle: Warhead* to realise it's actually tame, accessible and much more '*Who*ish' than you remember. But there's the constant pressure to be 'like *Doctor Who*' that keeps them from deviating too far from the format. What people say when they say they want it 'like it was on the telly' is that they want *notional Doctor Who*, like you remember it being from the seventies, but which it was never actually like. *Doctor Who*, on television, wasn't - on the whole, it's impossible to generalise - obsessed with old monsters, and was constantly changing, witty, surprising and inventive. *Doctor Who* 'on the telly' was far more 'like', say, *Mad Dogs and Englishmen* with Pink Poodles rewriting Tolkein than it was like *The Bodysnatchers*, with Professor Litefoot from *The Talons of Weng-Chiang* meeting the Zygons.

1998

The most remarkable thing about the New Adventures only became obvious after Virgin lost the licence and people started asking what the authors were up to these days. Of the British-based New Adventures authors who wrote more than one NA, only one hasn't received a TV credit. Since around 1998, there's barely been a day without at least one of the Virgin authors' or editors' names appearing on a British TV screen. Between them, Golden Roses and BAFTA awards have been won, soap operas steered, cult hits created, mainstream drama and comedy scripted. Virtually every Virgin *Who* author has gone on to write or co-write at least one non-*Who* book. A fair few are now full-time writers - and (outside of television, at least), there are far fewer of those in Britain than you'd think.

The primary reason for this is obvious: the New Adventures were one of the few places in Britain that took unsolicited manuscripts from aspiring authors. While TV companies occasionally launch competitions for new writers, there's no real, systematic way in which they encourage and develop new talent. As for books... it's pretty much unheard of these days to get a book commissioned without an agent, and agents are increasingly looking to represent people who've already been published. It's a vicious circle.

Peter Darvill-Evans' appeal for unsolicited manuscripts may have been, in part, done for less than noble motives. It was good publicity for the range, after all. And hiring new authors is always going to be cheaper than hiring established ones. But the end result was practically a parade of up and coming writing talent of the nineties, particularly if you include the *Decalogs*, and get to rope in Steven Moffat and Stephen Baxter.

BBC Books have found just as many new writers, and have been noticeably better at encouraging existing writers like Lloyd Rose, Mark Morris and Paul Magrs to contribute to the range. What they've not done, though, is develop that stable of talent. Virgin didn't just have the NA authors write *Doctor Who* books - to this day, they produce paperback episode guides for pretty much every TV show that deserves one, and they tend to be written by the *Who* authors. There were plenty of other avenues for *Doctor Who* authors to explore at Virgin, not quite all of them writing pornographic novels, and Virgin recognised they had a talented bunch of people. So far, BBC Books haven't tapped into that resource for the many other books they publish.

But these writers weren't, despite what some of the more negative NA reviews said, just science-fiction authors looking to get a book published wherever they could. Indeed, it's noticeable just how few of the authors have gone on to write SF. Paul Cornell has written a couple of mainstream SF novels, but only as part of a wide-ranging career - his day job, if you like, is as a writer on *Casualty*. Both *The League of Gentlemen* and *The Second Coming* could be, broadly, defined as 'telefantasy', but they're certainly not the hard SF that Darvill-Evans favoured with the early NAs. The NA authors have colonised soap opera in the UK - there's not one now that hasn't had an NA author or editor work on it. They've written non-genre sitcoms and drama series, for the most part. Part of that is because there isn't much telefantasy on British TV (predictably, perhaps, two NA authors, Gareth Roberts and Mark Gatiss both contributed to *Randall and Hopkirk (Deceased)*, the highest profile example of the genre), but mostly I think it reflects that the NA writers were writers at heart, not limited to just SF authors or *Doctor Who* fan-fictioneers.

Not that we weren't fans. Most of us seemed to write *Doctor Who* books because we loved *Doctor Who*, and saw a potential for telling stories within the framework it set up. In turn, it's not hard to imagine that *Doctor Who* has given many of these writers an understanding of how television works - all those *DWM* articles, *In-Vision* features and *Making of Doctor Who* chapters on the difference between a director and producer, the arcane art of the vision mixer, the uses and limitations of studio and OB work must have rubbed off.

It's tempting to see this as a 'lost generation' - that we missed out on *Doctor Who* on the telly in the nineties written by Russell Davies, Gareth Roberts, Mark Gatiss, Paul Cornell and Steven Moffat. But instead, we got to see the early work of a new generation of TV writing talent. *Doctor Who* only gained from the talents the NAs attracted.

1999

Whatever way you look at it, the Big Finish *Doctor Who* audios are something of a phenomenon.

There have been *Doctor Who* 'audio adventures' since the seventies - records like *Genesis of the Daleks* and *The Pestacons*, radio shows *Slipback*, *The Paradise of Death* and *The Ghosts of N-Space*. Radio would seem to be an excellent medium for *Doctor Who* - an SF show (for sake of argument) that's always been more interested in wit and big ideas than visual spectacle. Despite clichés to the contrary, while *Doctor Who*'s never been a big budget show, it could certainly have done more mindless action than it did. Part of the problem with *Doctor Who* on the radio is that there isn't really a natural slot for it - *The Paradise of Death* seemed distinctly uncomfortable on Radio 2, and just explaining where *Slipback* was broadcast is complicated enough.

There was already a market for *Doctor Who* audios - the Radio Collection had released 'lost' stories on tape and CD. BBV had taken another step, and started to release their stories exclusively on CD. The market for audio drama, spoken word and comedy is usually seen as car owners or people listening to Walkmen on the way to work. At the time, that was thought to be almost exclusively people with tape players, not

CDs. Big Finish had also started their Benny range of audios by adapting New Adventure novels, and knew that enough of an audience was there to make it viable.

But this was by no means a sure thing - none of the previous radio dramas had exactly set the world alight. The Big Finish audios on CD cost more than buying a story on VHS or DVD (if you shop around). There were plenty of other demands on the fan pound, too.

One relatively early casualty were the cassette releases. As most high street shops only stocked the tapes, this meant that since the first McGann season (when the format was dropped), the audios haven't had a significant high street presence. Apart from the comic shops, only larger branches of some book and record shops stock them. At the same time, selling a (higher priced) CD direct by mail order is far more profitable than selling a cassette in a shop.

As with the NAs, the audios quickly went monthly, and now there are two audios more months than not. The audios have been allowed into areas the books haven't - Terry Nation's estate have licenced the use of the Daleks, and the BBC have let them recast the Doctor for a series of one-off 'Unbound' adventures.

What we've increasingly seen, though, is a fragmentation in the *Doctor Who* audience. There's a model where all the various ranges could be brought together. When Gary Russell edited *DWM*, the comic strip featured the seventh Doctor, Ace and Benny. Now, the comic strip, audios, EDAs and Telos novellas have presented, in effect, four different eighth Doctor continuities. This isn't to criticise that approach - *Doctor Who's* strength has always been diversity, after all. And it's not to complain about 'canon' - it's not a question of worrying how all the ranges fit together. The main problem is that it's practically impossible to follow every strain of *Doctor Who*, and if you don't follow a range, you can quickly get alienated by its internal continuity. None of their stories are that convoluted, but Izzy, Charley and Compassion - the Doctor's companions at various times in various ranges - were all involved in complex time paradox/identity type stories that ran across half a dozen stories. There will always be people in the audience confused just to learn that the Doctor's got a companion called 'Anji' they've not heard of.

This fragmentation is a sign of success - the market seems to be able to bear all the ranges (whatever the reasons for Telos losing their licence, it wasn't poor sales). But it does mean that when two *Doctor Who* fans meet, they can both religiously follow the ongoing Eighth Doctor Adventures, yet not have a clue what the other one is talking about. We've got used to the idea of 'book fans' and 'audio fans'. It's going to be very interesting to see how the new TV series will affect this.

2000

What's essential to *Doctor Who*?

I don't think there's a right answer. The year 2000 saw people asking the question a lot. There were now all sorts of spin-offs that featured *Doctor Who* characters, but licenced from their creators, not the BBC. BBV had started the trend some years back with *Auton*, but by now had a whole portfolio of work featuring monsters created by Robert Holmes, Robert Banks Stewart and Pip and Jane Baker. Benny Summerfield featured in a range by Big Finish, who were also planning a range of Dalek audios without the Doctor.

'Essential' means just that - what elements of the series are necessary and sufficient to make it *Doctor Who*? It's not asking whether it would be nice to see the Brigadier, or whether a new Doctor should meet the Daleks - clearly you can tell a *Doctor Who* story without those. And it's not just a question of the *Doctor Who* logo: some of the later New Adventures didn't have a *Doctor Who* logo on them (and, of course, neither do many of the spin-offs). What is the bare minimum?

But it was also a question being asked in the BBC Books. This was the year that Gallifrey was destroyed in the EDAs, as part of new editor Justin Richards' plan to revamp the line. He set out his plans in a document to the writers where he posed the question of what was essential to *Doctor Who*. In doing so, he referred back to the television series, rather than tried to forge new solutions. (One of the interesting things about *Death Comes to Time* is that it decentres the Doctor - he's only part of a large ensemble cast - there are more radical ways of answering the question than looking back at the TV show.) But the document rightly points out that you don't need old monsters, you don't need a TARDIS, you don't need a companion, you don't need the Time Lords (introduced in something like the fiftieth story)... you don't even need the Doctor, as *Mission to the Unknown* and various spin-offs have proved.

Justin admitted he didn't want to go quite that far. What he did, in fact, was settle on a 'back to basics' model. The Doctor was a traveller in space and time, whose origin was a mystery. He had a TARDIS, a teenage girl who was a relative and a pair of companions. He couldn't pilot the ship properly. In 2000, though, the idea of *Doctor Who* without its past scandalised some people, who saw it as somehow a calculated attack on everything they believed in.

Doctor Who, to a large extent, had become its past. Justin argued that the important thing was, to paraphrase, that monsters came out of the sea, not that the third one on the left was called Sauvix and was played by Stuart Fell. *Doctor Who* storytelling can get bogged down in the details and literally lose the plot - again, that happened on TV, with stories like *Mawdryn Undead* and *Attack of the Cybermen* that just don't have a clear narrative, protagonists or characters whose motives are logical or articulated properly. To some, *Doctor Who* serials were a collection of facts to be logged, not a story where we care about the characters.

It was inevitable. *Doctor Who* on TV now looks monolithic. It's very tempting to imagine that there was a twenty-six year 'story arc' in place, in which the plan all along was to reveal that he was a Time Lord, and where monsters like the Cybermen, Ice Warriors and Sontarans were gradually introduced. But, of course, many of the creators of *Doctor Who* had limited awareness of the show's past. It's recently been suggested on rec.arts.drwho that The Key to Time season was a deliberate reference back to *The Keys of Marinus*. Both feature the Doctor running around after bits of device that control free will, but surely it's a coincidence - the write up in *The Making of Doctor Who* talks about it governing 'fairly', not controlling actions. If Williams had realised it had been done before (sort of), he almost certainly wouldn't have done it again.

The cutting edge of *Doctor Who*, the ongoing series, always looks subversive and dangerous, the past always looks like part of a grand tradition. 2000 also saw the growth of 'NAstalgia', a fondness for the New Adventures 'golden age' that those of us who were there to deflect the brickbats when the books actually came out find extremely ironic. Not to mention gratifying.

2001

BBCi have become major players on the *Doctor Who* scene. Because they're not selling anything, this isn't always obvious. But the BBC Cult site has quietly built up an impressive library of *Doctor Who* materials, and one that encompasses far more than the TV series. There are now Virgin novels archived online, there are reference books, telesnaps, plus all sorts of fun and games. Bearing in mind there is - or was - no series to push, that's pretty good going.

BBCi is funded by the licence fee, which means it's the one place that you can get BBC-endorsed *Doctor Who* for free. In the nineties - unavoidably - *Doctor Who* became *Doctor Who product*. Commitment to *Doctor Who* became measured in what you bought. It's barely possible to follow *Doctor Who* ranges with a great deal of effort, let alone without one. It's impossible to find the time and money to follow every strand of *Doctor Who* merchandise. If nothing else, it's impossible to define what counts as *Doctor Who* merchandise, now that half a dozen characters from the books have spun off into their own ranges. The result has alienated a lot of *Who* fans from much, if not most, of current *Doctor Who*.

While someone needs Internet access to get to the BBCi site, that's by no means an exclusive club these days. The big breakthrough for BBCi, the thing that made them realise what a big, loyal audience there was for *Doctor Who* stuff, was *Death Comes to Time*.

Getting rejected by Radio 4 was almost certainly the best thing that could have happened to *Death Comes to Time*. It's hard to see where Radio 4 could put it - they have regular slots for drama and comedy, but *Doctor Who* would sit rather uncomfortably in either of those. It's certainly possible to imagine *Doctor Who* written for the (to stereotype wildly) greying, middle class, female audience of Radio 4, and the channel did broadcast *Hitchhikers* (twenty-five years ago!) and *The League of Gentlemen*. However, it's not the perfect match, and it's hard to see how either the channel or *Doctor Who* would have gained from the broadcast.

BBCi, on the other hand, was a perfect fit. *Doctor Who* fans tend to be 'early adopters' - they get new technology before most people do. There was an active *Doctor Who* community online ten years before most people had even heard of the Internet. *Doctor Who* titles appeared on VHS among the first handful of BBC releases. BBV pioneered the CD-only format for audio drama, at a point when BBC Audio still thought it was a bit avant garde to release things like that on tape.

Death Comes to Time was the first *Doctor Who* story available everywhere in the world at exactly the same time. It's obviously easier to do that on the Internet than any other way, but it's becoming increasingly the done thing in the entertainment industry - although even *Harry Potter* and *Star Wars* haven't quite managed to get simultaneous release into all markets. Distribution glitches have meant that the books have vanished from whole continents for a couple of months, each territory releases the DVDs to a different schedule, and the BF audios and Telos novellas hit the physical problem of post services taking varying times to reach their customers. We're already getting people in Australia and North America worrying / complaining that the Russell T Davies series may take... gasp... weeks to make it over to them.

The pilot episode of *Death Comes to Time* got a huge number of hits. Debate has raged about exactly how many people visited the site. It's impossible to come to anything more than an informed estimate. What we *do* know is that the hit rate was something like forty or fifty times what the BBC was expecting, and it briefly crashed their servers. It got coverage on - ironically, given its origins - the prestigious *Today* programme on Radio 4. Most important of all, the BBC stopped thinking that *Doctor Who* was a relic from the seventies, and realised it had a role in the twenty-first century at the cutting edge of digital broadcasting.

2002

Doctor Who's fortieth year saw an environment where *Doctor Who* fans had never been so well served. There were the VHS and DVD releases, *DWM*, the Past Doctor and Eighth Doctor books, the Telos novellas, the Big Finish *Doctor Who* range, plus their Benny, Dalek and Sarah Jane ranges, BBV, the Radio Collection and Kaldor City. Spin-off comics from the EDAs (*Faction Paradox* and *Miranda*) had been announced. *Death Comes to Time* and *Real Time* were on BBCi. That's just the licenced stuff.

All of this was, broadly speaking, by the fans and for the fans. Indeed, by now, most *Doctor Who* writers have contributed to more than one of the ranges out there, making something of a mockery of those who'd try to see the industry as rival camps. What is perhaps most remarkable is how stable these ranges are - there's a *Doctor Who* audience out there, and while they're not as uncritical as some cynics have suggested, they are a reliable audience.

None of the *Doctor Who* ranges are spectacular successes - the *Doctor Who* DVDs are marvellous pieces of work (easily the best TV releases anywhere in the world, consistently nominated for awards), but they don't sell in vast numbers. The novels have run for over ten years and make a modest profit, they aren't bestsellers. The BF audios are successful, but there's no significant high street presence. Whenever *Doctor Who* makes the news, an interviewer will invariably express surprise that there's been a steady stream of books and CD plays for a decade.

This doesn't matter. By definition, these products will appeal only to a niche audience. To buy all the BF audios, you'd have to pay nearly £200 a year, and you'd have to keep track of various titles, ranges and release dates. Anyone who does that is a fan. The books require just as much commitment - even on a reduced schedule, nearly a million words of prose a year are released a year. A recent survey suggested that the average Briton reads three books a year. Reading is a minority interest nowadays, and even *Harry Potter and the Order of the Phoenix* was read by fewer people than watched *Battlefield*, the lowest-ever rated episode of *Doctor Who* on television.

What we have here is a golden age for fans. These are stories written with a specific audience, and - thanks to the Internet - there's more interaction between the writers and the audience than any other place in the world. It's led to a lively set of ranges that (at their best) can react to give the audience what they want. There have been hundreds of such stories, now, and there's such a diversity that - with echoes of the TV series - they defy easy categorisation or lazy generalisation.

What the current model lacks, though, is any way of reaching out to a wider audience. There's little or no attempt to reach out to the general reader or listener. This isn't anyone's fault - there isn't an efficient way to advertise to a market that may not even exist. There's an easier market to reach: existing fans who don't read, for example, the books. Again, though, it would be a very unperceptive *Doctor Who* fan who didn't realise that there *were* books. Efforts could be made to make the books more accessible to new readers - the books themselves are usually pretty good, but there are a lot of them, they all look the same. There need to be more stepping on points, the BBC needs to make it easier for people to take the first step to try them out.

There are new *Doctor Who* fans - many (a surprising number) of the current fans came to the series via the books. One section of the audience misses out entirely: children. I'm guessing that most people reading this first encountered *Doctor Who* as a child. Nowadays, how would anyone under the age of... well, what? - fifteen?... become a *Doctor Who* fan? In the age of *Harry Potter* and Philip Pullman, which of the two hundred *Doctor Who* books could we give a kid as a Christmas present? It's a significant gap, one that could be plugged, and that could only benefit *Doctor Who*.

2003

People haven't realised yet, but *this is it*.

The Russell Davies scripted version of *Doctor Who* on television isn't *a* revival of *Doctor Who* on television. It's *the* revival. Sure, franchises never die these days, and if *Lost in Space* can come back, then *Doctor Who* isn't destined for eternal oblivion. But this is the BBC putting their money where our mouth is: a primetime, live action, British-funded revival, written by a top TV dramatist and *Who* fan. It's not going to get better than this - because, frankly, it just doesn't get much better than this.

For the last fifteen years, the *Doctor Who* brand has been managed on a slow burn. The plan is to keep the fanbase happy, but just as importantly, it's to keep the brand alive. You can walk into a high street shop and see the *Doctor Who* logo on books, DVDs and the Radio Collection CDs. It's a living brand, and plenty of people still want *Doctor Who* products. But why has the BBC been keeping the brand alive? Surely, it's for just the eventuality that we're faced with now: the return of *Doctor Who* on television. The current sales become the minimum number the ninth Doctor novels will sell. And this sounds like great news for anyone who was worried about the books, or just concerned that gravity will eventually affect the *Doctor Who* lines.

After this, though... what? After the boom, will there be a bust? In the short to medium term, there won't be any more *Doctor Who* after this new show, unless it finally makes the leap to movies (something that's been promised pretty much every year since 1975!). The BBC priority won't be on keeping the brand alive, and their accountants will see (presumably) a slump in sales. We've been used to *Doctor Who* on a slow burn. We might now face a situation with *Doctor Who* burning brightly, for a few magnificent seasons.

But I'm certainly not complaining. This is what we wanted all along. Russell Davies is the perfect person to write the new series - even for the book fans who aren't actually that fussed about the return to TV (and who would actually be opposed if it clipped the wings of the ongoing novels). At the moment, we're at a very early stage - we're several months away from the script being written, for one thing - but it all sounds fantastic.

Russell Davies is promising us 'contemporary' *Doctor Who*, as opposed to retro, and that's exactly what we need. He's not going to show us how *Doctor Who* should have been done all these years, he's going to show us that *Doctor Who* can be something modern and relevant.

It is the *Doctor Who* I've waited my whole life to watch on television - one that's an uncompromised piece of drama, with the BBC fully behind it, with perhaps the best possible writer for the job depicting his vision of the show. Will it be all things to all men? No. Will sections of fandom be up in arms? Hell yes. Will *Doctor Who* catch the imagination of a whole new generation? Don't doubt it for a moment. We fans have kept the faith, we've kept the flame burning. *Doctor Who* should never have ended in the first place. Now he's going to return, and he is, to para-phrase the man himself, going to prove to us that we weren't mistaken in our beliefs. *Doctor Who's* coming back, and this time nothing's going to stop him reaching his full potential. It's going to be the biggest thing to hit British TV for years, and if the BBC play it properly, it could be the global mega franchise that *Doctor Who* has always threatened to become.

We've waited nearly fifteen years for *Doctor Who* to return to television. We've got used to waiting. Even the BBC's own publicity said it was 'about time' *Doctor Who* came back - in 1996, and it's nearly been back two or three times since. But somehow, I think the next year or two are going to be the most tantalising.

It's going to be worth the wait. And as ruby anniversary presents go, it's a pretty damn good one.

FIVE YEARS ON

2004

When that fortieth anniversary issue of *Enlightenment* was first published, it ended on the ultimate cliffhanger - *Doctor Who* was coming back to television.

Looking back, it surprises me how early the new TV show was announced - nearly eighteen months before it was broadcast. There was a drip feed of information, but so much of it only made it harder to work out what the end result would look like. Just when you could get your head around Christopher Eccleston fighting Autons, you learned that he'd be wearing a leather jacket... and Billie Piper would be the companion. It was very difficult to triangulate all this.

What I wrote back then was one of the last snapshots of *Doctor Who* as it was (well, as I saw it - not the same thing, of course) before the new era. My assertion that *Doctor Who* no longer revolved around a TV series, that there was a whole ecosystem of spin-offs and other media, may look a little quaint, now. At the same time, it's obvious that the novels, the audios and the comic strip have all been a big part of the mix for the new TV show. My 2004 self was a little worried that the new series might contradict the books - or, worse still, just ignore them. Five years on, it's all more complicated than I'd imagined: when the TV series gets Paul Cornell to adapt *Human Nature*, my head says it's clearly a celebration of the book, but my heart worries that the book just got decanonised. Then my head says 'hang on, *Human Nature's on television*', and head and heart perform the Ewok dance of victory.

It's hard to remember now just how nervous everyone was in 2004. Russell Davies was clearly the best man for the job... but was the job even possible? Balancing the demands of the fans with that of the mass audience, telling *Doctor Who* stories worth telling in forty five minutes to an audience used to gameshows and middlebrow emergency services drama, getting the BBC behind something...

I was commissioned to write the last eighth Doctor novel, and was specifically told to leave things open just in case the new series bombed and we were back where we'd been after six months or so. The more likely scenario was that the show would do OK, but wouldn't be renewed.

To be honest, that didn't hold much terror for me - it's what happened with McGann, after all, and that had provided a nice chunk of new material and a sales bump for the novels.

Just imagine that: the series ending at *The Parting of the Ways*. Eccleston turning into that bloke from *Casanova*, after a fascinating, spiky series that just couldn't match up to ITV's much-hyped hit of the year, *Celebrity Wrestling*. If we'd been offered *that* in 2004, we might have taken it. It's what the smart money assumed was going to happen. It's the lot of the telefantasy fan to see their beloved show killed off before its time, to the point that Joss Whedon's fans were campaigning to save *Dollhouse* before he'd even shot the pilot.

So, 2004 was a year of waiting, and of obsessing over any bit of news that was released.

2005

Looking at some of my *Enlightenment* columns from 2005, they were quite breathless. But... well, that's the only sensible response to what happened in 2005.

I'm proud of what I wrote for the '2003' section of the anniversary essay. I'm proud of the fact that I'm on record - in a *TV Zone* column - as predicting ten million viewers and that *Doctor Who* would universally be renowned as the best thing ever. That seemed crazy at the time. Part of me had that cult TV cringe/snarl thing - 'the mass audience aren't smart enough to love my show'. Well, that old canard's been put to the sword. I thought it would be. It's *Doctor Who*. It's the best thing ever. Of course it exceeded our wildest dreams; *of course* it won the Hugo Award and the TV Quick award in the same week; *of course* a Super Bowl-sized audience watched the Kylie episode; *of course* that's an army of Daleks invading the Earth for the season finale; *of course* when the Doctor announces his retirement, on live television, while winning his third consecutive National Television Award (but isn't actually there because he's in a sold-out, critically-acclaimed West End production of *Hamlet*) the newspapers stop the presses. Of course. It's just what *Doctor Who* is. It was always like this, wasn't it?

There was a war and we won.

The very smartest thing Russell Davies did was decide that his *Doctor Who* was meant to be on opposite *Ant and Dec* on Saturday night. It wouldn't be cult telly, it wouldn't be one of those shows that's great but can't quite find the right timeslot. The Saturday night thing has had all sorts of implications for the show - it meant, for example, that *Journey's End* felt more like *The X-Factor* final than an *X-Files* season finale - but the main thing is that it meant that *Doctor Who* was out and proud, not cowering in the corner hoping some critics would like it. It had to be the biggest thing on television or nothing at all.

Rewatching the Christopher Eccleston season is quite an odd experience. It seemed very confident, lavish and spiky at the time. The *Doctor Who Confidential* for *The End of the World*, where people queue up to say it's never, ever going to look as good as this or be so effects-intensive again is funny now in about a dozen different ways. You forget that the show had Simon Callow in it, and Tosh from *Torchwood*. Above all else, you realise that so much of the dynamism of the show is that no one making it really knows if it's going to work. They're literally working out how to make a show unlike anything else being made in the UK as they go along. Later seasons have a swagger about them - watch *Doomsday* or *The Runaway Bride* and they just *know* they're making the sort of television that people be talking about in twenty years. *Voyage of the Damned* just *knows* that a large chunk of the British population will take the day off, give each other presents and a big turkey dinner before settling down to watch it together.

The first season is bold, rather than confident. It's all-in, uncompromised stuff. Billie Piper is incredibly endearing, but also very clearly learning the ropes. Christopher Eccleston is extraordinary. What's *most* extraordinary is you see that Russell Davies is telling the truth when he says that he just writes for 'the Doctor' - you can see exactly how Tennant would play the same scripts, changing not a word but everything else. The grammar of the show hasn't really changed - the speed things move, the way that (like Grant Morrison's comics) Russell Davies will often skip over the dull middle bits and leave us to infer them.

What's most extraordinary now is that all the stuff we got worked up about seems so... *Doctor Who*. He wears a leather jacket and has feelings for his companion, we go back to see her mum, there are silly cameos, and the episodes are fifty minutes long. Well, yeah. And?

I think Christopher Eccleston is now 'my Doctor'. I'm a lifelong Tom man. Clearly, the great success of *Doctor Who* now is down to a whole bunch of people, and clearly Russell Davies is top of that list. But Christopher Eccleston is the one who perhaps risked the most, and the one who, right there on screen, untied the Gordian knot while squaring a circle while doing six impossible things before breakfast.

2006

In some parallel universe, presumably not the one where there are airships and Mickey's gran is alive, Easter 2006 saw the BBC launch Dale

Winton's *Celebrity Fencing*, a show in which ex members of Atomic Kitten and retired newsreaders learned to fight with rapiers. The surprise winner was 'that bloke who was Captain Jack'. Four million people watched it, and the delighted BBC commissioned a second series. The *Doctor Who* fans watched it because of John Barrowman, and their friends and workmates occasionally say they quite liked Christopher Eccleston and ask if there's going to be a new series.

Back here, the second series of *Doctor Who* consolidated the success of the first. Russell Davies clearly had a policy of nudging his audience along - notice how the first series had been wary of alien planets or past continuity (when things were referred to, like the creator of the Daleks or the Doctor's home planet, they weren't actually named). It was all quite grounded, and even with the science-fiction stuff (like *The End of the World* and *Father's Day*), it was all carefully kept at the ordinary, human level by filtering everything through Rose and her perspective. By contrast, the fourth series had *Planet of the Ood* and throwaway lines about *The Sensorites*.

The second season saw the show as sure as it could be that lots of people would be watching, and with the luxury of knowing there would be a third season. David Tennant was a much 'safer' Doctor than Eccleston, certainly the actor seemed much more comfortable with the role, and with the extra-curricular stuff that the role involved. *Doctor Who* was now an industry - literally, as the Cardiff production facilities became permanent. *Torchwood* and *Sarah Jane* both spun off from this second season. The sense is of *Doctor Who* blossoming. The special effects just make a quantum leap, the storytelling starts experimenting a little.

The original idea for the show - dare I say it, the one that Christopher Eccleston thought he'd signed up for - was reported to be a mini series written solely by Davies. Piecing together what's been said, it's basically the Russell Davies episodes of Series 1 except *Boom Town*, with Sontarans instead of Slitheen, and with a beginning, middle and a definite end. Taking those episodes as broadcast, there's a much higher ratio of social commentary and Rose-centric stuff. The safer, fan-favourite episodes - *The Unquiet Dead, Dalek, Father's Day* - are missing.

Plenty of shows launch expecting to last a year, do brilliantly, then have terrible problems when they survive (just ask any *Heroes* fan). Russell Davies was at something of an advantage - *Doctor Who* had run for years back in the day, and was clearly not a limited concept. The loss of Eccleston also meant the production team couldn't rest on their laurels - they had the same advantage losing Rose and gaining Martha the following year, and engineered the same change by losing Martha and gaining Donna for the fourth season.

As well as the boost from knowing the series was working, that the audience was there, Russell Davies had learned a few lessons. The production team were just getting more efficient at what they did - Eccleston and Piper, for example, spent a lot of the first season on set while special effects were prepared, and it had become clear that they could easily use stand-ins for that. *The Empty Child* had been scary, and Davies realised just how much he'd neglected that in his own scripts for the first season. There had been plenty of unsettling moments, but very few out and out equivalents of just saying 'boo!'. The second season is much, much more slick and smooth than the first, and while the fans and the general audience were starting to take the show for granted, clearly the production team weren't.

2007

We're living in the age of the geek in many ways. News coverage from Comicon is more extensive than that of the G8 summits. The new President of the United States gave Leonard Nimoy the Vulcan salute and collected Spider-Man comics. Movies and TV shows in the eighties used to have nerdy characters in the background, now we have shows like *Chuck* and *The Big Bang Theory* where the geeks are the protagonists. Shows like *Futurama* and *Robot Chicken* are basically stringed-together geeky touchstones and catchphrases, but even the handful of mainstream movies that aren't based on existing 'cult' series are full of in-jokes and 'easter eggs' (or, as Homer Simpson put it, 'Mmmmm... references'). The digital age has filled the Internet and DVDs with obscure stuff. There's real social capital now in knowing what else an actor has been in.

It's fitting that the new TV series has reaped the rewards of this. Reality has caught up with fandom, and 2007 saw a 1995 *Doctor Who* New Adventure novel adapted for television. Russell Davies continued to nudge *Doctor Who* and its mainstream audience along, further and further into fanboy territory. Everyone in Britain was a *Doctor Who* fanboy by 2007, and the third season is, for me, just about perfect *Doctor Who*. The third season certainly dips for a few episodes in the middle, but there aren't really *bad* episodes, just ones that should have been better. But for the most part, this is the *Doctor Who* I wanted on the telly. I first got that buzz with the last scene of *The End of the World*, but the 2007 season has whole episodes like that.

It was the year that saw the first major fan backlashes - heavy criticism of Helen Raynor's Dalek story, *Last of the Time Lords* and (in some circles) a great deal of hostility between fans of Rose and those of Martha. To me, a lot of this seems crazy. Plenty of fans have pointed out the nature of fandom is often like the squabbles in *Life of Brian* between the People's Front of Judea and the Popular People's Front. The nature of Internet discussion tends to emphasise snarkiness, claims of entitlement, polarized opinions and so on. It's much harder to celebrate and champion things. It's also all micro-management stuff - discussing one line, one decision, one moment, and not seeing the wood for the trees.

Perhaps, too, a lot of fans - and *Doctor Who* fans in particular - are so used to being underdogs and in a culty 'niche' that they can't cope with anything else. Not quite the old cliché of following a band until they make it big and 'sell out', but more that most of the great narratives of fandom are about how the studio don't understand the genius of the series or give it a chance, or trying to come up with ways to reach a new audience, or trying to avoid seeming childish. Perhaps *Doctor Who* itself, always celebrating awkwardness and argument, encourages us to be awkward and argue.

We're not used to winning, and we've won. We're not used to security, and we're secure. After three years, Russell Davies performing a miracle a week is going to just seem like the way things are. But only *Doctor Who* fans could watch *Human Nature* adapted for telly, *Blink*, *The Shakespeare Code*, Derek Jacobi as the Master and Kylie in a maid's outfit on Christmas Day all in the same year, and wonder where it all went wrong.

2008

The sheer volume of *Doctor Who* merchandise and coverage in the UK is extraordinary. The action figures range rivals the *Star Wars* one for its ability to convert background characters you can barely remember into plastic.

This is, oddly, something I didn't foresee. I say 'oddly' not because I believe myself to be an infallible oracle, but just because my fortieth anniversary essay kept banging on about merchandise and spin-offs, and it would seem obvious that a popular TV series would drag the spin-off toys and stuff along with it. I guessed that the new show would have healthy DVD sales and the BBC wouldn't have too much trouble selling books off the back of it. It surprises me, though, just how successful this side of *Doctor Who* has been. I think what caught me out was just how mainstream it all was - the action figures, for example, are not 'collector's items' like a lot of the American ones are. They're mass market, you-can-buy-them-in-supermarkets toys. I'm sure fanboys are buying them, but kids are too, and playing with them. You can't really miss the toys in their bright, fiery orange packaging.

The new *Doctor Who* stands out like that, bright and fiery. It's striking - virtually all the other science fiction and fantasy shows around at the moment are symphonies of grey and muted, natural colours. *Battlestar Galactica, Lord of the Rings, Lost, Fringe, Quantum of Solace...* even the later Harry Potter movies and most of the superhero movies have a washed-out, faded palette. There are splashes of colour in things that bombed like *Speed Racer*, ones that did better, like *Pushing Daisies* and *Iron Man*. There are some big exceptions, too: obviously there's *The Simpsons*, but there's also the *Star Wars* prequels - bright and flashy in a way the original movies never were.

A lot of this darkness, I think, is down to one of the main influences on SF of the last few decades: *Blade Runner*. In many ways, *Blade Runner* is the opposite of *Doctor Who* - pretentious, humourless, fashion-conscious, slow. It's convinced a generation of fanboys that if it's raining at night and someone's bleeding and mumbling something from a high school philosophy textbook, it's deeply profound art. Fans love 'darkness', but sitting in a dark coat, sulking and poking at the logic holes in pop culture is never as big and clever as it seems to the person doing it. And yet it's extraordinarily easy to cater for, if you're a film studio or television company.

The new *Doctor Who* stands out for so many reasons - it has an essential optimism and cleverness that's been missing in pop culture for a long time. *Doctor Who* is not flawless, though. Reading Russell Davies' account of writing the series, *The Writer's Tale*, it's clear that the creative figurehead of *Doctor Who* is acutely aware of that. At the same time, however, it's uncynical. The irony is that a show made by a publically-funded organization that spent fifteen years convinced nobody would watch it has emerged to unprecedented acclaim and commercial success. People are buying the toys because they love the show, not because the show was designed to sell toys.

Doctor Who is now very possibly the most successful show there's ever been on British television. And if I could sum up why in a word, the reason, I think, is because *Doctor Who* dares to be *colourful*.

THE MATRIX ARTICLES

Matrix was a *Doctor Who* fanzine published by Seventh Door Fanzines in Southport, in the North West of England. It was well-established by the time I first contributed to it, as was their sister publication, the fictionzine *Silver Carrier*. I submitted three stories to *Silver Carrier*, all of which were rejected. The stories that saw print were, generally, of a very, very high standard. Although one of them did contain the line 'with the sound of a giant awaking, the giant awoke'.

The early nineties was a boom time for British fanzines, particularly ones that had morphed into something that looked almost exactly like a mainstream magazine - A4, with a glossy colour cover. Fanzines like *In-Vision*, *Skaro*, *The Frame*, *DWB* and *Matrix* all had a niche in the ecosystem. Each issue of *In-Vision* was a blow-by-blow description of the making of a specific TV story. *Skaro* favoured personal responses. *The Frame* was glossy, impressive and concentrated on what had gone on behind the scenes. *DWB* was a fearless and occasionally demented newsletter. A lot of their writers and editors are names you'd recognise from *Doctor Who* spin-offs, and now the TV series.

Matrix, like all the others, published reviews and art and comment and so on, but its specialty was close reading - really nicely-researched, imaginative articles about the series. It was edited by Mark Jones.

I'd have been twenty-one when I started writing for *Matrix*. The first few articles were about *Doctor Who* continuity - histories of early space flight, the Cybermen and Mars. These were based on notes I'd been making for years. I'd made a number of half-hearted, vague attempts to expand on the timeline in Jean-Marc Lofficier's *The Programme Guide*. It was the purchase of an electric typewriter with a memory (and a four line liquid crystal display!) that allowed me to do something with that information. It was a way to slot in and rearrange the scattered bits of data without having to retype everything every time. The reason that those earliest articles are not reprinted in this volume is, of course, that everything ended up in the different versions of the book that's currently available as *AHistory*.

Another omission: my article on the Davison era, from *Matrix* #54, is a bit redundant with the other pieces in this volume, and so has been held over for a future installment of *Time, Unincorporated*.

The articles here were all written while I was studying English Literature at university, and there's a whiff of a seminar paper about many of them, I think. When I was twenty-three, I was commissioned to write *Just War*, a New Adventures novel - and I wasn't shy of mentioning my new writing career in my later articles.

Who Dares

From Matrix #50, Summer 1994

Recently a great number of articles have been published about the origins and sources of *Doctor Who*. While writers have often mentioned the influence of *Dan Dare* on the series, such mentions are little more than footnotes - you'd think from most articles that Newman, Lambert and Whitaker were trying to create a kiddie version of *Quatermass* or *The Avengers* (both of which certainly had a profound influence on the programme in the seventies, but on only a handful of sixties stories). Tulloch and Alvarado's *The Unfolding Text* has perhaps the longest comparison between *Dan Dare* and *Doctor Who* (p43-50) and they demonstrate the similarities between them, principally that the two started with an educational brief and they both quickly developed into moneyspinners, with a range of related books, toys and games. The comparison, I think goes far further than anyone has said so far.

First, a quick word about the *Eagle*. The first issue of the weekly comic was published in April 1950 (over three years before the first *Quatermass* serial and seven years before Sputnik), with a print run of almost a million copies. This sold out, and the circulation soared through the fifties (no one, it seems, knows exactly how high, but some estimates claim over three million - as many as watched *Battlefield* in 1989!). The undoubted highlight of the magazine was *Dan Dare*, created by Frank Hampson. Dan was a square-jawed English astronaut, totally committed to the values of the United Nations that by 1995 had harmonized the world under one government. Man had first landed on Mars thirty years ago, and was now on the verge of interstellar travel, but faced chronic food shortages and a population explosion on Earth. Hampson created an intricate world, with technical and political details worked out to the tiniest degree.

The earliest creators of *Doctor Who* almost seemed to be consciously ignoring *Dan Dare*. Both, though, were designed to appeal to the same audience: not just young boys, but their fathers as well (the *Eagle*, famously, was read by Cabinet ministers as well as their grandchildren). It isn't, I think, a coincidence that the first Dalek story, the one that ensured the series' success, borrows heavily from the first *Dan Dare* story. (It *is* a coincidence that neither have titles the fans can agree on - for convenience, I'll call the serial that ran in the *Eagle* from Volume 1, Number 1 to Volume 2, number 25 *The Pilot of the Future* and *Doctor Who* Serial B *The Daleks*.)

In *The Pilot of the Future*, all Earth's attempts to reach Venus are being thwarted by an unknown force. Many good men have been lost. Dan Dare and his team discover a way to land on Venus, but their ship develops a fault and crashes. The planet is a hostile jungle, crawling with strange lifeforms. Dare soon discovers a huge futuristic city and is captured by its inhabitants, the evil Treens. Escaping, he contacts with Therons, a race of blond pacifists. Ages before, they fought a century-long war with the Treens and ever since they have lived on opposite sides of the planet, the Treens gradually becoming more and more reliant on machinery. Dan leads a military force of Earthmen and Therons and captures the Treen's city. While the ending is different, the parallels with *The Daleks* are remarkable.

If that wasn't convincing enough, how about *The Reign of the Robots* (Volume 8, Number 8 to Volume 9, number 4). In this story, Dan and his team return to London after ten years in space. The Capital is deserted. As they wander past the familiar landmarks, they realise that the Treens have conquered the planet. The Treens boost their numbers using Elektrobots, robot servants, and Selektrobots, an elite force. Reaching the Treen control centre (amongst other things, the Mekon has set up a huge mining operation), Flamer Spry grabs a microphone and orders the Selektrobots to kill one another, and the Treens. The Mekon is defeated and his spacecraft destroyed.

Ignoring the ban on BEMs and the instructions to produce studio-bound educational stories, it really looks like Terry Nation took two of the most memorable *Dan Dare* adventures and adapted them for a TV budget. I'm not suggesting any plagiarism; I doubt Nation realised his influences - he merely thought back to what SF he had enjoyed as a child (he was 14 when the *Eagle* started).

Nation's next move was almost certainly conscious. Quickly recognizing the success of the Daleks, Nation set about marketing them. Knowing that evil couldn't be seen to triumph, he created (for *The Dalek Book*, the first-ever piece of *Doctor Who* merchandise) a team of heroic humans. Their leader 'Jeff Stone - a mineralogist' looks like Dan Dare's younger brother, complete with pointed chin and distinctive eyebrows. Another Dare clone, Meric Scrivener (!), appeared in the following year's *Dalek World*. Both books featured painted comic strips by Richard Jennings that imitated Hampson's style. *The Dalek World* even had another *Eagle* trademark - cutaway drawings of spacecraft and weapons. When *TV Century 21* was launched in 1965, it attempted to combine the production values of the *Eagle* with an array of recognizable characters from television - Terry Nation's Daleks were an obvious candidate for inclusion. The art was again supplied by Jennings, and an early story featured a metal-eating cloud, very similar to the Crimson Death in the 1958 story *The Phantom Fleet*. Incidentally, the design of the *TV21* Emperor Dalek bears a striking similarity to the Mekon. All this Dalekmania reflected back on the series and so Nation's *Daleks' Master Plan* featured the Space Special Security Service, another organization of square-jawed Dalek fighters (in *Rogue Planet*, incidentally, Dan comes face to face with a super computer called Orak).

Kit Pedlar supplied the introduction to a Dan Dare reprint volume in 1979 (*The Man From Nowhere*) admitting that the Cybermen were 'very like the Treens'. Likewise, three Dare stories - *Red Moon Mystery*, *Rogue Planet* and *Wandering World* - featured planets that wandered into a solar system (two of these attack Earth). Pedlar cheerfully admitted to reading the *Eagle* in the 1960s, so must have read *The Big City Caper* in 1965 in which an alien uses the Post Office Tower as a base of operations to conquer the world. Pedlar suggested, at around the same time, the idea that would become *The War Machines*.

It wasn't just Nation and Pedlar: in *The Earth Stealers* an evil corporation, 'Earth Redistribution Limited', move mankind to Mars to exploit them (*The Sun Makers*) and *The Web of Fear* featured webs trapping spacecraft. The imagery of the UNIT era owes just as much to *Dan Dare* (gleaming control rooms, stiff upper lip English soldiers fighting gun battles with exotic alien humanoid aliens) as it does to *Quatermass'* industrial towers and ancient evils.

Dan and Digby finally met the Doctor (all seven incarnations) in the *Comic Relief* comic in 1991, in a two-page strip drawn by John Ridgway. Terry Nation refused permission for the Daleks to appear (although something we can't see says 'Exterminate!'). Next year, Dare celebrates his forty-fifth anniversary and fans hope the BBC will finally get around to giving Zenith the money to make the TV series they first promised in 1990. Sound familiar?

The Quatermass Irrelevancy

From Matrix #51, Summer 1995

When Sydney Newman, David Whitaker and Verity Lambert were drawing up the format for *Doctor Who*, they aimed to emulate the success of the popular *Quatermass* serials of the 1950s. Or so fans now assume. The truth is that although we now have access to reams of BBC documentation about the early evolution of *Doctor Who*, *Quatermass* is only mentioned once. A report of April 25th 1962 (reprinted in *The First Doctor Handbook*) sent to Donald Wilson gives a brief survey of SF attempted by the BBC up to that point and concludes that Science Fiction 'has not shown itself capable of supporting a large population'. As suggested last issue in my article "Who Dares", *Quatermass* was not a huge influence on the early years of the programme. I will go on to commit further heresy: *Quatermass* was never really that much of an influence on *Doctor Who* at all.

It seems to be the case that Nigel Kneale was approached by David Whitaker to write for *Doctor Who* before the series started but he quickly declined, not wanting to write for children. This does not mean that Whitaker felt that the series was anything especially like *Quatermass*, as he contacted a number of other prominent SF writers (Arthur C Clarke and John Wyndham included) at around the same time in an attempt to involve them. What all those authors share in common is an ability to write a range of material, create convincing human characters and to make science palatable to a mass audience. *Doctor Who* quickly established itself as a whimsical, vaguely educational space fantasy, albeit with an occasional harder edge. The series was always intended for a Saturday late afternoon, family teatime audience - totally unlike *Quatermass*, which was famously 'not for those of a nervous disposition' and was shown in the late evening. *Doctor Who* was more like the *Pathfinders* serials or *Space School*.

It is important to note that just because a *Doctor Who* story includes elements similar to those seen in a *Quatermass* story, it doesn't follow that *Doctor Who* was influenced by *Quatermass*. True, the first three *Quatermass* serials are a part of television mythology and found a further audience in film adaptations. (*Quatermass and the Pit* was only remade in 1967 and this probably did influence one *Doctor Who* serial, more of that anon), but most of the themes and images that fans accuse *Doctor Who* of 'borrowing' from *Quatermass* are little more than SF clichés: a crashed rocket, a buried spaceship, radar screens tracking a UFO, an alien infection turning a man into a monster, vast spawning tanks, aliens in a familiar big city (one thing linking *Doctor Who* and *Quatermass* is that they were limited by their BBC budget and so the city was invariably London), scientists and military men clashing on principle, race memories, mind control, alien intelligences, fear of the unknown in space, a new advance awakening ancient evil powers. Yes, *Quatermass* had them all a decade before *Doctor Who* had even started, but HG Wells has most of them half a century before *Quatermass*.

What *Quatermass* and *Doctor Who* do have in common is that they take those standard SF tropes and use them in (hopefully) new and interesting ways. I would go so far as to admit that they do so in much the same way. Neither are really interested all that much in hard scientific details and rarely indulge in technobabble; instead they simply want to scare the pants off their audiences using evil alien forces in the same way as old storytellers used goblins and devils (indeed, both cheekily reverse this: goblins and devils were actually aliens all along!). *Quatermass* and (some) *Doctor Who* stories are simply reworkings of old fantastical motifs. This is hardly a startling or original point - in fact if there is anything that distinguishes British and American SF, it's that ours is pessimistic, more concerned with regression and fear of the unknown, whereas optimistic American SF stresses progress and the resilience of certain ideals. It is interesting that two American telefantasy series that have caught on recently in Britain more than they have in America, *Twin Peaks* and *The X-Files*, are noticeably more pessimistic than normal American fare (*Babylon 5*, to digress further, seems to pull both ways, optimism in the face of a grim future). *Quatermass* doesn't create this pessimistic tradition - I would suggest that it had more to do with the difference between the experiences of Britain and America in the two world wars. *Doctor Who*'s influence on British telefantasy is a great deal more pervasive anyway.

What elements, then, distinguish *Quatermass* from other telefantasy? *Quatermass* is especially concerned with science as 'light' against the 'dark' of ignorance - a polarity inherent in all four serials but which is explicitly made in the last one, where the radio telescope in the country represents a safe haven for men of reason in the face of urban social collapse. Space is a Pandora's Box that humans have opened by launching rockets: all four of the serials start with human spacecraft being destroyed. Space is not a final frontier, but an infinite, hostile nightmare. Alien beings are totally inscrutable - Quatermass manages to destroy them, but ultimately, we know nothing about where they came from or what motivated them. No alien is ever given a voice or a face or even humanoid form (instead they take control of humans). Mass hysteria features in all four serials: mobs storm gleaming factories, riot in London, smash up machinery. There is almost no room for comedy when human civilisation and society could collapse in a day. Humanity is fragile, not eternal.

Taking that as a list, it is almost impossible to find a *Doctor Who* story from the sixties that shares themes with *Quatermass*. By my reckoning, out of all the Hartnell and Troughton stories (about fifty of them), only five show the slightest resemblance: *The Dalek Invasion of Earth*, particularly the first four parts, had the grim mental domination of the Daleks over the Robomen (scenes admired by Kneale, according to an article in *The DWB Compendium*), and the human resistance are a flawed and rather weak bunch reduced to infighting and huddling underground in the face of an incomprehensible alien power; *The Web Planet* has, in the Animus, an inscrutable alien intelligence that can dominate by force of will; *The War Machines* has soldiers and the scientific establishment joined in fighting a non-human menace; both *The Abominable Snowmen* and its sequel *The Web of Fear* feature the Great Intelligence, another alien sentience that can dominate minds. In 1956, Nigel Kneale wrote a television story, 'The Creature' about a search in the Himalayas for the Yeti (filmed later as *Abominable Snowman*). Crucial scenes of *The Web of Fear* and the 1967 film version of *Quatermass and the Pit* are set in the London Underground.

All of these are quite tenuous links, to say the least, and all could probably be dismissed as shared SF clichés. *The Dalek Invasion of Earth* more closely resembles a film about the French Resistance than anything Nigel Kneale has ever written. Only one sixties story, to my mind, is consistently 'like *Quatermass*' - *Fury from the Deep*. In that story we have so many of Kneale's themes coming together: the story is set in the very near future where a scientific advance unleashes an ancient evil. The threat is faceless, voiceless, motiveless alien power. Ordinary men and women are threatened, a whole community is mentally dominated, people develop regressive yearnings - humans return to the sea and mobs smash machinery. Men revert to a primitive state. Like *Quatermass*, all the Doctor can do is refer to an old book on folklore and recognise the full horror of the situation. The whole way of human life is threatened and only an accidental discovery saves the day. At the end, the aliens are still as mysterious. I would also declare at this pint that I haven't seen *Fury from the Deep*, only read the book, seen the telesnaps and listened to the audio.

In an attempt to liken *Quatermass* and sixties *Doctor Who*, the absurd belief has grown up among fans that the BBC initially planned to cancel *Doctor Who* at the end of the sixth season and replace it with a new series of *Quatermass*. This myth is asserted time and time again in print, but it is based on a number of transparently false assumptions. It is true that

Nigel Kneale had plans for a fourth serial by 1969 (it was reported in a contemporary edition of the magazine *Supernatural*). The BBC, though, only started pre-production work on *Quatermass 4* in mid-1973 and even then the plug was quickly pulled for budgetary reasons. Like the fifties serials, *Quatermass 4* was to have been a self-contained prestige TV drama, not a running series and it was intended to have a nighttime adult slot. In no way could it have been a replacement for a cheap and cheerful Saturday afternoon family programme that was on for forty weeks of the year. It is possible that some members of the *Doctor Who* production team might have become involved in some capacity had the serial gone ahead, but there is absolutely no evidence for this. Eventually, of course, Euston Films made the serial (now just called *Quatermass*) for a reported £1.25M budget. The executive producer was Verity Lambert.

The seventh season of *Doctor Who*, it is argued, bears more than a passing resemblance to the *Quatermass* serials. This is true, but the case is often overstated. Indeed I've seen at least one fanzine article (by the normally reliable Anthony Brown in *DWB* #116) claim that 'it seems reasonable to suppose that had Kneale not objected, 1970 would have seen Professor Quatermass' visit to the Wenley Moor Cyclotron, and his return to the British Rocket Group to provide assistance to his successor once or twice removed, Professor Cornish'.

When the decision to exile the Doctor to Earth had been made, some members of the production team rewatched the *Quatermass* serials for inspiration. This is quite visible on screen. Suddenly, the Doctor faces ancient menaces: the Nestene have been active for a thousand million years, the Silurians are two hundred million years old, the Ambassadors of Death are infinitely more advanced, the Primords may be as old as the Earth itself. The aliens are also, generally, more inscrutable than before: we never discover the precise origins or purpose of the Ambassadors or the Primords - indeed those names are never used in dialogue. The Nestenes are equally enigmatic - we see a great deal more of their creations. Only the Silurians are anything like a traditional *Doctor Who* monster, and even they release terrifying race memories and an ancient 'alien virus' that kills indiscriminately. The settings of the stories are suddenly those of *Quatermass* - vast industrial complexes, space mission control rooms desolate moorland. But this is still unmistakably *Doctor Who* - the plots are not radically different from *The Seeds of Death* or *The Invasion* from the previous season, the monsters are still men in rubber suits (or sprouting fur) who eloquently express their desire to eradicate humanity. Mankind is occasionally represented as militant or xenophobic, but never irrational (unless contaminated with an alien disease or reverting to primal form). The Doctor's faith in human nature is always rewarded.

And where in *Quatermass* the disaster usually happens, at the end of each seventh season story disaster has been averted - on our Earth at least. Season Seven is certainly the nearest *Doctor Who* got to *Quatermass*, but it was seen as a failure and the changes in format for Season Eight erased virtually all the *Quatermass* paraphernalia. The Doctor no longer lives in the near future, he's a lot more chummy with the army, Liz has gone back to Cambridge, and the aliens are now more familiar - two disturbing seventh season aliens return in watered-down form, the regular villain is a charming renegade from the Doctor's own race. Is Azal's buried spacecraft a lift from *Quatermass and the Pit*? I doubt it - I've never seen it suggested that the ships in *The Power of the Daleks* or *The Visitation* are.

Admittedly, there are a couple of other parallels. By the time *The Daemons* was transmitted, the idea that 'God was a spaceman', that passing aliens had helped human civilisation on its way was almost passé - Von Daniken's books (*Chariots of the Gods*, etc) were bestsellers, and as evidenced by his other stories, Robert Sloman was clearly interested in writing about trendy seventies nonsense. All we can really say is that while some members of the *Doctor Who* production team and individual writers knew about *Quatermass*, and might use the same clichés from time to time, nowhere except for a few minutes in a couple of Season Seven stories does seventies *Doctor Who* 'feel like' *Quatermass*.

The Holmes/Hinchcliffe era was not dominated so much by 'Gothic' but specifically by 'possession' - a Gothic theme, of course, but also a common Science Fiction one. In virtually every story someone (usually Sarah) is hypnotized, duplicated, absorbed, brainwashed or turns into an alien. This does lead to some moments that are highly reminiscent of *The Quatermass Experiment* - especially in *The Ark in Space, Planet of Evil* and *The Seeds of Doom*. The *Doctor Who* budget, though, rarely runs to being able to afford a 'mob', so mass hysteria was out of the question, and other concerns of Kneale were left largely untouched.

Fans often forget that Holmes stayed on to edit Williams' first four stories. Every fan knows, though, and I would agree, that one of these serials is the nearest *Doctor Who* ever got to *Quatermass*. Like *Quatermass and the Pit, Image of the Fendahl* features an ancient skull, an alien force, man evolving from Martians, a bit of folklore, significant place names, a machine which can see into the past, a group of scientists. Unfortunately, Chris Boucher swears blind that he hasn't seen *Quatermass and the Pit* in any form. Elsewhere, he acknowledges his sources: he freely admits that *The Robots of Death* is partially based on Frank Herbert's *Dune* and that much of his *Blakes 7* dialogue is lifted from cowboy movies. *Image of the Fendahl* was simply, as Graham Williams said, 'archetypal fifties horror', with all its stereotyped props.

Contrasting *Quatermass and the Pit* and *Image of the Fendahl* is a great deal more instructive than comparing them, as it demonstrates how the two programmes take the same basic material and mould it to their own unique formats. The Martian capsule is unearthed in the heart of London, in full view of the public; Fetch Priory is miles from anywhere. This in itself is a vast difference: *Fendahl* is a traditional *Doctor Who* story - aliens menacing a small, isolated community. *Quatermass and the Pit* demonstrates how the full power of the State - Army, Police, Government, Scientific Establishment, Media even the man on the street - is helpless in the face of alien power. The scientists in *Quatermass* are on the side of good, desperately trying to keep civilization together. In *Doctor Who* they are a group of egotists, ranging from the misguided to the truly insane. The 'ordinary man' is represented in both stories, but in *Quatermass* we see a broad spectrum of people from black workmen to pub landlords, while in *Doctor Who* we only get a comedy poacher and his mad Ma. The main difference is the hero himself: the Doctor knows of the Fendahleen and can resist their power; *Quatermass* pieces together the clues, but is powerless. The Doctor laughs in the face of fear, *Quatermass* gibbers helplessly. If you don't believe me, don't just read plot summaries, see for yourself: both *Image of the Fendahl* and *Quatermass and the Pit* are out on BBC Video, and if you watch them together you'll recognise some similarities, and that they are both examples of the same genre, but they are very, very different kettles of fish.

Which Season Fifteen script is more 'like' *Quatermass* than any other seventies *Doctor Who* adventure, then? *The Invisible Enemy*. The early episodes at least feature all the *Quatermass* touchstones: pioneering space exploration, alien viruses, possessed humanity, a helpless protagonist - Tom's taken over and can't do anything about it (and how often can you say that?), an odd alien entity, scientists battling away, savage humanity somehow being immune, breeding tanks. Without K9 (who is only really ly a scientist's tool/bodyguard in this first story), the fantastic voyage and the rather camp costumes, the story might almost be *Quatermass: The Next Generation*. The Baker and Martin catchphrase for the story, 'contact has been made', even mirrors the title of the first episode of *The Quatermass Experiment*, 'Contact Has Been Established'.

And then, nothing. The nearest we get to *Quatermass* in the eighties is *The Awakening* and *Paradise Towers*, neither of which are particularly close. 'Bernard' and his British Rocket Group may get mentioned in *Remembrance of the Daleks*, but that story is a celebration of *Doctor Who's* past without even a glimmer of *Quatermass'* themes. None of the 'ancient evils' that popped up with almost embarrassing regularity in the McCoy years resemble those in *Quatermass* - Light probably came closest, but he's more closely related to Azal than anything else. Significantly, the (mostly fan-written) New Adventures have seen a number of *Quatermass*-influenced stories: *Cat's Cradle: Warhead, Nightshade, Love and War, The Pit* and *Shadowmind* particularly.

Once we strip away all the bog-standard SF clichés and start looking for a distinctive *Quatermass* 'tone' in a *Doctor Who* story, what are we left with? *Fury from the Deep* and the first half of *The Invisible Enemy*, bits of Season Seven (most notably episode six of both *Inferno* and *Doctor Who and the Silurians*, and the opening of *The Ambassadors of Death*). About ten episodes out of seven hundred. The link between *Quatermass* and *Doctor Who* is way off the mark, a race memory, a trace element harvested by fandom. Contact has not been established.

Special Report to All Operatives, Anti-Dalek Force

From Matrix #51, Summer 1995

From: Supreme Space General Trey Naitan
To: All Operatives, Anti-Dalek Force
Report Rating: Confidential - I don't want to see this leaked in a World Distributors Annual. Not after what happened last time.
Subject: Mission Procedures

Welcome to the Anti-Dalek Force. The ADF is committed to taking the fight to the Daleks, and as such many ~~suicide~~ missions are undertaken in the Seventh Galaxy. Much is at stake, and it is vital that ADF agents follow established procedure. Using the very latest computer brain thingies, we've analysed all previous encounters with the evil Daleks and have reached certain conclusions about the way we can fight their evil menace. Oh, I seem to have used the word 'evil' twice in that last sentence. Well, the Daleks are evil, that's why. Evil.

First of all, although the mission we send you on is vital to the future of the galaxy etc etc, and Earth is - as you'll have noticed - really overpopulated, we only ever send about five people on our space missions and we never give them any weapons better than handguns and grenades. There is a very good reason for this, but it is classified. Teams are carefully composed, making sure that there is only one explosives expert, one engineer, one Scotsman, one pretty lady, etc. This is so that if one of you were to die then the entire mission would be buggered, because you wouldn't be able to blow anything up or escape the planet.

The computer also picks people with tough-sounding names: each crew has a member called 'Tarrant', and everyone else will have a monosyllabic first name (Jeb, Dan, Roj, Cab, Karl) and a surname with a double consonant (Farrell, Sarran, Cattal, Calloway, Kennis).

Standard mission procedure is to crash on the target planet, a horrible radiation-soaked jungle/desert hellhole. One of you will inevitably die or be crippled but don't worry, it won't be the pretty lady. Statistically, it will be the captain. Standard procedure then is to flap about for a bit in a generally leaderless kind of way, arguing amongst yourselves and shouting a lot. Your communications equipment, etc, is all designed to break in the crash. Generally, the ship's Scotsman will become a bit paranoid and cynical about now. The pretty lady comes in handy, though, because she can help make drinks, mend things and administer first aid.

Scouting the planet will reveal the existence of a vast, deserted alien city. This is the last vestige of a once-great alien race and points to greater achievements in the past. The deformed/invisible/physically perfect natives will no doubt have spent the last few thousand years avoiding the hostile plant life, becoming naturally resistant to radiation and practicing their spear throwing. Unfortunately, despite centuries of technological innovation, mankind has yet to discover anything that can stop the standard wood spear (the cotton jumpsuit is the best our boffins can come up with), so you'll probably lose another crewmember at this point. It'll be the one that looks like Stuart Fell. You'll also discover that a mysterious race, known locally as 'the metal ones', has enslaved some locals and is involved in mining operations. Don't worry about this mystery just yet, just sit around your base wondering what to do next. Don't forget those radiation pills!

This is the point where you discover if the mission is important or not. If it is, the Doctor and his companion will turn up in the TARDIS. They always split up fairly early on, because the door to the TARDIS is blocked by falling rocks or somesuch. One of them meets the good people, and the other one meets the evil people. Now, this is where it gets tricky: evil people don't always look evil, sometimes they look good. Complicating matters even further, the reverse is also true. Generally, the nicer people look, the nastier they are, but even this isn't always true. Best just to let the Doctor sort it out. Usually the Doctor meets the good people, and usually you'll *be* the good people, so in other words, now is the point you'll meet the Doctor. First of all, be a bit rough with him (remember, if you convince him you're evil, he'll know you're the good guys really). Fill him in about the local situation: plague threatening entire universe, mysterious mining operations on the planet, the one-eyed metal men being worshipped as gods, oh and on a completely unrelated note, the space war with the Daleks isn't going so well etc. He won't be terribly interested in that, preferring to talk about the deserted city, but play along with him. At some point another spaceship will land in the next clearing. This will either be your reinforcements, or the Daleks.

Conversations can be tricky things, so here are a few stock phrases you might try using: 'whatever they are, the place is swarming with them', 'our mission must succeed, it is humanity's only hope', 'they're just primitives', 'we need to put our petty differences aside', 'what hope is there of that?', 'perhaps we could strike a deal with them', 'they've installed drilling equipment', 'mining operations', 'the plant life here is hostile', 'can we trust him? / we have no choice'. Try to spice up everyday speech by randomly inserting the words 'space', 'star' or 'Earth' into sentences, e.g. 'five star hours until dawn', 'we've been here two Earth months', 'our space radio was smashed into pieces when we crashed on this desolate hole'. If you need to express the urgency of the problem or importance of anything, then the words 'vital' and 'supreme' are useful, e.g. 'it is vital that the Supreme Commander of the Earth Star Force is informed of our new space mission directives'. The Doctor will immediately take command, much to the annoyance of the Scotsman. About twenty-four minutes, thirty seconds after he first arrives, you'll see your first Dalek. Now it's very important that you don't laugh. It is permissible to say 'those motorized dustbins' in a derisory way, but expect a lecture from the Doctor about how the Daleks are actually the most fearsome/scientifically advanced race in the universe.

At this point the Doctor will become concerned for his companion, and will take most of you to the Dalek base to find her. You'll spend the next two hours or so running around, setting up explosives, being captured, escaping by dressing up as a native, dodging hostile plant life, being sacrificed to local deities, getting basic science lessons (hot air rises, magnets are magnetic, etc). You'll discover that the Daleks aren't engaged in simple mining operations, but have something more elaborate planned. You'll also team up with the natives and the Daleks will threaten to unleash a plague or fire or something that will kill all life on the planet. At one point, you'll be trapped in a small room and the Daleks will slowly burn through by cutting a big square shape in the door. To be best off, you should tag along with the Doctor. If you are captured and subjected to the mind probe, then say 'I'd rather die than tell you anything, you motorized dustbins'. Don't be surprised if the Daleks take you up on this. If you're a coward, you will die, but if you are brave and foolhardy you probably won't - a paradox that has baffled our best scientists and theologians for years, but it's true. One of you will fall in love with the

Doctor's companion. Every so often the mission computer selects a traitor to join the crew. This helps spice up the action a bit, because you never really know who's on which side, whether they look evil or not. Occasionally, the Scotsman will start acting like a traitor, even though he never is. Don't worry, it will all sort itself out by the end. The Daleks will also set up a countdown to destroy the area/planet/galaxy at some point, but don't worry the Doctor always finds a way to shut that off at the last possible moment.

Remember those explosives you planted? Well, now they come in useful for blowing up the Daleks. The timing mechanism is, of course, broken. This is where the Scotsman justifies his place on the team. He'll decide to stop being so cynical and will sacrifice himself to save you all. As you watch the explosion, you'll ask the Doctor whether this means we've seen the last of the Daleks and he'll say that we haven't. You all just stand around for a bit watching more explosions. The bravest bloke and the pretty lady have survived, but neither of you will cop off with the companion, I'm afraid. Just steal one of the Daleks' own ships and return to Earth. We'll try not to shoot you down. Oh yes, and if you write your memoirs, don't forget that Terry Nation will get 60% of the profits.

Something Took Off From Mars...

From Matrix #52, Spring 1996

The Ambassadors of Death must rank as the most reworked story in the history of *Doctor Who*. David Whitaker had been commissioned soon after *The Enemy of the World* to write a story detailing man's first contact with aliens, with a twist: some property of the aliens' bodies meant that they would be lethal to humans on physical contact - this would inadvertently lead the two races to the brink of war. Before it reached the screen, in the words of Terrance Dicks, 'there were seventeen rewrites' and Whitaker had to adapt his scripts for the changing regular cast - Zoe was written in, Jamie was written out, the Doctor changed and the UNIT format was imposed upon the story.

Rumour has it that at one point the production team considered having Zoe accompany the new Doctor into exile - her replacement, fellow scientist Liz Shaw, was certainly a similar character and it's easy to picture Zoe saying her lines. The title of Whitaker's story changed from *Invaders from Mars*, *Carriers of Death* and *The Ambassadors*. It gained an extra episode. Finally, even the author changed: Malcolm Hulke was brought in to work on the scripts when Whitaker left Britain to work in Australia. So, the story was two years in the making; including Terrance

Dicks, it had three writers. Further changes were made by Dicks, Barry Letts and director Michael Ferguson when the filmed action sequences ran well over-budget. It would be a brave or foolish man that declared which bits were Whitaker, Hulke and which are remnants from earlier drafts.

Nevertheless, we can see a couple of similarities with other Whitaker stories. In his two Dalek scripts, the Troughton Doctor engages in some quite bizarre detective work: in *The Power of the Daleks* he discerns a coded message in a notice pinned up on a board, and in *The Evil of the Daleks* he traces someone and (incorrectly) guesses his first name from a matchbook. Here the Sherlock Holmes stuff is the Brigadier's job, and his forensics team manage to find where the Ambassadors are being kept by tracing the insecticide found in the soil on Cyril Shaps' shoes. Likewise, a couple of familiar Hulke themes crop up in the later episodes - the Doctor acts as a middleman between humanity and the aliens, the military plots to blow the aliens to bits, officialdom is weak, the man from the ministry dies horribly halfway through and it turns out that a mad general is behind it all. Within the UNIT format much of the rationale of the story becomes obsolete: this isn't a 'first contact', the Brigadier has been doing this sort of thing 'for several years'. It's also odd that both UNIT and Carrington's newly-formed Space Security Department exist - in many ways the Brigadier and Carrington are the same character, and it's tempting to think that in the earlier drafts Carrington got many of the Brigadier's lines. This might also explain why Carrington all but vanishes in the middle of the story. However, fan wisdom has it that Carrington was only introduced by Hulke, very late in the day.

Perhaps the story's complicated genesis is the reason why it has long had a reputation as a rather confused mess. In reality *The Ambassadors of Death* is a rather interesting thriller set in the near future, like *The Invasion* the year before. Like that story, most of the aliens live in a vast ship just on the extreme range of UNIT's missiles, and the story concentrates on the humans determined to exploit the aliens for their own purposes. The aliens themselves hardly appear, except as tools of the human plotters. The first episode rapidly sets up the premise for the new story, and we start right in the thick of the action. The moonshots were still underway at the time of broadcast - so in the first two minutes we have tense scenes at mission control, earnest TV journalists, all the iconography of the NASA launches. It's made clear that this is a few years into the future: now decontamination procedures only last an hour, not two days, there's a new miracle fuel, there are videophones and man has reached Mars. Michael Wisher tells us all about the problems with the Mars mission. The sixth season had a number of attempts to recreate the atmosphere of the moonshots - *The Wheel in Space* was set on one of the space stations that NASA had planned, *The Seeds of Death* and *The Space Pirates* projected the space programme a little further into the future, but this was the first time that a *Doctor Who* story had dealt with a space programme so close to home. The Procul Haremesque music as the Recovery ship docks with *Mars Probe Seven* evokes the recent *2001: A Space Odyssey*, another earnest attempt at realistic space fiction.

The Doctor is superb in this story and, as with most of the stories in the Pertwee era, some considerable effect is expended demonstrating that the Doctor is not simply a particularly gifted human scientist. While everyone else at space control reels on the floor as an alien sound blares from the loudspeakers, the Doctor stands firm and recognises it as a message. With a flick of his wrist, he can make objects appear and disappear, he can withstand G-forces that would kill any human and he builds devices that can project people forward in time or magnetise them to his car. Unusually, in this story the Doctor is the character who asks many of the questions that the audience want answers to, traditionally the role of his companions. He succeeds in simplifying the rocket science for the general audience and cuts through the technobabble (Cornish: 'do you have visual contact?', Doctor: 'If you mean "can I see it". Yes'). Pertwee exudes authority in only his third story, dominating a huge and interesting cast (over eighty cast members, nearly thirty of them speaking parts).

UNIT also do quite well. As the UNIT era progressed they were called upon less and less: by the end of Pertwee's reign, the Doctor would build a device to beat the baddy, and UNIT were there simply to explain the premise of the story to the Doctor, seal off the area and prove that the aliens were bulletproof. In the earlier stories they are frighteningly efficient - they operate a network of spies from a mobile HQ in *The Invasion* and here they display as much military might as the BBC budget will allow. Once a target is identified they swing into action, blasting away at the enemy, as they do in a long battle scene in the opening episode. The Brigadier also gets a rather fantastic fight scene in the last episode in which he punches someone over a clifftop! In other parts of the story he is reduced to being a foil for Cornish, the head of space research - and as the Brigadier observes on more than one occasion 'there's little we can do but wait'. The story is also notable for seeing the return of Benton, for the first time since *The Invasion*.

The title is a little misleading, as it is meant to be. At first, *The Ambassadors of Death* has all the hallmarks of a science fiction thriller: alien abductions, government cover-ups, high level military conspiracies, mysterious agents without backgrounds, men killed in bizarre circumstances, interference in a top secret research programme. But the cliches are all inverted: the alien abduction is literally that - men have abducted the aliens. This isn't a story about monsters invading Earth, but of Earthmen's reaction to the existence of aliens. Like both *The Invasion* and *The Enemy of the World*, *The Ambassadors of Death* charts the complex relationship between a number of people as a larger, esoteric plan comes to fruition, and much of the story concerns the baddy's attempts to murder his disloyal followers. General Carrington disappears from view for the middle episodes, the baddy's role taken by Reegan, and a couple of Carrington's key allies (Taltalian and Lennox) are killed without noticeably affecting the plan. It's left unclear exactly why they allied themselves with Carrington in the first place.

It must have been tricky for the audience to keep track of the story over seven weeks - it's tricky enough now that we are able to rewind it. It certainly seems to have confused Michael Ferguson - different characters discover the crucial information at different times, and late in the day things we have already been told are presented as big revelations. We realise that the astronauts are aliens after a couple of episodes, but it's a shock for Liz in episode six. Likewise, we know that Carrington is up to no good right from the first episode and it's not difficult to guess that he is 'the boss' that Reegan keeps referring to (the Doctor is 'not particularly' surprised that it's him), but the scene is played as if we don't already know in episode six. Perhaps worst of all, and again in the same episode, the Doctor reacts with shock when he learns that the aliens are ambassadors! Perhaps viewing the story in serial form, with a week between episodes, irons some discrepancies out, but in one sitting it is certainly tricky keeping up with the state of play on occasion. At the time, the audience figures held up quite well throughout the story (apart from a low rating for the last episode). The fourth episode of the story, helped no doubt by an overrunning Cup Final which pushed it into a later slot, achieved the show's highest viewing figures since *The Celestial Toymaker*.

While *Spearhead from Space* pointed the way to the punchier, more concise style of storytelling that would become the norm in the seventies, the remainder of the seventh series is a throwback to the more leisurely, some might say rambling, stories of the black and white era. Most of *The Ambassadors of Death* episode five is taken up with Reegan's attempts to sabotage the Doctor's rocket, an attempt eventually foiled by the Doctor in thirty seconds. That said, the action sequences are lavish and the cliffhangers are among the best in the show's history. Keeping the aliens at a distance really makes them, well, *alien*. Glimpsed behind slats, or in a moment after Liz removes one of their helmets, we never really find out much about them. Their voices are strange, disembodied; their vast spaceship mixes the mundane (a recreated quarantine area to keep the astronauts in) and a surreal CSO landscape. We hear that 'they have invaded our galaxy', and that 'they were on Mars before us', but only from Carrington we don't know whether they are even really Martians or not. We know they need radiation (2,102,462 rads of it) to live, but not why (or how). Although fans have expressed dissatisfaction with this obscurity, it's a deliberate device that only adds to the mystery, suspense and paranoia - it's a trick that *The X-Files* uses on a weekly basis nowadays, over twenty years later.

1966 and All That

From Matrix #52, Spring 1996

The historical stories were quickly phased out by the production team because they weren't popular with the writers, the actors or the public. Viewers would much rather watch the Daleks than stories set in the past. *The Gunfighters* was the low point, in teams of artistic merit and ratings.

Or so the story goes. It isn't true: the last historical was *The Highlanders*, made three years after the series started. Right up until then, roughly a third of stories were historicals. Then, suddenly, the genre completely disappeared.

Doctor Who was a very clever idea for a television series. One week it would encompass the appeal of *Dan Dare* and *Journey into Space* science fiction, the next that of historical serials such as *William Tell* and *The Adventures of Robin Hood*. At first it was planned that there would be a third type of story, those set 'sideways into lesser or greater dimensions, into non-gravitational existence or invisibility, etc'. In his introduction to the Titan script book of *The Crusade*, Stephen James Walker observes that the 'sideways idea was quickly dropped, with only three televised stories (*Inside the Spaceship*, *Planet of Giants* and, in part, *The Space Museum*) fitting into that category'. Arguably, *The Web Planet*'s insect world is another example.

It had become clear even before shooting had started that with limited studio facilities and visual effects technology, the 'sideways' stories would be expensive and difficult to script. The two remaining types, 'Future' and 'Past' quickly took over, and (excepting *Inside the Spaceship*) the stories of the first series alternated strictly between them.

The traditional fan view is expressed in Peter Haining's *The Key To Time*: 'February 8, 1964 - Because of the huge success of the Daleks, Verity Lambert and David Whitaker revise the style of *Doctor Who* and the third scheduled serial, *The Hidden Planet* by Malcolm Hulke, is dropped because it no longer fits the format.' This rather endearing view of the mechanics of television production is undermined by the facts - the second episode of the fourth serial had been recorded the day before, and *The Hidden Planet* wasn't finally rejected until 1965.

However, there was no denying the Daleks' success. The press were reporting that the BBC had been inundated by requests from children for their return, and it was clear that this aspect of the series was a huge success. Toy manufacturers and publishers quickly began to show an interest, an almost unprecedented state of affairs for a BBC programme. This clearly affected the production team: at this point, Terry Nation was writing *The Keys of Marinus*, but as soon as that had been completed he was commissioned to write a new Dalek adventure. It became clear that there was now another type of story: serials featuring the Daleks. The historicals had a place in this scheme - the BBC's declared aim was into entertain and inform, and it had been planned that the science fiction stories would have philosophical or educational purpose: the first Dalek story was a treatise on the ethics of war and pacifism. This, of course, didn't last, and the dreaded 'BEMs' quickly began to take over.

While *The Sensorites* might be seen as an examination of paranoia and insularity, it's more difficult to discern the moral wealth of *The Keys of Marinus* (although there is perhaps a recurring theme of law and legality). The historicals were useful balances to this - while all *Doctor Who* was action-based, the historicals were better placed to pose moral dilemmas, and educate their audience - as Verity Lambert says in her recent *DWM* interview, teachers would praise the educational value of the historicals - 'it was a wonderful way of teaching... these were interesting and also informative'. In terms of ratings there was no real distinction between the historical, science fiction and Dalek stories. Apart from the two-part *Inside the Spaceship*, the highest average rating for the first series went to *Marco Polo* with 9.5 million. The highest episode rating was 10.4 million, shared by five episodes (the last two episodes of the Dalek story, *Inside the Spaceship* 1, *Marco Polo* 7 and *The Keys of Marinus* 4 - honours neatly shared between the four types of story). After a very shaky start, with the first episode only gaining 4.4 million viewers and 114th place in the charts, *Doctor Who* began averaging about 6.5 million - by the seventh week, this was boosted to around 9.5 million by the loss of networked opposition and the advent of the Daleks. *Inside the Spaceship* narrowly missed the top twenty programmes. The ratings for the first series remained fairly steady, regardless of the story. The stories broadcast in the summer dropped back to around seven million, the decline starting in May, during *The Keys of Marinus* - perfectly normal, as fewer people watch television when the weather is good. Relative to other programmes, *Doctor Who* continued to do well, and although the average chart position slipped a little, a couple of the series' later episodes made the top twenty for the first time. The series as a whole averaged a respectable 8.08 million viewers.

The early public image of *Doctor Who* encompassed the historical stories. While the Daleks and the Voord generated some press attention, the first *Radio Times* cover was awarded to *Marco Polo*. Significantly, one of the three serials novelized in the sixties was the first Dalek story, the second was the science-fiction tale *The Web Planet* and the third was *The Crusade*, a historical.

The early plans for the second series blocked out by David Whitaker were to continue alternating 'future' and 'past' stories. Indeed, Whitaker suggested that there be a senior writer for each genre, and he nominated Terry Nation as the senior writer for futuristic stories. Whitaker himself was moving on, and although (as Philip MacDonald suggests in *DWM* #200) for Whitaker, 'the essence of *Doctor Who* had very little to do with monsters, spacecraft and the reversed polarity of the neutron flow', he found himself writing Dalek stories for comic strips, stage plays and a novel. As Dennis Spooner replaced Whitaker as story editor, not only was more comedy introduced, but the boundaries between the various genres began to blur. *Planet of Giants* was a sideways tale; *The Dalek Invasion of Earth* and *The Rescue* were purely futuristic; *The Romans* was pure historical, but *The Web Planet* contained both 'sideways' and 'futuristic'. *The Crusade* was another pure historical, and *The Space Museum* once again was a 'sideways future' tale.

The Chase and *The Time Meddler* were a new genre: the pseudohistorical. The third Dalek story contained a 'sideways' segment (the House of Horror), the pseudohistorical (the *Mary Celeste*), an alien planet (Aridus) and a segment set in Earth's future (Mechanus) - as well as a few other short sequences set in the modern day. It was the first story to completely ignore the genre boundaries established at the beginning of the show's production. *The Time Meddler* was a science fiction story set in the past, but much of the story resembles the old historical stories - we know that the Monk is an enigma, with a wristwatch, but we don't know that he has a time machine until the cliffhanger for the third episode, and even by that point we haven't learnt about his plans to change history. The second series was in many ways the peak of early *Who*'s popularity.

Publicity for the series opening concentrated on the return of the Daleks, and the ratings of *Planet of Giants* suffered as a result (although they were still nearly two million up on *The Reign of Terror*). Of only four episodes not in the top thirty, three are from this first story. It is clear from the figures that people would watch *Doctor Who* regardless of the genre of story. The two solid historicals, *The Romans* and *The Crusade* hold their

101

own with the two Dalek stories. *The Romans* episode 1 reached an record number 7 in the charts (equalled by *The Web Planet* 1 and *The Chase* 6 - and only beaten in the show's entire history by *The Ark in Space* 2).

In terms of audience appreciation, generally the historical stories are less popular than the science fiction ones, but it is only a matter of a couple of percentage points. In the sixties, the science of audience appreciation was not perfected, and it wasn't measured the same way it is now. Added to this, the audience appreciation figures are notoriously unreliable - indeed the fewer people watch a programme, the more they like it. This is not a contradiction in terms: if a programme is on in primetime, then by definition millions of people will have their televisions on. Faced with a choice of four channels (only two in the 1960s), any programme will pick up a couple of million casual viewers. If, on the other hand, it is on late at night, only a few hundred thousand people might be watching, but they've all had to stay up specially to do so. The chances are they want to see the programme. (That, incidentally, is why *Eldorado*'s appreciation index soared when the ratings collapsed: only the hardcore fans were watching it. Ten million people watched the first episode, and most of them hated it, and it scored the lowest ever rating of 29% - the average for most programmes nowadays being between 55-60%. Seven million people stopped watching, leaving three million who, by definition, thought that it was OK. The appreciation rating shot up to a still way below average 48%.)

Audience research done into Hartnell *Doctor Who* by the BBC found that the audience concentrated on the 'foam' stones and 'cardboard' walls, pouring scorn on the general shoddiness of the programme irrespective of the story itself. Marcus Hearn has found BBC research documents (reprinted in *DWM* #226) suggesting that audiences were 'not keen on *Doctor Who* going historical' and 'it seems that on the whole the TARDIS's journeys into the future and into space held more fascination than those into the past', but virtually everyone quoted in that article seems to have hated the programme wherever the TARDIS landed! *The Dalek Invasion of Earth* and *The Web Planet* are also mocked by the viewing panel. One of the few specific examples of praise went to Derek Francis as Nero and Hartnell himself in *The Romans*. A number of people preferred the historical to 'weirdies from outer space' - and while Marcus Hearn's narrative talks of 'the now-expected criticisms of historical stories', he quotes from a number of people who, in the words of one, 'prefers this type to the Daleks'. Opinion was clearly divided, but perhaps the best method of assessing whether the mass audience liked the story or not is seeing whether they tuned in the next week - and as noted the historicals show no significant difference from the futuristic ones.

During the third series, the ratings collapsed. For the first time since the first episode, *Doctor Who* dropped out of the top 100 programmes (during *The Ark*). The audience appreciation figures also slumped, as low as 38% (for *The Gunfighters*). This malaise affected the whole series - *The Gunfighters*, long thought to be the lowest-rated serial, managed to average 6.3 million viewers; the following story, *The Savages*, could only garner 4.9 million, with the last episode getting only 4.5 million. Audience appreciation figures dropped by an average of around 10%. Some individual episodes had particularly high or particularly low ratings: this, presumably, is due to unusual scheduling from ITV, or other external factors. It is safe, for example, to assume that "The Feast of Steven" [*The Daleks' Master Plan* 7] must have faced some stiff opposition from ITV, as it was broadcast on Christmas Day, losing over a million viewers and thirty chart places, recovering them the next week - these weren't people that hated the 'pantomime' episodes, they never tuned in to see it in the first place. Audience report after audience report talked of a series that had run out of ideas - again, their wrath was aimed as much at the Daleks and War Machines as Johnny Ringo and the Medicis.

As *Doctor Who* entered the national consciousness, journalists and newspaper cartoonists tended to concentrate on the monsters, particularly the Daleks. Toy manufacturers wanted to market Daleks, Zarbi and Mechanoid models, not Nero and King Richard dolls. While the series was never driven by the merchandise, aspiring writers for the series must have been very conscious just how much money Terry Nation was making from his creations - each new monster was wheeled out for the press, generating publicity for the series. Lloyd's vision of *Doctor Who* was a complete reworking of the series' format and it was adopted by every subsequent production team. Most obviously, and perhaps most radically, the Doctor himself changed, but virtually every other aspect of the show deceived a similar facelift: before this time, the female companions (Susan, Vicki, Dodo) had been schoolchildren, virtually interchangeable granddaughter-types to William Hartnell's Doctor (the only exception was Barbara, a school mistress). Now they became late-teen dollybirds - Polly was the first of the more glamorous breed of companions that would become the norm.

The role of the male companion remained unchanged - from Ian to Harry there was an unbroken line of young men whose job it was to handle the fight scenes, leaving the Doctor free to think. *The War Machines* introduced a new genre, the contemporary Earth story - many stories over the next decade would see the Doctor in the late twentieth century, battling state-of-the-art technology. The opening credits also changed.

At first, the historical remained: Gerry Davis said (in the introduction to *DWB*'s *The Highlanders* photonovel), 'At the time I was looking for historical stories that were based on identifiable areas of fiction, like *The Smugglers* which I set up with Brian Hayles, which was loosely based on "Doctor Syn". I always thought that if we were going to do a historical then there's no point going back to the Massacre of St Bartholomew, which is not well known and hardly the subject of romance... I loved *The Highlanders* because it allowed me to do a historical story as I felt they should be done. I always considered it a mistake to meet Napoleon and people whose faces and personalities are so well known.'

It's interesting that Davis makes no mention of education, talking instead of 'romance'. Despite Davis' fondness for *The Highlanders*, it had become clear that there was no room any more for historical stories in the new scheme of things. Perhaps the general decline in the popularity of historical television drama in favour of spy/detective series was also a factor: Troughton only took part in this one historical, and then the genre died out. What's interesting, though, is another format change: the Hartnell production teams had twice dropped the idea of having a companion from Earth's history, Katarina died in her second story and Ann Chaplet was dropped at a relatively late stage in favour of Dodo. It was felt that there was a problem plucking people from history, because history would have been changed (the fact that, by the same logic, history must have changed when, say, Ian and Barbara where taken was apparently never considered). Troughton, unlike any other Doctor, travelled with two characters from history, Jamie and Victoria.

It has sometimes been suggested the historical stories were dropped 'because the most interesting bits of history had already been used up'. This analysis is banal - the TARDIS only landed in about a dozen historical periods, and there were many potential eras left to visit. Perhaps the reason the historical died out so quickly is because the production team had run out of plots. There were only really three types of historical stories:

(1) Educational - The Doctor and companions explore an era, finding out what makes it tick. In these stories, the Doctor and his companions tended to be swept along by events. The stories are often sprawling travelogues, with the TARDIS crew splitting up and exploring various aspects of the time they have landed in. The audience often knows what is going to happen, which limits the dramatic potential - often the stories are building to a huge climax that we already know about (*The Romans*, *The Massacre of St Bartholomew's Eve*). To avoid this, the stories concentrate on the travellers attempts to stay alive, with the 'important' events going on around them as a sub-plot. So, in *The Reign of Terror*, Ian and Barbara deal with a spy network while Napoleon plots the downfall of

Robespierre, and in *Marco Polo* they expose a plot to kill the Khan. The problem with a lot of these stories is that the involvement of the TARDIS crew often looks incidental - things would chug along quite happily without them, and a lot of the interesting stuff happens off-stage. As one of the audience panel for *The Myth Makers* put it, 'Why not just show a programme of the Trojan War without the complication of *Doctor Who*?'

(2) You Can't Change History - There are three examples of a time traveller trying to alter established history in the *Doctor Who* historicals, and all are very different: Barbara's unsuccessful attempt to end human sacrifice in *The Aztecs*, the Monk fails to change the course of the Battle of Hastings in *The Time Meddler* and Steven can't save Ann Chaplet in *The Massacre of St Bartholomew's Eve*. The major disadvantage is that the audience already knows the end of the story and that history didn't change, making it something of a false dilemma. That said, each of these stories is actually rather good, makes intelligent use of the dramatic potential, and plays with out expectations. But there is a danger, like the *Star Trek* Prime Directive plots, that such stories might have become repetitive and artificial - this is not a debate we can identify with, and it is difficult to dramatise. Rather than an exploration of an era, it's a science fiction story in historical clothing. It is also tricky to rationalise: why can the Doctor interfere in the future of our present, but not the past? Why does the Monk think he will succeed? Why can the Doctor and Steven save Vicki but not Ann Chaplet? If you can't change history, why does the Doctor bother to stop anyone from trying?

(3) History is Wrong - the Doctor and companions discover that a commonly held view of history is incorrect. Often in the historicals, the Hollywood or popular image of events is critiqued, rather than actual history's - so *The Myth Makers* (the title being something of a giveaway) demonstrates the gap between the idealised sleek heroes and their earthy real-life counterparts. These stories became popular under John Wiles' producership, where they tended to be comedies, and are something of a neglected genre. While fans often see them as 'silly' this type of story often assumes that the audience is bright enough to spot the discrepancies between the original history and the glamourised version for themselves. Such stories tend to be more intelligent than the attempts of the pseudohistoricals to rewrite history - telling us that the Great Fire of London was started by Terileptils or that the Daleks caused the crew to evacuate Mary Celeste.

In practice, many of the historical stories contained a mixture of these elements - most notably *The Romans* which, far from being the 'spoof' of fan myth, actually veers between the harsh life of a slave in Ian and Barbara's subplots, to a 'real' explanation of the Great Fire of Rome and the Hans Christian Andersen fairy tales, to a pastiche of the toga epics of the time (*Ben Hur* and *Cleopatra* in particular), to a comedy subplot in which Vicki almost assassinates the Roman Emperor. In four episodes, the regulars cover a huge amount of ground, ranging from a slave auction and murder on a country road to the Imperial palace and the dawn of Christianity (which is beautifully and subtly handled - just compare it with the *Trek* episode *Bread and Circuses*, made a couple of years later). There is most certainly comedy (including one of Hartnell's best performances), but Ian and Barbara in particular are given some pretty grim choices. Perhaps unsurprisingly, it averaged over two million more viewers than the next most popular historical.

While there were only a few permutations of plot, the historical stories concentrated on character and dialogue. This has meant that they have aged rather better than their science fiction contemporaries which were reliant in places on rather primitive special effects. Julian Glover's King Richard, John Ringham's Tlotoxl and Michael Peake's Tavius all shine as fully-realised people, rather than cardboard characters. William Hartnell, freed from the need to memorise technobabble, shines in these stories - he's often given some wonderful comedy scenes, but is just as good at confronting the baddy. Now that these stories have emerged on video and audio, fans have come to realise that some of the best scripts and performances were in the historical stories. These were not the lightweights of fan myth, but some of the best made *Doctor Who* of the sixties. Nevertheless, the show moved on under Lloyd, and as far as we know, not a single historical story was considered until 1982.

John Nathan-Turner had looked into the show's past and remembered the Hartnell days. *100,000 BC* was repeated in 1981, and *The Programme Guide* and *Doctor Who Monthly* were making information about the series' past more accessible. In interviews, JNT justified his new four-person TARDIS crew by referring back to the original Hartnell line-up, and the two-parter *Black Orchid* was another result of this 'back to basics' policy. Although the ratings were good, the story was perhaps a little inconsequential, and the new script editor, Eric Saward, despite his interest in history, wasn't keen on repeating the experiment.

It was thirteen years before the next historical *Doctor Who* story, although oddly the game book *Rebel's Gamble* published by FASA in the mid-eighties was an historical set during the American Civil War. Even publishing twenty-four stories a year, with a fan audience in mind, the New and Missing Adventures were slow to publish pure historicals, although many of the books have been pseudohistorical. David McIntee submitted *White Darkness* as an historical, but Peter Darvill-Evans felt that the book needed an alien threat as a dramatic focus. McIntee's

Sanctuary, an examination of the Cathare heretics, was published in early 1995, and became the first historical for thirteen years. While he was writing this, my own historical story, *Just War* was commissioned. Rebecca Levene, series editor, advised me in a letter (dated 28/11/94) that 'I'm not averse to pure historicals, but they are much harder to make work. Because you lose the WOW! factor that science fiction can supply, you have to replace it with something else. Fascinating historical detail can help, but it isn't enough'. It became clear that the Doctor's involvement with events had to be rationalized and the 'vacuum' caused by the lack of science fiction elements needed to be addressed.

Whether *Sanctuary* and *Just War* are the beginning of a new trend or a couple of oddities, we won't know for a while. A number of the other authors have expressed an interest in the genre, although there are no historicals commissioned for 1996. We'll never see a return to the days in which one out of every three stories was an historical, but perhaps now fans are beginning to value the Hartnell historical and they realise that for the first few years, the Doctor's travels into the past were as much a part of the series as his journeys to distant planets.

Past Lives

From Matrix #52, Spring 1996

Virtually every *Doctor Who* fan knows that the Doctor, like every other Time Lord, potentially has thirteen incarnations, that William Hartnell played the first of these and that the character has regenerated six times. This is accepted without question, but the facts as presented in the series are by no means as clear cut.

The orthodoxy, of course, is expressed on a number of occasions, but these are surprisingly few: in *The Three Doctors* the Time Lords claim that the Hartnell Doctor is the 'earliest'; we learn that the Time Lords are limited to twelve regenerations in *The Deadly Assassin*, this is reinforced in *The Keeper of Traken*, *The Twin Dilemma* and *The Trial of a Time Lord*; in *Mawdryn Undead* the fifth Doctor claims to have eight regenerations remaining; in *The Five Doctors* the first Doctor sees the fifth Doctor and concludes 'so there are five of me now'; finally, in *Time and the Rani*, the Doctor talks of his 'seventh persona'. No unfamiliar early incarnations come to light when previous Doctors are lifted out of their timestreams in *The Three Doctors*, *The Five Doctors* or, heaven help us, *Dimensions in Time*. However, there have been a number of hints that the Hartnell Doctor was not the first. In the script for *The Destiny of Doctor Who*, the new Troughton Doctor confides to his astonished companions that he has 'renewed' himself before. Of course, in the transmitted version of the story, *The Power of the Daleks*, the line does not appear, but neither is it contradicted. In Part Four of *The Brain of Morbius*, Morbius succeeds in mentally regressing the Doctor back from his Baker incarnation, through Pertwee, Troughton and Hartnell, and the process does not stop there, we go on to see a further eight incarnations of the Doctor prior to Hartnell.

This is indisputable: however we might want to fit this scene into the continuity of the series as established elsewhere, here, as the sequence of mysterious faces appears on the scanner, Morbius shouts 'How long Doctor? How long have you lived? Your puny mind is powerless against the strength of Morbius! Back! Back to your beginning! Back!'. These are not the faces of Morbius. The production team at the time (who bear a remarkable resemblance to the earlier Doctors, probably because they posed for the photographs used in the sequence), definitely intended the faces to be those of earlier Doctors. Producer Philip Hinchcliffe said 'we tried to get famous actors for the photos of the Doctor. But because no-one would volunteer, we had to use backroom boys. And it is true to say that I attempted to imply that William Hartnell was not the first doctor'. In another Hinchcliffe story, *The Masque of Mandragora*, the Doctor and Sarah Jane discover the secondary control room, and one of the Doctor's old costumes. He has, he says, not used this room for a long time and as we have never seen the room or the costume before, the implication is that an unseen incarnation (presumably prior to Hartnell) used it.

Elsewhere, facts about the Doctor's past are more ambiguous: the Doctor seems vague about his age throughout his life, the figure varying wildly from story to story and incarnation to incarnation. In *The Deadly Assassin*, Runcible remarks that the Doctor has had a facelift and the Doctor replies that he has had 'several so far', although in the original script he had done so a more specific 'three times'. In *Silver Nemesis*, it's hinted that the Doctor might have been a contemporary of Rassilon, millions of years before, and various other hints in the Cartmel era (most of which were edited out), suggested that the Doctor was no longer even a Time Lord.

If there were eight Doctors before Hartnell, and Time Lords are limited to thirteen incarnations, then that would mean that Davison was the last. He does say that his regeneration 'feels different this time' - is this because he's just started a second regenerative cycle? This might explain why the Colin Baker Doctor's incarnation was unstable and why the McCoy Doctor claimed to be 'more than just a mere Time Lord'. It would also mean that the Watcher existed between the Doctor's twelfth and thirteenth incarnations. This, of course, is the same position that the

Valeyard occupies. Could the Watcher and Valeyard be created at the same time, one a distillation of good, the other a distillation of evil? On television we are never actually told that the Valeyard is from the Doctor's future (obviously it is the implication, and it's explicitly stated in the novelisation), all we are told is that the Valeyard wants his remaining incarnations, so what if he was a potential fifth Doctor? It would explain a number of anomalies: why the Valeyard doesn't know he'll lose the Trial, why he tries to kill his past self, why he survives the Trial after the Doctor has promised to mend his ways.

Are Time Lords really limited to twelve regenerations, anyway? We were originally told that the Time Lords could 'live forever barring accidents' (*The War Games*). Only later, in *The Deadly Assassin*, was it revealed that Time Lords only regenerate twelve times, but even in that same story the Master proves that it is possible to prolong life beyond this, and in *The Five Doctors* the Time Lords officially offer the Master a new regenerative cycle.

Additionally, we know that Time Lords are able to survive death by sheer force of will (Omega, Morbius and the Master all do so), and that it is possible to divert energy from other Time Lords to gain a new lease of life (Mawdryn, the Master and the Valeyard all planned to do this). Rassilon, we learn, has the secret of Perpetual Regeneration, so is truly immortal. The Time Lords appear to have given the Minyans the same gift. In *The Creature From the Pit*, the Doctor states that Time Lords have ninety lives - and that he's used one hundred and thirty. All this evidence suggests that the Doctor is not necessarily limited to thirteen incarnations.

We can piece together a great deal about the Doctor's early life, but much of it is contradictory and it is impossible to state outright that William Hartnell played the very first incarnation of the Doctor. We don't even know that it was the Hartnell Doctor who left Gallifrey. The Monk might recognise Hartnell when they meet, but the War Chief, Runcible and Drax all recognise the Doctor after he has regenerated. We have also found out that the Doctor traveled the cosmos for the Time Lords while still an official member of Gallifreyan society (*The Two Doctors*), but we don't know how often he did this of what he looked like at the time. (Again, Dastari recognizes the Doctor when they meet again, despite the fact that he has regenerated since.) Presumably, while acting in an official capacity the Doctor used a state-of-the-art TARDIS or a Time Ring, not the antique model he would later steal.

It is unclear whether the Doctor left Gallifrey because he was he exiled or of his own free will. The Doctor suggested in couple of early stories that one day he might return to his home planet, but had he already done so? We discover in *The Time Meddler* that the Doctor left his home planet at least fifty years before *An Unearthly Child*, but Susan is only fifteen - did the Doctor go back home after thirty-five years travelling the universe only to leave again, this time with his grandchild? If we take everything said in the series at face value, then the Doctor left Gallifrey when he was 236 years old, but was 309 when he attended a Tech Course with Drax - this would seem to suggest that the Hartnell incarnation also returned to Gallifrey, but after the television series had started. It's certainly *simpler* to suggest that the Doctor was simply being vague about his age, but would it be *right*?

In *The Two Doctors* we learn that the Doctor maintained contact with the Time Lords in his Troughton incarnation - was he ever really out of touch with Gallifrey? If the Doctor did regenerate several times before the series started, it might explain the contradictions in his early life - one incarnation could have been the mischievous, late-developing student; a second the serious young man who studied under K'anpo near the family home and learned the myths of Ancient Gallifrey; the third was a brilliant pioneer; a fourth a family man and father; another the Time Lord ambassador; yet another the political agitator who campaigned to ban Miniscopes. When the Pertwee Doctor is exiled to Earth he already knows Venusian Aikido - can we really picture Hartnell or Troughton acquiring fighting skills under a Venusian sensei? We know that the Doctor and Susan visited Venus before *An Unearthly Child*, but perhaps the Doctor wore a younger, more agile body at the time. The Time Lords might think that Hartnell was the earliest incarnation, but they have a very poor record of keeping track of renegade members of their species - the Master, Salyavin, Rani, Morbius and the Valeyard all manage to remain undetected. Perhaps the Doctor is an alias for a Time Lord who has secretly transgressed a number of Gallifreyan laws, in a number of incarnations. The Time Lord we know as the Doctor might have only adopted that name in his Hartnell incarnation - Hartnell would be 'the first Doctor', but the ninth (or more) incarnation of that Time Lord.

There are a number of other solutions that might explain away the contradictions. Several of the New Adventures have suggested that a leading Time Lord from the time of Rassilon (the Other) has infiltrated the Doctor's subconscious, but haven't revealed yet when this happened. If it was before *The Brain of Morbius*, then the faces might be those of the Other, rather than the Doctor. The faces might be potential Doctors like the ones we see in Episode Ten of *The War Games* or the Valeyard. The costume in the secondary control room might belong to the original owner of the TARDIS (another mysterious figure). Unlike the past lives theory, though, there is no evidence whatsoever on television that would support such speculation.

The Doctor is a mysterious figure, and every time we learn a fact about his past, it raises more questions than it answers. Although more than one New Adventure has had scenes set before the Doctor leaves Gallifrey, Missing Adventures authors are forbidden to set their novels before *An Unearthly Child*. There is no chance whatsoever that we'll see a Missing Adventure featuring the Hinchcliffe Doctor and Susan, a story in which the Gallacio Doctor visits Dastari or the Camfield Doctor gets Miniscopes banned. Phew. The Amblin Pilot is rumoured to depict the Doctor leaving Gallifrey, but this will apparently be the start of a new continuity, not that of the BBC series. In other words, we will probably never know the whole truth about the Doctor's past. Just remember, though, that we have actually seen incarnations of the Doctor before the Hartnell incarnation.

Seriously Silly

From Matrix #53, Autumn 1996

Ian Levine once declared that *Doctor Who* under Graham Williams was 'like *Fawlty Towers* in space'. Incredibly, the comment was meant as criticism.

The Williams era, of course, was the most successful in the show's long history. Now, almost twenty years on, the iconography of the period is still how the general public perceive the programme: the Doctor has curly hair, a long scarf, a robot dog and a scantily-clad companion. There is a general belief that *Doctor Who* was always a show with wobbly sets that didn't take itself too seriously. The Williams era was the one that finally got the show the cult American audience it had been trying to win for a decade. Back home it got some of the highest ratings the show has ever seen (and not all because of an ITV strike).

When *The Stones of Blood* won the DWAS season poll in 1978, Graham Williams noted that it got the lowest ratings of the year. He remarked that fans' appreciation of a story often seemed to be the opposite of what the general public thought. This was his own experience: despite the mainstream success the show was enjoying, and the overwhelming support the producer received from BBC management, the newly-organised fandom was united in condemnation of the current style of the show, believing that it was a 'betrayal' of what had gone before.

The pendulum is swinging back - people who were ten years old when Williams served as producer are writing and editing *DWM*, and manning the barricades in Williams' defence. The mood began shifting about five years ago, around the time *In-Vision* started covering the Williams era. Initially, as Gareth Roberts noted in *DWB* #121, we all went on about how postmodern it all was. In the immortal words of Tulloch and Alvarado (who never use one syllable where eight will do): 'Williams' intellectual tendency was to establish his signature as producer and capture the bonus audience by "spoof"... under the influence of Doug Adams as script editor, the "parody" signature became still more ambitious.' In other words, Williams wanted it funny, Adams wanted it funnier. But still, the old ways of discussing the stories prevail: 'Hey, everything is really shoddy and silly, but that's all part of the fun.'

The Williams stories are certainly fun, but they aren't badly made. First of all, let's knock one fan myth on the head very quickly. In *DWM* #60, the unattributed article "Future Times Past" credits JNT with the changes of the eighteenth season and looks forward to the nineteenth: 'A less obvious modification to the programme was the tightening of the continuity which became noticeable in every story'. Examples given include the use of the word 'Kasterborous' and praise that the Doctor and Romana's old outfits were seen on the hatstand. We are told that the stories linked together in a way entirely unlike the old Williams ones (the E-Space trilogy, for example), and the flashback sequence in *Logopolis* was great. The author clearly was looking the other way during the Williams era. The stories might not dovetail, but we see old coats on the hatstand, an entire season is linked and the following year it is again, more subtly - K9's laryngitis, the chess games, redecorating the TARDIS and Romana's attempts to fly the ship are all running subplots and jokes. There was even a flashback sequence planned for *Shada*. Continuity is respected and added to: *every* story in the fifteenth season adds something, great or small, to the Time Lord mythos (we learn that regeneration was something Time Lords learned in *Horror of Fang Rock*, and if *The Witch Lords* had gone ahead, we'd have had the vampires in that season, too). Incidentally, the *DWM* #60 article ended with the confident prediction 'it is thus very possible that the [nineteenth] season will end at the peak of Dennis Spooner's allegory of the dramatic W'. *Qué?*

Number Two: it betrayed Hinchcliffe and Holmes, and all that had gone before. Holmes was there throughout the fifteenth season. Most fans forget he was the script editor for the first three stories, that he wrote the fourth and the sixth is a sequel to one of his, using an old Holmes baddy. There might not have been that many returning monsters, but there weren't any in the thirteenth or fourteenth seasons either, apart from a radically different Master. When continuity is invoked, it works well - *The Invasion of Time* and *Destiny of the Daleks* stand on their own, but also fit in quite well with their prequels. The 'slide into silliness' is gradual. A lot of the violence has been toned down, but Humour has always been part of the show, especially when Holmes was writing. *Carnival of Monsters* and *The Time Warrior* are both 'Williamsesque', and Hinchcliffe had already begun to experiment with a lighter tone. *Talons* is usually seen as the pinnacle of Hinchcliffey Gothic Horror, but it's really the first Williams story, full of jokes, literary parodies and metafictional stuff. It wouldn't be out of place in Season Seventeen, alongside *City of Death*. Williams used a small group of mostly established authors (only Fisher and Adams are new boys).

Apart from its use of an old baddy, *Destiny of the Daleks* is, like most Dalek stories, a good example of the prevailing mood of the production team. You can see all the Cartmel themes in *Remembrance*, *Resurrection* is as Sawardesque as it gets (*none* of the characters have first names!) and *The Chase* is the second series in microcosm, dying to encompass everything from tragedy on a planetary scale to a ludicrous American tourist. *Destiny of the Daleks* has received a hammering over the years from critics of Williams, who have taken it as final proof of a malicious intent to trash the series and its most sacred icons - Trivialisation of the Daleks. Voices in its defence are few and far between. Craig Hinton isn't particularly averse to the Williams era, but this *DWM* review (issue #215) is unambiguous: '*Destiny of the Daleks* is one of the most embarrassing farragoes of sheer drivel I have ever sat through. It takes genius to muck things up on this scale, so stand up Messrs Nation, Adams, Grieve and Williams for writing, editing, directing and producing this nonsense.' It gets worse, believe it or not: 'so many faults, I don't know where to begin... undergraduate humour falls like a lead balloon... the ridiculous excuse for a regeneration sequence (is) nothing more than silliness... the Daleks shabby shadows of their past glory... *Destiny of the Daleks* is one of the worst stories ever made, with nothing to recommend it in the slightest'. The *DWB* thirtieth anniversary poll - the most comprehensive recent poll - wasn't quite so damning: the story came 90th (out of 158), with a rating of 64.26%. Not good, but better than *Day* (93rd), *Planet* (101st), *The Chase* (105th) and *Death* (120th). It's within slithering distance of *The Dalek Invasion of Earth* (82nd, 65.8%).

The story suffers because it doesn't compare terribly favorably with *Genesis of the Daleks*, its predecessor. *Genesis* was (and is) one of the best-remembered stories - helped by a repeat, a novelization (the all-time best-seller with over 125,000 copies sold, incidentally, according to Peter Darvill-Evans), an audio tape and its appearance in the Marks and Spencers anthology. The Daleks didn't appear for another four seasons, but managed to sustain enough interest to generate four Dalek Annuals in that period. There aren't many fans who would argue that *Genesis* is one of the series' highpoints, the only thing against it nowadays being its overfamiliarity (following another two repeats and a video release). In that *DWB* Poll, *Genesis* came 5th, with a rating of 90.71%. *Destiny of the Daleks* suffers from heightened fan expectation rather than any particular production failing. Fans in 1979 thought that all Dalek stories had been like *Genesis*, and if you wanted to write a fanzine article about how things were much better in the good old idealistic days, it was just as well if you could conveniently forget the rule rather than the exceptions. *Destiny* compares very well indeed with the two previous Terry Nation 70s Dalek stories - a comparison made very easy indeed, because all three have exactly the same plot, give or take a couple of elements.

The most common criticisms of *Destiny* have a sort of weary hypocrisy about them: the same fans that moan about Romana's regeneration were probably cheering when Tom Baker tried on his different costumes in *Robot*. It's a nice, lighthearted way of introducing the new, nice, lighthearted Romana. The direction (Ken Grieve) is really quite impressive: high and low camera angles, handhelds and imaginative location work all inject some pace and visual excitement into the story. The script balances the comedy with the horror - this is a story in which the Doctor genuinely thinks he's going to die. His confrontations with Davros don't match the big set pieces of *Genesis*, but they are still powerful. Take the beginning of Episode Three. Holed up in a room, with the Daleks about to break in, the Doctor's in fine form; laughing at Davros, while about to make the self sacrifice that Davros is incapable of. Watching the scenes, it's very tempting to imagine that the Davros dialogue is Terry Nation's while the Doctor has abandoned the script for a series of Baker/Adams asides ('You're misquoting Napoleon!').

Some fans (and Nation!) might object to the flippant replies to the usual guff about how the Daleks will conquer the universe, but Baker is acting on a human scale. Davros wants to know about the wars and fighting, but what about the sports news? At the some time, the Daleks and their creator are untouched: Davros isn't even listening to the Doctor, he's dreaming of exterminating billions. Outside, his creations have lined up prisoners and they are shooting them one by one. Never before have the Daleks done anything so personal: they've released plagues and planted bombs, but never before have they taken so much pleasure in killing unimportant individuals. It's a very clever scene, infinitely better scripted and played than the normal, butch rubbish about how the Daleks must be stopped but the timing mechanism is broken. Of course the Daleks must be defeated, but not at the cost of your sense of humour. This scene doesn't undermine the Daleks, it throws them into the sharpest possible contrast with the nice people like you and me.

The 'infamous taunt' (Jeremy Bentham, *In-Vision* #39) of the Doctor's, inviting the Daleks to climb up after him if they are so powerful, is hardly subversive. Quote Tulloch and Alvarado again: 'He is doing no more than pointing to the extreme implausibility of these ball-bearing monsters for anything other than the most unsophisticated child audience.' Whoever annotated my second-hand copy of *The Unfolding Text* has written *'and Terry Nation'* in the margin. No-one, surely, who watched *Destiny* hadn't noticed that the Daleks couldn't climb stairs or bend down to pick anything up. It's the oldest joke in the book, the weariest of crappy journalist cliches. (The joke still has some life in it: a couple of years ago, one if the letters in Viz complained that 'all these new ramps for the disabled are leaving us wide open to attack from the Daleks'.)

The Stairs Thing is the true Power of the Daleks. The whole of Britain suspended its disbelief, aware that the sucker arm, the twitching eyestalk, the hissing gun, the fifty-two (or however many) half tennis balls on the skirt and the grating 'exterminate' voice are so much more than the sum of their parts. When they were five, everyone saw a Dalek story, and even at that tender age they could see the problem. Groups in playgrounds from John o'Groats to Land's End reached the same conclusion and declared in all seriousness: 'If only the Daleks could climb stairs, they'd be unstoppable.' The Dalek design is a work of absurd genius, truly one of the great creations of television.

The Movellan design is no more ludicrous than Castrovalvan or Kinda haute couture. The Movellans are pretty ordinary-looking compared with most of the races seen in *Doctor Who* and *Blakes 7* at this time. The wigs are perhaps a mistake, but the multi-racial and androgynous Movellans are striking. If it seems highly unlikely that such a race would defeat the Daleks, then surely that's the point. Besides, Terry Nation never managed to create anything with the same appeal as the Daleks on any subsequent attempt: the Movellans join the long list that includes the Mechonoids, the Voord and the Kraals. Perhaps, deep down, fans are disappointed with *Destiny* because the Daleks and K9 didn't meet up.

What I don't understand about the criticism of the Williams era is the tired old 'the production values were crap' line. It isn't true. Compare the jungle in *The Creature from the Pit* with that in *Kinda* (the last attempt at anything so ambitious). One is on film, looks alien and is lavish, while the other looks like a dozen pot plants hastily arranged over studio flooring and cables. Bad design doesn't make a bad story, but it certainly doesn't help make it a good one. 'Oh, but *The Leisure Hive* is lavish compared with *The Horns of the Nimon*.' Fine, but it's an underrunning, underplotted, unfunny trifle compared with *City of Death*, the last (broadcast) showpiece story. There isn't a Williams story as shoddy as

Time-Flight, Timelash or *Meglos*. *The Leisure Hive* is a misleading place to look anyway, a deliberate ploy to make the new series look like something really different. It was a ploy, incidentally, that saw the audience drop from 10.4 million and 26th place for the last part of *Nimon* to 5.9 and 77th for *The Leisure Hive*. The audience weren't fooled - whereas Nimon's audience had grown, *The Leisure Hive*'s plummeted to 111th in the chart - the lowest since the very first episode! Naturally, the fans loved it, seeing it as a bold new era.

The modelwork in the Williams era is a triumph - presumably the production team felt that they had to try to match *Star Wars* in the spaceship stakes. It seems a fool's errand - until the Vardan ship passes overhead, the Movellan one buries itself or Scaroth's explodes over primeval Earth. The special effects reach new heights of ambition, and if they sometimes look like magnificent folly (Kroll, in all his manifestations), then surely that's better than not even trying. *Underworld* was perhaps the most effects-intensive programme the BBC had ever made. The special effects aren't as bad as you've been told, and for an emergency measure they work a lot better than *Captain Zep* (marketed as a showcase of state-of-the-art SFX) four years later. Only with the advent of CGI have they been bettered - nowadays programmes as diverse as the BBC evening news and *Babylon 5* regularly use the techniques pioneered in that story.

The Williams era is the most ambitious in the show's history. The Hinchcliffe era is great, underrated if anything, but there are only so many times that Sarah can get hypnotized, the Doctor can get knocked out and they run through the woods back to the TARDIS before the manor house explodes. Although fans will say they like *Doctor Who* because the TARDIS can land anywhere, two-thirds of all the stories are set on Earth. During the Williams era, including *Shada*, the TARDIS only visits Earth five times in eighteen stories - two of those in the 'handover period'. It gives a real universal scale to the stories. This isn't a series about trying to get a couple of teachers home or escaping exile, this is the story of two aliens and their robot dog. Why should they visit London every other week when a whole universe of delights awaits?

But good as the production, direction, acting and design are, the real strength of the Williams era is the scripting and characterisation. The scripts sing with jokes, from witty one liners to elaborate recurring sight gags. Rather than a mass of rubber-suited monsters, the Doctor meets one baddy, his henchman and his monster. These villains are well-rounded characters, played by actors and actresses sent in to bat against Tom. Many villains either were, or would be, big names or stalwarts of 'proper drama': Woodvine, Woolf, Glover, Sheard, Lill, Milton Johns, Cuthbertson, Peter Jeffrey, Dyall, Crowden, Neame. The villains don't want to blow up the universe because they are evil, they want the best for their people and don't care how many planets they have to destroy to get it. The Black Guardian might be the ultimate Black Hat, a Baddy who wants to set the two halves of the universe at war with one another, but he's only in the last minute of *The Armageddon Factor*. Compare him with the Marshall, who's mad and genocidal, but is given some Churchillian speeches and only wants to win the war against the planet that is drop- ping nuclear bombs on his civilization. The motives of the Williams bad- dies are clearly defined in the space of their first scene - we find out what they want and what the cost will be. Compare that with the Master: why does he want to blow up the universe or prevent the signing of Magna Carta? For that matter, why does he want to kill the Doctor? It's never explained beyond 'insanity' or 'revenge' .

I've not even mentioned Tom (at the height of his powers, an utterly unstoppable force capable of upstaging John Bloody Cleese and Julian Glover in the same story). Or Lalla (the only successful 'as bright as the Doctor' companion, after years of trying). Or K9 (a tin box that can out- act Iain Cuthbertson and Graham Crowden). I've not bothered with *City of Death*, everyone knows that no subsequent story came close to its genius - although it isn't the exception, and it's only the second-best Douglas Adams script. Rather than three seasons of irrelevant trivia between the monoliths of the Hinchcliffe and Good JNT stuff, the Williams era is a solid canon of work, within the established *Doctor Who* universe, well aware of the show's past, and the limitations of the format. Watch those tapes again, and imagine everyone in Britain sitting down to watch the story. *Doctor Who* wasn't 'cult viewing' back then, it was as big a phenomenon as *Heartbeat* or *Casualty* now. If the fans didn't like it, then they were the only ones.

Eighth Wonder

From Matrix #53, Autumn 1996

What are we to make of the eighth Doctor? If the Davison era had ended with *Castrovalva*, we'd know very little about the fifth Doctor. There are hints there, and we can see he's very different from his prede- cessor, but it's impossible to build up a rounded portrait, because he spends much of the story weak and confused after his regeneration. It's the same with McGann: we know the Doctor kisses girls now, and that he's half-human and that he knows about Gareth's exam. But, just as the pilot doesn't really give us much indication as to what a series would be like (unless the plan was to have twenty-six episodes set in the Cloister

Room), future writers have very few clues about the new Doctor based solely on the evidence of the movie. We can say that the eighth Doctor seems possessed of a sense of urgency, but is that because that's his new persona or because he knows the world will end at midnight?

We can see many traces of previous Doctors and fans are queuing up to say he looks like a young Hartnell (he doesn't - see *The Sixties* p13-15 for pictures of Hartnell in his twenties and thirties) or that his performance is reminiscent of Troughton or Tom (these fans seem unable to point to any actual line delivery or mannerism when challenged). Apparently he has the youth of Davison, the energy of McCoy, is capable of scathing comments worthy of Colin and he tinkers like Pertwee. This makes him sound like the Morbius monster, a crude patching together of bits of other people. It also smacks of fanboy desperation, the sort of thing you're meant to say that allows the eighth Doctor to slip into the established continuity. It also ignores McGann's contribution, something that can't be overlooked.

In fact, McGann is the problem. Many of the previous Doctors had a rather limited range, but this isn't a bad thing - the best Doctors turned this to their advantage. Tom, for instance, is capable of making any line he's given into a Bakerish Witticism. The writers soon began playing to the actor's strengths: McCoy was given less spluttering anger and more low menace, Troughton became less 'eccentric' and more fey. New and Missing Adventures writers find it fairly easy to write a line of dialogue that you can hear Pertwee saying, or a McCoyism. One of the frequent criticisms of the MAs is that the characterization isn't quite right, 'the Doctor sounds more like Tom Baker than Patrick Troughton', or 'that was the sort of thing Pertwee would do, Sylvester would have chosen a different method'. But, as the fans who assembled a makeshift Paul McGann collection on video at the beginning of the year know, anyone capable of playing both Marwood and Percy Toplis, who ended up in *Nice Town* but could have played the title role in *Sharpe*, has the range to play any potential Doctor from a slapstick spoonplaying twat to a lonely walker in eternity. McGann himself (*DWM* #238) has admitted that his interpretation of the Doctor remains nascent: 'I'm just finding my feet as I go along. At this stage it's a one-off anyway. If it does get picked up as a series then I'll be able to get my teeth into him.' This, of course, is the irony. At the time of writing, we don't know if there will be any more TV adventures. Even if there were, McGann might not be involved.

There will be plenty of eighth Doctor stories, though - he's already appearing in comic strips in *Radio Times* and *DWM*, Virgin will be publishing a novel, and BBC Books a range of novels featuring him. Fan fiction will soon be rolling off the presses. The writers and editors will have to reach their own conclusions about the new Doctor and 'what he's like'. The Virgin NA featuring the McGann Doctor will be written by the end of August 1996, but won't be published until April 1997. Spare a thought for the authors who will be writing stories in the full knowledge that during that time, the first full season might come and go on TV, and that their readers will have seen twenty-five times as much of the new Doctor.

The earliest *Star Trek: The Next Generation* novels and comic strips were written based on the series bible and publicity shots (thanks to the angle of one of those pictures, Troi is drawn taller than Riker at first in the comic). The author of the first novel, *Ghost Ship*, hadn't even seen *Encounter at Farpoint*. Reading the early novels and watching the TNG pilot now is to take a fascinating glimpse into what the show that might have been: Picard is a wise old man who sits on the bridge dispensing words of wisdom while his dynamic Number One beams down to the new civilizations. Riker is helped by the Amazonian security chief Natasha and his exotic telepathic lover, the talented diplomat Deanna Troi. All Data does is sit at the helm trading banter with Geordi, and Worf gets three lines, two of which are 'shields up'.

Picard and Doctor Crusher are almost certainly lovers, and Wesley Crusher may well be the Captain's son. The ship is full of the crew's families, who get marooned in the saucer section at the first sign of trouble. The Ferengi are cannibals, savage users who strip-mine planets and sell entire populations into slavery - they make the now-peaceful Klingons look as scary as the Royal Beast of Tara. The *Enterprise* is travelling ever outwards on an ongoing mission deep into the unexplored mass of the galaxy. In performance, of course, it was completely different.

All TV series, even - especially - those with a fixed idea of where they are going, change when an actor proves too good or bad at their job, or too expensive or isn't available that week. If things had gone to plan, then a perfectly ordinary mad bloke called Bob killed Laura, Sinclair's still in charge, Servalan only appeared in *Project Avalon* but Blake was there right until the end and Alan Rickman played Rimmer. I needn't have polluted the pages of *Matrix* with such trivia - in *Doctor Who* the same thing happened over and over again: BEMs were introduced, the eighth season revamps the UNIT concept, Harry Sullivan's role completely changes, and Philip Segal wanted Alan Rickman but couldn't afford him. It's difficult to imagine that in 1987 people could see the pratfalling, spoonplaying, gurning, malapropisming McCoy of *Time and the Rani* leading to stories like *Ghost Light*. So, if and when McGann reprises the role for a regular series, he'll have his chance to get his teeth into the part. He'll grow, develop, evolve. There will be points of similarity between the TV series and the 'non-canonical' stuff' - long before the movie, the New Adventures had a half-human snogger, a Gothic control room, a they've-killed-him-on-the-operating-table scene, a professional female companion in her thirties with an unhappy lovelife, a the-world-ends-at-midnight-1999 plot, a dying TARDIS and a beefed-up feral-eyed Master - but McGann's interpretation will significantly differ from Gary Russell's in *Dreadnought*, Warwick Gray's in the *DWM* strip, mine in *The Dying Days* or the BBC Book version. With all that in mind, do we know anything about the eighth Doctor? Are we to be condemned to a bunch of generic *Doctor Who* stories, or worse still, snog-of-the-week, I'm-half-human, *Withnail*-injoke books?

There are plenty of clues in the movie, many strands that are there already, or that could be developed. Obviously he shares all the classic character traits of the Doctor, all that 'neither cruel nor cowardly stuff', his love of life and of creation over destruction, his distaste for guns, his technical skill, his ability to adapt. There's plenty of talk about how the incarnations of the Doctor differ, but little about how virtually every line could have been spoken by virtually any other Doctor. Here, though, we are talking about differences.

In all my travels through space and time, and nearing the end of my seventh life, I was finally beginning to realise that you can never be too careful.

At face value, fans might have thought that the Doctor of *The Curse of Fenric* or *Ghost Light* had long learnt that lesson. While it can be over-emphasised, the seventh Doctor was certainly characterized by his fore-knowledge of events, his preplanning and the manipulation of others to achieve a set end. Whereas a previous Doctor might have landed on Terra Alpha or 1963 London at random, and then become embroiled in events, the seventh Doctor set the co-ordinates deliberately, and had at least some knowledge of what was going on. But the voiceover at the beginning of the movie has a double meaning. In many of the Cartmel stories (not least of which being his first novel, *Cat's Cradle: Warhead*), the Doctor's meticulous plan overlooks one small detail, and as a result of his miscalculation he is forced to save the day through brilliant improv-isation. You can never be too careful, because life is too complex, and you can never know everything about everything, even if you are a Time Lord. This never stopped him from trying.

The eighth Doctor has chosen another path. At no stage does he plan - he may have objectives (fix the TARDIS, close the Eye, stop the Master) but he improvises the solutions from the materials at hand. The scene in which he lures the motorcycle policeman over with jelly babies, to steal his gun, to threaten himself with it and to borrow the motorcycle is the most lauded and most successful example. Often as not, though, the new Doctor suffers a setback because he isn't playing the game two moves ahead. At the movie's climax, the Doctor taunts the Master, making him angry enough to accidentally prove that he wants to steal the Doctor's lives - 'I have wasted all my lives because of you!'. The short-term objective is achieved, Chang Lee realises that the Master is evil, but the Master's response is to kill Lee while the Doctor watches helplessly.

Imagine a ruthless McCoy in the same scene - he'd be one stage ahead, and would deliberately trick the Master into destroying the only thing that can facilitate his plan. He'd deliver the line 'how are you going to open the Eye now?' in a low menacing voice and the scene wouldn't be wildly different from the end of The Curse of Fenric. Ultimately, though, the result would be the same whether the Doctor plotted or not - the Doctor doesn't know that the Master can still use Grace to open the Eye.

One thing the eighth Doctor lacks that all his predecessors had to some degree or another is arrogance. Even the second and fifth Doctors became indignant when someone questioned their intelligence. All the other incarnations might almost be characterized by their assumption that they are better than the people they meet. The eighth incarnation has none of this - he is almost pedantically polite (count the number of times he says 'please', and note that he asks the motorcycle cop 'will you excuse me?' when he takes Grace aside).

He's also perfectly willing to be passive: when he and Grace arrive at ITAR, it is she that takes the lead, trying to persuade the guard, coming up with the 'Doctor Bowman' alias, making all the introductions. A previous incarnation might have strode in as if he owned the place. In this scene, the Doctor/companion body language is reversed, he trails after Grace, following her around - it's something that hasn't happened before. Many previous Doctors boast, and spend much of their time demonstrating how clever they are to their companions - the eighth incarnation downplays his achievements. The new Doctor seems to operate mainly on instinct, and his intuition is fine-tuned. At the hospital he has a sense of threat - 'get me out of here before they kill me again' - and even when he doesn't know the right answers he seems able to sense when someone is wrong: somehow he knows he isn't a genetic experiment, that there isn't a millennium effect and so on.

This does mean that he makes deductions that seem unexplainable. How does he know the world will end at midnight? How does he know the glass will bend? He has a number of traits that might be characterized as 'childlike'. Chief of these is a sense of wonder at spectacle - fireworks and monster movies. He lives in a kid's universe, full of storybook things (note that when he watches Frankenstein he takes the monster in his stride, but jumps when the woman screams). In Grace's house she scolds him, 'Only children believe in that crap.' The Doctor responds immediately with 'it was a childish dream that made you a doctor' - Grace's adult life, like everyone's, is based on beliefs fostered in her childhood. As all the things that make her an adult (her job, lover, scepticism) are removed she becomes part of the Doctor's world. The eighth is also the first Doctor to mention his parents, referring to both of them over the course of the movie.

The eighth Doctor also has difficulty prioritising. Philip Segal says, 'The scene in the movie that is a real tribute to [the production team's efforts to get the Doctor's character right] is the one where the Doctor is in the park and beginning to remember who he is. Just as Grace begins to get concerned about and into all this, the Doctor is suddenly off the subject and more interested in talking about how perfectly his shoes fit. That is *Doctor Who*.' It is certainly one of the movie's defining moments.

GRACE: Maybe you're the result of some weird genetic experiment?
DOCTOR: (*Shakes head, smiling*) I don't think so.
GRACE: But you have no recollection of family.
DOCTOR: No, no wait. I do I remember. (*He's becoming more animated*) I'm with my father: we're lying back in the grass, it's a warm Gallifieyan night -
GRACE: Gallifreyan?
DOCTOR: (*Hold his arms out in triumph*) Gallifrey! Yes - this must be where I live. Now, where is that?
GRACE: I've never heard of it. What do you remember?
DOCTOR: (*Shouting now*) A meteor storm! And the sky above us was dancing with lights - purple, green, brilliant yellow. (*reached a crescendo*) Yes!
GRACE: What?
DOCTOR: These shoes, they fit perfectly. Yes!

The Doctor tends to fix on things from moment to moment - and for that moment his shoes, his memory of home, the word Gallifrey, kissing Grace or whatever it happens to be - is the only thing that exists. It's slightly obsessive, pedantic behaviour. This is a Doctor who lives for the beauty of each moment, and who would take time out while being chased by Cybermen to stop and listen to birds singing.

While the Doctor has a nice line in deadpan - 'breathe in, Grace', 'they say that on my planet', 'oh, a good ten minutes away' - he's not a Doctor to indulge in (deliberate) physical comedy or word-play. He has something of a lack of humour when the stakes are high. In the ambulance he's full of scorn when Grace trades banter with the Master - 'Oh yes, very witty Grace. Freud would have taken me seriously.' He's bemused by her jokes, able to recognise but not understand her sarcasm. Later he reprimands the Master for changing into Time Lord robes while the world is at risk - 'time enough to change?' he shouts. Again it's an almost childlike 'take me seriously' sort of thing a precocious five year old would demand of his mother.

The Doctor isn't mad, of course. Humans might make him laugh for seeing patterns that aren't there, but that's because he can see the patterns that *are*. He explains as much to Grace while they ride through San Francisco: 'The universe hangs by such a fragile thread of coincidence. There is no point in trying to tamper with it unless, like me, you are a Time Lord.' It's this innate ability, along with his great scientific and historical knowledge and centuries of personal experience that informs his behaviour.

Grace is not a stupid woman - just the opposite, she's clearly more intelligent, talented and well-adjusted than any of the other humans in the movie - but she can't hope to understand what is going on, so her attempts to rationalise away what happens are doomed to failure. Meanwhile, the Doctor seems to work it all out on instinct alone.

What are we to make of the apparent new ability to see people's fates? How far can he see into people's souls? Grace talks about his 'glorious predictions, all your knowledge of what is going to happen to Gareth, to me, to this city'. The Doctor has an immense knowledge of history - enough to recognize Gareth as a youngster and know about his exam results, but that's no worse than the Puccini lines earlier on. Gareth is going to be a famous seismologist - perhaps he meets the Doctor in twenty years time and confides to him about his time at college.

Grace too is an exceptional woman: by her mid-thirties she's clearly a talented surgeon, she's rich, she's on the board of ITAR. It isn't much of a leap to imagine that she'll be famous one day. As far as I can see, the Doctor uses his great knowledge, rather than demonstrating a new psychic ability.

So the eighth Doctor acts impulsively, without planning. He lacks arrogance, instead demonstrating childlike qualities of wonder and boundless energy. Everything is done in earnest, with a passion. He fixes on things, and is capable of brilliant improvisation.

And then there is the last scene.

Twenty-four hours after his regeneration, without the urgency that has driven him up to this point, we get the best indication yet what a McGann Doctor would be like. His character has stabilized, in the same way that Davison's has at the end of *Castrovalva*. And it's an interesting scene. He lets Chang Lee keep the gold dust, either unaware of the gang member's former plans for it ('Power!') or else confident that Lee has changed. Once the kid leaves, watch out for the *differences* between Grace and the Doctor. Throughout the movie they have almost been set up as equals - they are the same height, the same apparent age, they even have the same hairdo. This last scene would seem to emphasize this equality: for the first time, when the Doctor asks someone to come with him, she replies 'you come with me'. The Doctor says he's tempted, but look closely: he's staring out over the city, not at Grace. She's 'finally met the right guy', he likes the fireworks.

Besides, Grace and the audience know that the Doctor won't stay. They kiss, then walk their separate ways. The Doctor bounds over to the TARDIS. He is a model of romantic restraint as he stands by the TARDIS door. His expression is utterly inscrutable - the flutter of his eyelids might indicate regret, but his mouth is almost smiling, There is passion there, energy, intelligence, but they are perfectly balanced and controlled. Cut to Grace, as she waves and mouths goodbye. Without changing his expression or looking back, the Doctor steps into the TARDIS and it dematerialises. Cut to Grace, whose shoulders are slumped. She sighs and stands perfectly still. She's lost her job, her boyfriend, she's seen wonders she'll never see again and the Doctor has gone forever.

And we cut to the TARDIS interior where the Doctor is fixing the console, thinking about what he'll do next ('where to now?', 'where was I?'). *In A Dream* is back on the record player, there's a fresh cup of tea on the table by his chair and he's not finished reading *The Time Machine*. There isn't the slightest evidence that he's thought of Grace since he stepped back inside.

As ever, then, the Doctor's living in the present, excited about the future, not dwelling on his past.

The Nth Doctor

From Matrix #54, Summer 1997

Jean-Marc Lofficier's latest book contains an introduction that does my job for me: it explains that what he is doing is subjective, that the story titles are made up by him, and he notes carefully where he's altered the scripts (an editing process that includes changing the names of the main characters on a couple of occasions). So, I can't reprimand him for trying to reconcile the unmade scripts with established *Who* lore, he already knows it's as futile as trying to reconcile the Janssen *Fugitive* with the Harrison Ford version. He even - bless him - mentions me by name as someone who's likely to disagree with his personal opinions.

So I can concentrate on the new material itself, and there's a lot of it in the public domain for the first time. About half the book is devoted to the various Johnny Byrne scripts, mostly drafts and reworkings of *The Last of the Time Lords* outline that appeared in *DWB* many years ago. I've never been a fan of Byrne's TV work on the series, not even *Traken*, and nothing in the first half of the book makes the Green Light / Coast to Coast / Daltenreys script sound any more appealing. When interviewed for the book, Byrne concedes that his film was 'very late 80s' and would need to be totally revamped for the 90s audience. As with all the storylines presented in *The Nth Doctor*, it's impossible to say what another draft of the script, a talented cast, a brilliant director and a multi-million dollar budget would have done with the material, but the renegade cyborg Time Lord plot is quite reminiscent of a lot of the generic 80s action-SF films which form a major part of any given HMV sale nowadays. When I try to visualize it, it reminds me of stuff like *Masters of the Universe*, *Spacehunter, Battle Beyond the Stars* and *Star Trek V*. Mindless fun, but not *Doctor Who*.

This movie wasn't written with a specific actor in mind to play the Doctor (other than he'd be a 'famous face') and it suffers a lot from having to keep its options open so that anyone from Dudley Moore to Donald Sutherland could take the lead. Almost ten years on, *The Return of Varnax* is a footnote, not something that deserves 121 pages devoting to it.

The Dark Dimension is covered, and it's clearly far too ambitious for the projected Bill Baggs-sized budget. The interview with Tony Harding suggests that if it had been made, virtually everything would have been downsized anyway. Because of that - like the BBC themselves - I found it difficult to worry too much about what it would have been like. For some reason I could only picture *Dimensions in Time*. I agree with Lofficier's opinion: *The Dark Dimension* reads like an early New Adventure and fans *might* have liked it. The fact that Graeme Harper and Tom Baker would have been involved would almost certainly have been enough to keep me happy.

The American TV scripts are a completely different kettle of fish, and here Lofficier's personal (if somewhat peripheral) involvement with the project means that the coverage gets better. Three scripts are detailed.

The first, written by Denny Martin Flinn (*Star Trek VI*) would have been directed by Leonard Nimoy and the part of the Doctor would have been offered to Pierce Brosnan, a casting decision apparently 'proved to be correct considering his later success as James Bond'. Whether Brosnan was actually approached isn't clear and the project fell through when the rights expired. The script as presented here is a whirlwind tour of the universe. The TARDIS visits (takes a deep breath) the Death Zone and Rassilon's Tomb, the Mermaid Tavern in 1593, Ancient Egypt, the Pacific in 1937, an alien night club, even more Ancient Egypt, the British Museum, the Transylvania of Vlad the Impaler, the Time Lord Academy, the Ottoman Empire, the *Titanic* (which we see sinking), the Lake District (complete with Meddling Monk), a lonely planet, the Moulin Rouge, a bleak far future Earth, a planet of Amazon women, Carnaby Street (a sequence in which the fourth Doctor appears), a Who concert (geddit?) in the 60s and the Master's hideout, a city on an asteroid. Many of the locations would have required huge sets and hundreds of extras. Flinn admits he followed the maxim 'never worry about the budget, that's the producer's job' but what he's written would seem to be unfilmable on fifty million dollars, let alone five. The script also features five versions of the Doctor. It reads more like the whole first season than the pilot episode! Worst of all, though, is that behind all the changing scenery is a fairly standard 'quest' story, as an evil renegade Time Lord (Mandrake) tries to assemble the Key to Time for some evil purpose or other. Lofficier praises the script's 'pacing and character' but this doesn't really come across in his synopsis. In his introduction, Lofficier has already told us that the script extracts 'have been selected for their relevance to the *Doctor Who* universe, rather than for their literary merits'. It means we don't really get a feeling for the tone of the stories, and we have to rely on Lofficier's opinion and other clues as to whether they would have been any good.

Personally, I find Brosnan uncharismatic - I liked *GoldenEye*, but I don't even think he's terribly good in the part he was clearly born to play. He'd have been dreadfully miscast as the Doctor, if they'd ever asked him. I'm pretty sure that this movie would have been hated by the fans for its superficial script, and I doubt the new viewer would have found much to engage them.

The next script was the first that Segal was involved with, and it was right on the verge of shooting (with McGann) when it was pulled by Amblin. The story was written by John Leekley, and it's the one that all the rumours were about - the Master's the Doctor's half brother and is in charge of the spider-Daleks and so on. The basic setup of the series is completely revamped: the Master is the Gallifieyan defence minister who has sold out his people to the Daleks, the Doctor is a rookie at the Academy and the President's grandson. The Doctor's half human, and by the end of the movie he's set off on a search for his explorer father, lost somewhere in the cosmos.

This version of *Doctor Who* would have been a very different series from the BBC one and by definition a lot of fans wouldn't have liked the rebooting. The script strips the Doctor of all of his mystery - we know where he comes from, why he travels the universe, all about his family. The pernicious influence of Joseph Campbell - whose study of the 'world monomyth' *The Hero With a Thousand Faces* has been a profound influence on Hollywood ever since *Star Wars* made a billion at the box office - is felt throughout the script. Like many writers who've read Campbell, Leekley clearly thinks that having it turn out that one of the other characters is related to the hero is both necessary and sufficient to give any story 'mythic resonance'. So, we have all the Campbell elements present from The Call to Adventure to The Freedom To Live: the blasted landscape full of noble savages and fierce monsters, the old man dying so that the young man can take his place, the hero rediscovering something about his lost parents, exile from a pastoral paradise. Campbell's overrated and *Star Wars* is all-pervading: viewers who've read *Hero With A Thousand Faces* would have been expecting the 'Atonement with the Father' around Act Six, everyone else would just think Leekley's nicked it all from the *Star Wars* trilogy.

The Doctor himself is the thing that comes off worst from being squeezed into the generic Campbell template - he isn't an ancient, infinitely wise father figure, but a young man who needs a spirit guide to tell him what's happening (a concept that conveniently allows the script writer a way to explain the plot to the audience in a mystical, pseudoenigmatic way - Kosh, Al, Zordon, that hologram thing in the first series of *Seaquest* all fulfill the some function). It's a weakening of a character who, in the BBC series, had always been a spirit guide to others. Leekley has made the show-killing mistake of making the Doctor into Luke instead of Obi-Wan.

But, given that it's a betrayal of all that *Doctor Who* stands for, blah blah, this version could have really worked. It's a much tighter script than any of the previous versions: the action is confined to Gallifrey, London during the Blitz and Skaro. All three locations are well-drawn and important to the plot, with a small but strong group of characters. *The Invasion of Time* and *Genesis of the Daleks* are seamlessly knitted together, portraying a genuinely quite epic Dalek Invasion of Gallifrey. Unlike the broadcast movie, we travel though space and time, getting a real sense that the universe is a big place full of Good and Evil.

Despite the mythic saga baggage, the Master and the other Gallifreyans are well-drawn, Olympian people. The Daleks are nasty, and recognizable despite their complete makeover. The half-human business is important, there are monsters and the ending both makes sense and opens up the action for a full series. If nothing else, it's interesting to read as Segal's vision of *Who* and this script clearly informs the broadcast movie, even explaining away some of the plot holes.

On the other hand the final script, by Robert DeLaurentis, reads as a dreadful watered-down version of the Leekley script. The 'Daleks' are still there, but as 'armoured human cyborgs' (Cybermen, in fact). The plot is much the same, but with a tacked on 1995 segment. The character-driven action of the earlier script has become a much less interesting race-against-time action adventure (the Master is building time-travelling warships for the Daleks). It's all a lot less focused and the characters are stereotypes instead of archetypes. It falls messily between Leekley's uncompromising 'mythic' script and the glossy 80s Byrne version, and makes the fatal mistake of abandoning the 'quintessential Englishness' without replacing it with anything.

It's already clear that 'fan opinion' of the McGann movie depends on whether it spawns a series or not. If it fails in that basic task, we'll all start the inquest: the script was weak, the ending was rubbish, no time travel, no monsters, poor continuity. So, if we judge that story by how successful it is at persuading Fox to make more, how are we to judge seven first draft film scripts that couldn't even get themselves past the earliest stages of preproduction? Whatever you think of the McGann movie, I can't believe you'll prefer any of the alternatives presented in *The Nth Doctor*. The Leekley script is an interesting 'might have been', but it's a different - quintessentially American - series with only some of the names the same. Most of the other storylines feel very similar to each other, and are rambling and unfocussed attempts to spend a big budget rather than tell a good story.

None, though, are quite as terrible as the unsolicited story outline the Lofficiers presented to Segal as a 'springboard' story to reconcile the BBC and Universal continuities. The story appears in an Appendix and was originally a 'submitted' (or, to use the English vernacular, 'rejected') New Adventure which starts: 'We open on the planet Deva Loka, home of the peaceful, native-American-like Kinda. The alien villainess Zodin steals the fourth segment of the mythical all-powerful Key to Time after killing its guardian, the Kinda's high priest.' Come back David Hasslehoff, all is forgiven.

THE ENLIGHTENMENT COLUMNS

One of the first things I did at the University of York was get what in those days was called an 'E-Mail address'. This was coming up for twenty years ago, when it was best for people in the UK to go online in the morning - because in the afternoon the Americans woke up and the entire Internet slowed down as they logged on. I would brave the lightning storms and vicious trilobites of that primeval Earth to get to the computer room. There were no webpages or hyperlinks in those days, but there was already a vibrant online fan community. We would discuss *Star Trek*, *Twin Peaks* and - this may not come as a surprise - *Doctor Who*.

Before long, I discovered a group of fans from York University who were already online and discussing *Doctor Who*. Very excitedly, I made contact … only to learn they were all at York University in Toronto. They were members of the Doctor Who Information Network, and their group published the fanzine *Enlightenment*.

Now that we've reached an age of webpages and podcasts and so on, *Enlightenment* remains an old-school A4 printed fanzine, with reviews and commentary and whimsy, plus some fantastic fan art. It even has a news section that's stayed relevant in the Internet age by neatly condensing and rumour-controlling the mass of *Doctor Who* coverage out there.

It was ten years before I contributed to *Enlightenment*; I was asked to write a regular column, and it's appeared in more issues than not ever since. Unlike my *Matrix* articles, these columns are far more relaxed and tend to be a lot shorter. I've tried to bring a British perspective to the magazine, and in recent years this has led me to chronicle just how big that *Doctor Who* has become in the UK, now.

Enlightenment often runs themed issues - so occasionally my column accommodates that and becomes a top ten list, an examination of a particular season, etc. It's fairly obvious when that's happening, but I mention this for benefit of anyone who might wonder - for instance - why I suddenly felt the urge to write *Torchwood* reviews. More often, I simply write what's on my mind. In instances where the exact event being covered remains obscure, however, I've added some Historical Notes.

I've always loved *Doctor Who*, and I really do like the new TV series, so it's great to have a forum where I get to celebrate it. I'm very grateful to the editor of *Enlightenment*, Graeme Burk, for the opportunity.

It's Adric-riffic!

From Enlightenment #104, June/July 2001

As *Doctor Who* approaches its fortieth anniversary, it stands at an important crossroads, one that will see it either make the leap into a new millennium, or slowly wither away, as it fails to retain the fanbase. The release schedule of the BBC, Big Finish and BBV suggest a healthy market at the moment, but we have to take on some important lessons if *Doctor Who* is to retain relevance to a modern audience.

But never mind all that, what about Adric?

The other day I was sorting out some of my old stuff and I found an old school exercise book full of book reviews. And, yes, as long as I've been reading, I've been reading *Who* books. There weren't anything like the number of *Who* reviews I was expecting - virtually the only thing I can remember writing at primary school was a 'diary' every Monday that was meant to be a description of my weekend, but which week in week out consisted entirely of a description of that Friday's episode of the *Godzilla* cartoon (how do you spell 'Godzooky'?) and book reviews. Luckily for future Parkin scholars, my younger incarnation carefully put the date at the top of every review. Only one of the twenty or so books I reviewed in this exercise book was a *Doctor Who* one. I can only assume that there are three or four volumes of exclusively *Who*-related jotters in another box.

So, there it is... 25th May 1982 (I was ten), a review of *The Keeper of Traken* novelisation. One that even includes the word 'novelisation', proving I was an avid reader of *DWW* at the time. And which also proves I'd bought, read and come to a critical understanding of the book the week it came out.

And there it is, in my appalling handwriting (what's even more appalling is that my handwriting's even more appalling now): "My favourite character was Adric."

When I read that, I instinctively checked over my shoulder to make sure none of my fanboy pals had seen. How could I ever have thought that? Heresy! He waddles instead of walking, he deserved to be blown up and only got the job... ahem, well, OK, I'd better not saddle *Enlightenment* with a lawsuit on my first day here.

But I've recently rewatched *The Keeper of Traken*, and Adric's really good in it. There's the lingering suspicion that he's got all of Romana's lines - he gets to correct the Doctor about what the TARDIS console says, he gets to build that gadget that messes around with the Source. But there are also some nice Adric-only character touches - he picks a lock, he seems very eager to prove himself. It's also a bit scary that it's over twenty years old, now - when *The Five Doctors* came along, twenty years seemed like a geological age. Now we're almost at the twentieth anniversary of *The Five Doctors* itself. Yikes. It means, of course, that last October we passed the twentieth anniversary of Adric's first appearance.

As we scrape away the topsoil and uncover the archaeological layer that was 1981, we find that Adric works really well with the fourth Doctor. It's a stretch to say Tom and Matthew Waterhouse spark off each other - just the opposite: the Doctor ignores him, seems preoccupied. We might presume that Tom was bored, counting the days until he was leaving, missing working with Lalla and John Leeson, he's still quite ill. Perhaps. But it suits the tone of the end of Season Eighteen, as the end of an era looms. Everyone watching knows that; the Doctor certainly seems to. The actor playing Adric was a fanboy, and gets to play out every fanboy's dream. It's not surprising that he seems almost deferential to the Doctor. It's the last time that would happen, and it seems right somehow. Even in a story like Traken, where the Doctor basically just stands around for ninety minutes while some stuff happens, the title character's the centre of attention. Adric works well as a solo companion for Tom... a role he has for only a matter of a few weeks.

It's a common problem, I think - even though the producer knew there was a new Doctor on the way, the new companion suits the current one down to the ground: Peri is great in her two stories with Davison - she complains about things a lot, but that just contrasts with the ever-patient fifth Doctor. She also has a lot to complain about in those stories, to be fair. When the sixth Doctor comes along and is moody and whines a lot, and Peri's doing the same, for no obvious reason a lot of the time, it just stops being any fun to watch... and people stopped watching. Mel, on the other hand, does suit the sixth Doctor's theatricality. But stick her opposite McCoy and suddenly it tips over into panto. As we'd see, the seventh Doctor needed a companion like Ace to ground him, to give him a more paternal role.

Gosh, don't get me wrong - Matthew Waterhouse is as awful as the Canadian libel laws allow me to express. It's just that in the scripts for Season Eighteen - and Terrance Dicks novelisations, as my perceptive ten-year old self noted - the problems aren't apparent. Adric gets good, meaty roles in every story he's in bar *State of Decay*. Like Nyssa, there's a lot of potential there. Like Nyssa, the next season would lay bare the problems of casting and writing, and a change (or two) of script editors would see a lot of the original concepts for them trampled over - in *Traken*, Adric's keen to see our universe, he's eager to impress people. By *Earthshock*, he's in his bedroom sulking that he wants to go home.

But I can certainly see why I identified with Adric when I was ten, just the same as Benny appealed to me when I was at university. So... Adric, the great missed opportunity of *Doctor Who*? Lance Parkin (aged 10) hasn't convinced Lance Parkin (approaching 30) of that. But he's made me watch some *Doctor Who* again. So I can't have changed that much.

Feels Just Like Starting Over

From Enlightenment #105, August/September 2001

Doctor Who has had a lot of pilots lately, a lot of 'new first episodes', where people set out their stall. I've been greedy and written two - *The Dying Days* was an attempt to show what Virgin could have done with the eighth Doctor, given a chance. *The Infinity Doctors* was an attempt to ground the *Who* books in a more novelistic framework. Other people have had a stab, too - the audios had *Sirens of Time* and *Storm Warning*, the books had *The Eight Doctors* and *The Burning*, there was the McGann movie, and last, but not least, there was *Death Comes to Time*.

The TV Movie is an interesting one. I enjoyed it, but writing *The Dying Days* I realised what a useless pilot it is. It gives no sense at all of who the Doctor is, or what a 'typical' adventure is. It spends a great deal of time introducing Grace, then leaves her behind at the end. *The Dying Days* was an attempt to include everything *The TV Movie* didn't have - the English countryside, scary monsters, a sense of playfulness, the Doctor in charge, acting courageously. You can imagine the Fox people sitting around going 'well, OK, so the premise is that every week some baddy tries to steal this Eye thing'. Instead of exploring the universe, the most wondrous thing is the TARDIS set. I still enjoy the movie, but five years on, it's not hard to see why it didn't go to series. It's also a bit shocking just how lightweight McGann is in the role. He would have been good, I'm sure, but he wasn't *that* good in *The TV Movie*.

The Eight Doctors and *The Sirens of Time* both explore the universe, and both do so the same way - every available Doctor has a series of short encounters around a crisis on a Gallifrey where the phrases 'artron energy' and 'transduction barrier' are never far from the lips. Neither are well-regarded by fans, despite, presumably being designed to be 'fan-pleasing'. If *The Eight Doctors* was meant as an introduction to the series, it fails - it's meant to be a greatest hits album, but it comes across more like a series of weak cover versions.

The past is a problem. We can all reel off all the facts about the old show... but what would a new audience make of it? There's been a real backlash against 'continuity' lately - the latest orthodoxy is that stories shouldn't rely on being propped up by the past. You can use the Cybermen, say, but the novelty has worn off - fans won't automatically add points for including them... in fact, they may knock points off. *The Burning* anticipated this - Justin's back to basics approach ditched absolutely everything but the Doctor. No TARDIS, no continuity references at all (except one: 'when I say run'), no companion, no monsters... the fact that he managed to convince people it was 'traditional' was a remarkable achievement. *Storm Warning* lacks continuity references, and it's a traditional tale, but it appears very old-fashioned by comparison.

Death Comes to Time takes a different approach - it starts with a lovely *Bagpuss*-style monologue, and a minute or so in, the penny drops. They're retelling the background to *Underworld*. At least, that's what the fanboy bit of your brain tells you. But it establishes that the Time Lords aren't quite the same as they were on TV - the idea of them wandering abroad, trying to redeem themselves for the mistakes of the past is a beautiful one, but the exact opposite of the TV series. Before we're out of that monologue, the whole background of the series has been redefined. While the Doctor spends the first five minutes in *Storm Warning* rearranging his shelves in the TARDIS and talking to himself, *Death Comes to Time* throws you straight into the action and establishes the threat the Doctor will confront. But then we get back to basics - evil aliens are attacking a peaceful planet, and the Doctor arrives to help the oppressed defeat the invaders. For the fans, tellingly, it's the novelty that's confusing - Antimony is not a confusing character. He's a companion who asks questions and hits people. This is not complicated. But then you try working out backstory and where this fits in with the books, and you add a bit of nineties fan revisionism (that the Doctor was never violent and has never travelled with a companion who's violent), and you end up with your head hurting, reeling around unable to do anything but spew gratuitous continuity references. Just like the K1 robot. The casual viewer, I contend, would 'get it' very easily - Antimony is the Doctor's companion. He does companion things. *Death Comes to Time* makes perfect sense until you try to make it fit. Not everything is explained - but that's the point. It's the ultimate 'I'll explain later' story.

But when is a continuity reference a continuity reference? A couple of online responses about *Death Comes to Time* have suggested it was a mistake to reference the Time Lords, one person even wondered how a 'casual viewer' would understand that it was the TARDIS materialising at the end of the pre-credit sequence. To me, this is getting a little puritanical - the 'casual viewer', in the UK at least, remembers the TARDIS and the Daleks, a companion they fancied, they understand the premise of the show, they can even tell you the Doctor's a Time Lord.

A lot of recent movies have revamped old TV shows and cult films - so many, in fact, that *Charlie's Angels* starts with a joke reference to the trend. The first, and still most successful, was the original *Mission: Impossible* film. And the model that it, and *Lost in Space, Shaft, Charlie's Angels* and most of the others have followed is simple - keep the theme tune, keep the three things people remember most about the original, and ruthlessly dump absolutely everything else. *Mission: Impossible* appalled the fans of the TV show, expecting to see a movie about a team operating for the government, and finding a Tom Cruise vehicle, with the three things you remember - the rubber masks, the self-destructing tape and the daring heist. Everything else ran ruthlessly over of the original: not only was Phelps - shock! - the baddy, he was *played by someone else.*

If you're going to spend £75 million on a movie, you're going to have to appeal beyond the 20,000 people that buy *DWM*. And the way to do that is to pick an actor with box office draw and to emphasise spectacle in the trailer. It'll be nice to keep the fans on side - they can generate buzz, spread word of mouth, and buy all the action figures. But in the end, we're not an important part of that equation. We'd hate it. The people that accused *Death Comes to Time* of being a rip-off of *The Phantom Menace* - simply for having some baddies invading a planet and a bit of cod-mysticism (which is actually closer to *The Matrix* than *The Phantom Menace*) - would be horrified. But it wouldn't be *for* us.

If a *Doctor Who* movie came along, it would have the theme tune, the police box, the Daleks and... what? The frock coat, probably. It would be a kinetic action film, heavy on special effects, borrowing from whatever had been big the year before, set to a soft rock soundtrack. We all want to reach the promised land of *Doctor Who* returning to our screens - but I bet we won't like it when we get there, and see all our sacred cows turned into burgers.

2001: A Who Odyssey

From Enlightenment #106, October/November 2001

This year, I think, has been a vintage year for *Doctor Who*. That's not always obvious, because it's also been the year when it became impossible to follow every new *Doctor Who* adventure. There are, now, at least eleven sets of people making *Doctor Who* and related drama CDs. Including the charity publications and self-published books, there are half a dozen different sets of books around. Even if you had the money, it's very unlikely you've got the time to read them all and enjoy them. So, people are picking and choosing, staying loyal to a range, or following authors or Doctors.

So, my top ten tries to pick and choose from the various ranges, to come up with the best ten new (or newish) *Doctor Who* things around at the moment. They're in alphabetical order, and I've tried to pick at least something from each range. But it's meant hard choices... no room for the Benny audios or BBV, despite some lovely work. No place for *Henrietta Street*, *Bloodtide*, *The Barnacled Baby* or the DWM coverage of the tenth anniversary of the NAs. And no room for *Exploration Earth*, which was, as near as dammit, a new Tom Baker and Sarah story. In the end, this isn't a strict top ten, just evidence that our cup runneth over.

THE CAVES OF ANDROZANI DVD - A great story, and one I'll wager features on more than one other top ten list in this issue. It's never looked better, of course: DVD is finally a format that's better than watching it on the telly the first time round. *Caves* bears up better than some other stories are going to in the harsh clarity of digital remastering, too. But what really makes the DVD are the extras, which add a whole new layer to the story. It's got one of the most interesting commentaries on any DVD, including the big Hollywood movies, to date. A good story just got better.

THE CITY OF THE DEAD - A new author, and distinctive voice, and a stunning debut. If you've neglected the EDAs for a while, then shame on you - but make amends by reading *The City of the Dead*. Lloyd Rose has brought a whole new perspective to the format, and it's one of the few *Who* books so mature that it makes you forget it's a TV tie-in series. The follow-up has already been commissioned. There's a new generation of *Who* writers, now - ones who never worked for Virgin. We're starting to see the emergence of a whole new perspective on the series. With a great chunk of the readership born in the eighties, seventies nostalgia isn't going to fly much longer, and the way of things is that the nineties are already starting to look a bit naff (*Terminator 2* is now as much of a nineties period piece as *Terminator* is of the eighties) - *The City of the Dead* is one book that proves there's a better way.

DEATH COMES TO TIME - Ten million hits and counting... *Death Comes to Time* proved that *Doctor Who* was still viable beyond fandom, it proved that the BBC would make *Doctor Who* if the circumstances were right. And now, after a decade of telling us that *Doctor Who* was a bit of cheap seventies nonsense, the BBC are now talking about webcasts, CGI and a megafranchise.

THE DOCTOR'S EFFECTS - A self-published book by Steve Cambden, where he interviews his BBC special effects colleagues. And there's a wealth of new material there, from a perspective that's been ignored or parodied for years. For a start, there are a lot of previously unpublished photos. It's an honest, simple account, and far more entertaining than the average *Who* interview these days.

OUTPOST GALLIFREY - The best place to find *Doctor Who* news there's ever been. A website that's authoritative and comprehensive, this has everything you need - from the differences between the Region 1 and Region 2 DVDs to the latest rumours on the new TV series. *Doctor Who's* an incredibly diverse and diffuse place, but amazingly this site brings it all together. The message boards are the model of civility and polite discussion, too, with none of the factionalism that seems to be programmed into the rest of online fandom. It's an extraordinary piece of work, and every fan ought to be checking it every day.

KALDOR CITY - Seedy, funny and fast-paced, *Kaldor City* just shows what a wealth of fan talent there is out there. Alistair Lock, one of the heroes of the BF line, does a stunning job on sound design and production. Paul Darrow is, of course, perfect as the paranoid and barmy 'security consultant' Kaston Iago, with a great line in lunatic advice ('Remove all red paintings from this room, they attract psychopaths').

MISSING PIECES - The ultimate charity anthology, despite incredibly stiff competition from the likes of *Walking in Eternity* and *The Cat Who Walked Through Time*. It's enormous, and while, by its nature, it's going to be hit and miss, there are enough hits to fill a couple of *Decalog*s. The writers are a good mix of pros and talented amateurs. And I've not even mentioned the pictures.

ADRIAN SALMON'S ARTWORK - Adrian's hardly burst onto the scene this year, but his work for the Time Team feature in *DWM* brings those stories to life in a way a couple of dreary screen grabs just couldn't. He's also the ideal candidate for cover artist of the new Benny range from Big Finish, and his stylised, almost deco, designs for them are just gorgeous.

THE STONES OF VENICE - A Paul Magrs book brought to life, in all its glory. A Doctor and companion discussing the state of the baddy's carpets, an evocative setting, a real sense of fun and dynamism. *Doctor Who* was never, ever like this on television, but you listen to *The Stones of*

Venice and you wish it had been.

THE YEAR OF INTELLIGENT TIGERS - Kate Orman returns! Always regarded as one of the crème de la crème of the *Who* authors, while paradoxically taken for granted, Kate's been away for a couple of years, but has come back with a perfect slice of post-colonial *Who*. *Set Piece* was the thinking man's *The Chase*, but *Tigers* is the thinking man's *Kinda*. Self-contained, with nothing you could call a continuity reference, it plugs in perfectly to the Justin Era EDAs and is as good an SF novel as you'll read this year.

Trading Ethnicities

From Enlightenment #107, December 2001

'Anji Kapoor.' For those that don't know, that's the name of the Doctor's latest companion in the Eighth Doctor Adventure novels. I've just (and I mean 'just' - in the last few hours) finished the first draft of *Trading Futures*, my first book with Anji in it, which is coming out in April next year.

As her name suggests, Anji's Asian... well, already we're hitting problems with terms here. Her grandparents originally came from Pakistan but Anji, and her parents, lived their whole lives in the UK. And 'Asian' in the UK means 'from the Indian Subcontinent', not Japan/China/Korea.

There's been criticism recently on some of the Internet message boards that we're not 'addressing' Anji's background enough in the books. It's true that it's not been a major aspect of her characterisation... but then she was drawn up that way. The writers' guidelines specifically say she's not religious.

Why *would* Anji's parents' religion make that much difference to her adventures with the Doctor? We don't really know anything much about any of the previous companions' beliefs. We know about the rituals Leela's tribe had, but Leela's atheism is a key part of her character. As for the other companions... well, Katarina was a handmaiden in a temple. Steven said he was a Protestant in *The Massacre*. Peri wears a St Christopher, but it's stretching things to suggest that makes her particularly religious. Victoria and Jamie come from times where Christian worship was taken for granted... but there's not a mention of it in the series, that I can recall. Roz and Chris worship Justice, a Goddess, but again, that's mainly so they can swear imaginatively in times of stress. Benny... well, not that you'd know it, but Benny's a lapsed Catholic. Her guilt over that is one of the Doctor's main weapons against the Hoothi in *Love and War*. Subsequent books never mentioned her religion again (indeed I was asked to remove a reference to it in *Just War*).

Part of the problem is the Doctor. The Doctor is always right. He's knowledgeable, well-travelled, he always has the right answer. So if a companion asked the Doctor whether God existed and what form He took, the Doctor could probably, to coin a phrase, give them His phone number. It's not something we could ever see, because ultimately if there is an answer to one of the greatest philosophical questions humanity has ever asked, it's not going to appear in a show about a funny man in a time travelling police box.

But why do some people think that Anji's race and religion is going to be more important to her than, say, Mel's is to Mel?

In the end, it cuts to the heart of *Doctor Who*, a series very much rooted in the adventure narratives of the Victorian era. *Boy's Own* stories, with a dash of Jules Verne. A lot of science fiction is about dressing up old narratives about plucky white men fighting off primitive savages. A lot of science fiction uses race to signify alien-ness. Back in the thirties, it meant Flash Gordon going to the planet of the Black People, but not much has changed. *Star Trek*'s Vulcans are almost invariably played by Jewish actors, the Klingons were Hispanic, now they're black. Aliens are mainly characterised by a slight physical difference, eating disgusting food and holding strange beliefs, expressed in weird ceremonies. The jokes about Klingon food are exactly the same as the curry "jokes" in seventies British sitcoms. In *Enterprise*, one of the running jokes is that the Vulcans think the humans 'smell funny', for heaven's sake.

Ironically, modern Western society seems far more open to change and influence than the 'tolerant' utopian Federation. Since *Star Trek* started, British culture has gone from fear of the new arrivals to embracing Asian culture. The national dish of Britain is curry, now, but there are no mentions in *Star Trek* of popping down to the nge'Soj (that's your actual Klingon), just the same old jokes about foreign food tasting nasty. In any major Western city you can eat a different cuisine at a different restaurant every week of the year... despite its replicators, humans in *Star Trek* aren't anything like as adventurous. They're probably the sort of people who think pizzas are 'foreign food'.

Religion in *Doctor Who* means worshipping a false god and performing human sacrifices. There are a couple of vicars... one of whom turns out to be the Master. Churches are there to blow up at the end of the story. 'Faith-based organisations' include the Cult of Demnos, the Fish People sacrificing passers-by to their Octopus and the High Priests of Kroll. In the end, *Doctor Who* is not the right tool to be examining Hinduism with.

Britain is a secular society, and *Doctor Who* is a secular programme. Anji has lived in Britain all her life, she was educated there. Her race and religion may be an important part of who she is... but in Anji's case, her gender, her job, her age, her friends are more important. Are Anji's creators colour-blind, or exceptionally naïve? Well, unsurprisingly, I don't think so. In the end, as an Asian woman living in modern Britain, Anji is not a particularly rare or unusual creature, and there is no reason at all why she should wear her ethnicity on her sleeve.

Fifth Doctor II: Electric Boogaloo

From Enlightenment #108, February/March 2002

I've worked with Peter Davison.

I wasn't at the recording of *Primeval*, so I've not met him, but I've written a *Doctor Who* story which he has performed. I've also written a fifth-seventh Doctor MA entitled *Cold Fusion*, and co-written 'A Town Called Eternity' - a short story for *Short Trips and Side Steps*. But I've always had a nagging sensation that the era wasn't right. Now, it's not uncommon in fandom - for many fanboys my age, *Doctor Who* was Tom, K9, Romana and jokes, and they were all gone in the space of a year. I could just about remember Pertwee, and of course I had *The Making of Doctor Who* and the Target novels to tell me that the Doctor had regenerated before... but this was the first I'd been fully aware of. Fans from the eighties (or seeing the show abroad in syndication) were encouraged to see the current Doctor as 'just the latest in a long line'... but for a British fan in 1981 it was a big deal. Reading a couple of the entries in the DWM *Fifth Doctor Special* that just came out, it really seems like a couple of my fellow fanboys retain deep scars from what they call, perfectly straight-faced, a 'trauma'.

I missed Tom, K9 and Lalla, but that wasn't what nagged at me. What strikes me about the fifth Doctor era on TV is that there's a ton of potential there, but the show rarely gets round to realising it. A lot of it feels terribly unfinished.

During the hiatus in 1985-6, one of the papers asked the actors who'd played the Doctor whether they'd go back. Davison said he'd love to - but in fifteen to twenty years time, when he was old enough. Although it's very hard to believe it, Davison is now the same age Jon Pertwee had been when he took the role, and only a couple of years younger than Hartnell was in 1963. Or, to put it another way, at twenty-nine, Peter Davison was younger than I am now when he was cast. Davison is candid about it - he thought he was too young, but knew that three years as *Doctor Who* would propel him into more 'leading man' roles. Without *Doctor Who*, he wouldn't have got *Campion* or *A Very Peculiar Practice*.

But now he's back, playing the Doctor, old enough to be the Doctor. The second fifth Doctor era, begun with the very first Missing Adventure, *Goth Opera*, continued by the PDAs and the Big Finish audios has (as of *Primeval*) more stories in it than his era on TV.

And Davison's return is slightly different from the others. Paul McGann's return is an odd one - the only Doctor defined in other media, the eighth Doctor has been characterised by this fragmentation, the sense that somehow Charlie and Sam and Izzy and Grace and Benny and Stacy and Larna don't quite fit together, but also that they must do, somehow. The eighth Doctor has a rich, multimedia existence, and - with all respect to him - while some people have been working on eighth Doctor stories for years and years, Paul McGann's prior contribution was a couple of days shooting a half-finished script in early 1996. Sylvester McCoy recreates his era perfectly, makes fifteen years ago seem like yesterday. Colin Baker also sounds the same, but he's on the same mission he's been on since 1985 - to prove that it wasn't his fault. Amiable, a convention regular, the only Doctor to have written a *Doctor Who* story, in many ways the instigator of the whole of New Who - it was *Summoned by Shadows* that launched BBV, and made people realise there was a market for new *Who* product (and which demonstrated once and for all that Colin was great if he wasn't wearing that damn coat) - Colin is clearly making huge efforts in his BFs. He's the one that's really trying to redefine his Doctor, to make amends. It's no coincidence, I think, that his are among the consistently best-regarded of the audios.

Davison is different. He just doesn't sound like the fifth Doctor any more. The thing that most defined him on TV, his youth (whether it's 'youthful exuberance' or Bidmead's 'old man trapped in a young body') just can't be a factor. And the great three-way creative rift that was the dynamic of his era - Davison's understated performance vs. Saward's cynicism vs. JNT's desire to market the show with guest stars and explicit appeals to foreign stations - isn't there either. Plus, BF don't have (nor, I gather, do they particularly want) Tegan, which means they have to come up with Doctor-companion teams that stretch the 'rules' a little, because we never quite saw them on TV - the fifth Doctor solo with Nyssa, Turlough or Peri. (Oddly, perhaps, the past Doctor books had already fixed on the Doctor and just-Turlough combination as one worth exploring more). All this combines to mean that writers of BF audios can't do what they can with, say, McCoy and simply recreate the past.

So, twenty years on, there's an all-new Davison era, one that can't pastiche the early eighties stuff, at least not, by the evidence, terribly successfully. In both the books and the audios, the results have been very mixed. But that's interesting in itself. One thing that shines through on every Davison audio is how terrific Davison himself is. When I say that I think his performance in *Primeval* is one of his very best as the Doctor, I'm not being immodest - it's got very, very little to do with me.

I feel terribly old to realise it's twenty years since *Kinda*. When *The Five Doctors* was first broadcast, a twenty year anniversary sounded like a geological age. Next year it's the twentieth anniversary of the twentieth anniversary story. Eek. But instead of being a historical footnote, or where it went wrong, or where it was last right, in 2002, we're once again slap bang in the middle of the Davison era.

Must There be a Doctor?

From Enlightenment #109, April/May 2002

The first thing Justin Richards asked his authors when he became the consultant editor of the BBC book range was the big question: 'If we were setting up *Doctor Who* today, how would we do it?' He then set about identifying the core elements of the series. Gradually whittling away the Daleks, the Time Lords, UNIT, the two hearts, the companions … all the continuity, in fact, until we're left with the Doctor.

2000 was Year Zero, when continuity was ditched in favour of concentrating on the most important thing of all: keeping the Doctor, a wonderful, funny, intelligent, rational, kind, selfless and self-aware being who is both more and less than human, central and important. But even then, Justin noted that *The Keys of Marinus* 3 and 4 are *Doctor Who*, and they don't have the Doctor in them. *Mission to the Unknown* doesn't. And now, there's *Dalek Empire*, the Benny adventures, *The Faction Paradox Protocols* … so he came to a rather shocking conclusion:

'Nothing is sacrosanct - even the Doctor or the TARDIS can be dropped and the result could still be *Doctor Who*.'

Whoa.

It sounds like insanity. Taking the Doctor out of *Doctor Who*… what would be left? What would be the point? Wouldn't that be throwing away the baby with the bathwater? And what's wrong with bathwater? In the end, the EDAs didn't take that one last step.

In the last year, though, two other franchises have done just that. *Smallville* has told some of the best Superman stories there have been…

without having Superman, Lois or Metropolis, and with Lex Luthor as Clark Kent's best friend. *Enterprise... Enterprise* is doing everything it can to avoid calling itself *Star Trek*. Look at the opening titles for both - it might seem superficial, but it's an important exercise, it's a statement of priorities. The opening credits of *Enterprise* stress man's evolving quest for exploration, that it's 'been a long time, getting from there to here'. The connection isn't backwards from Kirk or Picard to Archer, it's from the history we know of, via our immediate future. And the Trekkers hate it, for the most part, because they've realised that they've been cut out of the will. *Enterprise* is an exciting action adventure series that's gone out of its way to celebrate the spirit of *Star Trek*, but also just as far to blank out the letter of *Star Trek*. Just about everything that was established about the period has, by now, been actively contradicted.

In both cases, the brand was the problem. The set-up was a fantastic one - man making their first steps out into a complex universe, exploring strange new worlds and going where no-one has gone before; a young man growing up in a small town, who has godlike powers but can't work up the nerve to ask a girl out. But the public perceptions of the general public - and, just as importantly, the perceptions of the executives who commission shows - of *Star Trek* and Superman is that they're a bit old-fashioned, a bit hokey. The problem with *Star Trek* is that people have expectations about what it can and - more importantly - can't be.

However familiar the convention, there's just no sane reason why a man with Superman's abilities would wander around in tights and a bright cape; it's a throwback to early comics that were printed in primary colours and written for six year olds. Superman literally doesn't fly for a modern audience. The calculation has been made that more people will watch the programme if it *isn't* called Superman than if it is. As a Superman fan, albeit one who's rarely seen him done properly, I love *Smallville* - and it's obvious that the people making it love Superman. It's what's needed to bring the concept I love to a new, more sophisticated, audience. And it's the highest-rated new show of the year, getting twice the viewers *Buffy* used to in the same spot.

If you were to start making *Star Trek* today, you'd concentrate on the sense of wonder, the exploration, the physical realities of living in a confined space. And Superman can be just as much of a hero. You can have an intense working knowledge of the past, but you can't afford a moment of nostalgia, and you can't compromise.

The format of *Doctor Who* is perfect. A time traveller who can go anywhere in time and space, who can look like anyone. You can tell any sort of story you want, and someone else will later can come along and tell any sort of story *they* want.

Except, of course... you can't have hanky panky, the Doctor isn't half human, he doesn't have motorbike chases, he doesn't kiss women, he most certainly isn't a woman, or black, or American. Is the problem with *Doctor Who... Doctor Who* itself? Are the forty years' worth of continuity, nostalgia and convention the problem? Do the expectations of what *Doctor Who* is like mean that it would be perpetually unable to escape a fanboy ghetto? Every time there's a new development in the books, there's angry denouncing of it as a 'betrayal' from one quarter or another. And this isn't just a books thing - the one element that's seemed to define fandom, right from fandom's origins in the mid-seventies, has been that most fans seem to hate the current show.

But ignore the fans for the moment. If you were really making *Doctor Who* now... wouldn't you have to start from the beginning? Change some of the premises of the programme? *Death Comes to Time* takes the Time Lords and completely reinvents them - they're the godlike beings of *The War Games*, but they daren't interfere because their powers are just so great. They atone for their previous sins by wandering the universe, setting wrongs right. That, instantly, is a situation far more interesting, dynamic and (over-used word alert) mythic than a bunch of old men who sit around doing nothing until the Doctor shows up.

The big revolution in telefantasy during the nineties was that you could make it about people - *Buffy*, *The X-Files* and even *Babylon 5* were far more about relationships then spaceships. If you were making it now... well, wouldn't it be more of an ensemble piece? Not just the Doctor, but a few companions and a few friends - plus regular places he visited, and people he confided in. Perhaps have a sense of a community of time travellers. Maybe even give the Doctor a family? Call it *Time and Relative* or *Time Lord*. Have story arcs.

You're probably thinking it could all go horribly wrong - but then, anything could. Think about why you don't like the idea. If the answer is 'because that's just not *Doctor Who*', stop and wonder if that's such a bad thing. *Doctor Who* constantly changed to fit the times it was broadcast, more than any other show. If it's to succeed after a nearly fifteen-year gap, perhaps a complete shift in emphasis, a complete rebranding, is exactly what is needed.

The spirit of *Doctor Who* is far more important, interesting and enduring than what the show's called. And perhaps it's best if the makers are honest about their intentions from the word go. Perhaps more people will watch *Doctor Who* that way...

Jumping the Shark

From Enlightenment #110, June/July 2002

When did *Doctor Who* jump the shark?

For those that don't understand the question, 'jump the shark' is a phrase that's recently come into use to describe that moment you can pinpoint when a television show went wrong. The beginning of the end - something happens that shows that the people who've made it have lost the plot, or run out of stories or begun to rely on gimmicks. It comes from *Happy Days*, which started out as a small-scale sitcom about life for a bunch of (weirdly anachronistic and, it has to be said, peculiarly old) fifties teens... and eventually ended up with the Fonz slapping on some waterskis and leaping over a shark. The show had changed, grown bloated on success and lost much of what had made it appealing in the first place.

Doctor Who went wrong on TV. There's nothing unusual about that - it ran for twenty-six years, it had a good innings, and the demise can't be blamed solely on the quality of the programme itself. Almost sadistic scheduling and a remarkable lack of support from senior management did far more to kill off the programme than any particular story or event. But the fact that *Doctor Who* ended as shadow of its former self is indisputable - what had once dominated Saturday evenings and fuelled the games in every playground in Britain on a Monday morning had dwindled to a few million viewers, many of whom seemed to be watching it solely to have something to moan about in *DWB* letters pages.

It's a bit churlish to ask the question in a JNT tribute issue, isn't it? *Doctor Who* ended on his watch, after all. There are three points that came in quick succession which fans might reasonably say looked like a shark being jumped to them - Davison becoming Colin (or, more precisely, the show going overnight from *The Caves of Androzani* to *The Twin Dilemma*); *Attack of the Cybermen* (where viewers literally deserted the show in droves - for the first time a whole third of the audience left and never came back), and, lastly, the BBC deciding that the solution to this problem was to cast Bonnie Langford as the companion.

Perhaps the roots of this lie a little earlier - the series had looked back at its own past before *The Five Doctors*, but it had never quite had a story that rested quite so firmly on its laurels. If it is Nathan-Turner's fault, then, well, if you look very closely at that *endless* panning shot of Brighton Beach at the beginning of *The Leisure Hive*, you'll see someone jumping over a shark. JNT came in, briefed to change *Doctor Who*, and perhaps he did so without fully understanding that the 'Monty Python humour' was actually the baby, not the bathwater.

But JNT's era had a lot of highlights, and rallied towards the end, even after being dealt a pretty poor hand. What if the show jumped the shark before then? When did the rot set in? Well, with *Doctor Who* it's a tricky one - the show literally wasn't the same show in 1989 as it was in 1963. Or any other given year. No other television drama has ever managed to change every single person in front and behind the cameras and still keep running as long. Even before the Doctor regenerated for the first time, all his companions had changed, then changed again. The producers, script editors and writers had all been replaced. What we think of as 'traditional' *Doctor Who* - the Terrance Dicks stuff about Time Lords, UNIT and sprightly yellow roadsters - really only started a third of the way through the episodes.

The obvious jump-the-shark point, I think, is *The Dalek Invasion of Earth*. Seriously. It's the point when the 'original' TARDIS crew is broken up. More importantly, the return of the Daleks marked a shift in emphasis for the series away from small studio-based stories to ones that relied on spectacle and gimmicks. The return of the Daleks themselves saw a show already starting to rely on its greatest hits - while also abandoning everything we knew about the Daleks in their first story to make them cliched nasty monsters (they even use flying saucers!). The second season ended with *The Chase* and *The Time Meddler*, two stories that were basically about how silly *Doctor Who* was. Meanwhile the ratings soared, piling all sorts of expectations and pressure on what had always been imagined as a quiet little show. The next couple of years were spent bringing back the Daleks and trying to get them to do bigger things, and the rest of the show became all rather secondary to that.

So there you go: November 1964. It was all downhill from there.

Which is silly.

Perhaps the problem here is with the 'jump the shark' concept, not *Doctor Who*. Some shows jump the shark. *Moonlighting* did. *Lois and Clark* did. *Blakes 7* did. *Voyager* did the moment the Maquis put on Federation uniforms (that's in the *pilot*, folks). There was one point where it all went wrong, and never recovered. *Doctor Who*'s decline was more gradual, and entirely unnecessary - there was plenty of life left in the concept yet. So much so that there are now more books, more comic strips and by the end of next year there will be more audio stories than there ever were on television. And, more importantly, the programme's format allowed it to change and survive. In the end, *Doctor Who* doesn't jump the shark, it *is* a shark - an animal that can hold its own against any other, but which drowns the moment it stops moving forwards.

Something for Posterity

Enlightenment #111, August/September 2002

Amazon in the UK recently had a half-price sale of the BBC Radio Collection, and I picked up a few titles. I have to confess, I hadn't bought many of them before, but as I sat listening to *The Daleks' Master Plan*, I found myself wondering what the people involved with it would have thought back in 1965 if you'd told them that in more than thirty-five years' time people would be able to buy the soundtrack to the story they were making. By 1965, there were albums of some British radio shows, but - as far as I can tell, I'm not an expert - they tended to be compilations of highlights. There were a couple of *Hancock* albums, a couple of *Round the Hornes*, a few more *Goon Show* ones. It just wasn't the industry it's become, there wasn't the demand for purity of the text (*The Daleks' Master Plan* comes with a Peter Purves narration to explain what's going on... but one of the hidden extras is the soundtrack without the commentary). The only 'permanent' stories were the three books (*The Daleks*, *The Crusades* and *The Web Planet*) and, perhaps, the Cushing films. In 1965, *Doctor Who* was something that was on once, then it was gone. Ever since I was a fan, the exact opposite has been the case - there's been a series of novels, lists of old stories in books and magazines. Nowadays, fans come to the series as something that's completely available, usually in a variety of formats: *Genesis of the Daleks* has been available in three audio formats, for heaven's sake... not to mention a novelisation and a script. It's not out on DVD, but it's the most repeated story (in the UK) and it was out on video.

Doctor Who now is an instant, self-perpetuating archive. Before the ink is dry on the books, they've been reviewed in a dozen magazines and fanzines (not to mention the websites), and the *I, Who* entry has been written up. The books sit on fans' shelves, and I'd wager that on most of them they're in some kind of order. OK, some books are hard to find - I've been amazed how many people who've read *The Dying Days* on the BBC site didn't read it as a book - but they're permanent. They're going to be there until your mum / wife / children / executors throw them away. Even then, they'll just end up on some other shelf somewhere. People don't like destroying books. All the *Who* books will eventually fall apart (the Virgin ones before the others, given the quality of the bindings), but part of the deal with a book is that there will always be some library somewhere with a copy.

Every fan knows that the *Who* releases are only part of the 'Radio Collection' because the BBC threw away the TV episodes. What they don't often take into account is that the BBC were, on balance, entirely sensible to throw them away. They'd never been repeated, they were bulky and difficult to store, and once colour TV came along, there was no demand at all for black and white. There were the first, primitive, home video recorders, but basically only Elvis Presley had one. The idea that, in 2002, there would be a demand to see old episodes of *Doctor Who* bewilders the BBC in 2002, so you can see why they didn't give in much thought in 1972.

Who's going to endure from the recent past? Which writers, which musicians and film-makers will define the twentieth century in, say, the twenty-second? If we were going to guess now... well, I'd guess Tolkien's in with more chance than - to pick a name - Iris Murdoch, or any of the other 'literary' authors. George Lucas might make it, but Tarantino won't. *Doctor Who*, of course, stated in 1965 that by Vicki's time, there was going to be a museum dedicated to The Beatles in Liverpool. An absurd suggestion at the time, a joke, but it's about the only prediction the show's got right (so far). It's very difficult to imagine that The Beatles won't deserve a chapter in a book on twentieth century culture. But then... everyone read Kipling and thought Charlie Chaplin was the funniest thing there had ever been, and a couple of generations on, we just don't understand the appeal.

Famously, posterity cheats people. The only rule seems to be that the greatest writers of the age are condemned to anonymity, while people relatively unknown in their day become lauded. Blake, Melville and George Eliot were nobodies in their day. Ask anyone in 1900 what the most famous vampire novel was, and they'd look at you funny and tell you *Verney the Vampire*. There were exceptions - Shakespeare was always popular, but again the idea that, four hundred years on, he'd be seen as way ahead of his contemporaries, way ahead of any other playwright, would have been laughable.

When Dennis Spooner wrote *The Daleks' Master Plan* episode nine ('Golden Death') and Douglas Camfield directed it, and Peter Butterworth played the Monk, I can't imagine for a minute that they thought they were doing anything for posterity. But here we are, most of us - I guess - not even born when they made it, able to listen to it, after all their deaths. I doubt, somehow, that *The Daleks' Master Plan* will rank as the greatest play of our age in some twenty-second century textbook. But they've managed to get me to spend £15 on a sound-only recording of the episode nearly forty years on, and it was meant to be utterly throwaway. Let's not bet against them just yet!

Notes From the Audiotape Underground

From Enlightenment #112, October/November 2002

There have always been *Doctor Who* audios.

Back in the days before videos, there were some fans with tape recorders who recorded the soundtracks of *Doctor Who*. Some of the more technically-minded came up with recordings straight from the aerial, rather than doing what I did and pushing a tape recorder next to a speaker. My family was late coming to the wonders of the VCR - although I think it's fair to say I've made up for lost time since. My copy of *Resurrection of the Daleks*, uniquely, had a phone ringing in the background of the mind probe scene followed by my audio debut as 'boy who tells his friend that he really ought to know by now not to phone me when *Doctor Who* is on'.

There were two advantages of audio copies. First, they were remarkably cheap and easy to copy. No need to get a friend and his video round, or all that weird faffing around with leads where you realise that the mathematicians are wrong: two sets of leads fitting into four sockets actually leads to about ten thousand possible combinations, none of which give you sound and video at the same time. Fans - or at least fans down my way - swapped audio tapes for nothing. Audio copies didn't degenerate as they got copied down like videos. By no means was every story covered, but there were some real gems - *City of Death*, for example. And one of us found someone with some sixties stuff, and all they wanted in return was a copy of *Hitchhikers*.

It's weird how the market for videotapes was around before the technology was, isn't it? There were all those novelisations, a few albums of soundtracks. The late seventies also saw those photobooks - the *Star Trek* ones are the best known over here, but there were plenty of them. A full set of colour photos from the film, turned into a sort of comic strip. They were the equivalent of punchcards compared with floppy disks. But audio soundtracks seemed like the nearest it was possible to get to having the old stories - it was clear to those of us that studied them carefully, that the audios had stuff in that just wasn't mentioned in the books.

But the main advantage with audios was that... well, *Doctor Who* always looked better on audio. Sure, you needed a helping hand from the Target novelisations sometimes to get a good handle on what the monsters looked like, and even what was going on in some scenes, but a story like *Tomb of the Cybermen* is gorgeous on audio. I love it on telly,

148

don't get me wrong, but on audio the scary bits really were as scary as all the fuss at the time suggested. No foam, no wires, no dummies. Just a steady, suspense-filled script. In audio form you get the purest performances. There are no flashy (or trashy) visuals to get in the way - just the script, interpreted by the cast.

The Celestial Toymaker (I only found out years later that this was one of the rarest soundtracks) just didn't work. Oddly, though, I assumed that this was because it was so visually stunning that the pictures must have spoken for themselves. This was before the novel, so I had to go from the description in Doctor Who Weekly. I wasn't much the wiser, I have to say. All I know is that, now I've seen the surviving episode, I'm in no hurry for the crack fandom SWAT teams to swoop into some foreign TV station's archive and recover the rest.

In many ways, audio is the perfect medium for Doctor Who, a show that has always relied on writing (particularly wit) in a way that few other 'science fiction' shows ever did. Doctor Who is also a show that's always thrived when there's a gap for the imagination of the audience. Those lovely throwaway lines, like the Filipino army advancing on Reykjavik. On audio, every line evokes. Every monster stays as a series of glimpses and hints - we never get that big reveal where we see the costume in all its 'glory'. The thing that makes the companion scream is scarier than anything the BBC could show us at teatime.

That said, some stories are irredeemable, whatever the medium. The Twin Dilemma, which I taped as the dawn of a new era, is... and I know this is difficult to imagine... even worse when you can't see it. Yes, you read it here first - there is something worse than the Doctor's coat, Hugo's tunic and a baddy that looks like he's been wrapped in a carpet. And that's not being distracted by all that and having to hear just the dialogue. Of course, any masochists out there only have to get their video copy and turn the picture off. But you have been warned.

It Seemed Like Such a Good Idea at the Time (and the Rani)

From Enlightenment #113, December 2002

It's fifteen years since Time and the Rani was shown in the UK.

This isn't a column about how old we're all getting, although that is worth remarking on in passing - fifteen years is a whole childhood. Fifteen years before Time and the Rani, they were just starting to film The Three Doctors. Fifteen years before that, it was the week before the first

Sputnik was launched. *Time and the Rani* was a long time ago.

Time and the Rani, remarkably, was meant to represent a fresh start, a clean break, a new chapter. *Doctor Who* had suffered for a few years, this was the story that would put things back on track.

Oh dear.

It wasn't a huge surprise to fans that it didn't even manage to live up to almost non-existent expectations. The 'new page' started off with JNT and Bonnie Langford's names on it - the two people who'd come to embody what was wrong with the show. Sylvester McCoy wasn't famous, but he was well-known - as a 'wacky' kids' performer. There wasn't a script editor until after all the scripts were commissioned - and *Time and the Rani* was written by Pip and Jane Baker, the exact opposite of fan favourites. Kate O'Mara would represent a bit of glamour and star power... but again, she was a returning element, and hardly a demonstration that the show was moving away from superficiality and glitz.

The trailer was great, though. It really seemed to get things right - the TARDIS in space, the hint of a monster, the Doctor regenerating, Mel in her bubble. Some nifty camera angles and special effects. Ten seconds that hinted at something good. The trouble being they'd taken the only decent ten seconds out of the ninety minutes and run them together.

Fifteen (sorry, that still makes me go 'eep') years on, I've rewatched it. And I know what the main problem is. It's not anything to do with the acting, the production or the script. Hell, don't get me wrong, there are problems there, problems so bad that they start at 'appalling' and get as low as 'series-killing'. But the main problem is that it starts off from a false premise: that it's possible to tell a *Doctor Who* story by numbers.

Most Doctors are given a fairly straightforward debut story. *The Power of the Daleks*, for example - the Doctor may be new, but the Daleks recognise him, and he can still beat them. The archetype, though, is *Robot* - a story that would be ridiculously light in any other context, but which introduces us to the new Doctor by showing us how he reacts to a 'typical' *Doctor Who* story. It's written by Terrance Dicks, who'd only co-written one story beforehand - but even back then was 'Mr Doctor Who'.

Time and the Rani tries to pull off the same trick, but fails. But I can well imagine that at the script stage, it must have looked great. The problem is a familiar one, now - while *Robot* referred out to Cold War paranoia and King Kong, *Time and the Rani* doesn't look any further than the last issue of *DWM*. We get an exciting shot of the TARDIS in space, a new title sequence, the return of an old baddy, kisses to the past like a glimpse of the TARDIS tool kit, a montage of old costumes before the new one makes its appearance. We don't see the monster properly, we only see what it sees and a hint of a clawed hand and foot. There's a lone resist-

ance leader, a helpless puppet leader. There are monsters in the basement, there's something nasty in the loft, and there's a countdown at the
end to save the planet.

And it must have felt like *Doctor Who* to the suits that read the scripts.
But, as ever, a lot of the people that do that job don't understand the
appeal. The movie version of *Lost in Space*, for example, looks great on
paper. The script hits all the points those film-writing seminars say it
should. The casting looked to cover all the demographics. The studio
thought they had a new *Star Wars* on their hands, that it was utterly fool-
proof. The cast were optioned for six sequels.

And we know what happened there.

Time and the Rani is the same. On paper, it hits all the points. On the
screen, it sucks.

Fifteen years was a long time ago, but it's a moral that still applies - if
you're writing a *Doctor Who* story, be it for telly, film, book or audio, you
can't just trade on some 'spirit of *Doctor Who*'. *Doctor Who* has its cliches
- but they are there to be subverted. It's impossible to tell a *Doctor Who*
story by numbers, because the whole appeal is novelty, whimsy and
eccentricity - things that can't be quantified. With *Robot*, Terrance Dicks
wasn't following a formula, he was subverting expectation, playing
against precisely those cliches and space opera cliches that *Time and the
Rani* happily dances into.

Are the Books Doomed?

From Enlightenment #114, February/March 2003

I love the *Doctor Who* books. I did before I wrote for them.

For me - and I mean absolutely no disrespect to anyone else, from
BBCi, Telos, Big Finish, the Restoration Team, *DWM* or any of the other
people, professional or otherwise, involved in any capacity in producing
Doctor Who stuff - the books, specifically the Eighth Doctor Adventures,
are 'where it's at', they're the ongoing story. There are now far more
books than there were TV adventures. They've often been at least as
good as the very best TV stories, and they've rarely plumbed the same
depths as the worst. They've got far closer to realising the potential of the
most diverse and complex fictional format ever devised.

Anyone whose *Doctor Who* doesn't include *The Also People*, *Human
Nature* or *Camera Obscura* has a *Doctor Who* that's poorer and less interesting than mine, which does. But the books seem to be in trouble now,
and it must look even worse on the other side of the Atlantic.

American distribution has always been a problem for the BBC Books.

They launched the range without, apparently, being aware that the US and Canadian market accounted for a third of the total sales. Glitches have meant that books (usually the key 'arc' books, as luck would have it), haven't shown up in North America. Most British companies dream of 'breaking the American market'. We have music acts who would kill to. It must look awfully like the BBC broke the market, then decided to fix it. The demand is still there - news that the BBC books are half price in US Borders stories have lead, literally, to queues of people buying them up. The Borders announcement has been taken as some terrible nail in the coffin - in fact, it's a blindingly obvious consequence of the distribution deal collapsing a year ago: if a shop can't get copies, they can't sell them. The problem has never been demand, it's always been supply. Of course sales will fall if there are no books in the shops.

The halving of the schedule has been seen as another nail in the coffin. Again, this might not be a bad thing. A couple of years ago in the UK, the VHS releases went from one a month to one every two months, and sales picked up. The logic must be that the books will do the same. Behind the scenes, the BBC have always run the books with a skeleton staff - Virgin thought they'd cut it to the bone with three full-time editors on the staff dedicated to the *Who* books. The *Who* books are put together by about as many part-timers, freelancers and people with other responsibilities. It's an amazing testament to the dedication of these people that the books come out at all. When the BBC wanted special anniversary books without wanting to hire extra staff, something had to give. So it was decided to release about a million words of fiction in 2003, rather than two million. It's still more than the *Buffy*, *Star Wars* or *Star Trek* fans will get. Even if the books were to end, it would be impossible to call this failure - there's an enormous body of work there, a genuine publishing phenomenon.

Going to one book a month may be a good thing. Two books a month is an enormous commitment of readers' time, if not their money. People were falling behind, people were skipping books. If a shop just has one copy of each BBC book, that's now three or four shelves dedicated to them.

It does feel remarkably like winding the range down, though. I've been assured this isn't the case, and I know for a fact that Justin Richards, the editor, is commissioning books well into 2004 already.

The worst thing about all this is that the EDAs last year were the best they've ever been at the BBC, with a great mix of newbies, old hacks like me and people who are relatively new. All the polls show that the books under Justin's editorship are among the best-regarded of the lot. The work is undermined, though, by stupid decisions like making the books harder for shops to return. From the beginning of 2001, UK shops were told the BBC wouldn't take unsold stock back. The result? The shops order less copies, so they don't get stuck with them, then only reorder if there's a demand. The books sell almost all their copies in the first month. What typically happens now is that the shops order a few, sell them, then reorder... and they don't come in until they arrive with the next batch. So, for virtually the whole first month, the key sales period, unless you got in fast, you can't buy the book in a shop. If sales have fallen (and mine haven't, as far as I can tell from my royalty statements), then that is the reason, not Sabbath, not Anji.

It really, really doesn't matter how good the books are, if you can't actually buy them.

We're in an age, now, with direct access to the readership. At one point, the *Telepress* (the BBC Books mailing list) had over three thousand subscribers. That's an extraordinary, direct route straight to the readership, the sort of thing conmen promise the Internet can deliver. It was tragically neglected and allowed to fall into disuse. Meanwhile, fans have produced spin-offs (licenced and unlicenced), and have embraced the Internet as a way to get to the audience. Is the irony now that the BBC's vast marketing and licencing arms are a handicap? Is the BBC a plodding dinosaur, in a new age of little scurrying mammals like Telos, BF, Mad Norwegian and Comeuppance Comics, who can identify and exploit a niche in the market before the BBC can even get round to scheduling a meeting of all the relevant departments? The niche is still there - and the BBC ought to be the best-placed to exploit it. When Telos, literally run by two people passionate about *Doctor Who*, selling a premium product mainly by mail order, can manage comparable sales and better international distribution than the BBC, one of the world's biggest media corporations, you know that there's a problem. And it's not with the demand.

Death by Niche

From Enlightenment #115, April/May 2003

When is a niche not a niche?

Doctor Who is a niche, and the *Doctor Who* books, videos and audios are all niches within that niche. We're in something of a developed market, now - a polite way of saying that the books, audios and videos are all finding niches within those niches of niches.

OK... that's eight uses of the word 'niche' in three lines. Nine. I'll stop now. But the *Doctor Who* scene seems to be settling down into a period of selling products to very specialised subsets. It's an old marketing adage that it's easy to get an existing customer to buy something else than to find a new customer. But the *Doctor Who* market now seems to be taking this to absurd lengths. Worse than that, we're being told this is the only way to go.

How can you make more money selling to a thousand people than to ten thousand? Easy - you charge those thousand people more money. The amount of money needed to buy all the new product has shot up in the last couple of years. Not a problem, you say - you don't buy everything, so it's no skin off your nose if the BBC bring out a £40 hardcover (I won't even attempt to convert that into Canadian dollars, out of consideration for the more faint-hearted of you), because you won't buy it. If Big Finish want to bring out four things costing £15 a month, it doesn't matter if you don't buy any of them.

But that's the problem - fandom isn't 'fandom', now, it's about half a dozen groups who rarely interact and are losing common frames of reference. The fan community has always shared a culture - and we still do, to an extent, but now the people who only listen to the Big Finish audios and the people that only read the EDAs could be talking about a different series. The things they like, the priorities they have, the selling points, the agenda of the ranges... it doesn't matter that the two ranges are far closer than most people usually allow for (if nothing else they're written by exactly the same people, barring about half a dozen names on each side). The fact is that for the last couple of years, the BF people have had their Internet mailing lists, the books people have got theirs, and people visiting one from the other marvel at the weird customs and attitudes of the foreign land they find themselves in.

Part of this is just capitalism - the idea of The Competition. EDA vs. BF is as Pepsi vs. Coke, DC vs. Marvel or Apple vs. IBM. But the main reason is economic, I think - it's beyond most wallets to buy *everything*. So you make choices. And people tend to follow a range, rather than, say, pick and choose the books and audios individually. Part of it is the way fandom is organised - rec.arts.drwho was a general forum for all *Doctor Who* discussion. I've been there for a while, and there never was a golden age... but the last couple of years have seen the neighbourhood go completely to pot. So we all retreated into mailing lists, and that meant we had to specialise - a general list would generate too much traffic.

The market has reacted accordingly. The Benny books are a case in point. They've gone from mass-market, generally available paperbacks to slightly-more-expensive ones you could only get in specialist outlets or via mail order and now we get limited edition hardbacks for £15. OK... these books are a spin-off of a spin-off of a spin-off of a spin-off of a spin-off of a spin-off of a television series. The laws of diminishing returns are going to kick in at some point, and no-one would expect the Benny book *A Life of Surprises* to be seen by as many people as *City of Death*. But how many *new* readers did *A Life of Surprises* bring to the Benny fold? It was limited to 1000 copies and cost as much as a DVD. My guess at that new reader tally? Less than ten. Benny's a great character, but in the current form, only the people that already know that will ever know that.

Doctor Who books are never going to sell in the millions, or even in the hundreds of thousands. But the existing fans are there. There are literally about a dozen subsets, all buying a Benny books here, *Books of the War* there, *Dalek Empires*, BBVs... surely one product, one that's cheap and plentiful enough, can unite all these fandoms and push the sales into five figures?

But *Doctor Who* is going the same way as Benny - the books are getting harder to find, even in the UK. The 'entry price' is going up. After the books, the next cheapest option is the Telos novellas - for £10. How many new readers will come along? Not many. And let's make no mistake whatsoever - the *Doctor Who* novels have created *thousands* of new fans, or energised old ones to return. Go onto the BBC Boards, where the average age seems to be in the teens. *Doctor Who* is great, and there are whole new generations who are discovering that for themselves.

But we're being marketed ever-more-expensive, ever more specialised products.

We're told this is inevitable, that this is the only model for *Doctor Who* these days. But that's completely wrong. *Doctor Who* is a great idea for a series; it's one that's endured for decades, one where the official magazine is soon going to have run longer than the series, one where there are more books than original TV stories. It deserves better than to be the preserve of an aging, ever-diminishing group of die-hards. Without mass-market books, there will be no new fans. And then it's just a question of when *Doctor Who* dies - when *Doctor Who* becomes a group of small puddles, each of which is drying up.

There is another way - we've seen webcasts (free), comics (cheap) and there's more hints that the TV series (free) is being actively considered. *Doctor Who* doesn't have to be the preserve of a thousand people with the wallets to keep up. *Doctor Who* is good enough to be seen by millions - and whenever it's free and a quality product, that's exactly what happens. There is another way, and don't let anyone tell you any different.

McGann to Return!

From Enlightenment #120, February/March 2004

The 'exclusive' news on ITV's teletext service on 17 January was that Paul McGann was returning to play the Doctor, for a short while, in the new TV series. It was the headline news, based on an interview with Mal Young. The problem being that the interview itself said nothing of the sort, and didn't even mention McGann. What Mal Young said was:

"He will regenerate but we will bring it up to date, modernise the storytelling. People will expect great monsters, battles and saving the world."

We're into semantics. Does that mean we will see the regeneration, or that the Doctor will be played by a different actor the next time we see him? My interpretation is that it's far more likely to mean the latter. We're still in the very early stages of the new series. Scripts haven't been written yet - meaning the budget must be, at best, not quite finalised. They've not even started looking for a ninth Doctor, mainly because they don't know the exact shooting schedule, so they can't begin to discuss availability. If that's the case, how can they have told Paul McGann when to show up? If McGann isn't under contract, Mal Young would be rather foolish to say the BBC were lavishing money on the new series and that McGann would definitely appear - it's practically handing McGann's agent a blank cheque. It would also be peculiar for McGann to accept the role of the Doctor on terms that Colin Baker baulked at in 1987 - to appear just long enough for him to be bumped off.

What Paul McGann's thinking might be is rather interesting, though. A number of actors - notably Tom Baker, Paul Nicholls and Anthony Stewart Head - have done the rather actorly thing of modestly declaring they doubt they'd be approached, but adding, y'know, if they were, they wouldn't say no. For years now, we've seen a number of actors and their agents whispering that they're 'in the running' to play the Doctor, and it's a game that's only going to increase now there's actually a race.

Paul McGann has gone, in the space of a couple of years, from someone who didn't want to do a DVD commentary for his story lest he be identified with the role, to someone who's crossing the Atlantic to make a convention appearance. What are we to make of this? Has the weight of being 'the current Doctor' now been lifted, so he feels more comfortable with the role? Both Tom Baker and Peter Davison spent the first decade after leaving the show keeping a quiet distance from the fan circuit, but the decade after that, they've been far happier with the association. The other possibility is exactly the opposite: is Paul McGann starting to lobby for the lead role in the new series? Not just a cameo where he falls over and turns into the new Doctor - is he trying to be the star of the new show? If so, will he get it?

The argument has nothing to do with continuity. Fans of the books, audios and *DWM* strip have already had an 'eighth Doctor era' that's longer than Tom Baker's tenure, and plenty has happened to this incarnation. If McGann was to return, it seems unlikely (to put it mildly) that he'd bring Fitz or Charley with him. But, even without bringing that sort of thing, there would be an issue: *The TV Movie* will be nearly ten years old by the time the new series appears. McGann looks older. The implication will be that he's at least been up to something. But even *that's* not the issue. If you're going to do something new and different, then why cast the same lead actor? This won't be Phillip Segal's vision of *Doctor Who*... why would the new production team feel bound to include 'his' Doctor? There's nothing contractual forcing them to use McGann. There's no great public association with McGann and the role - the BBC's anniversary documentary managed to ignore him entirely. One amusing snippet about *The TV Movie* is that the BBC weren't keen to have Sylvester McCoy in the show - they actually wanted to show *Tom Baker* regenerate into McGann.

A separate, but relevant, question is whether Paul McGann is the best man for the job. There's a degree of loyalty among many fans towards who they see as the 'incumbent' (regardless of how that's defined), and he plays the 'current' Doctor for both EDA and BF fans. A lot of the pros - myself included - have a vested interest in keeping people thinking of Paul McGann as the current Doctor, because it makes at least some sections of fandom more interested in stories featuring him.

But is there really a groundswell of support for him? Time has not been kind to *The TV Movie*, and the character of the 'eighth Doctor' in both the books and audios has been significantly changed from McGann's initial interpretation. While there have been high points, and fan favourite stories, in the McGann audios, his return to the role just hasn't had the galvanising effect some fans predicted. The authors of the books, for example, don't seem to have rushed to adopt any new insights or facets McGann has brought to the role. The consensus on the McGann seasons - and it's always hard to say this with any accuracy - seems to be that they're a bit patchy, and that McGann is brilliant in some, lacklustre in others. He doesn't dominate proceedings or bestride the franchise. The books and audios have diverged to the point that they now have fictional reasons for the fact they seem to operate in entirely different universes. The fact the books and audios have *different* explanations for the divergence is as clear proof as you need that McGann's return to the role has done nothing to unify *Doctor Who*.

Ultimately, whatever the semantic arguments about the Mal Young quote, the end result is that we're going to get a new Doctor pretty sharpish when the new show returns. Does Paul McGann want to change the new producers' minds, and will he be able to? One thing's for certain - this isn't the last time we'll read an interview this year where certain quotes are open to interpretation.

The Essential Eccleston

From Enlightenment #121, April/May 2004

Christopher Eccleston doesn't spell his name with an 'e' at the end. That's the first thing a fan should know, to avoid any 'Peter Davidson' type embarrassment.

This is an extraordinary piece of casting. Christopher Eccleston is a British actor known mainly for serious, gritty roles. It's a bit like if JNT had cast a young Robert DeNiro to be the fifth Doctor in 1981. He's relatively well known in the UK. Not a household name, perhaps, but certainly a heavyweight actor, someone who brings prestige to a production. He genuinely is a Shakespearean actor, rather than - as with pretty much every actor - someone who was once in a Shakespeare play.

If he has a reputation, though, it's for rather dour roles, ones with a social realistic bent. He's not an obvious choice to play *Doctor Who*. The names bandied about in the press were either comedians who do a bit of acting, like Stephen Fry, Alan Davies and Eddie Izzard or at the very least actors with a lot of comedy under their belt, like Bill Nighy or (shudder) Anthony Stewart Head. Despite appearances in *The League of Gentlemen*, *Linda Green* and *24 Hour Party People* (a wonderful, uncredited cameo - he doesn't play Boethius, whatever the IMDB says, he plays a tramp who quotes Boethius), Eccleston's CV is very short on light roles. Think Robert Carlyle... but without *The Full Monty*. This is a fascinating piece of casting, because it's a big indicator that Russell T Davies is making good on his promise that this is going to be a contemporary take on *Doctor Who*. Christopher Eccleston is easily the best actor to be cast in the role. Easily. It's disorientating to imagine a *The Nine Doctors* where he shares scenes with Sylvester McCoy, and they're nominally playing the same part.

OK... so what's he been in, and where is he Doctorish?

There's no one thing you can look at and see him as a proto-Doctor.

If you want to see him in the lead role of a great series, track down *Our Friends in the North*. He plays Nicky Hutchinson, a young dreamer from Newcastle. The series tracks more than thirty years in the life of Nicky and his friends. Eccleston's is perhaps the central performance in a heavyweight cast. The range he demonstrates is extraordinary. If you have to watch only one episode, watch the last. The very last shot, a monologue from Eccleston, is one of the most beautiful pieces of television I've ever seen, all the more magnificent because it just isn't the moment of closure it seems to be.

But it's not *Doctor Who*. If you want to see him adopt a Home Counties accent in a fantasy film, check out *Death and the Compass*. The film is a piece of sub-David Lynch rubbish, based on a great short story by Jorge Luis Borges. A young Eccleston has a triple role in the movie, and is just about the only memorable thing in there. Again, the last scene is one to watch.

Another SF film is *28 Days Later*. Eccleston plays a paranoid army Major in a post-apocalyptic Britain. Again, it's hard to see his performance as the Doctor being anything like this, but again, he's easily the most memorable actor in the film.

So... where to go? The obvious place, especially given that it's now out on DVD on both sides of the Atlantic, is *The Second Coming*. This is a fantasy serial written by... Russell T Davies, and Eccleston plays Steven Baxter, a man from Manchester who wakes up to discover he's the new messiah. Despite the writer and lead actor, the new *Doctor Who* is unlikely to be anything like the series, but it's one of the best pieces of contemporary British drama, it shows how Russell Davies can build up tension, create warm characters and use the bare minimum of special effects as part of telling a compelling story. It's Eccleston at his warmest and most sympathetic... and there's still a nice edge to the performance that never quite leaves you at ease. My guess is that new *Doctor Who* will look a lot more like this than like *Time and the Rani*.

Christopher Eccleston is not an obvious choice for the role, and part of me is worried. This anxiety is, of course, fantastic. He's not a safe choice. This isn't going to be a safe, twee or retro series - any attempt to make it one would be crushed by Eccleston's performance. The best analogy is Patrick Stewart in *TNG* - an actor so good it adds new gravitas to the series, and demands and attracts strong writing and supporting cast. It's important to add one thing, at this point: *only more so*. Eccleston is a far, far better actor than Patrick Stewart, and far more highly regarded and better known than Stewart was in 1987. The actors they cast as the villains are really going to have to be heavyweights. As Davies has said, Eccleston's casting raises the bar for the series.

The casting does seem at odds with Davies' declaration that the new show will take some cues from *Buffy*. If you sent a casting director out with a brief to look for an actor who was the completely opposite of *Buffy*, they'd come back with Christopher Eccleston.

It's unclear why Eccleston has taken the role - it's way off his normal type of work, and he's got a film career. Is he a fan? Is he looking to change his image? Does he see it as a stepping stone to a higher profile in America?

Whatever the case, the new series of *Doctor Who* just became even more interesting. It's not playing it safe, and it's going to be incredible.

A Failure of Management

From Enlightenment #122, June/July 2004

It's very refreshing to see the senior BBC management behind the new *Doctor Who* series. Very senior people indeed, like Mal Young, haven't just commissioned the show, they've gone on the record in interviews and press releases to support it. There's the very clear sense that the whole of the BBC is behind the new series. Teletext and BBCi have been leading their Entertainment sections with *Doctor Who* stories - one last week announced 'Fans back Billie', the story quoting a DWAS spokesman. Reports have it that pretty much every arm of the Corporation has been mobilised to come up with something to tie in with the new show. The series hasn't started filming yet, it won't be on for months, possibly around a year, and the BBC have already made it perhaps the biggest thing on British TV. It's going to be expensive, it's going to be high profile, and the management are clearly keeping a very close eye on the show.

In Colin Baker's era, things were different. There have been any number of conspiracy theories over the 'hiatus' and the subsequent death of the show. These have ranged from it being a question of resources (*Doctor Who* sacrificed to make way for *EastEnders*), to one of personal antipathy for the show from decision makers, bordering on the irrational. A recent variant on this theory has blamed a lurid - and implausible - personal feud between Michael Grade and Colin Baker himself.

In the end, Colin Baker probably has it right. The problem was that *Doctor Who* didn't have a champion at the BBC. People had their own pet projects, and wouldn't get any credit for keeping *Doctor Who* afloat. Even John Nathan-Turner was trying to move on to make a show he'd created. It was a little too early for commercial considerations to over-ride creative ones at the BBC, and it was a little too early for BBC Enterprises to demonstrate what a huge money-spinner the show could be.

What it comes down to, though, is a failure of management. This wasn't at the big strategic level: the BBC were perfectly within their rights to cancel *Doctor Who* if they thought they had something better to spend their resources on instead. To us fans, it seems fairly straightforward that a much-loved show which continues to be a success and which made about five times what it cost to make in merchandising and foreign sales should be recommissioned. But, objectively, you can't really argue that if they lost *Doctor Who* but won *EastEnders*, then the BBC got a pretty sweet deal. Of course, the BBC can, did and will make both *EastEnders* and *Doctor Who* - it was never a straight either/or.

The real failure at the BBC seems to me to have been at the day-to-day level. There doesn't, for example, seem to have been much of a search for the sixth Doctor. This isn't to blame Colin Baker for impressing a producer, but you'd think the senior management would have a close eye on the casting process. There seems to have been either complacency (the idea the show could get on with itself) or active neglect. We've all heard Eric Saward's complaint that he was told to put more comedy into the twenty-third season, but was never given any more constructive advice. Seven or eight years before, the line managers at the BBC would jot notes warning that the script they'd just read should pay more attention to the companions. One for *The Pirate Planet* warned that Romana was becoming a generic companion with the phrase 'it's like Leela all over again'. There's no evidence that JNT's superiors ever paid that close attention.

Obviously, having managers breathing down your neck can be a mixed blessing at best. But the hiatus caught the production team completely by surprise - indeed, embarrassingly, the fans knew before the producer that the show was being taken off. It's not good management to close something down without warning, or trying to fix it. Perhaps JNT got plenty of memos and warnings - but he, his script editor and his lead actor have all said different. The fact that a show could be very publically criticised by management, taken off the air, then come back with exactly the same producer, script editor, stars and writers is telling. Michael Grade was happy to tell the papers that *Doctor Who* was tired and the new season was a ratings flop. There was rather less indication that anyone at the BBC wanted to mend what was broken.

The contrast with the new series couldn't be greater. We know the production team have the full confidence of the management. Indeed, the management seem to have struck a very healthy balance between trusting the best people to do the best job, and being involved in all the big decisions. If only the management then had been as good as the management now.

Fashion, Sense

From Enlightenment #123, August/September 2004

Is it an uproar? It's hard to say, but the unveiling of the ninth Doctor's costume has provoked a lot of discussion. For the last ten years, we've all had the idea that the Doctor wears Victorian clothes, and has to dress somewhere between Dickens and Oscar Wilde. The new Doctors in *The TV Movie*, the Gatiss Who Night incarnation and *Shalka* all go for variations on the frock coat and cravat theme. The various Doctors of *The Curse of Fatal Death* all wear exactly the same costume. All four have gone for what they see as a 'generic' *Doctor Who* look. The expectation was that the ninth Doctor would do the same - to the point where the BBCi site put up pictures of Eccleston in past roles where he had to wear a frilly shirt.

The twist being, of course, that none of the first seven Doctors wore anything like this 'generic' Doctor costume. If you're reading this, you don't need me to review what the various incarnations wore. Some were dandies, some were scruffy; some had 'costumes', others wore clothes; some stood out, some were subdued. There wasn't one 'look' - indeed, with the possible exception of Troughton, all the Doctors wore clothes that seemed designed to distinguish them from their predecessor, not to make them look the same.

So the leather jacket has proved to be something of a Rorschach test for individual fans. Responses on the most open, unmoderated forum online, rec.arts.drwho, were characteristically fast and forthright. The jacket 'made the Doctor look gay', 'it's trendy, like the Matrix', 'he's not the Doctor, he's the Fonz'. Three responses there that make you wonder if you're sharing the same reality as the people posting them, but which are very telling and point to some deepseated beliefs, fears and prejudices held by a lot of fans. Feelings that perhaps we all have, at least a little.

Assume for the moment that the Doctor was wearing a Fonz-style leather jacket. A glimpse at even a blurry photo would demonstrate that he isn't, but, for sake of argument, let's imagine he was. The show will air in 2005. *Happy Days* was set fifty years before that. It means that the Fonz's outfit is exactly as 'historical' as Hartnell's Edwardian gear was in 1963. It's the sort of thing the audience's grandparents might have worn. The idea it's a costume straight out of *The Matrix* has no connection with reality, but some fans genuinely seemed to have looked at the screen grabs and newspaper photos of a short, battered jacket and seen an ankle-length glossy coat. It is perhaps a truism that one should never ask a *Doctor Who* fan for fashion advice, but this is an extraordinary mistake for these people to make.

Both, I think, point to the fear that this new *Doctor Who* will be 'trendy'. *Doctor Who* was never 'cool'. We forget now that in the UK it was mainstream family drama at a couple of points (mid-Hartnell and mid-Tom), but even then it was a show for the bookish, nerdy kids, and it's been comfortably deep in geek territory for so long that it's hard to imagine it as something the whole family can enjoy on a Saturday night. *Doctor Who* always shamelessly stole from things that were popular at the time, but it somehow never stayed in the same place long enough to look like a fashion victim. The nineties saw rumours of a sassy, womanising Doctor and a TARDIS with rapping lips, and this version of *Doctor Who* - one that jettisons the appeal of the show for a quick buck - has always been a great fear of fans. *Doctor Who* wouldn't be the first old TV show to be revived as an entirely terrible vehicle for some Hollywood star. Some have seen evidence of a 'star ego' at work in Eccleston's choice of costume and his justification that fancy clothes didn't suit him.

If that seems silly, then some of the other objections to the leather jacket have been surreal. It's interesting to see the doublethink that comes into play. There are fans who hold the belief that the new Doctor is gay, citing the twin pieces of evidence that Russell Davies is gay and Eccleston's wearing a leather jacket. Some fans are worried that the Doctor and his lovely female companion will have sex, based on comments from Eccleston that they have an 'interesting relationship'. Incredibly, there are some fans who believe both these things. He's both too gay, and too straight. It sounds like a contradiction, but it's actually consistent. What we have here is evidence of a great and familiar anxiety among a substantial set of *Who* fans - that the Doctor will be a sexual being in some way. The arguments here are well rehearsed, and seem to boil down to the idea that it makes the Doctor 'too ordinary'. It would perhaps be disingenuous to draw conclusions about the psychological development of fans who utterly insist that their hero be entirely sexless.

A few people objected on the grounds that the Doctor wouldn't wear something made from a dead animal. When they were reminded of the second Doctor's big fur coat, the response came back immediately: that was fake fur. There's another fan prejudice: anything from 1963-89 gets the benefit of the doubt, it's 'proper *Doctor Who*'. Anything new is treated with the greatest suspicion, and seen as evidence that this new series will be, and I'm quoting, 'a bastardised version of the show we love'.

In the end, it's a jacket. We love *Doctor Who*, and we extrapolate our hopes and fears for the new series from the snippets of information. As these snippets are reported on and analysed, they take on a life of their own. But watch the BBC Wales interview, where Russell says he loves *Doctor Who* and gives enough information for the fans to realise that the opening scene of the first episode is going to be a classic moment - in both the sense that it's going to be instantly memorable for a new generation of viewers and that it's a retelling of one of the key moments of the old show. Anyone watching that couldn't possibly believe that *Doctor Who*'s in anything but the safest hands, could they? It's a clear case of not being able to see the wood for the trees. Or, in this case, the Autons for the leather.

Abstinence Makes the Heart Grow Fonder

From Enlightenment #127, April/May 2005

Preface: The first episode of the revived Doctor Who was leaked onto the internet a couple of weeks before it was shown in the UK, and the culprit was someone working at a Canadian broadcaster. This piece is a response to the question of whether or not I was going to treat myself to a sneak peak of the new series...

I haven't downloaded *Rose* and watched it.

As you may guess, this is not because I don't want to see it. And it's not because it's illegal (which it is, the only question is which is the most serious law it's breaking, and how often that law's been tested). And it's not even because it's not what the production team would want me to do. It's because last week, the billboards went up across the UK, twenty foot high. The first time I saw one, I slammed on the brakes of my car. Thankfully, so did the person behind me. I've just seen the fifty second trailer, the 'trip of a lifetime' one. I have tears in my eyes. There you go, I'll be the one to admit it. It wasn't seeing the Doctor, it wasn't seeing the inside of the TARDIS, it wasn't even the image of the Dalek ship (I'm assuming) scraping the Houses of Parliament. It was the announcement at the end:

'Doctor Who coming soon to Saturdays on BBC1'.

And this is the crux of it, that's what's changed, and that's why I won't be downloading.

Doctor Who isn't coming *back*. There has been more *Doctor Who* in the last fifteen years than in the fifteen years before that. A fact that's just been rammed home to me as I work on the revised version of *A History of the Universe*. The Virgin version of the book covered *Doctor Who* from

1963 to 1996. The new one covers it from 1963 to 2005. It's twice as long. The *Doctor Who* since 1989 - give or take ninety minutes in 1996 - has one thing in common: it's for the fans, by the fans. It's been wonderful, but it's been fanboys huddled together (or at computer screens).

Please, please don't misunderstand me - the fact that 'the New Adventures changed my life' is about as true for me as it is for anyone. I think the ongoing *Doctor Who* book range is extraordinary and marvellous and all the TV show has to do is be anything like as good as the best NAs or EDAs... well, I hope you get the point. We've not just kept the flame, we've handed it back, brighter than it was.

But this is something else. We don't need to huddle - *Doctor Who* is coming soon to Saturdays on BBC1. I've mentioned the billboards, I've mentioned the trailers. I haven't mentioned the magazine covers, the fact that it made the front cover of *The Times*, the fact that *The Sun* had a pull out and keep parade of new monsters, Billie on the front of a lads mag, the barrage of interviews and features on TV, the fact that serious review programmes are giving over whole editions to the comeback. *Private Eye* has two joke features and a cartoon about the return of *Doctor Who* this week - three years ago, you'd be lucky if *Dreamwatch* gave the show that much coverage.

The great thing about this is that *everyone* gets to see what we love. It's going to be huge, and we were right. All these years, we've known that if the BBC got behind the show, put some money in, got some good writers and actors, then it would be the best show on the telly. And the *trailer* is the best show on the telly. It literally explodes onto the screen, then afterwards the announcer comes on to say that next is *DIY SOS* and after that *Traffic Cops*, and you feel a bit embarrassed for her.

Doctor Who has stopped being cult viewing. It's mass entertainment again, and I'm not downloading it for the same reason that I'd rather be at a stadium watching a rock band than furtively listening to a cassette pirated the week before the album came out. I want to be there when everyone else is. I want to hear the announcer say the words, I want to hear that music, knowing that the audience for *Doctor Who* just *squared*.

Canadians only have to wait another week. If I lived in the US, well, I might be more inclined to download it. Although I didn't buy that pirate VHS of *The Phantom Menace*. Er... actually, I crossed an ocean to watch it in a cinema. That's worse, isn't it? But if I just wanted a new *Doctor Who* story... well, they aren't hard to come by. I want *Doctor Who* back where it belongs. It's not a game for the fans, now, it's not just for us and for all our usual fanboy oneupmanship of who is more in the know than who. I'm not trying to get at anyone who's come to a different choice. I don't feel morally superior or judgemental. But I've chosen to wait.

We fans are not onlookers, we still have a role to play. The night after it's on, we can jam the BBC switchboards, burst the BBC postbag and crash the BBC servers, thereby telling them that we want more of this.

The Incredible Week

From Enlightenment #128, June/July 2005

It was the greatest week *Doctor Who* has ever seen.

A wave of hype larger than the one for *The Phantom Menace*. Constant trailers, every single BBC programme (and quite a few on the other channels) with interviews and clips. An eye-popping montage on the Jonathan Ross show. Billboards, magazine covers. If it hadn't worked, it wasn't for want of trying. Everyone in Britain knew that *Doctor Who* was coming back, but would they watch?

Before *Rose* was shown, *Doctor Who* was seen as an expensive gamble. One ITV executive openly questioned whether an audience existed for it, pointed out that the days of ten million people watching TV on a Saturday night were long gone, and was too modest to point out that *Ant and Dec's Saturday Night Takeaway* had never, ever been beaten by anything that the BBC had put on opposite it. The bookies were certain that *Ant and Dec* would win the night. The BBC said they expected about six or seven million viewers. There was nothing like it on television, and in the world of TV that's not seen as a good thing at all.

And then *Doctor Who* destroyed every single one of those certainties. *Doctor Who* became, in an instant, the most popular drama on British TV, it even outrated some episodes of *EastEnders* and *Coronation Street*. The other high profile BBC launch, *Strictly Dance Fever*, was seen by the BBC as a surefire winner. They hoped that at least some of the people watching it would stick around for *Doctor Who*. It got almost exactly half the number of viewers. *Doctor Who* got its highest ever chart position, the highest audience appreciation index. Overnight, *Doctor Who* was a national institution that everyone was talking about, and it hadn't just beaten the opposition, it had humiliated it. The BBC had delayed announcing the death of a former Prime Minister so as not to spoil the mood. Now they were telling the Scots that if *Doctor Who* overran, they wouldn't show the beginning of next week's football match, and it seemed entirely reasonable. The headlines on Monday morning said it all '*Doctor Who* exterminates opposition'.

Wait a second. The *headlines*?

Doctor Who made the front page of the British papers three times that week. The most spectacular came towards the end of it:

DOCTOR WHO QUITS!
Pope given last rites.

Wait a second. *Doctor Who quits?*
Rumours had surfaced a couple of days before - and it's only now we're beginning to find out the whole truth. There would be a second series - the BBC had promised not to make a decision for a month, but the sheer impact of the first episode made the announcement inevitable. But Christopher Eccleston - who had put to the sword the Great Lie of the Eighties (that three years wasn't long enough to establish yourself as the Doctor) before his first episode had even been broadcast - would not be returning. The TV news and the papers were full of rumours - and (perhaps the most bizarre thing of all) they were turning to *Doctor Who* message boards and Internet sites for pointers.

Then *The End of the World* was shown. A spectacular episode, colourful and silly, but with as many special effects, jokes, insight into the Doctor's psyche, character-building moments for the companion and cute cameos as any given previous decade of *Doctor Who*. And it started to dawn on the people watching that *Rose* wasn't a sugar-buzzed, superfast, wacky, modern take on *Doctor Who*... it was just easing us in. The ratings held firm, and now *Ant and Dec* was just that show that *Doctor Who* beat every week.

What a week. *Doctor Who* fans will never have another one quite like it. The sense of anticipation and trepidation, an utterly comprehensive victory over anyone, ever, who'd doubted *Doctor Who* could do it. Then the sense that defeat would be snatched from the jaws of victory. Then the knowledge that there were at least another twenty-six episodes to go, and that this was just the beginning.

Since then... well, *Rose* was so long ago, now. *Doctor Who* is the most popular non-soap drama on British TV. It's the show that everyone's watching, part of the national consciousness. Kids love it, fans love it. Even my sister loves it. It's going to be the centrepiece of the Christmas Day schedule. Next year, between *Doctor Who* and *Casanova*, Russell Davies could well sweep the BAFTAs. There is a very real chance that two Doctors will go head to head for Best Actor. If Billie Piper doesn't get Best Actress, then it'll be a travesty. *Doctor Who* crushed *Ant and Dec*, so there probably isn't a word in the English language for what it did to ITV's replacement for them, *Celebrity Wrestling* - it got more than twice the viewers, and reduced ITV to its second or third worst primetime audience share in the channel's history. Three weeks later, ITV pulled the show. Walking down the streets of my home city of York with Mike

Doran this month, we saw Dalek teapots and wedding cakes (the latter very much a 2005 model, all gold and knobbly). We saw *Doctor Who* novels for sale in supermarkets, and DVDs at the top of the charts. *Doctor Who* is everywhere, it's cool, and with the release of Billie's Greatest Hits, it's even dictating terms to the music industry.

If I'd have written this six months ago, as a prediction of what would happen, my editor would have rejected it as mad fanboy nonsense. *Doctor Who* fans may never see a week like it again. But... wow. *Doctor Who* is back, and it's bigger and better than even we could have imagined.

Don't Forget
It's Also Christmas

Enlightenment #129, August/September 2005

A date for the diary: December 24th this year looks like Doctor Who Eve.

The week following *The Parting of the Ways*, the BBC started trailing *The Christmas Invasion*. This was apparently before the script had even been completed; it was certainly before filming had started. It comprised clips of the highlights of the first season, culminating in the regeneration. The BBC had run daily trailers for *The Parting of the Ways*, but this truly was unprecedented. Remember that they waited until about three weeks before *Rose* was broadcast before running their first substantial TV trail for it.

There's been a lot of coverage of the start of filming and a couple of substantial press interviews for Billie. *Blue Peter* ran a competition to design a monster, and that's led to Russell Davies, David Tennant and a Dalek making appearances.

The wave of merchandise has begun breaking over us. The new *Doctor Who Annual* is here, an almost pitch-perfect book that acts as an ideal gift for youngsters and a pastiche of the seventies annuals for the older fans. It's far too early to say how it's going to sell, but 'better than people expected' seems likely - the first two shops I went looking for it had sold out by the lunchtime of release. Next month is going to hurt the wallet. The next three ninth Doctor novels (and presumably last, before they become the TDAs). Many toys. Battling Daleks, Christopher Eccleston Walkie Talkies and the Sonic Screwdriver pen, which I'm guessing will grace the pockets of more than one person reading this. Don't forget to leave room for the mighty DVD box set. No doubt you've pre-ordered it.

Like the papers report the Queen has. Her Majesty has always been a fan of *Doctor Who*, she said it was her favourite show when she visited the Radiophonic Workshop. (She's a fan of fantasy TV in general - Paul McCartney tells the story of how she quickly wrapped up his audience with her 'because *Twin Peaks* is on in a minute'.) Will she find the easter eggs herself or get a flunky to do it?

It's interesting that at this stage, the merchandise is very heavily Eccleston-branded. These are souvenirs of this year's triumph, not scene-setting for the tenth Doctor's era. And why not? How much of this has been because merchandisers didn't have time to adapt to the new Doctor, it doesn't matter - this has been *Doctor Who*'s year, in no small part because of Christopher Eccleston, and it's nice to see that he's not been swept under the carpet or rebranded away just yet. The actor may or may not feel differently - no doubt we'll find out sooner or later. Personally, I'm glad that his 'era' isn't quite over just yet.

The National Television Awards are open to a public vote, and allow the public to vote for Eccleston, Piper and *Doctor Who* in the Best Actor, Actress and TV series categories. It seems like a foregone conclusion. As I've said before, the more heavyweight test will be the BAFTAs, and the question there would seem to be not if it wins, but how many. Between it and *Casanova*, Russell Davies would seem to have it sewn up. As with the Oscars and Emmys, there will be some playing around with categories, but it's not hard to imagine an Eccleston, Piper, *Doctor Who*, Russell Davies landslide.

It's very easy to get carried away by the hype. But there's a huge gamble here, and a bit of mis-scheduling or Tennant just not gelling with the public, and the tenth Doctor's era could be in a lot of trouble very quickly. I'm not too worried. The production team is certainly not going to be lulled into complacency, and they've got a degree of security, now. Not to mention Stephen Fry writing for it. By then, half the target audience will recognise the Doctor as that bloke out of the new *Harry Potter* movie. Expectations are high, perhaps unrealistically so, but *Doctor Who*'s a good show and ITV have already tried everything they've got to stop people watching, except scheduling *Coronation Street* against it. It says something about how far we've come since the late eighties that, as they plan their Christmas schedules, they'd hesitate before even doing that.

The production team have proved a lot already. They've learned on their feet. What lessons have they learned, how will they build on success without stagnating? What's changed and what's stayed the same? How significant is it that there's still no sale to a US station? This time next year, where will *Doctor Who* be? I think it's safe to say that anyone trying that exercise last year would have fallen short of the mark.

So I'm going to make a crazy prediction.

Perhaps the most peculiar Christmas tradition here in the UK is the race for the Christmas Number One single. That week is the week when the most pop singles are sold, and it's very competitive. Now, if I've thought of this, someone else will have done. Expect a dance remix of the *Doctor Who* theme to be a strong contender. Billie's brief career as the British Britney has been packaged up as a greatest hits album. (I was a bit surprised to learn that one song I thought was by Britney, 'Day and Night', was actually Billie. Then again, I'm hardly Mr Pop.) The Christmas Number One would be the perfect cap for a year when *Doctor Who* turned every piece of received wisdom on its head and exceeded every expectation.

Historical Note: Alas, Doctor Who has yet to score a number one single - although when Kylie released a single called '2 Hearts' just before appearing in Voyage of the Damned, I did wonder if it was a tie-in designed to get the Christmas Number One.

AHistorical

From Enlightenment #132, February/March 2006

This month sees the publication of my book *AHistory*. This is the revised *A History of the Universe*, and this time round it's published by Mad Norwegian. It's not simply a revision, it's an almost complete rewrite of the book, it covers about twice as many stories as the previous version, and it's the only single volume *Doctor Who* reference book that covers the TV show, the books and the audios. It also took roughly twice as long to write as anyone involved thought it would (each month of delay bringing a new batch of stories to cover, of course, which didn't help)... and, of course, there was the slight matter of a new television series coming along just as we thought we were finishing up.

AHistory covers a lot of ground - so much so that eventually I gave in and accepted the offer of help from my editor Lars Pearson. I think, on the whole, any non-fiction book benefits from being co-authored. *AHistory* certainly has. If nothing else, it actually got the book finished, and secured at least the last vestige of my sanity. This book's the longest one I've ever written (and I co-wrote a *Star Trek* guide book that covered every *Star Trek* story ever screened, and that was a slab).

I have to admit I'm awaiting the online discussion with a little trepidation. I'm very happy with the book... but it's the sort of work where people could fixate on one error / omission / decision they disagree with, and I'm sure - given the nature of *Doctor Who* fans, bless us - that every single person that reads it will find an example. Already, people have complained because it doesn't include the last few PDAs or EDAs, or *The Christmas Invasion* (they weren't published or broadcast when the book was finished, which seems like a pretty good excuse). Some people have lobbied for the comic strips to be included... we thought about it, but it would have almost certainly taken another year to write. Even just limiting the scope to the *DWM* comic strip would have added tens of thousands of words and a fair few months.

In the end, though, I've always taken people talking about a book to be a very good sign. It shows they care. In the last year, quite naturally, a lot of attention has shifted from the books, audios and spin-offs and to the new TV series. Word of mouth is important, and if people are talking about something else, then sales can only suffer. There seems to be some sort of correlation between the amount of discussion online and the success of a book and the survival of a range. When people howled in protest at the destruction of Gallifrey in the EDA *The Ancestor Cell*, other people flocked to the EDAs to see what the fuss was about. People seem keen to read *AHistory*, pre-orders have been very healthy indeed, there's been a steady stream of discussion and interest on Outpost Gallifrey, and when I did a couple of signings for *The Gallifrey Chronicles*, about half the people asked me about it.

The first version of the book, a fan version published by Seventh Door only covered the TV series. The second version covered the New Adventures and the first few Missing Adventures. In both cases, I'm sure most readers were familiar with a lot of the material. Sure, the appeal of a reference book is to unearth new snippets and pieces of trivia. Some people have followed all of *Doctor Who*, in all the media. I'll be perfectly honest and admit that I haven't been able to manage that, and I've written for most of them by now! I think *AHistory* will be map out a lot of unfamiliar territory.

The book was commissioned at the Gallifrey convention in 2003. In retrospect, that was the exact point where the *Doctor Who* spin-off industry was peaking. With no TV series in sight, we had a new ninth Doctor in the webcasts, and... well, you can probably reel off a list of the spin-offs. I make it nine publishers with *Doctor Who* or related ranges of books, comics or audios around and active at that point (and I have the nagging feeling I've missed one out). Most of those have now fallen by the wayside, and last year was all about Eccleston and Piper. I'm certainly not complaining - just looking at the Christmas schedules in the UK, or the DVD charts, and *Doctor Who* has gone from being a hobby for a few thousand people to pretty much the epicentre of popular culture here. But

Doctor Who never went away, and I hope that, among the other things it does, *AHistory* serves as a good record of the highs and lows, but above all else the sheer breadth and energy of the *Doctor Who* universe, and its writers, in the last fifteen years.

Historical Note: By and large, everyone was very nice about the new version of AHistory - so my fears about the book being lasered into a smoking crater because of a mistake or two were unfounded.

Even Cleverer Still

From Enlightenment #133, April/May 2006

The first thing to do is get *Doctor Who*'s US launch into perspective. The US has five or six times the population of the UK, so it's natural to assume that when *Doctor Who* was shown in the States it was seen by an unprecedented, vast number of people. But the television audience in the US is extremely fragmented. When *Rose* was first shown in the UK, it got 45% of the people whose TVs were on watching - the week *Doctor Who* debuted on the Sci-Fi Channel, the main networks got the following average audience share: Fox and CBS got 13% each, ABC 10% and NBC got 9%. Exactly 45% between them. The Sci-Fi Channel, on cable, has a tiny average share by comparison (roughly equivalent to ITV4's in the UK). Preliminary figures have *Doctor Who* getting around 1.8 million viewers. Or, to put it another way, in a country with five times as many people, *Doctor Who* musters about the same number of actual viewers as *Doctor Who Confidential*, the digital channel 'making of' series, did in the UK last year.

So... it's been a huge flop? No, not at all. The two biggest shows on Sci-Fi are *Battlestar Galactica* and *Stargate-SG1*, and they were shown on Friday evening, the same night as *Doctor Who*. The week before *Doctor Who* debuted, they got around two million viewers. *Doctor Who* might be in a small pond, but it's a big fish - the fourth highest rated show on Sci-Fi barely got a million viewers. Unlike both *Battlestar Galactica* and *Stargate*, *Doctor Who*'s also attracted a vast amount of free publicity for the cable channel across the Internet, in the local and national newspapers and in *TV Guide*. Almost all of the coverage stressed the drama credentials of Russell T Davies (an American version of *Queer as Folk* ran for five seasons, only finishing last summer), and on how the new version has a much higher budget than the one people might vaguely remember from years ago.

So... what did the people watching it think? Well, one clue is that Sci-

Fi showed the first two episodes on the same night, and the audience actually went up a little for the second episode. So, whatever they thought, the people who watched didn't turn over in droves. As I'm writing this, it's only a couple of days since it was shown, and we have to rely on the Internet for more specific reaction. This is not always the most useful barometer, but some themes are developing.

First of all, a great tranche of *Battlestar Galactica* fans have taken against the show. *Doctor Who*'s debut came the same week that it was announced that Season Three of their show was going to be delayed. Fans of *BSG* have associated the two, and somehow blame *Doctor Who* for the delay. This atmosphere of rivalry wasn't helped the following week when it was announced that four *Doctor Who* episodes were nominated for the Hugo Awards. One *BSG* episode was, too (and the first one, *33*, won last year).

There are people complaining that there are too many adverts and that the broadcast quality wasn't very good compared with the DVD. There's also criticism of the special effects. On the whole, though, the reaction seems overwhelmingly positive. The iPod joke (actually hacked at by the channel, who've cut a few lines, apparently for timing reasons) has gone down well.

A lot of people have seen the episodes already - cunningly, they've somehow managed to acquire the episodes on DVD. Most assert that the series gets stronger as it goes on. Among those who are seeing the new series (or, indeed, *Doctor Who*) for the first time, there seems to be some confusion about what *Doctor Who* is. The fact it's funny is being misinterpreted as being 'childish' and 'dumb'. The Sci-Fi audience is perhaps used to its resonances with contemporary politics being writ large, and a lot seem to miss the subtexts in *Doctor Who*. The feature review on the much-visited Ain't-it-Cool site accuses the episodes of stealing from *Minority Report* and *Terminator 2*, which is true (although you have to think about why for a good few minutes), but sort of the point - *Doctor Who* trades on intertextual stuff, homages and so on. It was doing what *The Simpsons* did years ago, just as playfully, but with a poker face. British audiences know this... the American one will 'get it' soon, but a lot haven't quite got it, yet.

The Sci-Fi Channel, as noted, is a niche. *Doctor Who* was written with a mainstream family Saturday night audience in mind. It's not that surprising that an audience used to the more 'serious' gung-ho antics of *Stargate* and *BSG* might be a little bewildered. Interestingly, *Doctor Who*'s first week saw it directly opposite the last episode for a while of *Monk*. I'd contend that *Monk* - witty, eccentric, well-acted, *good* - is actually much more 'like' *Doctor Who* than *Stargate* is. If a segment of the *Monk* audience (which is pretty hefty) finds *Doctor Who* instead, something very, very interesting might happen to the ratings. But would they even think to look on Sci-Fi?

There are some strange cultural things in there - a couple of people have commented on the fact that the relationship between Mickey and Rose is interracial. It's not, as yet, proved controversial per se with American posters... but some have assumed it 'must have been a big deal' in the UK or that it's part of a political agenda. The US is notoriously sensitive to portrayals of homosexuality, and it's 'a big deal' there - *Brokeback Mountain* has been a real cause celebre. In this country there was so much going on in *The Parting of the Ways* that it's possible to forget that the Doctor and another man kissed. We might predict that it won't go quite so unnoticed in the States.

Another thing that's ridiculous if you're British is the idea, expressed in more than one place by more than one person, that Billie Piper is 'fat'. It's extraordinary until you see just how emaciated some of the American female stars of telefantasy are - remember that a few years ago, Amber Benson was celebrated by *Buffy* fans as being a celebration of 'bigger sized women'. On American film and TV, the trend really is for women who appear, and often sadly are, anorexic.

Ending on a lighter note, there's a golden rule on the Internet - never, ever call yourself an expert. One poster on the Sci-Fi Board boasts that he's an 'expert in Liverpoolian accents', but Eccleston's is too much even for him. Fantastic!

Historical Note: Gratifyingly, the bit with Jack kissing the Doctor stayed in the US Sci-Fi broadcast of "The Parting of the Ways" - it's in all the PBS repeats too, come to think of it - and there doesn't seem to have been any fuss about it.

The Golden Age of Radio (Times)

From Enlightenment #134, July 2006

We're living in the golden age of *Doctor Who*. In fact, it's practically a cliché in fan circles to say as much, now.

We can measure it one way - *Radio Times* covers. *Radio Times* is one of the biggest selling magazines in the UK, and getting a cover is - or is meant to be - something of a rare honour. *Doctor Who*'s had six since the relaunch. No other show has anything like that. The Christmas issue is almost invariably the bestselling magazine of the year in the UK; it's usually a generic painted Christmas scene on that cover, but last year it was a TARDIS in a snowglobe. No series, that I recall, has ever had two consecutive Christmas covers, not even *EastEnders* at its eighties peak of success. I wouldn't bet against a *Doctor Who* cover this year, not least because the editor has said that 'by far' the biggest selling individual issues last year were the three *Doctor Who* ones.

Tom Baker's era didn't earn a single *Radio Times* cover. During the whole of the eighties, *Doctor Who* had one. This week, the companion, 'TV's hottest actress' earns one in her own right. The second series has, very slightly, outperformed the first on just about every week. The change of lead actors has been achieved without damaging the show, the novelty didn't wear off between seasons, the revamped Cybermen have proved a hit with kids. It's grown a little, with a huge amount of merchandise, almost all of which is genuinely hard to find. *Doctor Who Adventures*, with its dinky free gifts, seems to sell shelf loads every fortnight. We needn't have worried. Perhaps best of all, the show hasn't overheated. *Doctor Who* gets great ratings, share and audience appreciation, but it all seems sustainable, not the sort of bubble of hype that has to burst.

So where next? How does it get *Radio Times* covers next year?

What's the old monster that could make the Radio Times cover next year? There was some discussion about this last issue, and the obvious answer isn't the Sontarans or Ice Warriors - it's 'dinosaurs'. *Doctor Who* facing down a T-Rex on the cover next year, I bet you. They'll bring their pals the Silurians along, I'm sure, but don't doubt for a minute who'll get top billing. It's so obvious, particularly given that the BBC made *Walking With Dinosaurs*, that it's perhaps surprising they've resisted this long.

The Master might be a draw... but probably not on his own. First, he'd bring with him the knowledge that the Doctor isn't the last of the Time Lords (if the Face of Boe's message isn't 'you are not alone', I'll eat my hat). A story where the Master's after the last TARDIS in the universe - and the last Time Lord body, if he still needs one of those - would make for a great battle with high stakes. Could the Doctor really kill the only other one of his kind to stop him? You don't doubt the Master would.

He'd have to be played by someone quite heavyweight. Personally, I'd be happy to see Eric Roberts back in the role. Not because of any particular need for continuity - he did a good job, camp and thuggish, and would actually fit in really nicely. I doubt it would happen. They've missed the chance to do the obvious and get Anthony Stewart Head in, which is probably for the best, but we've also seen Masters played by Jonathan Pryce and Derek Jacobi in recent years. It is bizarre, isn't it, how just as the Doctor has to be played by a 'name' now, the Master is seen as the role for the Shakespearean heavyweights?

Ian McKellen or... no: Christopher Lee as the Master. Oh, yes.

I think this is the other obvious route for the show to go down - big name guest stars. The new series hasn't been afraid of them, just as the old series wasn't, but it's tended to be more 'familiar faces' than huge stars. Zoe Wanamaker, Don Warrington and Simon Pegg are great, but I doubt that droves of people tuned in because they were on the show. Peter Kay - a huge household name here, if not anywhere outside the UK - has paved the way for 'event casting'. Obviously, anyone who's ever seen a series run its course is right to get a little nervous at this point - 'star guests' are usually a sign that the show's out of ideas and needs gimmicks, and it usually distorts the storytelling. With *Doctor Who*, though, it could just be a sign of the sort of profile the show has and its ability to, er, absorb whatever's thrown at it.

Russell Davies has mused publicly about a 'Hollywood guest star' for the show. Does he have someone in mind? Kate Winslet's an old show-biz pal, she was game to do the sitcom *Extras* and - always an important factor - has young kids she might want to impress. That's the safe bet, but there could be someone out there who's just a ridiculously big movie star, or an absurdly heavyweight actor who could be reeled in. It's difficult to come up with names, pretty much by definition.

Doctor Who might not have the novelty value of the return of the show, the Daleks or the Cybermen next time round, but it'll find something to wow the *Radio Times* readership. The irony is, of course, that David Tennant and Billie Piper are now superleague telly stars in their own right, and *Doctor Who*'s bigger than both of them.

Historical Note: Since I wrote this, Doctor Who continues to average four or five Radio Times covers a year.

Legacy Issues

From Enlightenment #135, October 2006

A year since the original full-length novels ended, what is their legacy?

I have a vested interest in the question, of course. It would be very easy now to relegate the books and audios to the same place where the DC Comics Jim Kirk commanded the *Excelsior* and Saavik was his science officer go. Certainly, elements within BBC Books, and latterly some of the fans, seemed to lose interest towards the end. That said, readers certainly weren't allergic to the sight of them. The last regular EDA, *The Gallifrey Chronicles*, was easily my bestselling BBC Book - selling twice what *The Infinity Doctors*, my second, did.

Personally, I think there's still a market for them. When I read Lloyd

Rose describing the ninth Doctor as a man whose leather jacket is a hard shell over a surprisingly fragile body, it makes me want to read a book by her. The themes of loss, companionship and the emphasis on character we had in the ninth Doctor's season on television would seem natural subjects for the novels. The elephant in the room is the Time War. While I tend to think it's probably best left in the imaginations of the people watching, there's a certain logic in the idea of a great ten-book epic charting the War, showing the eighth Doctor becoming the ninth in an epic battle with the Daleks. It's not hard to imagine it would sell. At the moment, ironically, it's the older fans who aren't being catered for by the books - they aren't excluded, on the whole, from the new series novels, but neither are they getting things targeted right at them. The right books would do very well, I think.

While I firmly believe that full-length adult *Doctor Who* novels will be published again one day, there's no clear prospect of that now, and the BBC are selling a lot more tenth Doctor hardbacks than Past Doctor paperbacks. Inevitably, now we're looking forwards to the tenth Doctor's second season on television, so continuing the eighth Doctor novels doesn't seem to be much of a priority. So it's regrettable, but we can start talking about the books in the past tense. The novels ran for fifteen years; there were more New Adventures, Missing Adventures, Eighth Doctor Adventures and Past Doctor Adventures than original TV stories. They remained where *Doctor Who* was at during the period the show was off TV. A rough back of the envelope calculation, and I reckon there are over three million of them in print, so you'd hope they'd have some lasting effect - even if it's just 'taking up a lot of shelf space'.

The most obvious legacy is the stable of writers - with the pick of anyone writing for TV today, the new TV series (executive produced by the author of *Damaged Goods*), picked people like Paul Cornell, Gareth Roberts and Mark Gatiss. All people with impressive TV credits, but who got an early break at Virgin. Peter Darvill-Evans' policy of seeking out young, cheap writers, which the BBC Books and Big Finish inherited, really did keep pushing new people forwards. And while many of us discovered by that process are now seasoned old hacks, the last EDA, *Fear Itself* by Nick Wallace, demonstrated that there were still people out there with a stunning debut in them. Phil Purser-Hallard's *Faction Paradox* book *Of the City of the Saved...* was another great book. There's something *wrong* that now such people don't get a chance to write *Doctor Who* stories.

The novels' legacy isn't as placeholders, or as a footnote. The new TV series is, in many ways, a continuation of the NAs (particularly) and EDAs rather than the original series. There are far more stories 'like' the new TV series in the books than in the original TV show. The most regrettable aspect of the books, in a way, was that the people who'd actually buy them were older fans, and this meant the books could never have the family audience the TV series enjoys.

At the same time, this was their great strength - it allowed those of us writing them to stretch things a little. The idea that *Doctor Who* could have stories featuring people with thoughts and feelings was shocking fifteen years ago, misinterpreted as 'angst'. It was somehow seen as 'wrong' to allude to the fact that human beings sometimes had and enjoyed sex. It was utterly taboo to imagine that those human beings might be the same gender. The format of a *Doctor Who* story was something to be adhered to and repeated, not something to be subverted or deconstructed. The companion was there to be rescued or educated, not to have any independent life. Perhaps the most shocking thing about the new TV series is that most older fans, thanks to the books, just take it for granted that these elements are part of a modern *Doctor Who* series.

Russell Davies is a very smart writer. He didn't need the NAs to make a *Doctor Who* that worked in the twenty-first century. But he had them, and used them. Watching an episode produced by Russell, written by Matt Jones and script edited by Simon Winstone, with occult stuff colliding with a cyberpunky psi-powersy space station belonging to the Earth Empire facing an evil from before the time, it's not all that fanciful to suggest that the influence of the books is a lasting one.

Kneale Before Who

From Enlightenment #136, November 2006

It was announced on Halloween that Nigel Kneale had died a couple of days earlier, at the age of eighty-four. Most famous for *Quatermass*, he remained an active writer until a very few years ago, and his name popped up in a number of surprising places - as the screenwriter for the 1960s *First Men in the Moon*, and for episodes of *Sharpe*. I have a book with one of his scripts in called *The Television Playwrights*, but a word that ought to seem impossibly pompous is actually as good a fit as any.

Kneale was a visionary, and as a number of the tributes have suggested, if he'd written novels instead of television, there's a very good chance his name would appear alongside those of John Wyndham, JG Ballard, Aldous Huxley and Christopher Priest in a list of British literary writers who used the fantastic to make serious points about the state and future of humanity. They didn't write science fiction, per se, but the science fiction canon is all the richer for having them there.

Kneale's influence on *Doctor Who* is one of the Things We All Know About Doctor Who, but whether there was much of a direct influence (before Mark Gatiss' New Adventure novel *Nightshade*, at any rate) is more debatable. Various researchers like David Howe, Stephen James Walker and Andrew Pixley have pored over the early production documents and the only mention of *Quatermass* is in a list of previous science fiction shows.

Ten years ago, I wrote an article for the fanzine *Matrix* that tried to argue that *Doctor Who* fans had overstated the case that *Quatermass* was a particular influence on *Doctor Who*. There were points of comparison, certainly, but a lot of the things fans held up as clear 'homage' to Kneale's work were often little more than standard tropes of horror stories, and the various stories from the seventies that claimed human development was influenced by aliens often bore far more resemblance to Von Daniken's bestseller *Chariots of the Gods?* or the monolith from *2001: A Space Odyssey* than anything else. It's easy to spot things from some *Doctor Who* stories that are a bit like things in *Quatermass*, but they tend to be rather generic: men watching meteorites on radar screens, or chasing through refineries where alien processes are secretly at work. There are things that seem to have far more of a direct influence - Dan Dare, HG Wells, James Bond (if nothing else, a quick comparison of prose styles reveals Terrance Dicks is a fan of Fleming). One giveaway is that there's very rarely such a thing as a 'mad scientist' in Kneale's world. Scientists can be driven mad as their exploration uncovers some deep horror as the truth, but scientists are bastions of the rational, and almost always heroic figures in his work.

Quatermass and *Doctor Who* are both interesting for merging supernatural horror with a scientific explanation - other stories by Kneale like *The Road* and *The Stone Tape* were essentially classic ghost stories given a scientific sheen. But that's not to say that one led directly to the other.

Rather than look back, perhaps we should see how Nigel Kneale's work might influence *Doctor Who* in the future. The production team of the new TV series has learned a great deal about the mechanics of making telefantasy in the early twenty-first century, and they fully admit they're learning, for example, about how to use CGI to tell a story. While even the soaps have small CG budgets nowadays, this isn't a skill many makers of British TV drama have had to worry too much about - it's no coincidence that most of the Mill's previous work was in movies, documentaries and adverts. While critics of CGI have claimed that the greats of the past wouldn't have used it, that's clearly nonsense - Orson Welles and David Lean, say, used every special effects trick available. Nigel Kneale made imaginative use of new technology.

179

In terms of the writing, the great lesson that Russell T Davies seems to have learned is to make the stories scarier. This doesn't mean blood and overt violence - leave that to *Torchwood*! - but just deeply unnerving things. The clockwork man under the bed isn't something that scares grown ups, but it's terrifying for children, and it's not hard to imagine that when today's eight year olds are grumpy gits my age, they'll be fondly remembering the sleepness nights that image gave them. Kneale excelled in scary stuff going on just offscreen - the rats in an episode of *Beasts* are heard, never seen, and it makes the story claustrophobic, rather than one where they occasionally cut to stock footage of rats. There's a brutal murder in *The Year of the Sex Olympics* that happens (just about) entirely off screen. Kneale had a very strong visual sense, a very strong sense of how television was made, but he was also a genius at knowing what he didn't need to depict.

With a championing of science (it's been light on mad scientists, with only one so far) and a sense of horror as individuals confront the fantastic, the new *Doctor Who* series might not be quite in the footsteps of Nigel Kneale, but it's on the right track. Nigel Kneale didn't like *Doctor Who* - he objected to it scaring children (which it still does), but also that it was 'a producer's idea', meaning one to fill a demographic and a timeslot rather than anything writer-driven. The new series, of course, is very much seen as being 'authored' by Russell Davies, and the power the success of the show has given the production team within the BBC could well be the most remarkable of its achievements.

Perhaps what the show needs is to take a little bit more - the sense of 'warning' that Kneale's work often provides, the idea that we need to remain vigilant against superstition. Some of the youngest members of *Doctor Who*'s audience will live to see the twenty-second century, and it would be nice to see the show act as a primer for living in an age where cloning, men on Mars and possibly great environmental disruption take place. The ambition Kneale demonstrates, the way he can spin-a story from a simple, powerful idea - *The Road* is a great example, and deserves tracking down rather than me spoiling it here. Anyone who's interested in writing for television could learn a thing or two from reading one of Nigel Kneale's scripts. His influence on *Doctor Who* may be indirect, but he understood that television could be scary, ambitious and relevant - three words that ought to be watchwords for any *Doctor Who* story.

Who's Next

From Enlightenment #137, December 2006

In the USA, Fox News thinks there's a 'War on Christmas' - if such a thing was fought in the UK, then *Doctor Who* has already won it this year. The *Radio Times* cover (which I've talked about before) must be a sure thing - not only is the centrepiece of the Christmas Day BBC1 schedule the *Doctor Who* special, but *Torchwood*'s finale and the Sarah Jane Smith pilot will also be on in the same week. Every toyshop is brimming with *Doctor Who* stuff - my local Toys 'R' Us has a huge *Doctor Who* display in the space usually reserved for that month's big movie. Significantly, a lot of the stores' Christmas television adverts mention *Doctor Who* products.

It's very tempting to see this as the peak. It's hard to believe now that there were jitters that the show might take a hit from Christopher Eccleston leaving. Fans have perhaps underestimated how many people were watching new *Who* for Rose - significantly, both BBC1 and main rivals ITV1 have a Billie Piper series as part of their Christmas lineups. Freema Agyeman has a deeply unenviable task, and if this series doesn't hit the heights, fairly or not, she's going to get the blame as the most visible difference between Series Two and Three.

Doctor Who's main problem now is where it can possibly go next, how it can do anything but go down. It won every award it was nominated for - except, perversely, some of the special effects and other craft ones. Ratings, audience share and Audience Appreciation all maintained (or even slightly improved) on Series One's fantastic results. It's changed the debate, it means the BBC now have a '*Doctor Who* slot' on Saturday night. The OK performance of *Robin Hood* (about five or six million a week, audience appreciation in the 70s) which the BBC would have been delighted with two years ago, demonstrates just how hard it is to get eight, nine or ten million people watching. *Torchwood*'s audience has settled down from the literally unprecedented levels the premiere got, but it's still beating first-run *Lost* on satellite.

Doctor Who is the best drama on British television, it will continue to win awards. Paul Cornell picked up a Hugo on behalf of Steven Moffat for *The Empty Child*... he should have just asked them to save the bother and hand over the one for *The Girl in the Fireplace* while he was there. It wins, or it's a travesty. But the year *Doctor Who* doesn't win a BAFTA, or the week ITV actually win the timeslot, and that hasn't happened yet, but will, it looks like failure. The papers ran the story '*Who* ratings down' this year... and, of course, didn't retract it when the ratings, defying all TV gravity, picked up almost straight away. The Daleks and Cybermen were both huge draws the first, second and third times... will they really be on the fourth and fifth? (That's not a spoiler, by the way, but... c'mon.) Does the show have another 'name' baddy that could draw people in (again, I've talked about that in a previous column)? And could there be any sweeter irony that Michael Grade left the BBC this November (anniversary week!) with the papers citing *Doctor Who* as the great BBC achievement of his time in office?

The positive thing is that the enthusiasm for *Doctor Who* seems to be broad-based and genuine, not the product of hype. The BBC have, remarkably, marketed it very well, but as countless movies (and, to some extent, *Robin Hood*) have discovered, you can 'penetrate' all you want with a marketing campaign, it doesn't mean that people will watch or buy the toys. *Doctor Who* figures are everywhere at the moment, including supermarket shelves... but not for long. People genuinely are buying the action figures, the Cyberman voice changers and the remote control K9 (the last of those aren't cheap, either - £40). It feels like parents choosing to buy their kids those toys, rather than being caught up in a *Jingle All the Way*-mass hysteria that there will be shortages and their kids will miss out. It's affection, not a fad. Already we now that there's going to be a market in 2025 for New Who retro stuff. If we don't already, that's going to be the point where we old time fans feel decrepit.

So... what's left? Is the only way down?

No.

There's another challenge for Russell Davies, now, and perhaps the most emotionally difficult of all. He has to start thinking about the succession.

Russell T Davies has been the powerhouse for the revival, literally the reason the BBC brought it back, and the creative force that has reinterpreted something in a way that's kept the vast majority of fans happy, made the series a media darling, a show that can win BAFTAs and Hugos in the same year, given it mass appeal and made it bigger than *Harry Potter*... and oh my God, can you imagine anyone typing those sentences with a straight face even on the morning that *Rose* was due to premiere?

But he won't be there forever. Rumour has it that he wants to quit after Series Four (the fact that the BBC haven't formally commissioned Series Four would make that an incredibly presumptive thing for any other British TV producer to think, but... well, it's about the safest bet you could make that we'll see Series Four). The BBC must be very tempted to call it quits after that. That would be 55 episodes, and there is currently only one adult non-soap BBC drama running that has reached that tally, *Silent Witness* (they're making a new series of *Waking the Dead*, and that will pass the milestone in 2007). *Who* has already had a good innings. But *Doctor Who* can last indefinitely, if someone of the same calibre is the executive producer. There aren't many, but they exist. Paul Abbott is the obvious one - he's a fan, he almost wrote for the first season, and the BBC would kill to get him working for them on something like this. Steven Moffat and his wife Sue Vertue (a respected TV producer) would be a dream team. Casting the net further, Joss Whedon's currently writing comics and not making a *Wonder Woman* movie. There are candidates.

Doctor Who feels like Russell Davies' baby, now. And that's to *Who* fans fully aware of the forty-year heritage. Imagine what it must be like being Russell Davies - it must be almost impossible for him to imagine handing it over. There must also be the great fear of anyone handing over to a successor: that they'll do better than you did. Plenty of company directors or restaurant owners or magazine editors or presidents must be quietly pleased when the next guy drops the ball. It's far easier to imagine a Jackson-less *Hobbit* movie than a Davies-less new *Who*. He's turned the show into the most authored piece of television we have in the UK. The most obvious successor would be a 'steady as she goes' candidate who tried to replicate the winning formula, but it would be a pale imitation - the trick with Russell Davies' stuff has always been in seeing what he can get away with.

But that's his job now - find and anoint a successor who's equal to or better than him. His legacy shouldn't be 55 episodes, it should be a *Doctor Who* that's set up to still be running when kids watching don't quite believe that their parents were actually there the night when the Doctor first met Rose.

Canon 2.0

From Enlightenment #141, October 2007

I've been thinking about *Doctor Who* and canon... no, no... come back. I think I've got something new to say.

While the online debates tend to go over the same ground - in a nutshell, someone asks if the books are canon, someone says 'no', someone says 'well I count them in my personal canon', someone says 'personal canon' is a contradiction in terms, someone says the production team has never ruled on it and there's no consensus because there's no ultimate authority, and someone suggests that there ought to be - the fact that the question is debated so often indicates that the canon debate does matter to people, even if about one in five people apparently hasn't noticed there's only one 'n' in the word.

In the olden days, the battle lines were simple enough - most of the people who liked the books thought they were canon, most of the people who didn't thought they 'didn't count' or 'weren't real *Doctor Who*'. The debate was old when the Internet was half its present size - in 1996 I armed a spaceship in *Cold Fusion* with 'cannon threads', and I think the joke was an old one even then.

But now there's a new impetus to the question - new fans who've come to *Doctor Who* to discover that there are hundreds of novels and audios out there, and keen to find out things about the Doctor's past and Gallifrey. The books dealt with these surprisingly rarely, but always seemed to add big things when they did. If new fans like the tenth Doctor and want to find out stuff about Gallifrey, should they 'count' the books?

On the Sci-Fi Board, when answering questions about the books, posters frequently refer to the non TV stuff as 'fan fic'. Clearly, whatever you think about the books or BFs, that's not an accurate description - or at the very least there should be some way of distinguishing between the professional, licenced stuff and the not. You wouldn't call, say, the *Star Trek* animated series or the novelisations of the movies 'fan fic'.

Likewise, someone - a dullard with plenty of time on their hands, pre-sumably - has gone through every single *Doctor Who* Wikipedia entry and added a line about 'the canonicity of spin-offs is uncertain'. But, to me, a *Doctor Who* 'spin-off' is a series that's not *Doctor Who* that uses char-acters who were in *Doctor Who*. There are literally over a dozen of those - *Faction Paradox*, the Dalek *TV21* strip, good old Benny (who's been around now as long as *Doctor Who* had when he met K9) and so on - but the NAs, say, aren't a 'spin-off'. They're *Doctor Who*, but in another media.

I see why 'fan fic' and 'spin-off' are being used there - as shorthand for 'something that's not the TV series'. But the terms don't work, because they're words that already mean something else in a *Doctor Who* context. The body of work of Doctor Who And Related Literature sprawls, and lumping everything that's not the TV series - from the Cushing movies to *Torchwood* to *Damaged Goods* to something on a website about Nyssa getting it on with Giles from *Buffy* - as 'spin-off' isn't very useful.

The 'canon debate' is long and nuanced. But when someone who's started watching *Doctor Who* this year on Sci-Fi, say, asks 'are the New Adventures canon?', they're looking for a simple answer. The simple answer, of course, is 'the BBC approved them, but even the people in the BBC aware of the canon debate are fundamentally disengaged from it'. Which falls into the category of being true but unhelpful.

An analogy... one that's not terribly contentious in the UK or Canada.

Creationists use the fact that evolution is 'a theory' as proof that it's somehow just an idea, untestable, something vague, unproven and up for grabs. Because one of the everyday definitions of the word 'theory' is just that. But, as Richard Dawkins and others point out, a scientific 'theory' isn't just a vague idea someone's had, it's more like a legal case, with evidence, defence, debate, testing, review, appeals over time as new evidence comes to light and so on. The problem Creationists identify is with the word 'theory', not with the case for evolution.

Dawkins, when faced with the 'evolution, it's just a theory' line came up with an elegant reply: 'evolution is a fact, as that word is commonly understood'.

While far more interested in entertaining their audience than sticking rigidly to every detail established in every previous story, the current makers of *Doctor Who* on TV are aware of the novels, a great many of them contributed to the books, the books introduced and developed ideas that the TV series used or adapted. The books (and audios and comic strips, but let's keep it simple) are part of the resources and past that the TV series now draws on.

So, to pick just one example: a major plot point of *The Christmas Invasion* is that the TARDIS translates through telepathy and it only works when the Doctor's nearby and part of the circuit. There's nothing, at all, in the old TV show to suggest that. But that's what's established in the New Adventures - there's a section of *Set Piece* that makes it explicit, for example, and the book has a scene very like the one in *The Christmas Invasion*. This isn't a case of Russell Davies consciously lifting a specific bit from one of the books, or even 'quoting', as he did with the Oncoming Storm or kronkburger references. It's that he 'knows' that's how the TARDIS translates, and built a scenario around that. In the same way that the makers of *Logopolis* 'knew' that the thing that disguises the TARDIS is 'the chameleon circuit', even though the term had never been used on TV before. It's very possible that neither writer realised they were doing something that hadn't been established on TV before.

The new TV series is, in many ways and in not all of them coincidentally, more 'like' the books than it is like the old TV series. There have been apparent contradictions between the books and the new TV series... but no more than there have been contradictions between the old TV series and the new TV series, and nothing fundamental.

Or, in other words, the books are treated in exactly the same way as the old TV series is - as grist to the mill, as a potential source of ideas.

So... here's my thought: while it's a nuanced debate, and some of the details are up for grabs, the novels are canon 'as that word is commonly understood'.

Peak Practice

From Enlightenment #144, March 2008

That has to be the peak, surely?

The immense ratings (the second most-watched piece of television in the UK last year, with an audience that was proportionately as large as the Super Bowl audience in the US). The media saturation, helped along by Kylie, that - among many other things - saw the *Times* newspaper wish its readership a 'Merry Foxydoctormas'. The shops full of - and having to constantly replenish - *Doctor Who* books, toys, games and trinkets.

Christmas Day 2007 has to have been the point when *Doctor Who* reached its zenith.

I have begun to wonder if I'm in some sort of Sam Tyler / Pincher Martin-style lurid waking dream where my passing thoughts turn into great clunking concrete laden with symbolic meaning. How else to explain that on Christmas Eve, I was in a queue of ten shoppers in WH Smiths and I was the only one that wasn't buying a *Doctor Who* thing? Every way I turn, there's *Doctor Who* - there are literally walls of *Doctor Who* toys in Toys 'R' Us and the *Doctor Who Annual* was one of the ten bestselling books in the UK last year. *Doctor Who* is the most downloaded BBC show. Go to the cinema and there are trailers for it. Turn on *Top Gear* or *Extras* and there's suddenly some *Doctor Who*. There's even Peter Davison joining in. There's more *Doctor Who* in the external world now than there is in my brain. And that's a lot of *Doctor Who*.

I went to see the *Doctor Who* exhibition in Manchester. It was packed, but that's not the anecdote: on the tram back home I suddenly heard the old ladies in the seat behind say 'and of course that Martha's moved over to *Torchwood*'. Its universal popularity can be summed up most efficiently by noting that it's the first show to win a Hugo and TV Quick Award in the same week. Luckily, to break up the sheer relentless *Who*ness, there's also *Torchwood* and the frankly marvellous *Sarah Jane Adventures*.

It's not just that it's *Doctor Who*, it's that it's *my Doctor Who*. Honestly, guys at Cardiff, having Kylie Minogue's name flying past in the opening credits and a cameo would have done me. The maid's uniform and knee-length kinky boots were... well, I was going to say 'excessive', but I think 'thank you' might be more appropriate. I saw *The Shakespeare Code* with a roomful of Shakespearean scholars. And you know what? They *did* punch the air. What can they possibly do for me next? Here's my number one wish: they should make *Human Nature* for television, with all the reverence and craft of a serious literary adaptation.

Oh.

But we have to face the fact that Christmas Day might have been the peak. Not because of gloom and pessimism, just that when more people watch *Doctor Who* than watched every soccer game or every 2007 episode of *Coronation Street* (more people than watched anything, at all, that Michael Grade has commissioned since he took over ITV, schadenfreude fans) and when an episode of *Doctor Who* becomes a bona fide brings-the-nation-together event... well, where else is there to go? It'll be huge and fun and great and the golden age isn't over... but last Christmas was the high water mark. Yeah?

There's only one thing that makes me hesitate: that I've thought that before, half a dozen times. Nothing could beat the excitement of *Rose / Dalek / The Parting of the Ways / The Christmas Invasion...* the list goes on. The show didn't just survive the departure of the incredible Christopher Eccleston, it went from strength to strength. While I knew I would miss Jackie more than I missed Rose, my nagging fear was that a lot of people were watching for Billie, but that vanished when people - civilians! - started telling me how much they liked Martha.

So where will they go next?

I don't know. The danger, as with any long-running series, is to change but not to kill the golden goose. *Doctor Who* has been immensely adept at this so far, but it's led a charmed life. A lesser production team would have fallen into self-parody or would just remake their greatest hits. Their main problem might well be an audience who've got used to miracles, who mistake the symphonic structure of the series, with themes and echoes, as a show repeating itself.

Realising that having a new regular character shakes things up, they've engineered that this year, rather than have it forced on them. They may be starting to creak a little under the weight of their mythology - but, then, if they were pandering to that (or driven at all by merchandise), they'd have brought the Cybermen back last year. This is not a lazy show. The series dips when it's not ambitious and trying something new. That's always been the case. What's fascinating about the new series is how they've gradually eased an audience that used to think *Neighbours* was a bit 'out there', to a point where there's nothing more natural than them watching Kylie and a little red conker man being chased by angel robots around a spaceship that looks like the *Titanic*. As the episode said, Christmas is the time of year when, traditionally, giant alien ships crash into London.

The fourth series may be a little overshadowed by the 'gap year', the sense that the 'specials' are next year. That's an interesting way to shake things up, for both the people making and for the people watching. It also allows Russell Davies and David Tennant to try a couple of other things.

2009 won't exactly be a drought, though - it's a year with four TV movies and six months of *Sarah Jane* and *Torchwood*.

The Sarah Jane Adventures has been the unsung triumph of the year, for my money. A clever fusion of seventies kids science fiction and the more soapy stuff kids are used to now. And, unlike *Doctor Who*, it's got a chance to change. A twelve year old who watched *Rose* is fifteen or sixteen this year. It would be nice to see *Sarah Jane* grow up with its juvenile leads. It's a superb kids show now, but the prospect of it growing up with its audience (like *Harry Potter* sort of did) and evolving into a show about older teenagers - a real 'British *Buffy*' - is really something to look forward to.

Torchwood Reviews: "Meat" and "Adam"

From Enlightenment #145, May 2008

There were a number of peculiar things about the first season of *Torchwood*. The most glaring was that it was a show built around Captain Jack - a carefree, reckless and above all else *fun* character, but who was here portrayed as brooding, dark, conflicted and generally *Angel*-like. 'We need someone to play a troubled, subdued character... get me John Barrowman!'. If the first season of *Torchwood* knew what it wanted to be, it had a very odd way of showing it. While the episodes were able to surprise, it was often because the pay-off ignored the set-up, or because the regulars acted completely inconsistently from one scene to the next. It was a show that managed to have one episode which genuinely seemed torn about whether it was *Thunderbirds* or *Friday the 13th*, where the most plausible, character-led, grounded moment was a fight between a cyborg and a pterodactyl.

The second season has calmed down a lot and sorted out the regular characters. It's got everyone bantering and being a bit more self aware. Just by doing that, it's become a very solid show, one that's a lot more fun and a lot less frustrating.

Meat is a good example of what *Torchwood* is like, now. Someone's selling mysterious meat, and it turns out it's alien. The team tracks the source of the meat to a big warehouse... which is filled with a giant blobby alien that regenerates the flesh that's carved off it. The team is very sympathetic to the beast, which breaks loose and they have to kill it. It sounds odd to say it, but the plotting is a little generic - this could easily be an *X-Files* or *Angel* story. The regular cast make the story work, particularly Gwen's partner Rhys, who's right in the middle of events because he runs a van hire company and the bad guys are using his vans; Owen, who's tasked with euthanising the creature; and Jack, the one who empathises most with it. The bloodstreaked walls and aprons get across the horror of the situation nicely.

There's little wrong with the episode, but it highlights one problem that the show hasn't worked out, yet - what people think about the alien stuff. With *The X-Files*, it was very clear: the aliens were out there, glimpsed in folklore, covered up by governments. Contact with them was rare, weird, dangerous. There was always a clear line between the everyday and the uncanny, and Mulder and Scully were guarding that line. Their fight was entirely secret. *Buffy* and *Angel* had a more public model, but their demons were more like criminals - either gangs who hung out away from regular people, or the loner types who look just like you and me. The regular people of Sunnydale sort of knew they were there, often close to home - like the suburban drug problem - but kept their heads down. Buffy and her pals were the neighbourhood watch. And, as that suggests, the bad guys were usually metaphors or symbols of some real-life problem or anxiety.

In both cases, the shows were genre shows with supernatural elements. *The X-Files* was a detective thriller show, *Buffy* was a teen soap. The key thing was that the ordinary and supernatural were separate things, and that the heroes were between the two worlds, but by day they were at least trying to be perfectly ordinary.

Torchwood's relationship with the supernatural/science fiction stuff is all over the place. Some of that is *Doctor Who*'s fault. *Torchwood* is, technically, set in a Britain where the Master got elected Prime Minister on a 'defence against aliens' platform and it's now traditional for a big spaceship to appear over London at Christmas. There have been more, and more destructive, alien attacks in *Doctor Who*'s London recently than, say, terrorist attacks in ours. So for characters in *Torchwood* to be surprised that aliens exist is about as odd as having an episode of *Spooks* where no one's heard of Al-Qaeda.

The problem is this: are aliens weird in Cardiff or not? The show has it every which way it can, with some people collecting alien artifacts, others incredulous that aliens might even exist. Some people living in Cardiff are still surprised that the Weevils exist, even though there seem to be more Weevils in their city than heterosexuals. It means that the Torchwood team members themselves are often the weirdest thing in the episode, the ones who are most consciously setting themselves apart from the mundane world. The aliens are always blending in, lying low, concealed in some innocuous object... it's the covert ops unit who are the ones crashing around in fancy vehicles and costumes.

It's not just internal logic - if everyone accepts aliens exist, Torchwood just becomes a perfectly sensible specialist law enforcement team - it has implications for the show, and what it's about. This not-thought-throughness affects other areas of the show. The tension between Rhys and Gwen is based, it seems, on the premise that she used to be safe when her job only involved breaking up pub fights and catching armed robbers.

What it boils down to is that *Meat* doesn't really feel 'true'. In modern Britain, it's hard enough selling meat to a pie factory if you're a farmer raising cows and selling them in a cattle market. In *Torchwood*, a man in a hired van shows up with a slab of something unidentified and there's no problem.

It's an entertaining hour of television, but, like *Primeval*, it's not really 'about' anything. Or, rather, it feels like it's about to be about something. If *Meat* had been an *X-Files* episode, it would have concentrated a lot more on the visceral horror of the situation. If it had been a *Buffy* episode, it would have been a satire on the meat industry.

Adam is a much better episode, one that, ironically feels much less generic. Ironically, because it shares the same basic plot as the *Star Trek: The Next Generation* episode *Conundrum* - there's a new member of the 'regular' cast whom our heroes think has always been there, but the audience realise is an infiltrator.

The *Torchwood* episode takes the concept further and deeper than *Conundrum*. That story had Riker and Ro, who normally didn't like each other, going to bed. *Adam* starts with some lovely role reversal like that - literally, Tosh and Owen swap personalities. This is great fun, and the regulars clearly relish playing against type. There is the distinct sense that Burn Gorman is the secret star of the show, and here he's almost ridiculously sweet as a mild-mannered version of Owen.

But we're soon into something much more interesting. We see the Gwen and Rhys relationship stretched and challenged precisely by the side effect of some tiny little alien trick, which makes her forget about him. It's a much more effective way of dramatizing Rhys' fear of 'losing her' than yet another scene where he's moaning as she gets ready to go to work.

... and then there's the Jack stuff: the flashbacks to the fifty-first century (if you see what I mean) and Jack's childhood. Little bits of the character's Secret Backstory that's been hinted at since *The Empty Child*. Again, if you watch a lot of American SF, none of the scenes where the character stands in one of his own memories explaining that this was the day when blah blah is shockingly new or radical. But *Adam* really works as an episode, really gets the character stuff right, gets that mundane/alien divide right.

The second season of *Torchwood* has righted a lot of the wrongs, but there's often a spark missing that prevents the show from being truly great. It still doesn't quite know what it is, it still isn't as down and dirty as it seems to want to be. It needs more episodes like *Adam*, ones that stretch the cast by giving them human things to do while confronting them with clear, clever, alien threats. The most frustrating thing about *Torchwood* is that you know, watching an episode like *Adam*, that this could be the best show on TV.

Let the Backlash Begin

From Enlightenment #146, July 2008

Preface: This article was written the week that Steven Moffat was formally announced as Russell T Davies' successor as producer.

Doctor Who is going to make me rich.

I've been trying to work how for years, but I've finally worked out how to pull it off: I've trademarked the phrase 'Is this really the same Steven Moffat who gave us *Blink*?'. Now, every time anyone uses that phrase on the Internet, they have to pay me a dollar. Canadian, preferably at the moment, but American, Australian, whatever... my earnings forecast for the second quarter of 2010 just rocketed.

I need to stress at the outset that I think Steven Moffat will do a brilliant job. I suppose there's always the risk that he's going to turn out to be Brown to Russell Davies' Blair, and that the wheels will come off within the first year, and then it's novels, audios and podcasts for fifteen years - but I doubt it. Ironically, I think the thing that worries me most - and even this doesn't worry me all that much - is that his episodes have all been so out of the ordinary. They've taken the time travel stuff and done fun, weird things with them. What we've not had from Moffat is an episode like *Smith and Jones*, a template for a straightforward *Doctor Who* adventure that builds things up and shows us. They can't *all* be like Moffat episodes, can they?

Steven Moffat's episodes are marvellous - I mean, that's obvious and neither he or you need me to point that out - but they're working within the rules that Russell Davies has set down. Moffat's been able to squeeze that extra little drop out of the format. That said, his biggest contribution to the show was absolutely central: to get away with the scariness and creepiness in *The Empty Child*, so that Russell Davies added 'terrifying kids' to his list of things a *Doctor Who* episode should do.

Here, the Gordon Brown parallel might be appropriate. People from all over the political spectrum thought Brown would be like Tony Blair but without the 'spin and hype', which they broadly defined as 'the stuff I don't like about Blair'. The policies were good, the argument ran, it was the presentation and implementation that didn't quite work. One might argue that politics *is* presentation and implementation, of course.

Most *Who* fans seem to love the new version but have a couple of reservations. Whatever those reservations are, they seem to think Steven Moffat will sort them out. There certainly seems to be a chunk of fandom who assume that Steven Moffat is going to strip away the list of things they don't like about Russell Davies' era - the gay stuff, mainly, but the 'deus ex machina' stuff, too. Ironically, they picture Moffat flying in, all glowy, and making it all right.

The thing is... anyone who's looking for less flirty innuendo and an end to stories where the Doctor gets surrounded in a shiny special effect, then just makes everything better, should probably not pin their hopes on the writer of *The Doctor Dances*.

Then again, I love the *Who* revival. I love the episodes, but I also love the success, the way it's just become central to British consciousness. One of the things Gordon Brown asked for a couple of months back was 'a national conversation about the issues that people are really talking about' and *The Times* snapped back with 'what people are talking about is how surprised they are that Catherine Tate's good in *Doctor Who*'. On bulletin boards like Outpost Gallifrey, there are dozens of posts from old time fans just delighted that their kids want Daleks for Christmas. Someone has a sig about how he watched *Time Crash* with his son and was able to say 'that's my Doctor' and... I'm man enough to admit I well up at the thought of it. There was a war and we... won. Russell Davies did that. It's a scale of achievement that makes his OBE look a bit stingy, really. He's got the Cardiff connection, so make him Prince of Wales, that's what I say. At the very least, marry him off to Prince William. Perhaps when I imagine Moffat *Who* just being a continuation of Davies *Who*, I'm doing exactly the same thing as the moany RTD-Must-Go types - projecting what I want to see and all my assumptions onto Steven Moffat.

But I also never underestimate just how hard it is to make television. One actor delivers one line wrong, and the whole thing can collapse. Whatever the budget, there's never enough time; there are always moments where you just have to go with what you've got. As I've said before, we've become used to casual miracles with the new *Doctor Who* -

its lowest points are still exciting, funny and scary. And its highs... television is rarely any better.

I'm in America at the moment. I recently watched *Silence in the Library* on Sci-Fi, and just as Dr Moon says 'what you have to understand is that the world of your nightmares is the real one', they flashed up a 'coming next, *Stargate Atlantis*' banner. I struggled to find an analogy that expressed what this was like. Got there in the end: it's like ordering a meal at the Savoy, and having a Michelin starred chef serve it, and just as the Kobe beef melts on your tongue, just as you wash it down with the Yquem, the waiter brings in a chipped saucer with a poo on it and tells you it's for dessert. Last year, Sci-Fi put *Flash Gordon* on afterwards, and amazingly they didn't all die of shame. *Doctor Who* is, consistently, the best made, most ambitious, most surprising, most exciting, funniest, most involving show on television.

Steven Moffat wrote that episode, but it didn't happen independently of Russell Davies, or despite of him. It was Davies, above all, who's carefully moved the general audience along until they can watch a complex, layered, weird story about time travel, virtual realities, alien libraries and murderous shadows and just think it's the most natural thing in the world.

Now Russell Davies has worked his final wonder - he's ensured the succession. The show will survive the loss of Davies, just as it survived the departure of Eccleston and then Piper, just as it will survive the departure of Tennant.

Steven Moffat has inherited the best and worst job in the world. In his *Lying in the Gutters* column, comics journalist Rich Johnston noted that some of the fan reaction to Russell Davies has been a bit like someone watching Ali beat Foreman, then complaining Ali had a pimple. The backlash will start, there will always be fans that moan.

Hence my moneymaking scheme. I invite people to look out for the phrase 'is this really the same Steven Moffat who gave us *Blink*?'. It will first appear when the new companion is cast. Or when Moffat assures an interviewer that, if anything, there will be even more gay characters when he's in charge, or 'betrays' the fans by making an offhand remark about how we're all bonkers in the nut. If every episode was like *Blink*, fans would complain that every episode was like *Blink* - as Chandler noted once in *Friends*, 'I've so many fifties, I can't close my wallet' doesn't actually qualify as a 'problem', but people will complain anyway. The Doctor Moffat casts will be too old, too young, too much like David Tennant, not enough like him... possibly all in the same Internet post.

Underlying it all is a very simple truth: Russell Davies only made it *look* easy. As *Primeval* and *Robin Hood* and even *Torchwood* have demonstrated, even with *Doctor Who* there as a template, it's not easy doing what *Doctor Who* has been doing with Russell Davies in charge. Steven Moffat is going to be magnificent... and that's just as well, because that's what the *Doctor Who* audience take for granted, now.

Doctor Who Special

From Enlightenment #148, November 2008

There are times when *Doctor Who* survived a crisis - the show could easily, and justifiably, have been cancelled in 1966 or 1969. There are times when *Doctor Who* was in the right place to surf a wave and failed to - the 1996 TV movie managed to land on stony ground in *The X-Files*, *Independence Day* and *Buffy* era, by almost willfully failing to be like any of those things, despite *Doctor Who* being like all of them; the books I love so much completely failed to be the new *Harry Potter*.

There's only one point, though, where *Doctor Who* had a great hand and failed to play it, and that was around the twentieth anniversary. It's hard to see what actually happened between the end of 1983 and the end of 1985 as anything but a worst case scenario, because it was all going so well - high ratings, press attention, Longleat, the first home video, a solid set of publications (books and magazine), thriving fandom, blossoming success in North America. It was difficult to be anything other than optimistic.

We can all see now that the seeds of the show's decline were there. In retrospect Colin Baker's probably not miscast, but the sixth Doctor's a huge problem. There's also a reliance on the past, but it's the superficialities of the past - 'bringing back the Sea Devils' for its own sake, for instance, rather than working out what was so great about the Sea Devils that people remembered them from more than a decade ago. It's no coincidence that *Doctor Who* fandom had coalesced at this point - that so many of the 'big name fans' from nowadays had already had things published. The readers of *The Programme Guide*, DWM, *Doctor Who - A Celebration*, the members of DWAS, were all looking back, demanding and expecting the return of 'old friends', forcing *Doctor Who* to look backwards, shackling it to its past.

It's easy to blame fans for the problem. Indeed, it's easier now than ever - the memos that have recently come to light, featured in *The Trial of a Time Lord* DVD set, make it clear that the original 'hiatus' was an across-the-board rethinking of the BBC popular drama budget. It was only after *Doctor Who* fans accused the BBC of singling out their show that Michael Grade singled it out. It's chicken and egg to say whether that's caused by

194

the fans or Grade, the very public fuss backed Grade into a position where he was more and more hostile to the show.

But here's where the fans were right and the BBC were wrong: *Doctor Who* was special. There was a potential there that the BBC were completely blind to, and which other shows that were affected, like *Juliet Bravo* and *District Nurse* just didn't have. The difference is obvious, now. *Doctor Who has huge potential as a franchise.* It was always one of the show's proudest boasts that it was 'shown in over 65 countries', but now we have a better term, one that was in usage by 1983 but only by marketing and advertising specialists: *Doctor Who* was one of television's biggest *brands*.

Doctor Who has always been so far ahead of the curve, it's been almost embarrassing. It was by no means the only show to have tie-in books, annuals and toys, but they appeared very soon after the television show, and have been steady sellers ever since. *Doctor Who* was 'multimedia' in an age when people didn't think of using the term (possibly because Latin was still taught in schools and 'media' is already the plural). The mid-eighties was the dawn of the television era we live in now - shows with an immense afterlife, repeated on cable channels, released endlessly on home video, with a cloud of books and toys and T-shirts around them. *Doctor Who* probably has more 'icons' than any other TV show, from the logo (logos!) and TARDIS on down.

Unfortunately, there was another problem - the BBC weren't equipped to exploit this situation. The BBC is not a commercial organization. *Doctor Who* had always been an exception because it was a BBC show that made money, but this was almost despite the BBC's best efforts. When the show was cancelled, it came to light that *Doctor Who* raised five times more for the BBC than it cost to make. Douglas Adams famously wrote to the BBC pointing this out, and was told that their accountants didn't count things like that - as Adams noted that that was a great argument for getting rid of the accountants, not *Doctor Who*. Unlike Adams' own *Hitchhikers Guide to the Galaxy*, or *Monty Python*, *Doctor Who* had always been an in-house production, put together by staff members, there were no creators who would benefit from entrepreneurial spirit. The exception being Terry Nation, of course, who'd made a fortune from the Daleks. John Nathan-Turner had that spirit, and much good it did him. Play their cards right, and the BBC could have made *Doctor Who* into the franchise that *Star Trek* became in the late eighties. That isn't what happened.

But the accountants were right, in their Vogon logic kind of way, because *Doctor Who*'s success cut against the message the BBC was trying to send. The problem was that the BBC made it their prime goal to keep the licence fee, to resist advertising. 1983 had been the year of a massive Conservative landslide, and the Thatcher government returned with a solid agenda against unions and closed shops, for deregulation, competition, the free market and an end to subsidizing unprofitable businesses. The BBC looked for all the world like a bastion of everything the Tories were against. Grade had been hired from commercial television specifically to counter this threat, to emphasise the unique qualities of the BBC. He cut foreign (American, that is) imported shows from primetime, he introduced *EastEnders* (which is still the only BBC show a lot of older viewers watch). The emphasis was on prestige shows, documentaries, encouraging new talent, and the message was that the BBC was changing and relevant and absolutely had to be funded by the licence fee.

And that's the irony. Any other broadcaster in the world would have jumped at the chance to make a show that brought in five times what it cost to make, was becoming a cult hit in America and which was riding high, beloved, at home. The BBC could have spun it the right way - what ITV show could have inspired a Longleat? They could have forged alliances with PBS in the US and flown the flag for Britain.

1983 saw the beginning of a pattern that would take twenty years to get out of - *Doctor Who* was exactly the show the BBC needed, wanted and talked incessantly about finding, but they just couldn't see it.

I Predict 2013

From Enlightenment #149, January 2009

So... the fiftieth anniversary. Not long now - five years away. Or it's the twenty-fifth anniversary of *Remembrance of the Daleks*, if you really want to feel old.

Five years has always been a long time in *Doctor Who* land. It's almost exactly an 'era', and the changes both on screen and behind the scenes between, say, the fifteenth anniversary story (*The Stones of Blood*) and the twentieth (*The Five Doctors*) and the twenty-fifth (*Silver Nemesis*) are really quite striking.

It's exactly five years since the new series was announced. I think it's safe to say that Russell Davies has exceeded not just the average fanboy's expectation but even the weirdest fans' opium-fuelled visions. Back in 2003, *Scream of the Shalka* looked like the dream ticket. The Russell Davies era isn't exactly over, but it's ending on a high. *Journey's End* was the first-ever episode of *Doctor Who* to finish as the most-watched show of the week, and it had an AI index of 90%. *DWM* readers voted it the top episode of the year, also giving it 90%. The final result: fans and main-stream viewers united, the show at its ratings and creative peak. If any-one had have predicted where we are now, they'd have been laughed out of court.

So it would be a real mug who tried to predict where we'll be by the fiftieth.

Here goes.

I'm assuming the show's still on. That might be the big mistake. As I said a couple of issues back, Russell Davies has only made it look easy. You only need to look at *Primeval*, *Robin Hood* or arguably even *Torchwood* for examples of how talented TV people can fail to quite get things to spark, even with a template to work from. Of all the people in the world, though, the Cardiff production team and Steven Moffat understand best that Russell Davies didn't just happen to be around when *Doctor Who* was successful.

The show would have to make a series of pretty spectacular wrong turns to get killed off before 2013. The only realistic worst case scenario, I think, is that it's turned into *Robin Hood* - a steady performer that's just not catching on like it ought to. The best case scenario is... well... that it's still where it is now. Seriously, when you're the number one show, when Super Bowl-equivalent audiences tune in and it has more appreciative audiences and more awards than any other show, where is there to go? I think, realistically, by 2013 things will have settled down a little. *Doctor Who*'s here to stay, but it's a little more steady than it used to be, not quite as eventful. People have started to take it for granted. Fans like it, but what they're really raving about is BBCi's new feature where you can use CG to create your own original stories from a library of footage and an effects toolbox.

By the fiftieth anniversary, Steven Moffat has overseen as many episodes as Russell Davies. The eleventh Doctor has been and gone. Daniel Radcliffe's still too young to be the twelfth. We know that Moffat hasn't shown much apparent interest in *Torchwood* and the *Sarah Jane* youngsters will be comfortably in their twenties. I suspect the spin-off shows have gone. I imagine that *DWM* is still there, much the same and one of the few magazines that's not been affected by the Internet. I imag-ine that there's an action figure for virtually every TV character since 1963 and they've announced the Benny figure. On-demand printing, electronic books and home printers that can fabricate bound books have meant a proliferation in small presses generally, and *Doctor Who* books specifically. Fans are buying season sets for the classic series on Tu Ray, the successor to Blu-Ray. Big Finish announce that they've dropped physical CDs in favour of downloads.

In 2012, whether we admitted it or not, we wiped a tear away when David Tennant donned the costume for the first time in years so that he could light the Olympic Flame. Sure, he's put on a lot of weight, but he's still a fan favourite. Reaction to the news that he and Russell Davies had been lured back to write *The Four Doctors* was more mixed - while everyone on Who Kloud agrees that the Russell Davies era was the golden age and the show's a shadow of its former self, what Davies said in *Writer's Tale III* still rankles. Now we know exactly why Eccleston left, we can see why his return for the special isn't a problem. There's a worry among the River Singers that Davies will settle the Rose Question one way or another. The rumour is that the anniversary special brings back Gallifrey and that McGann makes a cameo appearance.

There you go: a cut out and keep guide to the world of 2013. If history is any guide, the only thing we can say for sure is that it's impossible to say where *Doctor Who* will be in five years time. I'm pretty confident that fans will be arguing whether the books are canon in 2013 - actually, I'm pretty confident that will happen even if the direst 2012 apocalyptic predictions come true and that after the Mayan calendar ends, humanity is reduced to a population of twelve people in mud huts. Beyond that... well, I'm looking forward to finding out.

Historical Note: My predictive powers can be summed up this way - I said Daniel Radcliffe would still be too young to play the Doctor in 2013. Between writing that and the column being printed, Matt Smith was cast. He's the exact age Radcliffe will be in 2013.

WRITING THE EYELESS

People often ask me for advice about writing *Doctor Who* books.

These questions break down into two categories, really - the first is a practical one, specifically about the *Doctor Who* novels: 'Who do I write to at the BBC? What do they want? What's the secret to getting commissioned? What's the appropriate level of bribe?'. The harsh truth of the matter is that the BBC aren't looking for new writers at the moment. They return, unread, any unsolicited submissions they get. The secret of my success with *The Eyeless*? I don't know. I've written a fair few *Doctor Who* books in the past, and I'd let the BBC know years ago that I'd be happy to do so again, but hadn't had any real contact with them for ages until Justin Richards (the Creative Consultant of the *Doctor Who* books) phoned me up out of the blue. So the only advice I can offer at the moment is 'sit by your phone and wait for Justin Richards to ring'. Not terribly helpful, sorry.

There is a second set of questions, and they boil down to 'how do you write a novel?'. People are very interested in the general process. I suspect this is because of that old expression 'everyone has a novel in them'. I don't necessarily think everyone does really have a novel in them - on my darker days, I wonder if some published novelists do - but I think it's certainly an area of creative expression, and having a way of expressing yourself creatively is valuable. Particularly if, like me, you can't really draw, dance, sing or play an instrument. And lots of novels get published every year, and someone's writing them.

One thing that has surprised me as a writer is how many of the techniques and tricks that can be used in one sort of story can be used in another. I'll explain the sort of heuristics that I use. You can trust this advice, because I know fancy-schmancy words like 'heuristics' and 'schmancy'.

Before I really start wibbling away, I should probably admit that the best practical advice I can give anyone who wants to improve their writing is to read this book: *The Creative Writing Coursebook: Forty Authors Share Advice and Exercises for Fiction and Poetry* (2001, ISBN: 978-0333782255).

Now... one 'how to' book a lot of people tend to end up mentioning is Robert McKee's *Story: Substance, Structure, Style and the Principles of*

Screenwriting (1997, ISBN: 978-0060391683). That's a great book and it's a good read... but it's mainly about how to write a Hollywood movie. It's a little like going on a bodybuilding course with Arnold Schwarzenegger, when what you really need when you're starting out is a bit of walking and perhaps a swim a couple of times a week. For us mortals, McKee's book is probably better as a tool for analysing the formulae of American cinema than as a place to find hints and tips to improve our own writing. It's cool to learn stuff like that the twenty-third minute is often the crucial one for a traditional Hollywood film, though.

(The twenty-third minute was the traditional place to put the moment when the Protagonist of the story is presented with The Call to Adventure. In other words, you spend the first twenty-two minutes showing us the everyday life of the main characters and establishing what the status quo is... then the hero gets a chance to change it. In the twenty-third minute of *Star Wars*, Luke sees Leia's message; in *Back to the Future* it's when Marty sees the time machine for the first time. The hero doesn't leap into action even then, at first he (almost always) decides to stay home because... well, buy McKee's book to find out. After you've checked all your movie DVDs to see what happens in the twenty-third minute, of course.)

The *Coursebook* has all sorts of exercise and insights. It's a much more practical and everyday than McKee's if you're just starting out, and is based on the UEA creative writing course. It was co-edited by Paul Magrs, who by an amazing coincidence has also written - amongst many other things - *Doctor Who* books like *Sick Building*, *The Scarlet Empress* and *Mad Dogs and Englishmen*.

The Synopsis

So... what's it take to get a *Doctor Who* book, specifically, commissioned? The guidelines are deceptively simple. In no particular order:

1. A tenth Doctor book should be between 50,000 and 55,000 words long. You have to be able to write it in six months, perhaps less.

2. It can't feature any old *Doctor Who* monsters or anything like that. Not even stuff from the new series.

(No exceptions, no excuses - Virgin used to say this in their writers' guidelines, too, and apparently about half of the submissions they got started something like, 'I know you said no old monsters, but when you read my book, *Valeyard of the Daleks*, you're sure to make an exception.' They never did make that exception. The BBC want you to come up with your own ideas. Yes, there have been authors allowed to bring back old monsters - but not many, and never with their first book.)

3. You'd always be told which companion the Doctor would be travelling with.

4. Like the TV series, the audience for the *Doctor Who* books includes children these days. When you're coming up with your story, bear that in mind. As a rule of thumb, the book should feature nothing unsuitable for an intelligent twelve year old.
(It's safe to say that this is the source of most confusion and consternation among fans, particularly the fans of the New Adventures and Eighth Doctor Adventures, which were often pitched at adult fans. In the end, this is pretty much the easiest instruction to follow.)

5. Your book has to be completely standalone - it can't be the sequel to a previous story, or just the first book of a trilogy, or just setting something up. Imagine that, for some of the audience, this is the very first *Doctor Who* story your reader has ever seen or read.
What the editors are looking for is a 1000 word synopsis of your novel (that's about two sides of single-spaced A4 paper). The purpose of the synopsis is to give a detailed breakdown of the story, and to get across the flavour of your book.
Hopefully you've read that last paragraph and think it sounds a bit tricky. That's because it really is quite tricky. It's an art, not a science, and every author approaches it differently. For now, think of it this way... this is your one chance. You have to come up with something that, in a thousand words, is - all by itself - enough to persuade someone to commission the book. A good way of thinking about this is 'if I handed my synopsis to another author, would they be able to write the book from it?'.
Now, what I've done here is lay out the guidelines I was given. There were no sealed orders to be kept away from the eyes of muggles or whatever. You've been told what I was told.
I already know what most people trying to write a synopsis will get wrong. The guidelines are very simple, but people will ignore one or more of them. Say, for the purpose of the exercise, that you're asked to use Donna as a companion. Someone, somewhere has decided they don't like Donna, so they'll use Martha. Well... send that into Justin, he'd reject it out of hand. Or, if he was feeling kind, ask you to rewrite it for Donna. Someone's decided that they're doing it for fun, so they've put the Daleks in it... well, again, instant rejection. Or, if the idea's great, a very swift email saying 'try doing the same story, but with new monsters'. If

it was a good Dalek story, that should be almost impossible.

The rules are transparent, and non-negotiable. If you find yourself negotiating with them, you're doing something wrong.

These days, it's never been easier to be a writer - you don't even have to set up your own blog, just comment on someone else's. What's more difficult is to be *read*. Writing a novel isn't a thought experiment. It's a series of concrete choices. You decide to do one thing, not to do ten others. The end result isn't a vague set of ideas about what your story should be, it's the story. Which is great... because the great enemy of the writer is the idea that writing is what you are, not what you do. You wouldn't call yourself a plumber if you had vague ambitions one day to do some plumbing. You're a writer if you write.

The best hint I can give if you're coming up with any story - try to come up with a really strong, simple, central idea and then try building on that. *Father's Day*, for example: Rose realises that if she can go back in time, she can save her father's life. *Dalek*: someone has a single Dalek locked up in their basement. These stories don't write themselves, not a bit of it, but straight away you can see the possibilities, you can see the potential for drama. You can already see that saving Pete Tyler is going to have consequences that Rose hasn't foreseen and picture the moment when that Dalek gets free.

Try to play around a little, bring your own ideas to the story. There's no point saying 'oh, I want to do a story just like the ones where the Doctor met Charles Dickens and Shakespeare and Agatha Christie but with [insert name of another writer]', because Mark Gatiss and Gareth Roberts already did that. If they want to hire someone garethrobert-sesque, they already have a number to call.

What's the synopsis for, you ask? Well... the rules are different when you're writing for a series with lots of different authors, particularly one based on a TV series that the books are running alongside. If you're an established author writing your own standalone book, with your own characters and so on, your publisher probably won't require you to write a synopsis.

But *The Eyeless* is one of three *Doctor Who* books that came out on the same day, and that's the day after a television episode. It's the thirtysomethingth book of the range. The tenth Doctor books aren't a 'series' like the New Adventures and eighth Doctor books, which told an ongoing story, instead they're all self-contained adventures... but they are all part of a range, and lots of people read them all.

The synopsis is a quick way to make sure that the stories are all sufficiently different. In a series that's been running as long as *Doctor Who*, it's very easy to come up with an historical character or setting or type of monster that's been in a story before (it's harder not to, at times). All series and genres have formulae and only tell certain types of stories. *Doctor Who* is a great deal more flexible than most (Paul Cornell once said 'the format is there's no format'), but I don't think I'm being massively controversial when I say that there are some old stalwarts - the alien invasion; the base under siege; the planet that seems nice but is secretly ruled by aliens; the everyday object that turns deadly as part of the invasion plans; a shipwrecked alien having to kill to survive. In any given year, the Doctor will face evil insects, evil robots and aliens disguised as people. There will be stories set in the past, present and future. It's the rules.

Individual writers, though, won't know what the other writers are up to. Not at first. Now, obviously part of my job is to come up with something... well, let's be polite and call it 'original'. It's not original in the true sense of the word - it's more like coming up with something that you assume no one else will be doing at the moment. If the editor has a synopsis he can say things like 'don't end it with a big shoot out, a lot of books recently have done the same' or something like that.

Once the book is commissioned, the synopsis is very useful to the various marketing and sales people. The cover has to be designed while the book is still being written, so the artist has to work from the synopsis.

There may be people - other writers, even - who read that and think that novelists shouldn't be worried about commercial stuff. Surely, they say, novelists are artists and should be free range and organic and dancing around meadows, and so what I've just described makes me the writing equivalent of a battery hen. No wonder these books end up in supermarkets.

Well, they're wrong for any number of reasons, but let's just pick one: once it's been approved, the synopsis actually frees me from all the 'commercial stuff'. I can get on with my writing, confident that all the marketing and publicity and editorial people know what they'll be getting and are happy with it. That's all sorted out before I've written a word my readers will read.

But I also think there are at least two obvious advantages to having a synopsis whatever you're writing. I think new and aspiring writers should at least try writing a synopsis before they set out trying to write a novel.

Firstly, it's much, much easier to change a synopsis than a novel. This is obviously true physically - if you write and rewrite and edit 10,000 words, then throw it away and write another 10,000 words, that all takes time. Weeks, at least. But I think the main advantage is an emotional one: you can get very fond of your writing. There's a bit of description you really love, or a joke, or a character... but that section of the book isn't working. Instead of biting the bullet and throwing it away and starting again, you get the urge to tinker and juggle things around and rework. It becomes all too easy to throw good money after bad.

It's very hard to get emotionally attached to a synopsis. The ending doesn't work? Come up with a different one. In the end, you're changing a couple of sentences, not a couple of chapters. And the prose is usually pretty functional.

Secondly, it's easier to see the problems. Novels are big and complex and take months to write. You make thousands of little decisions, all the time, and it's very easy to end up drifting a little off course. Sometimes you'll end up in a more interesting place - often, though, you'll just be getting lost.

But even before you set off, if you have the plot laid out in front of you, you can see where the problems are likely to be. There are always weak moments. Bits where you write 'she decides to trust the Doctor' when there's no real reason for her to do that other than you need them to work together now, or 'the Doctor suddenly reveals that', where what you're really saying is that the Doctor doesn't earn the knowledge, he's kind of known it all along.

Top tip: when you're plotting anything at all, if the word 'suddenly' appears, you're probably doing something wrong.

The trick isn't always to eliminate plot holes, it's often to understand where they are and hide them. Authors use the same basic trick as stage magicians - misdirection. Look at my right hand. My right hand is doing something really interesting with a handkerchief, ooh ooh, look at my right hand. While you're busy looking at that, my left hand is slipping the playing card into your pocket. Telling a story is exactly the same sort of thing - controlling and limiting the information the audience is receiving. Getting you to ask the wrong question while withholding the one piece of information you really, really need to see what's really happening.

There's a massive plot hole in the greatest movie of all time, *Star Wars*. A stupid one. One that defies all logic. One that you've probably never noticed (although the writer of the radio version did and tried to plug it). Our heroes depart from the Death Star and Princess Leia says that the escape was too easy, that they're clearly being tracked. Then she says... let's go to the Rebel base. The one that the Imperials have spent the whole movie looking for and have no other way of locating. They lead the Death Star to Yavin. And know that's exactly what they're doing. Which is pretty dumb.

Now, George Lucas is a genius. He distracts the audience with the space battle, the mourning for Ben, Han teasing Luke about Leia. That bit of the movie works brilliantly as a nice, short gap between the action of the Death Star escape and the big space battle at the end. Even though it's people just sitting around, it moves so fast and there's so much else going on, you've probably seen that movie loads of times and never noticed the 'plot hole'. Although I'd wager a lot of you will be telling your mates about it now. It is, in the end, basically the same trick that Schwarzenegger uses in *Last Action Hero* when he's surrounded by an army of mobsters - he points behind them and shouts 'look - an elephant', then runs away while everyone's looking for it.

Writers point at a lot of imaginary elephants.

The synopsis allows an author to see the story laid out without the distractions, allows him to see if there's stuff that doesn't work. There's then the choice of either fixing it, or burying it. In the case of *Star Wars*, getting the Death Star to Yavin for the final act was the important thing, and made for a much better story than any alternative way of doing things.

I saw a lot of synopses for the New Adventures when I was researching the Virgin version of *A History of the Universe*. Some writers, like Andrew Cartmel, sent in vast chunky things - I think the one for *Warchild* was about thirty pages, complete with dialogue samples and so on. He clearly preferred to have it all mapped out before he started. Gareth Roberts and Ben Aaronovitch preferred two or three pages, get the strong basic idea down, then build on it.

Writers all write differently. Some authors swear blind that they just start writing and don't know where the characters will take them. That sounds reckless and crazy to me, like jumping off a cliff and then trying to work out what to do next.

What a lot of writers do when they're starting out is concentrate on the least important stuff - the setting, the backstory of the characters. The setting and the shape of the monsters are basically dressing. The important thing is the structure of a novel, its plot - what happens and when. The trick of a novel, really, is working out when the audience finds out information. Writers keep information back. They either gradually introduce it, or keep some vital point either obscure or out of the equation so they can come back and surprise you with it later.

The typical *Doctor Who* story has the Doctor arriving to find some monsters menacing a group of nice people. The Doctor discovers that the monsters have a bigger plan than just menacing those people - the running joke on some *Doctor Who* discussion boards is that every blurb for a *Doctor Who* book seems to include the phrase 'but not everything is as it seems'.

For *The Eyeless*, I was keen to tell a story where everything was *exactly* as it seems. The problem is set out right at the beginning, there are no real twists and turns. The issue is solving the problem, not simple redefining it away.

I was keen to do a type of story that *Doctor Who* does surprisingly rarely - what I call the *Guns of Navarone*-type story. Basically, it's a mission, with the characters having to get past all obstacles to reach their objective. I also really wanted to tell a psychological story - one that explored the Doctor's character a bit, tested him. Now, there are limits to what you can do. Not because Cardiff are mean and don't let you, but simply because *Doctor Who* is a running serial. You can't change him all that much. What would you want to change him for, anyway, when he's the Doctor? He's great. What you can do, though, is reveal stuff about him, challenge him, see him how others see him.

I wanted to play with the themes of the new series, wanted to make it distinctly a tenth Doctor story, not just a generic one. A lot of the new series is set on modern-day Earth, with pop-culture references and a soap opera thing going on with the companions and their families. The brief was to stay away from all that - so, bye bye any story featuring a pregnant Lucy Saxon and the Space Pig and a visit from Torchwood: 2020 where Maria Jackson's on the team and K9's the boss. Instead of those trappings, I had to think about what the new series was about. I've tried to pick up on the themes of the new show and, if you're looking, you'll spot a few things like lines of dialogue that quote the television series.

I was writing a book in which the Doctor travels on his own. And what we've discovered time and time again (actually starting in the New Adventures, and first articulated in Paul Cornell's *Love and War*) is that the Doctor needs a companion. When we see him in *Rose*, say, or *The Runaway Bride*, without a companion, he doesn't have the checks and balances he usually has. He's not a human being, he's acutely aware of the bigger picture, and that can make him act a little... inhumanely. Think of him surrounded by fire, wiping out the Racnoss at the end of *The Runaway Bride*. That's the Doctor on his own, if he's not careful.

Here, it's taken me the equivalent of two and a bit sides of A4 just to set out what I was trying to do. You can imagine that explaining all that, while structuring it in the form of a *Doctor Who* story, explaining who all the characters are and what happens was something of a challenge. It's very easy to waffle on. As Pascal said, 'I'm sorry for the long letter, I didn't have time to write a short one.' It must be a good quote, because it's constantly ascribed to Twain, Churchill and Voltaire.

By the 23rd of November - appropriately enough - the synopsis had been batted back and forth to Justin a couple of times and between us we'd got the two page synopsis for a book I called *The Hidden Fortress* into a fit state to send to the *Doctor Who* production office in Cardiff for approval.

Now... I'll be perfectly honest, I've no idea about the process that goes on at Cardiff. None at all. They could have a trained monkey with a rubber stamp, they could have a crack team of fifty *Doctor Who* book-approving specialists working over every line. They might have fifty trained monkeys - that would be cool, although probably a bit of a waste of licence-payers' money. I didn't have any direct contact, I didn't get to visit the set or anything like that.

What I do know is that at some stage in the process, Russell Davies looks at the synopses - and that's presumably why they're two pages long, now, because he's got plenty of other things to worry about.

I got two notes back, and this was all within a couple of days (around the 26th of November). I was keen to take advantage of the Doctor being on his own, wanted the hook of 'this is too dangerous a mission to take a companion on', but the note came back that the Doctor takes his companions to plenty of dangerous places. The story didn't change one bit, but the marketing hook, if you like, did.

One thing I know that came back from Russell Davies himself was that the title should be *The Eyeless*, after the monsters in the book. It's a much better title than *The Hidden Fortress*, not least because the Fortress in the book isn't hidden. That led to a slight structural change - originally the Eyeless showed up out of the blue at the halfway point. Now they were in the title, that reminded me a little too much of *The Sontaran Experiment*, a two-part story which has the cliffhanger at the end of the first episode of 'it's... a Sontaran' (the working title of that story was *The Destructors*, which would have maintained the surprise). So I added a couple of things that mean the Eyeless show up a lot earlier in my book.

Russell Davies knows what he's talking about, to the point that it's mildly insulting for me to point that out. In other news: Lewis Hamilton can drive cars and Pavarotti was an above-average singer. At this stage, I hadn't signed a contract. If he'd said something I profoundly and utterly disagreed about, I could have walked away. He was right, on both counts.

As soon as that came through, Justin gave the formal go-ahead. This was around the beginning of December. *The Eyeless* was commissioned, contracts would be drawn up. I could start work actually writing the thing. My deadline was the end of June.

The Protagonist

OK... so what elements build up to make a story?

There are probably writers who'd baulk at that question. Then again, there are certainly guidebooks for writers which make it seem like all you have to do is assemble a couple of prefabricated Epiphanies and Inciting Incidents and then Bob's Your Uncle, you have a story.

There are elements common to virtually all stories. I don't want anyone who is hoping to be a writer to think that these are a set of magic keys that will enable anyone to tell a great story. They aren't, but they are things to think about. If, when you're planning or writing a story, you keep what I say in mind, it'll help you. I hope.

It's commonly claimed that there are only five types of story. Or seven. Or four. Or is it ten? Well... I think there's probably only one type of story. Every story ever written can be summed up in a sentence: 'someone doesn't get what they bargained for'. Or, as fellow *Doctor Who* author Simon Bucher-Jones once put it: 'Surprise!'.

Basically, every story is about someone encountering something new and the story is about the implications for that someone as they deal with the new thing. It doesn't have to be a Faustian pact, but most stories have at least *some* element like that - a deal with the devil where something that seems to give easy satisfaction turns out to have dire consequences. Science fiction is often - not always - about someone living in a world with a new piece of technology. A love story is about someone meeting a new potential lover. A thriller features someone discovering a new plot against their government. Most stories have someone going about their everyday - perhaps slightly *too* mundane - existence, then being thrust into a far more exciting, dangerous place. It doesn't have to be physical danger (although that certainly helps if you're writing a *Doctor Who* story) or on a grand scale.

This will either sound deeply profound to you, or be such an incredible generalisation that it has no real value. So... in order to be practical, let's talk about that 'someone'.

Every story needs a protagonist. The protagonist is simply the main person whose story we're following. The person whose story it is. They're the 'hero', although they don't have to be heroic or even remotely likeable.

I probably don't need to give examples of heroes in stories. Often, the author helps you along by naming them in the title. There's no great mystery who the protagonists of *Gulliver's Travels* or *Tom Jones* or *Hamlet* or *Harry Potter and the Goblet of Fire* are. There are multi-protagonist stories - at various times in, say, *Pulp Fiction* we're following a different character. Even there, it's always pretty clear that this is the Vince Vega bit or the Butch bit. There are stories where the protagonist changes from scene to scene, so the term becomes pretty meaningless. A good example of that is the TV series *The Wire*.

In some stories, it's not always clear who the protagonist is. Who's the hero of *The Phantom Menace*, for example? The poster makes you think this is Anakin's story, loyalty has you backing Obi-Wan, Qui-Gon's in the most scenes, and it's probably Amidala's 'story', in the sense that it's her world being invaded. Ultimately, the clue's in the title again, and it's Darth Sidious. The big reveal of the movie (so big that a lot of people apparently don't see it) is that every single thing the good guys have done, every victory they have won, has only strengthened Sidious. So it's no wonder people were confused, particularly when the protagonist of the original trilogy is so clearly defined, central and heroic as Luke Skywalker.

Anyone can come up with a 'hero' for their story. I think, unconsciously or not, a lot of would-be writers believe that coming up with the protagonist is a bit like generating a role-playing character - you pick hish / her appearance, special skills and so on. It's the easy part, in a way. It's also fun. The bane of a lot of SF writing is stories with amazing, colourful, eccentric characters... who then get slotted into rubbish, generic stories.

What's interesting about *Doctor Who* is that you're forced to do things the other way round. For *Doctor Who* authors the protagonist is - to the first approximation, anyway - always going to be the Doctor. Which means you spend your time trying to come up with silly and thrilling things for him to do, not agonising about what his magic sword is called.

In *Doctor Who* the companion is often nearly as important. Sometimes - very rarely - he / she is the protagonist. The protagonist of the episode *Rose*, for example is... well, it's not difficult to guess from the title. Some fans, on first viewing, felt the first episode was a very light *Doctor Who* story... and indeed it was. It was about Rose meeting the Doctor, not the Doctor fighting Autons.

But the companion's role is usually in the subplot. A subplot is what it sounds like - basically a secondary storyline that runs alongside the main one. It's usually there to compare and contrast with the main plot - so in *Pride and Prejudice*, say, we see what happens to the other sisters so we appreciate what happens to Elizabeth all the more. In *Doctor Who*, the typical story involves the Doctor and companion landing on a planet where there's a conflict and splitting up. The Doctor ends up with one faction, the companion with another. That way, we see both sides of the conflict. Often the Doctor is off dealing with the cause - the monsters who've invaded, say - while the companion is down on the ground and witnesses the effects - the suffering the monsters are inflicting on the native population. It's a neat way to do things. It also allows a writer to break up the tone a bit and just... well, cut away from the main action.

Instead of talking about what makes a protagonist interesting, let's think about what the protagonist is there in the story for.

Here's the key sentence, so memorise it:

'A story is the set of choices its protagonist makes.'

This sounds ridiculously reductive. It is. You can't really sum up the whole of human literature in a sentence. What you can do, though, is bring clarity to your *own* storytelling if you keep that sentence in mind. But what does that mean, what implications does that have, and why is it directly related to why some - misguided, wrong - *Doctor Who* fans don't like Tinkerbell Jesus?

Protagonists want something. Often the most sophisticated stories have protagonists with the most simple desires - 'revenge' or 'true love'. Robert McKee makes a useful distinction between Conscious and Unconscious desires. In the standard Hollywood formula movie, what the hero *says* he wants invariably turns out not to be the thing he *actually* wants. Indeed, many Hollywood movies are precisely about the revelation of what the Unconscious (and invariably 'true') desire is. The busy executive doesn't *really* want the money and status he's working so hard to earn at the start of the movie, he really wants some special time with his kids - and the movie is about him coming to realise that he'd rather see his kid's baseball game than get that promotion. (I'd pay good money to see a movie which ends with a businessman saying 'stuff my kids, I choose the money', by the way - that is, after all, the choice most Hollywood execs have made.)

A story is basically about the Protagonist pursuing his object of desire - with varying degrees of application, luck and success.

Now, in a running series, the emphasis is a little different. Sherlock Holmes wants to solve the case in hand, Batman wants to track down the supervillain, the Doctor wants to defeat the monsters. They want the same thing next time. And the next. And the next. There's no psychological progression. The stories are variations on the theme, the best ones are the ones rich in imaginative detail.

We've got a taste for heroes with more of an inner life these days, and so authors of running series tend to concentrate a lot more on the psychology than they did when the characters were created. *Batman* writers over the last twenty years or so have wrestled with the question 'what sort of man would dress up as a bat to fight criminals?'. The problem they have is... er... no-one would do that. It's a barmy thing to do, and by definition, you're not going to make any great insight into human nature by asking the question. The character just can't bear the load. To paraphrase Charlie Brooker, it's not a good idea to do a story where Postman Pat goes postal. It's why *The Killing Joke* is Alan Moore's least successful work, in my opinion.

But the Doctor has a desire, it's perfectly conscious and it's 'find out what the monsters are really up to and defeat them'.

During the story the Protagonist has to make choices to attain his desire. Big choices and little choices. He doesn't always realise at the time which are the big choices and which are the little ones. The recent *Doctor Who* episode *Turn Left* is a great example of a story where a trivial decision has literally universe-shattering consequences. If Donna turns her car one way, she meets the Doctor. If she doesn't, she doesn't.

Often the hero is the hero precisely because they have insight - folk tales commonly have the hero realising that the smelly old tramp is really a great warrior or god in disguise. Captain Kirk, Batman, Sherlock Holmes and the Doctor can all walk into a room and realise that an everyday item that's been on public display for years without anyone paying it any attention is actually some amazing and unique item that's the key to winning the day.

But real life isn't like that very often, and most stories don't work quite like that. Usually stories feature a choice that you probably won't be faced with, but might. Let's say you find a bag of money in your back garden... do you keep it? Do you tell your partner? How do you spend it without anyone noticing? What happens when the owner shows up? Hitchcock's movies were brilliant at plunging normal people into increasingly perilous situations because each sensible choice they made exposed them to more harm.

Soap operas basically have an engine that throws out a dozen decisions an episode - very simple moral dilemmas, usually, like 'should that character have an affair?' or 'should that character steal that money?' or 'should that character reveal a secret?'. The choices are all laid out, they're usually 'yes/no' decisions and they're all simple to understand.

If you watch the soap, you know something about the characters - that character's a bit thick, that one is always unlucky in love, that one is one bad day away from becoming a drunk. Those two things together - simple decisions, made by well-defined characters - mean that millions of people watch the soaps, and millions of people can kind of see everything coming, and millions of people shout out at the telly things like 'don't do it, he's a love rat' or 'don't do it, you'll hurt your best friend'. Not all writers will consciously do this - every writer is different. But I think even the most sophisticated or literary writers, by accident or design, use this technique. They just dress it up in posher clothes.

Right, here's another assertion: 'For a story to work, the reader has to understand the decisions the protagonist is faced with, and why the protagonist makes the choices he does.' If you get that right, you'll write a good story. And if you bash the piano keys in the right way, you'll be a great concert pianist.

The audience doesn't have to agree with the decision the Protagonist makes, it doesn't have to be the decision *they* would make. The audience often know more than the character ('don't marry him... he's only with you for the money and he killed his last wife!' - if the Protagonist had that information, you'd hope they'd factor it in to their decision). The audience *do* have to find it convincing that the Protagonist made the decision.

The hardest decision for an author to make convincing is often the very first one. The biggest choice is what, as I've said, Joseph Campbell terms The Call to Adventure. There will come a point in most stories where the protagonist is, well... basically invited into the story. When a horror movie starts with a group of teenagers deciding that, gosh, the most sensible thing to shelter from the rain is go into the spooky house where all those teenagers got killed ten years ago that very night... the audience groans. Horror movies still tell those stories, but invariably make a postmodern joke about what a stupid decision it is.

In *Star Wars*, Ben asks Luke to come with him to Alderaan and learn the ways of the Force. Luke, of course...

... refuses.

Campbell notes that most heroes refuse once - the pull of their ordinary life is too strong, or they need a better incentive to take a risk. George Lucas is a devotee of Campbell. I'd go as far as to say that you can't really understand *Star Wars* unless you've read 'The Impact of Science on Myth', which is a 1961 essay that basically says 'someone really needs to invent *Star Wars*'. (One *Star Wars* fan I said this to hasn't spoken to me since, because he hasn't read it and felt I was calling his very *Star Wars* fanitude into question. It's not as though it's difficult to find.) Having read his Campbell, Lucas has Luke refusing The Call to Adventure and deciding to stay on Tatooine... then his aunt and uncle are murdered, and he realises where his destiny lies.

In *Doctor Who* there isn't always a call to adventure - it's implicit in the series. When the villager says 'oh Doctor, these Daleks came along and they're hurting us, can you help?'... the Doctor doesn't exactly agonise about the decision. This is unusual - James Bond and Sherlock Holmes usually start by being offered a mission or case. They always decide to take it, but they do *consciously* decide. Even Superman usually gets a line like 'looks like I'll be a few minutes late for dinner with Lois' as he swoops in to catch a bad guy he's spotted.

All these choices lead somewhere, and that's the end of the story. Now... I'm going to skip to that. I'll do what I do when I'm writing and worry about the middle bit after that.

The key thing that audiences always like at the end of a story is a sense of justice. Not necessarily a happy ending, but an ending that fits the story. Protagonists have a desire. The story ends with them reaching a level of understanding about their desire - usually they win the girl, defeat the bad guy, solve the crime, that sort of thing. Unhappy endings see their desire thwarted or revealed as futile or unsatisfactory.

I got in terrible trouble with my *Doctor Who* book *The Gallifrey Chronicles*, because it ends before the Doctor defeats the monsters. I knew I would get in trouble when I wrote it. We know the Doctor will win, but *we want to see him do it*.

Audiences used to like to see the Protagonist just get handed the reward he deserved. Plays and novels of the eighteenth and nineteen century often ended with good, kind characters suddenly inheriting a great deal of money, or being married off to someone good-looking who was barely in the story up to that point, or facing some sudden form of external justice and being dragged away.

Even that seems naturalistic compared with Greek and Roman plays, which often ended with a god coming down and pointing at each of the main cast in turn, making definitive pronouncements on who was to get what reward and what punishment.

So, in *Orestes*, the play's going about its business until suddenly, at the end, literally without warning, the god Apollo appears and says (after a deep breath, one assumes):

'Menelaus, calm thy excited mood; I am Phoebus, the son of Latona, who draw nigh to call thee by name, and thou no less, Orestes, who, sword in hand, art keeping guard on yonder maid, that thou mayst hear what have come to say. Helen, whom all thy eagerness failed to destroy, when thou wert seeking to anger Menelaus, is here as ye see in the enfolding air, rescued from death instead of slain by thee. 'Twas I that saved her and snatched her from beneath thy sword at the bidding of her father Zeus; for she his child must put on immortality, and take her place with Castor and Polydeuces in the bosom of the sky, a saviour to mariners. Choose thee then another bride and take her to thy home, for the gods by means of Helen's loveliness embroiled Troy and Hellas, causing death thereby, that they might lighten mother Earth of the outrage done her by the increase of man's number. Such is Helen's end.

But as for thee, Orestes, thou must cross the frontier of this land and dwell for one whole year on Parrhasian soil, which from thy flight thither shall be called the land of Orestes by Azanians and Arcadians; and when thou returnest thence to the city of Athens, submit to be brought to trial by "the Avenging Three" for thy mother's murder, for the gods will be umpires between you and will pass a most righteous sentence on thee upon the hill of Ares, where thou art to win thy case. Likewise, it is ordained, Orestes, that thou shalt wed Hermione, at whose neck thou art pointing thy sword; Neoptolemus shall never marry her, though he thinks he will; for his death is fated to o'ertake him by a Delphian sword, when he claims satisfaction of me for the death of his father Achilles. Bestow thy sister's hand on Pylades, to whom thou didst formerly promise her; the life awaiting him henceforth is one of bliss.

Menelaus, leave Orestes to rule Argos; go thou and reign o'er Sparta, keeping it as the dowry of a wife, who till this day ne'er ceased exposing thee to toils innumerable. Between Orestes and the citizens, I, who forced his mother's murder on him, will bring about a reconciliation.' [Note: this is 1910 EP Coleridge translation, which is in the public domain.]

You don't see that sort of thing on *EastEnders*. The characters don't all shout out 'push off, we're in the middle of something, here', they accept the judgement and the play ends.

The god appearing at the end to pass judgement was as much a convention of drama then as things like opening credits sequences or montages are now. The audience knew to expect it, it was a highlight. There would be mechanisms that allowed the god to make a spectacular entrance - they'd float down or spring up, or appear to materialise. It was all about the special effects, even then.

A god came out of a machine. Or, in Latin, *deus ex machina*.

Deus ex machina is a dirty phrase, now. It's come to mean a quick and easy 'cheat' ending. In the end of the *Day of the Triffids* movie, it turns out Triffids dissolve in salt water. In *Superman: The Movie*, Superman suddenly acquires the ability to turn back time. It feels unfair if some external force just arrives to solve the problem - like that bit in *Monty Python and the Holy Grail* where they're being chased by a cartoon monster and the animator suddenly drops dead and the monster vanishes. HG Wells just about gets away with all the Martians dying of the flu in *The War of the Worlds*, but it's not entirely satisfying. It feels too easy.

Some *Doctor Who* fans have complained that the end of *Last of the Time*

Lords was a 'deus ex machina' ending. The Doctor literally descends as a god and passes judgement. I don't think it's a fair criticism. (I think what happens *doesn't* come out the blue, it's engineered by the Doctor using elements that have been set up previously in the story. Russell Davies plays tricks with the convention - just look at *Journey's End*, where character after character pulls out artifacts of amazing power that represent an easy solution... then they don't work.) The reason the fans don't like it, though, is that they think it feels like a cheat.

Nowadays we like stories where the fate of the Protagonist is down to the choices we see him make.

Modern audiences like the Protagonist to win his own battles. He can recruit allies, he can pull things out of his hat. The Protagonist can cheat... but his author can't. Writers have to explain who the Protagonist is, the choices he faces, the skills and tools he possesses and why he makes the choices he does.

So, after all that, a bit of writing advice: When you're planning or writing a story, always look at the choices your Protagonist is making.

Answer these questions:

1) Is it clear to the reader what the choice is and what the potential consequences of the choice are?

2) Is it clear how the Protagonist came to the decision they did? Is it consistent with what we've been told about the Protagonist? Is it consistent with what the Protagonist desires?

3) Is there a better choice to be made, and if so, why isn't the Protagonist making it? (One question I often find myself asking is - 'why don't they just get help?'. It's a joke in the *Doctor Who* episode *Blink* - nine times out of ten, characters in contemporary drama never call the police when they ought to.)

Now... real writing isn't like a checklist. Go on instinct. Write the damn story. But if something isn't ringing true or working or feels forced, or too sudden, or unconvincing... take a step back. Look at your Protagonist, what they desire, the choices they are making. If you know who your Protagonist is and how they reach the decisions they do, you'll find that getting your story to work is a lot easier.

The Middle Bit

Having dealt with the beginning and end of a story, now I'll talk a bit about the middle.

DWM in the early eighties was obsessed with something called 'the dramatic W'. The articles that mentioned this mystical sigil seemed to think it meant that a series could veer wildly from something dramatic to something that was undramatic. Or something rubbish to something good. Which was actually quite a handy way of discussing *Doctor Who* in the early eighties, of course.

But I, and I'm sure a lot of other people reading, sensed that ideally writers should probably not alternate between great, exciting things and rubbish, dull ones. They should stick to 'great and exciting'. So what is the 'dramatic W' and, more to the point, how can it help perk up your writing?

An example. Imagine a *Doctor Who* scene which starts with the Doctor exploring a lovely, happy garden and discovering the monster. The scene ends with the monster chasing him. Things go downhill, and so let's represent that with this symbol: \ .

Or the opposite: the Doctor's being chased by a horde of monsters, it ends with him getting out of danger, closing and locking the door behind him. Starts off bad, ends up good. Or, / if we felt the need to represent it visually.

Now that's good for the Doctor, but bad for the monsters - but, remember, the Doctor is the protagonist, we're charting his progress. His 'desire' in those scenes is that classic Shakespearean theme 'not wanting to be eaten by a monster'.

Let's imagine a couple of scenes between those first two.

So... after the scene where the Doctor finds the monster, we have a new scene which starts with him being chased. He dodges around, finds a safe cave. The monster doesn't follow him in. Things are looking up for the Doctor. So: / .

But wait... in the next scene, the Doctor realises that the monster didn't follow him in because it knew there was a horde of monsters in here. Run, Doctor, run! And things have gone downhill, so let's represent that as \ .

Then we get the final scene where the Doctor escapes.

OK... what was all that forward-slash, backslash nonsense about? Well, if I put those four symbols in order:

\ / \ /

... and that's the 'dramatic W'. At the end of each scene, the Doctor is manifestly either better or worse off than he was at the beginning of the scene.

That movement is pretty much the definition of drama, and it's often called a 'reversal of fortune'.

'Hang on', you're saying, 'drama doesn't just alternate wildly from scenes with characters doing well to scenes with characters doing badly'. And, of course, you're right. 'Reversal' is a little bit of a misnomer.

Sticking with *Doctor Who*-style action-adventure for a moment (just because what happens is usually nice and visible), you could imagine a sequence of scenes where the Doctor has to escape the monster which goes:

1. The Doctor is running from a monster and runs straight into the path of another monster.

2. The Doctor is now being trapped between two monsters. He leaps for safety... and finds himself in a nest of monsters. He is now being chased by four monsters.

3. The Doctor is now being chased by four monsters. He reaches a dead end.

The Doctor's situation goes from bad to worse to even worse... but the point is that there's progression. The alterative would be four very similar scenes where the Doctor's just being chased by a monster.

The Empire Strikes Back is a movie where virtually every scene ends with the good guys worse off than they were at the beginning of the scene. Even when, say, Luke escapes the Wampa's cave, the scene ends with him injured and in the middle of a deadly blizzard. There are slight upturns and good luck - but they're often undercut. The Falcon escapes the Star Destroyers... but Boba Fett is following them. Luke finds Yoda... who refuses to teach him.

If you've ever written something that just seems to noodle along aimlessly, it's probably because you've got scenes with no reversal of fortune. Things just sort of happen, characters just sit there, or are going around in circles. The story doesn't progress. The telltale sign is that you've written something (either in the synopsis or the story itself) that says something like 'after a day or so exploring, they still hadn't got anywhere' or which has characters sitting around waiting for something to happen to them.

Gareth Roberts once told me that he'd read a *Coronation Street* script with two scenes that started with the direction 'Deirdre is still bored', which is pretty much a textbook way to not go about things.

Now, you can do great things with boredom - the best episodes of *One Foot in the Grave*, for example, were often based around being stuck in one place. But things happened. Part of the joke is that even the tiniest things happening seem like epic victories and defeats. The post comes... but Victor discovers it's a bunch of bills and junk mail.

Most writing - even with *Doctor Who* stories - is more subtle and small-scale than the first example I gave. But it tends to work with reversals of fortune.

An important thing to note: 'good' here isn't a complex ethical question, it's simply defined as 'gets the protagonist closer to his goals'. You could have a movie with a murderer as a protagonist, and it would be 'good' if he evaded the security to get closer to his innocent victim. It would be 'bad' if the police brought him in for questioning.

The protagonist in *Doctor Who* is the Doctor. His 'desire' is, broadly, to find out what is really going on and put a stop to it with the minimum of casualties. If there's a scene where he finds a book in a library that mentions that there were mysterious lights in the sky one night in 1737 and after that the moor got a reputation for being haunted, it means he's a step closer to that goal. Even though he's not in any immediate danger, even though it's a quiet, quite passive scene.

The character doesn't need to know the exact significance at that moment, but it's always best if the audience gets some kind of clue. The best moments are often the ones where fortune swings the wrong way: the last cliffhanger of *Horror of Fang Rock*, for example, which has the Doctor declaring 'we've not locked the beast out, we've locked it in'.

The reality is that writers don't sit around drawing slashes to work out where they are on the dramatic W. They don't usually sit around going 'my Protagonist is'. Nor should writers do that - it sounds ghastly and mechanical. And the sad truth is that writing isn't as simple as knowing this stuff. I know the gymnast who just fell off the parallel bars in the Olympics shouldn't have, but that doesn't make me an Olympic gymnast.

But thinking about your existing story in those terms can often (not always) be a useful way of figuring out what's not working.

Naming Characters

It's a weird one. At one level, naming characters is fairly trivial. What your character is called doesn't really affect the story all that much. I'm a firm believer in the theory that if you can remember the name of the lead character in an action film, the makers have done something wrong. (*Broken Arrow* takes this to the extreme of having the audience find out the names of the male and female leads as the last lines of the movie.)

For long-running characters, it seems to be more important. There's clearly a resonance to 'Sherlock Holmes' or 'Dracula' that must be, in part, because their names are so distinctive. Would Kylie Minogue smell so sweet if she'd been called something less unusual, something that didn't sound like a team in the UEFA cup? I'd still fancy a sniff, I think. Some of this is clearly just our familiarity, rather than because they've got weird names - you can't really get more ordinary names than Elizabeth Taylor, Bruce Willis or Richard Burton.

'Hardy and Laurel' sounds discordant, but there's no particular reason why, it's just that we're used to it being the other way round. Some things are cultural. The name 'Kevin' in the US is Costner and Kline and Bacon. In the UK, it's still Gerbil.

Other names are just at hand. The name 'Dalek', famously - if, almost certainly, fictitiously - emerged when Terry Nation saw a phonebook that ran DAL-EK (or DAL-LEK). The most famous example of that is probably James Bond. Ian Fleming had an ornithology book by a 'James Bond' on his shelf - that's why Pierce Brosnan poses as an ornithologist in *Die Another Day*. Elsewhere, Fleming used the names of friends and acquaintances - not always amusing them in the way that he hoped.

I named a character in *Emmerdale* after a friend, once... and then (after I'd left the show) the character was revealed to be a golddigging ex-prostitute. Oops. Hilariously, when I tried to name a character 'Mark Clapham', I was warned not to use any more joke names. This, I think, might have been for the very episode where Gareth Roberts introduced a character called Roger Blake.

It's very hard to find an 'ordinary name' (this is a person called 'Lance Parkin' speaking of course... people always confuse me with Lars Pearson and Lawrence Miles, making *Warlords of Utopia*, - written by me, published by Lars, edited by Lawrence - like some weird *Three Doctors*-type special). The temptation is always to go weird and Pythonesque - Celia Molestrangler, that kind of thing. Or terrible puns - Howard Chaykin's *Angel and the Ape* has a policeman called Detective Kommicks. One of the things Vic and Bob always used to do so well was find ordinary names for their characters. A talking Labrador was 'Greg Mitchell'. Douglas Adams managed to have characters called Arthur Dent and Zaphod Beeblebrox in the same scene.

There are practical considerations - on the whole, you want to avoid characters with similar names, just so the audience don't get confused. TV shows often try to avoid characters with the same name as the actors, to prevent confusion on the studio floor. You want to avoid libeling anyone. (Barbara Cartland got very offended by the novel *Fatherland*, when she learned she was still writing romances in a parallel universe where the Nazis won.)

You want the names to be nice and memorable, to suit the characters without going the Restoration comedy route that would have seen Jack Harkness called something like Roger Proudcock.

So... how do I come up with my names? A lot of the time, characters just grow into their placeholder name. This has happened to me with pets in the past, and I suspect it's the power of the label - soon, they've 'become' that name.

The names in mine usually mean something, even if it's something trivial. All the names in my Big Finish play *Davros* are from *Diff'rent Strokes*, for example. The ones in *The Dying Days* are almost all place names from *The War of the Worlds*. I often use vaguely punny names, and don't explain them - in *Father Time*, Ferran is a corruption of Ferdinand, for example, and Klade is an anagram.

The reason the Eyeless are called that is explained in the book, and it's not the obvious explanation. *The Eyeless* has quite a small cast. A lot of the names are short, almost fragments of other names, because the planet is small and broken. This isn't some code to break or anything, and I hope now I've said this, it's not distracting, but - for example - there's a character 'Jeffip' whom I originally pictured as being sort-of played by David Bowie. His name's a mashed up version of 'Phillip Jeffries', the character Bowie played in *Fire Walk With Me*. In the event, I heard Bowie was in Season Four, so Jeffip ended up played by someone else. Regular readers of mine will be able to work out who. Regular viewers will note that Bowie didn't show up in Season Four. 'Gyll' is meant to be reminiscent of 'Gyllenhaal'. The planet Arcopolis is basically a city of Arcologies, if that's not a contradiction in terms, but the word also echoes with Ark and Arc and Arcadia.

Audience

I've written *Doctor Who* novels before, but *The Eyeless* is a little different. My last one, *The Gallifrey Chronicles*, was the last of the regular novels to feature the eighth Doctor (the 'EDAs'), and came out about halfway through the run of Christopher Eccleston's season. I was in an odd situation with that book - trying to write a novel that celebrated and wrapped up an ongoing story that was effectively over two hundred books long, while also being acutely aware that a new show with a fresh approach would be on the scene. It's my bestselling *Doctor Who* novel to date - although my *Emmerdale* books sold more - and while I don't have the figures, I've been told that *The Gallifrey Chronicles* ended up as the bestselling EDA of the lot.

The books featuring the new Doctors, though, are in a different league. I'm pretty sure that virtually everyone who bought *The Gallifrey Chronicles* was an old-school fanboy. These were people who'd read the books at one point or another tuning in to the series finale, and the audience for the books then was - pretty much by definition - the hardcore fanbase of *Doctor Who*.

The big difference nowadays is that the *Doctor Who* books are truly mainstream. In a competitive marketplace the three *Doctor Who* novels will be among the bestsellers this Christmas. The books are even available as three-for-two offers in bookshops. So, a great big chunk of my readership won't be *Doctor Who* fanboys, just people who enjoy the TV show and the previous books. For the first time, a chunk of my readership will be children.

Does an author have a picture of their readership in their head when they're writing and does that affect what the author writes? Well... yes.

It's easy to imagine that things divide up neatly between 'art' and 'commerce', but the fact is that every person buying any book has made a commercial decision, and has done so, in part, because a publisher has carefully offered them a product and persuaded them to buy it. Now, some authors may want to distance themselves from that process, to create an uncompromised, unalloyed work of pure art and form... but that just means that someone else has to do the marketing for them. Or, I suspect is more often the case, that the book is so 'uncompromised' that even the author's cat hasn't read it. And *The Eyeless* is a *Doctor Who* novel and part of an existing range, when all's said and done.

So... how do I picture my audience? This is the first time I've written this down, so don't get the idea that I've been drawing up Venn diagrams or anything.

I think readers of *The Eyeless* will mostly fall into one of three categories: the old-school fanboys who've been *Doctor Who* fans for years and who may well have a book by me already; more casual adult readers who like the TV show and end up giving the book a try; and younger readers.

The first thing to point out is that while it's tempting to imagine that these groups will place competing demands on the book, they want mostly the same thing: a good *Doctor Who* story. They want a novel which is at least competently written, with interesting characters and ideas, a story that hooks them, some stuff that scares them, makes them laugh and makes them think.

What's quite interesting is that all three groups there tend to prefer 'a solid story' over more literary qualities. I'm a writer, I've got a Masters degree in English Literature, I tend to get a bit poncey about imagery and turns of phrases when I read (and when I write, of course). I find it very difficult to read books with just 'functional' prose. A lot of people who read tie-in stuff seem to want more meat-and-potatoes writing, almost as if it's a straightforward account of what happened to their favourite characters. They want a story with a beginning, middle and end (in that order), and they don't want an author getting in the way of it with poetry and metafiction.

I'm generalising wildly. Just because you read tie-in novels doesn't mean you only read tie-in novels. It doesn't mean you approach every single book wanting exactly the same thing. When I read, say, William Shatner's *Collision Course*, I did not read it looking for exactly the same thing as I did when I read, say, Nicholas Christopher's *Bestiary*.

I enjoyed both books, I'm a big fan of both authors and have the secret desire to be both of them when I grow up. I recommend both books. They're very different. My point is that I didn't go into *Collision Course* expecting literary fiction. As Jonathan Ross said, if you play money to see Tim Burton's *Planet of the Apes* movie, you shouldn't complain when it's got a load of apes in it all being very Tim Burtony.

Of the three audience groups, it's that last one, 'younger readers', which is the tricky one for me. It's also the one that scares fanboys most. The thing that scares fanboys is the thought that if you're doing something 'for kids', it means you have to compromise and tone down and rule out and bowdlerise. The thing that scares me is that... well, writing for kids is way harder than writing for fanboys.

Fanboys see it as a censorship issue or a 'ratings' one. As it happens, the NSAs are meant to be 'suitable for twelve year olds'. Or, in movie terms, PG-13. They can be as dark and violent as *The Dark Knight* or *Casino Royale*... both of which, I'd say, are at the upper end of how dark *Doctor Who* should get. We can't use swear words... again, I don't really see how that would ever really cripple a *Doctor Who* story. You can't use swear words on primetime TV, either. As for sex... well, again, it's not traditionally what *Doctor Who* does. In the olden days (with all due respect to slashers and ficcers and shippers), the show was ridiculously asexual. I think I'm right that the first truly *romantic* kiss in the show's history is in Season Twenty-Five and *The Greatest Show in the Galaxy* (Jo and Cliff share a kiss at the end of *The Green Death*, but on screen it looks so chaste that it's hard to count it). Even nowadays, it's 'saucy' rather than explicit - the show now acknowledges that sex exists, and not just between a married man and his lady wife. This 'sauce' is filthy at times. Jackie

Tyler's 'you could always splash out on a taxi or... whatever' being a great example. And the thing is... all these restrictions were in place before, with the EDAs.

A Young Adult book like *The Eyeless* is not 'a children's book' in the Victorian sense.

Back in the day, humans had a larval stage, childhood, that suddenly ended at sixteen or eighteen and then they were adults. Nowadays, you're a kid until you're about eleven, you hit adulthood at some point around thirty. Many, many things that were 'for kids' are now 'for a much broader audience than kids'. Comic books, action figures, video games, ice cream, wearing football shirts on the street, watching cartoons, superhero movies, fantasy novels, pop music, bikes. We can argue whether that's a good or healthy thing. We can argue whether it infantilises our culture. More to the point, we can argue it while dressed as a Klingon, eating Retro Edition Wispa bars, playing Jet Set Wii-lly while sitting on furniture made of Lego.

The idea that things that were once the exclusive preserve of kids haven't been for twenty years seems to confuse a lot of people - British MP Keith Vaz, for example, didn't really seem to get what the '12' in a 12 rating meant when he said he wouldn't let his 11 year old watch *The Dark Knight*.

Part of the problem with - let's say - comics is that many of the things that used to rely on a casual ever-churning generation of kids are now the exclusive preserve of aging fanboys. *Doctor Who* had this problem in the nineties.

I'm an aging fanboy, so I think it's wonderful on any number of levels.

That said... *Doctor Who* is watched by a lot of children, now. That's a great thing. The books are available in supermarkets. That's a great thing. The BBC has a brand to protect and a duty to abide by taste and decency rules.

The obvious example of a YA book is *Harry Potter* - a range with a huge appeal to adults. Probably more adults than kids. It's 'the children's own series that adults adore'. If you're an aging fanboy, you've already worked out where I'm going with this - because that was the quote on the back of many of the *Doctor Who* Target novelisations in the seventies.

Doctor Who was consciously designed as a show that that kids and their parents could both watch and enjoy. As the years went by, a third distinct demographic emerged - the older fans of the show. But all *Harry Potter* did in the late nineties was locate a hole in the market that *Doctor Who* and *Star Wars* filled back in my day.

The BBC have always identified the 'YA' market as one to go for. In his very first set of guidelines for the Eighth Doctor Adventures, Justin

Richards, the series editor, namechecked *His Dark Materials* and *Stormbreaker* as things that were 'like *Doctor Who*'. The NSAs aren't 'aimed at eight year olds'. They're aimed at the *Doctor Who* audience.

The best way to put it is that a *Doctor Who* author *also* has to appeal to children, now. You don't have to lose anything, you do have another thing to think about and factor in.

I've 'got away' with stuff in *The Eyeless* that, in all honesty, I wasn't sure I would do. I have a fairly gruesome dead body, a child waiving a knife and references to pregnancy. Nothing, at all, got cut for 'ratings' reasons (unlike *Father Time* and *The Gallifrey Chronicles*, as it happens). The only thing that changed 'for the kids' was that I sped up the opening a little, got to the action a little faster than I did in my first draft. That was on the advice of Justin Richards, my editor... although to be fair, two or three of the people that read the draft suggested the same thing. In practical terms, there are about two pages of description of the cityscape 'missing'.

So... 'kids'. I imagine my youngest reader as being about ten or eleven, but those would be really smart, bright ten year olds, ones who were big fans of *Doctor Who*. I think the 'typical' younger reader of the NSAs is about thirteen. And I wouldn't know how to aim a book at 'thirteen year olds' - I'm thinking specifically about a thirteen year old *reader*. Someone who reads a lot, probably, who loves reading. So this is someone inquisitive, who likes learning things, solving puzzles, thinking things through.

In all honesty, smart thirteen year olds are going to be smarter and more literate than a dumb adult. They will know bigger words and more science and history.

The difference isn't in the word choice, it's in the world they live in. *Doctor Who* is, basically, about a man who fights what scares us. What scares me? Well, it's not insects or reptiles or any of the phobic stuff *Doctor Who* monsters usually represent. It's the idea that I won't be able to pay the mortgage, for one. Interest rates. The credit crunch. I was going to say that's not exactly the topic for SF action-adventure, but then I remembered that the running story in *Captain America* while I was writing *The Eyeless* is an elaborate supervillain plot to undermine the credit market, thus destabilising the US economy to lever in a third-party Presidential candidate.

I have a different perspective on the world and people than I did when I was thirteen. There would be something deeply wrong with me if I didn't.

For *The Eyeless*, what I've tried to do is take a cue from Philip Pullman - who, in turn, took his cue from Blake's *Songs of Innocence and Experience*.

A child and adult can look at the same event and see two completely different things. Neither is right or wrong, particularly, but adults are often better at seeing the hidden agendas and reading into situations - of looking out for what's *not* being said. There's plenty left unsaid in *The Eyeless* that the younger readers won't spot, but which the adult readers can't miss.

The net effect of all this: I've written a *Doctor Who* book in the exact style and manner I've written *Doctor Who* books in the past. The idea that a lot of my readers are younger or more casual than back in the day has actually kept me honest - I can't throw in an injoke or rely on the goodwill of people who know *Doctor Who* (or Lance Parkin). I've had to make sure those characters work, that the story makes sense and so on. I think, to put it another way, having a more mainstream audience has only made the book stronger - for all my readers.

Timeline

I'm going to run through a quick timeline of the commissioning and writing process for *The Eyeless*, to give a sense of what happens, when and how long everything takes. It's something that people often ask me about, and it is normally (and should be) an invisible part of the process.

I got an initial email from Justin Richards, the consulting editor for the *Doctor Who* range, on the 6th of November, 2007, asking if I was busy. Suspecting that, if not, he would have something that would keep me busy, I eagerly replied.

He wanted me to write a tenth Doctor book. I had an idea for one all ready and waiting. I proceeded to explain that it was the Doctor and Donna meeting Jane Austen. The Slitheen were active in Bath during the Regency, setting up an auction for an old superweapon from the Time War. Because they were in the past, zips hadn't been invented, so the Slitheen had button-up foreheads. Donna hasn't read any Jane Austen - she proceeds to tell Austen the plot of her favourite book, which is *Bridget Jones' Diary*.

Justin told me that if I'd just shut up a minute, they were looking for a book where the Doctor was travelling on his own, they wanted it set anywhere but Earth, and that under no circumstances was I to use old monsters.

Hmmmm.

In circumstances like this, a writer has to adopt, adapt and improve. So, naturally, I looked at my proposal and said 'OK. About this superweapon... '

Justin is very good at giving guidance - what the *Doctor Who* books are after is a story with a strong hook. That ought to be a given, of course, but with something like my earlier book *Trading Futures*, there's a more like a 'high concept' than a strong story '*Doctor Who* spoofs James Bond'. *The Gallifrey Chronicles* has quite a simple idea at its heart ('the Doctor discovers who destroyed his home planet... turns out it was him'), but it's not a standalone story. *Father Time*'s got a strong story hook - the Doctor literally is left holding the baby, Miranda, and has to protect her from enemies from the far future who are hunting her.

A couple of days later, I had a new idea and got in touch with Justin. We exchanged emails, Justin clarified a couple of points, we honed the idea. The basic story hook stayed exactly the same throughout this and it's right there in the blurb on the back of the finished book - the Doctor lands on a dead planet dominated by an alien fortress, intent on decommissioning the weapon at the heart of the Fortress.

He wouldn't let me use the Daleks. I suspected this would be the case, but I felt I should ask. I asked if it could show the Fall of Arcadia from the Time War, mentioned by the Doctor, and was quietly told that it was best if I didn't. The TV people are telling those stories, and want to tell them on TV - they certainly don't want to end up contradicting anything that's in a novel. This actually strengthens the books. We have to come up with our own ideas.

Coming up with a story that will sustain a novel is an odd process, and it's not something that I can break down into formulae. What I've found is that once you've got a few strong ideas, other things start to snap into place.

With a *Doctor Who* novel, of course, a lot of things are sketched in for you beforehand. I've also got notebooks full of ideas and bits of ideas going back years. There's an aircar chase scene that I wanted to put into *Cold Fusion* (which I wrote in 1996), and which has been in contention for most of my *Doctor Who* books since. It was very nearly in *The Eyeless*, but I played around with the ending a bit at a very late stage and lost the scene.

I've had the idea for the monsters for a long time. I had a clear picture of them, a little scene plotted out in my head, and that's made it onto the page pretty well untouched (page 116, to be precise).

The setting is a *Jetsons*-style futuristic city - you know the sort of thing - but one that's fallen into ruin. I just like the images that creates, all this amazing utopian promise, now rusting and collapsed.

I read a couple of articles years ago by Stephen Baxter about the human legacy - what we'd leave behind. The answers are a bit sad and strange. As the weather erodes everything away, in a million years or so the only structures that would be left are the absolute rock solid things like suspension bridge supports. The main evidence for mankind will be the cuttings in rock for railways and roads. Oh, and there would be a thin fossil layer of refined metal, pollution and nuclear waste. Baxter dramatizes this in his book *Evolution*.

There was clearly something in the air that makes this idea current. As I started writing *The Eyeless*, I found out about *The World Without Us*, a book that imagines what would happen if human beings just vanished today. The conclusion of that book is that, even in seven million years, the faces on Mount Rushmore will be recognizable. It starts out, though, just documenting what happens for the first few years as a city falls apart. The movies *I Am Legend* and *WALL-E* came out at roughly the same time; dealing with the same imagery, the BBC revived *Survivors*. There's always apocalyptic fiction, of course, but the current brand - almost certainly an imaginative bashing together of War on Terror anxiety and eco-guilt - is quite distinctive.

These things happen, there's a zeitgeist and people all end up doing things independently that look like they've been comparing notes. Sometimes, the reason's obvious - there was a lot of stuff set in China in 2008, like *Kung Fu Panda*, because everyone knew about the Beijing Olympics (this raises the prospect of 2012 being the year of movies like *Pub Fight Badger*, of course). It may be as simple as we're all watching the same stuff. You can see the NA/EDAs go through phases of *Terminator 2/Warhammer 40,000* gung-ho action, *X-Files*-style mysteries, *Babylon 5* knock-off future wars that are a bit rubbish when you actually get there, before ending up all Joss Whedon.

A lot of my writer pals are watching *The Wire* and reading *Death Note* right now. You have been warned.

The superweapon... well, ultimately, these devices are always McGuffins. This one is a pretty ultimate ultimate weapon, though, as these things go. As the Doctor says at one point in the book, 'It's a weapon that would give your run-of-the-mill ultimate weapon an inferiority complex.'

These are all elements that would end up in the story, but they're not the story...

This is going to sound arrogant and horrible, so imagine me saying it in gently ironic tones: I don't find writing a *Doctor Who* book all that difficult. Douglas Adams had that quote about how writing was about sitting there until your forehead bleeds... I prefer former BBC political correspondent John Cole's line that the hardest part isn't getting words on a page, it's keeping your bottom on the seat. It's very easy to get distracted, particularly when it's oh so easy to justify watching a DVD, popping out to Borders or just staring out the window as 'research'.

John Cole made his remark in the pre-Internet age, if anyone now can imagine such an epoch. Now you can be quite happily sat at your computer with the document open and still be involved in displacement activities.

I am, apparently, a fast writer. A fair few professional writers say they manage about a thousand words a day. Now... this isn't anything to get hung up about. If you write five hundred words a day and they're good, that's pretty handy. Most people have actual jobs and friends and family, that sort of thing, so it's hard to make time to write at all. If you want to be a writer, you have to work out a way to find that time, of course. *The Eyeless* is 55,000 words long, and that's at the lower end of novel-length. A thousand words a day is two months with a few days off for good behaviour, assuming you're doing nothing else.

My record is about 15,000 words in a day - the first great surge of activity on *The Dying Days*, where I had a really, really clear idea of what I had to do (and, more to the point, a deadline of five weeks to do it). All cylinders blazing, the first burst, or with a real mastery of the material, I can do something like 6000 words in a day. My record the other way... well, I've thrown away whole chapters of books on more than one occasion, so probably something like minus 5000 words. With books that completely fail to take root - such as my *Prisoner* novella, and my Great American Novel that I've been writing for three years now and refer to, dreadingly, as *The Whale Oil Book* - I must be averaging less than ten words a day. On the whole, I reckon I write about 2500 words a day on average. The best trick I've found is to try to do a novel at the same time as a non-fiction book - they don't really feel like the same kind of thing when you're writing, so you can displace from 'writing' to 'writing something else'.

This time I had a couple of extra challenges. The first was the length. It became very clear to me that *The Eyeless* couldn't be paced at quite the way my other books had been. *The Gallifrey Chronicles*, to be honest, is probably more frenetic, but it had a lot to do. The pace of *Doctor Who* TV stories just kept speeding up. Watch *The Web Planet* and it's hard to shake the idea that Tennant and Donna would get to halfway through episode three by the opening credits (virtually every 'sting' that comes just before the opening credits now would have been the episode one cliffhanger even in the eighties). It's no coincidence that the 'typical' story started at six or seven episodes long, dropped to four, was dropping to three in the late eighties and is now fifty minutes. There's just as much 'story' in, say, *Planet of the Ood* as a Troughton six-parter, probably more.

As a digression... it's interesting that while TV is getting shorter and punchier, novels are getting longer and longer. Technology allows this -

word processors let authors store more (the completed *Eyeless* book would fit on half an old floppy disk, it barely registers on a flashdrive), it allows editors to edit faster. Books get emailed, not posted. An author doesn't cross out mistakes or have to retype pages, or have one manuscript that they can't, at any cost, leave on the bus. It's pretty amazing to think that in the Target book days, someone at a printers was fitting together little metal letters to make up each page in turn, then running the press, then rearranging the letters on the frame to make the next set of pages. All of this means that these days a long book costs about the same for everyone as a short one.

Long story short (see what I did there?), if I'd paced *The Eyeless* like an old Past Doctor book, it would have felt like a short, light, slow Past Doctor book. The book starts out with quite a slow build, establishing the setting. I very quickly found myself splicing scenes together - instead of two scenes where the Doctor walks down a corridor, then into a room and starts talking to someone, we have what *The West Wing* production team took to calling 'pedalogues': the Doctor and someone walking down a corridor, talking as they go. The advice scriptwriters get is to start the scene as late as possible and finish it as soon as possible. I found myself doing that a lot.

This is all great for the book. It's very focused, there's not much you could mistake for padding. It was quite tricky, though - not least because if you're writing with everything tightly packed like that, it becomes very difficult to change things around when you need to.

The other issue was that this book was marketed as YA. In practical terms, although I was very determined just to write a *Doctor Who* book (and not paralyse myself by endlessly second-guessing what 'Cardiff' wanted or whether kids would like it), I did have 'older children will be reading this' at the back of my mind. I knew my Philip Pullman, and figured that if Young Adult books allow kids to not just go around with knives, but to stab God with them, that the 'ratings' issue wouldn't be too much of a problem. But I did want to read up on what was popular, mainly - I have to admit - so I could use it as precedent. ('Justin, in *Silverfin*, a girl pins Bond down with her thighs and a eel squirts out of a dead man's mouth, so it's clearly acceptable for the younger readers...')

I had a clear idea of how my book started, I'd already started assembling phrases and images and jokes and so on.

It's always good to read. If you want to be a writer, read more, and read more widely. As I wrote *The Eyeless*, I relaxed by reading. And what happened is what always happens when something's working: I'd be reading something completely unrelated to my book, and a factoid or quotation or bit of history would suddenly leap out as something to look at. This happens a lot with me. Either it's some amazingly powerful unconscious, holistic thing, or I just become completely blinkered and uncritical. I was reading *Life, the Universe and Everything* when the *exact* quote I needed appeared, a lovely turn of phrase from Douglas Adams I'd never noticed in the dozen or so times I'd read the book before. It's in *The Eyeless*, with all due credit.

I try to give every book its own 'voice'. It's hard to describe - it's to do with pace and the length of sentences. *The Infinity Doctors*, say, has loads of descriptive passages and dwells on little details. *Trading Futures* skates over things really fast (there were quite a lot of long, dense books in the previous batch of EDAs, and I just thought people would appreciate one they could gulp down in two sittings). This 'voice' is all about the internal logic of the story. In *One Fine Day in the Middle of the Night*, Christopher Brookmyre talks about the bullet-deadliness quotient, the idea that every bullet fired in a movie has to be equally deadly. You can have movies where each shot is lethal, you can have a movie where machine guns are spraying a room and no one gets hurt, but you can't have a movie where one minute guns are deadly and the next minute they're not.

He's right and I think there are lots of equivalents in fiction. Kissing someone is far more significant in *Doctor Who* than having sex with them and their sister would be in *Skins*. Each story has its own level of meting out justice, the relationship between what they do and the punishment they get. There are Child Spunkiness Quotients, Adultery Forgiveness Quotients, Swearing Quotients, Quip and Eloquence Quotients, Character Disposable Income And Free Time Quotients, Recovery Time From Injury Quotients. You create a world, with rules. The trick is, as Brookmyre says, to stay consistent within those rules.

Some books, I really struggle with finding those balances. If I had to describe the writing process, that's the word I would use: 'balancing'. Writing is about making lots of choices - choosing a path, which means not choosing other paths. You have to work out if you're telling your audience too much or not enough. A lot of this is instinctive, but writing itself is a sort of 'guided instinctive' process. You go on your instincts... then go back and make sure.

Finding the 'voice' for *The Eyeless* was fairly smooth. While I would eventually edit a few things down, I pretty much had the first sixty five pages or so done and dusted inside a week. Gosh, everything was going so smoothly. I'd have it done by Christmas at this rate.

By moving so quickly, I had got a little ahead of myself. I had my synopsis. But I wasn't just religiously following that. No plan survives initial contact with the enemy.

The synopsis I'd written, the one Justin and I had worked through, the one that Russell Davies had read and approved, was two pages long. It wasn't meant to contain every single thing the book would. Editors know that. The idea is that when you hand the book in, the editor can look at the synopsis and go 'yeah, that's what we commissioned'. Basically it's so, down the line, the marketing people, the cover designer, the sales reps, the press and publicity people... they all know, months before the book actually exists, what they'll be getting.

Tales grow in the telling.

The thing a lot of non-writers ask is 'where do you get your ideas?'. It's the wrong question to ask. Ideas are easy, it's stringing them together in a coherent way that's the challenge. What I've found is that to string ideas together, the process of writing is more like a set of heuristics... 'solutions to problems'.

There are a variety of strategies a writer adopts. Again, as I've said before, very little of this is conscious, particularly when everything's working. It's not a matter of sitting and calculating - you don't catch a ball by calculating a parabola, you do it on instinct. Or, in my case, you fumble and drop the ball because you lack even basic hand-eye co-ordination.

The basic problem to solve is that there's a set of specific story points you want to make - people who study drama tend to call these 'beats'. If you want to make the point that a character is cool in a crisis... well, the golden rule is that you don't just write 'Steve was great in a crisis', you have a scene where we all see Steve coping well in a crisis (and, by way of contrast, other people coping badly). 'Show not tell.' And the difference between fiction and real life is that everything in fiction is there for a reason, and is making a specific point - the art of it is to make it feel like real life, and the irony is that necessitates hundreds of different contrivances and conventions. So, for example, people in real life don't speak in any way at all like people speak in the movies - unless the real life people are quoting from movies. The biggest con job of all, the most artificial and convention-bound, is the story that's 'realistic'.

Things change as the writer turns his ideas into an actual book, and that was certainly true of *The Eyeless*.

One character, Dela, isn't even mentioned in the proposal and just ended up becoming a major character. This often happens - stories work much better if there are two people in a room, arguing and explaining things. As I said, I was splicing scenes together, keeping things pacey and efficient. I needed characters to hit three 'beats' - to do three things - and it turned out that Dela could do all three, and suddenly was there in my book, a rounded character.

Another character, Alsa, started out as one thing and ended up as exactly the same character but playing a completely different, much more interesting and involved role in the story. She started out as a character who, along with her friend Gar, followed the Doctor around. Their role was essentially to comment on what the Doctor was doing, ask each other questions. As I wrote the book, I realised that Alsa was my antagonist - she was the villain of the book, the person who is the greatest obstacle for the Doctor. The book altered quite substantially once I understood the active role she'd take in the story. Gar, on the other hand, ended up with far less than I was expecting. I thought the two of them would be a double act, and get pretty much equal time. He completely disappears from the audiobook version.

The thing is... synopses are always a bit of a fudge. Legend has it that the outline for the Paul McGann movie ends with something like 'and then the Doctor gets back to the TARDIS and stops the Master in his own inimitable style'. That's the whole last act basically down as 'TBC'. And the last act is a bit of a mess, probably not coincidentally. If nothing else, if you've not pinned it down, every random passing executive can pitch in and add a suggestion like 'wouldn't it be great if they went into, like, a time orbit?' and he'll be too senior for anyone to express their natural, healthy reaction to the idea, which is basically to re-enact that bit with Heath Ledger and the pencil.

There will always be things you've not fully worked out in your synopsis. You'll have things like 'and then the Doctor gets through the impenetrable forcefield and meets the Guardian who tells him the way to the Old City' or something, without knowing how he does that literally, by definition, impossible thing or what the hell a Guardian is or looks like. In that case, it's basically deferring your imagination. You'll explain later.

There are two simple problems there: coming up with a trick for the Doctor to perform to get past the forcefield while trying to maintain suspense, and playing fair with your readers. 'Oh look, a button that deactivates the forcefield' is a bit rubbish, but so's 'I'll plug my sonic screwdriver into the tachyon emitters and send a plasmotic pulse.' Ideally, you want some way that the reader could guess - 'oh, he uses the crystal he picked up in the forest in the first chapter' or just make a fight of it. The Doctor gets past five traps a story, there are over a thousand *Doctor Who* stories, so it's tricky coming up with a novel way of getting past a trap. As I said a while back, stories are about choices. If your protagonist gets past the trap by making a clever, characteristic choice, it's always going to be more satisfying than if he does it by luck or coincidence.

Likewise, the Doctor's met lots of monsters - a number of them called

'Guardian', for that matter, like Mavic Chen, Guardian of the Solar System (except on Sunday, when he's merely an Observer, joke copyright Jim Smith), the Guardian of the Doomsday Weapon, not forgetting the Black, White, er... hang on, I think I can do this from memory, Gold, Azure, Red, Crystal and Beige Guardians. Was there a Pink Guardian? Somehow, you feel there ought to be in the *Doctor Who* universe. Pink could play him or her.

These are basically just three pipe problems. You spend a day going 'the Guardian's a big lizard... nah... she's a little girl... nah... he's Stephen Fry in a *UFO*-style purple tinfoil wig... yeah... er... nah' until you hit on an idea that just works. It is, in all honesty, a ridiculous way to make a living, and to justify it, authors work themselves up until things like this seem like the Schleswig-Holstein Question or trying to prove that P=NP.

These aren't structural problems. At the end of the day, it doesn't really matter what the Guardian looks like from a story point of view. The story beat is only that the Doctor needs to meet someone who can tell him about the Old City. If the book was running over the word count, or was dragging a bit, you could ditch the whole forcefield/Guardian bit and have the Doctor find a signpost marked 'to the Old City'.

If you're writing a book and you change your mind, you only have to edit a few sentences. Or, and this is the great thing with novels, you can defer everything to your readers: 'she was the most beautiful woman imaginable'. OK readers... get imagining. On TV, you have to be more concrete - you have to cast that woman, so you end up with the most beautiful woman by the standards of the casting director who's available and agrees to the fee. Not really the same. But even on TV, the writer can palm a load of the heavy lifting off onto the director or designers. You type 'it's a futuristic control room' and get on with things, leaving some other guy to design and build the damn thing.

Ten days or so into the writing of *The Eyeless*, I hit a structural problem that can basically be summed up by saying that the middle of the book was proving to be better than the big finale I had planned.

I'd whizzed through the book at this point, and at one point seriously thought I'd have it all done by Christmas. Bear in mind that my deadline was June - and what the secret editors never like to share is that these deadlines always have a little bit of a buffer built in, because writers are prone to miss deadlines. When I handed in one of my first professional magazine articles, the editor said 'this is on time, it's about what you were briefed to write about and it's the word count we agreed'. I said something along the lines of 'well... duh', and he told me 'no - if we only get *one* of those, we're happy'. Note that 'well-written' doesn't factor into that.

But now it was mid-January and I'd stalled. I'd kept writing... I now had about two-thirds of the book, but I wasn't that happy with the last couple of chapters and I only had a scattered impression of where I was going. I knew I had structural problems, I knew I'd be throwing out a lot of what I was writing, which I always dislike doing. This sounds strange, but there are two basic writing techniques, I think: writers who throw down twice as much as they need onto the page, knowing they'll carve away at it and get it into shape; or writers who only commit things to paper when they're broadly happy with it, so end up putting half as much as they need, then adding things to get it into shape. I'm definitely the latter.

When Kate Orman and Jon Blum started writing their first novel featuring the eighth Doctor - *Vampire Science* - they were asked to use Grace, the companion introduced in the Paul McGann TVM. After they'd written a couple of chapters, the BBC got in touch to tell them that it wasn't possible to use Grace for rights reasons. This was, then, something that affected the novel's structure, plus they had to rework and revise the book to fit in the new companion, Sam.

Structural problems usually aren't the result of something external like that, it's usually something the author realises isn't working about their book. The Alsa thing I mentioned is quite a good example. Changing her role in the book changed a fair amount of other things. I wrote earlier about how a story is about choices - we see far more of her choices, the reasoning behind them and so on. All that meant that she had to be in different places at different times and all of that has knock-on effects.

The first ten days or so writing *The Eyeless*, I was writing stuff that was setting up the story and it was fairly straightforward. The opening section has the Doctor arriving and doing a little bit of exploring. Now... there was a complication. In a normal *Doctor Who* story, there's a companion, and it's the perfect set up: an older, experienced character can answer all the questions the companion has. And because the companion is an audience identification figure, the companion asks all the questions the audience would, if they were there.

The Doctor is travelling without a companion in *The Eyeless*. The easiest thing to do would be to have him meet someone early on who can act as a sort of temporary stand-in for a companion. I wasn't interested in doing that - I had an opportunity to have the Doctor alone, and hooking him up with someone would cancel all that out. And I didn't have the option the TV series has exercised a couple of times now, to have a stellar celebrity guest star as a one-time companion.

But I'd known all along that the Doctor wasn't going to have a companion, and that was all part of the plan. You'll see how I got on when you read the book. The irony was that my writing slowed down once I got past that phase and to the easy bit where the Doctor met up with other characters.

In the synopsis, this was a fairly brief encounter - the Doctor would meet them and move on. Even when I was drawing up the synopsis, though, I suspected that this would be an area of the book that would expand. It always happens - there will be some part of the story that just comes alive and presents all sorts of dramatic opportunities. Then there are always parts of the synopsis that seemed like really great ideas that would fill fifty scintillating pages which you realise you can cover in one chapter, one scene or even a single line... if it needs to be in there at all.

One thing that dropped out - I originally wanted the Eyeless to have a caste system, with clearly-defined roles. One would be a pilot, one would be a telepath, one would be a leader, some would be warriors and so on. That's completely missing from the finished book for a couple of reasons. First, it's a bit of a rubbish science-fiction cliché. I'm not saying it couldn't be done, or hasn't been done - there's meaty stuff to be had about 'we've all got our part to play' and individual vs. society stuff, which are nice big themes for any book, and were already part of what my book is talking about. I was originally going to explore that using the Eyeless characters. Those are still themes of the novel, but there were just better characters to tell that story with.

Second, though, it was just taking far too long to explain the set up. I was literally creating a convoluted problem for myself, then taking forever to solve it. The problems in the rest of the book are fairly straightforward and easy to relate to real life. I'll probably write a SF novel at some point where there are aliens with a strict caste structure - one of the great things about writing is that you end up recycling your old ideas sooner or later - but it'll be a book all about that.

My big structural problem came when it became obvious that the human survivors the Doctor meets are actually big identification figures... and that one of the problems with the book was that there were precious few identification figures.

It coincided with me realising that the bulk of the second half of the book wasn't going to work. Remember that bit with the big grabby robot arm thing in *Planet of the Ood*? That hadn't been shown at the time I was writing *The Eyeless*, but the whole of the second half of the book was going to be like that - relentless action. It was something I knew would be a challenge, and not quite right or sane for a piece of prose. There's a piece of received wisdom that there has never, ever been a great car chase in a novel. I can't think of one. I'd probably look in Ian Fleming to find it. The idea was to take something that would work really well in a movie and try to make it work in a book.

Yeah... it quickly became obvious that I couldn't get it to work. Whenever I tried, what I was doing sounded like the subtitles for an action film.

So, I had a couple of problems. The action bit didn't work and I wanted to expand the role of the people the Doctor met. The problem: the location of the story switches, and definitively moves away from those people for the second half of the book. For the first time, it was a problem for me that the Doctor didn't have a companion. In a normal *Doctor Who* book, the narrative can be in two places at once - the Doctor in one location, the companion in another. That's actually what happens in most *Doctor Who* stories.

The Eyeless is more like first person narration, in a way - the Doctor's in virtually every scene. Which has the advantage that it feels nice and immediate and that you're in the heart of the action, but the disadvantage that it's hard and vaguely boring whenever you cut away from what the Doctor's doing. I suspect I'm not the only person who has been reading a *Doctor Who* book and decided to skip ahead when there's half a chapter about the colonists (or whoever) and the Doctor and companion aren't in that bit. It's called *Doctor Who*, not *The Colonists*.

Originally what I planned was for the Doctor to be in and out of the Fortress pretty quickly... that had to change. The air car chase sequence that I've dropped from pretty much every *Doctor Who* book since *Cold Fusion* got dropped again. Alsa's new role was working nicely, and helping to show off the Eyeless themselves. To be honest, what I was writing was OK, and would have made for a functional *Doctor Who* book, but... well, this was my first tenth Doctor book, I had plenty of time, and I wanted it to be special, if I could manage that.

This wasn't exactly a looming disaster, but I was finding it frustrating. So I sent the book out to a few people, hoping they'd be able to tell me where I was going wrong.

The people who read through it are credited in the book, and absolutely every single one of them immeasurably improved the story. It's no exaggeration, for example, to say that Jon Blum gave me both the best joke in the book (the 'down the pub' one) and one of the best scenes ('begone, shift!').

A lot of the time, people would say things I knew already, either deep down or just because they were obvious. This is often the most helpful criticism of all - a lot of what a writer does is, as I've mentioned, papering over cracks and he needs to know what he's got away with. There were a couple of plot logic things I'd been avoiding thinking about, but everyone agreed I had to address. The blurb for the book - which I'd written pretty much when I'd started - talks about the weapon at the heart of the Fortress and asks 'What is the true nature of the weapon?'. This seemed like a very good question. I knew what the weapon *had* done, I knew what it looked like, but I didn't know its 'true nature'. It changed over and over as I was writing the book, from just a straightforward big radiation-burst thing through to ideas so exotic they looked remarkably like they didn't make any sense at all. The trick was to find something strange, big and vaguely plausible, but which worked in a way I could easily explain. The final version is kind of hard-sciencey, in a *Doctor Who* way.

As with so much science fictiony stuff, you want an explanation that's both bizarre, over-the-top and yet which is simple enough to get your head around. It would be difficult, for example, to actually build a ring-world or an ansible or a transporter or whatever, but it's simple enough to explain what they are and what they do, and why it would be cool to get your hands on one.

Another problem... and I think this is pretty common with a lot of writers: faced with a second half of a book that was a problem, I just went back and refined and revised the stuff I'd already written. It was something to do, but every time I polished the beginning of the book, the gap between the lovely first half and the scrappy second half just became more and more pronounced.

I think it was Lloyd Rose who first pinpointed that there were two distinct problems I was facing in the second half. The first one I knew, but was too close to the story to see as a big problem: I'd set up an interesting group of characters, then had the Doctor just walk away from them. It was essentially a bit of a waste. The second was something I hadn't spotted at all, but which was absolutely fundamental. Plenty of stuff was happening to the Doctor - quite big emotional beats, real challenges and so on - but they were just happening very episodically, there was no real sense of things getting harder for him, or any development at all.

The mistake I'd made is something I've already talked about here - the idea of the Protagonist and his choices. I was giving the Doctor a sequence of physical challenges, and these were getting trickier and trickier. The emotional beats, though, were all at one level (broadly 'gosh, how will I beat this physical challenge in time?'). Part of this is the problem with the Doctor as a character generally - he's a thousand years old, he's been through so much. It's hard (arrogant, even) to imagine that your story is finally the one that really puts him through the ringer or threatens to break him. He's resistant to any kind of change, really - even when something extraordinarily traumatic happens to him (Rose leaving is the best example recently, perhaps ever) he should be back to being the

Doctor pretty quickly. He's not far away from that in *The Runaway Bride*, which literally starts before the tears he's shed over Rose have hit the ground, and three episodes into the season, when he mentions Rose to Martha and it's still a sore point, it feels a little 'off', I think.

Mark Clapham noted the places where the 'influence' of *The Subtle Knife* on my book was straying into legal territory and wondered if the characters were a little too 'normal', given their circumstances. Mark Jones and I had a long phone call where we talked through the plot logic of just about every element of the book, including - again - the psychology of the other characters. Kate Orman and Lloyd Rose set me straight about when the tenth Doctor wears his glasses.

Everyone asked why the Eyeless were called the Eyeless.

The second half of the book began snapping into place, but it took a long time. It's quite intricately plotted - very tightly focused on the Doctor, but with stuff going on close by that's affecting the action. At every stage, there's a tension between moving the story along and dwelling on things.

I had my own notes, too. Three pages of my big notebook were taken up with bullet points that needed addressing - these were often big things or just references or lines or words I wanted to fit in the book somewhere. Many of these look pretty obscure:

'Sunlight = plants'
'Handful joke'
'why no survivor guilt'
'No H in "Antony Gormley".'
'callous to boys, not girls'
'how Eyeless can see?'
'Casino Royale'
'Civilisation Zero?'
'Museums rotting'
'Urban jungle'

The upshot of this was that I had to completely restructure the second half of the book, and there was a lot to fit in there. The irony is that I recently re-read the synopsis, and the end result is pretty much exactly the same as both the first draft and the published book.

I'd got a second draft I was relatively happy with by March 10th. I think I could have got away with this version of the book - it was the first complete draft. For the first time, the ending felt satisfying - although it still wasn't quite right. I sent this revised version to people, saying that it was 'still missing that special sauce'.

I also had a secret weapon: Phil Purser-Hallard. On the Jade Pagoda mailing list (which is all about the *Doctor Who* novels - in theory at least; be warned that the list once got into a fight over whether the argument they were having was circular or, as one person suggested, triangular), PPH's reviews of my books were always incredibly perceptive and constructive. Eventually I realised that if he reviewed my books at the manuscript stage, I'd end up with much better published books. I only emailed Philip the book when it was at this stage, because I knew I wanted a fresh eye on it. As ever, I got another great list of tweaks and suggestions.

A piece of television has hundreds of people making direct creative contributions, it's actually quite tricky to see 'authored' TV - *Doctor Who*, of course, is now an exception. But even shows with 'showrunners' whose names you know aren't created by one person, not even one writer. *The Eyeless* is 'more me own work' than a television episode would be; even so, there are dozens of people on the production side (editors, copy editors and so on...) and plenty of people who were happy to give me their time and perspective while writing. Thanks, everyone.

So, I delivered the official first draft of *The Eyeless* to Justin on May 16th. I say 'official first draft' because, well, these things are hard to define. Back in the day, an author (or his or her secretary!) would type out a manuscript and it would be a very solid, defined thing. Now it's a computer file, and I went back and forth changing as much as I wanted, whenever I wanted.

For the record, Justin was getting a fourth draft, I think. By the end of December, I had just about everything done but the ending. I sent it around to people and waited for feedback from them - in part because I needed that feedback to help crystallize that ending for me.

By mid-March, I'd got a much better second half and an ending that worked but which I wasn't completely happy with.

There was a much stronger draft by the end of April, thanks in large part to all the people who'd read it and commented. The ending was a lot better, but still not quite right.

By 'ending' I really mean the 'third act' - the whole last bit of the story, where all the cards are on the table, all the plans are in the open and reaching a critical point. Every *Doctor Who* story has one - in the olden days, it was the whole last episode. Now it's that last, frantic ten minutes or so. I say every *Doctor Who* story, but *The Mark of the Rani* and *The Ambassadors of Death* both just sort of stop.

One of the things I wanted to avoid was what I'll call '*The World Is Not Enough* problem'. There are two main baddies in that movie. They kill off the most interesting one first, then the last act is Bond beating the less-interesting one. And, as it turns out, in an extremely dull way - literally they push a prop back and forth until the bad guy dies. I really have three sets of antagonists by the end, and spent a long time juggling the order in which - spoiler alert - the Doctor sorts them out.

I wrote one ending and it was literally, almost word for word, the ending of *Watchmen*. Which has a great ending, but one with the slight disadvantage - for my purposes, if not the reading public's - of not being something I wrote.

There was also a separate question of the actual last scene. I had four or five different versions of this, all basically the same scene, played differently. These were nothing like the end I'd described in the synopsis - that no longer fit the book. In *Doctor Who* there's always a problem with this last bit - you want the Doctor back in the TARDIS, ready for his next adventure. If you're not careful, you end up finishing with a pretty redundant bit - the Doctor and companion walking back to the ship saying, effectively, 'well, that was exciting, wasn't it?'.

Around May 10th, it came to me exactly what the very last scene needed to be. This, though I say it myself, had everything - a nice echo of some things Russell Davies wrote (no, it's not someone shouting 'Paul McGann doesn't count!'), the Doctor doing something clever only the Doctor can do, a sense of the story coming full circle to an extent, and a real sense of closure. Coming up with that ending was a real 'eureka' moment, and quite a relief.

As is the way with these things, once I knew what to write, writing it was pretty straightforward. It quickly expanded to become the whole last chapter - as I was already bumping against my word count, I then had to go back and did a bit of trimming to fit it in. This sounds blithe and untroubled, but I'd been trying to find this last scene since the end of December, getting increasingly worried. Writing endings is a little like doing a balance sheet, it all has to fit together and add up, while leaving nothing out. Some of my favourite authors are hopeless at endings, and I think it's because they're reluctant to leave the wonderful world and the characters they've created. I understand that feeling, certainly.

It's also because life never has neat endings. One of the best endings of anything, ever, is the end of *Our Friends in the North*. It feels like a culmination of the thirty-year journey we've been on. It's superbly written, with an exceptional performance by Christopher Eccleston (as it also stars Daniel Craig, *Our Friends in the North* now feels like a story not even Paul Magrs dare write - the Doctor and James Bond growing up in the sixties as Geordie best friends). If you nitpick it, then the end only feels like things have changed, but it's incredibly cathartic and emotional.

Endings are tricky, and I speak from experience.

So, I went through a process to write *The Eyeless*. I had to identify, define and solve problems. Part of my job was to make the final book seamless and untroubled and to make that process pretty much invisible. If you ever watch a film and go 'that was a great bit of direction' or 'what a great special effect'... it wasn't. Not in the normal course of things. Reading should be a bit like driving a car - if you can hear the engine rattling, something's gone wrong. We're all very savvy and postmodern and meta and well-informed now, but the paradox of my job is that, at its root, what I'm trying to do is to distract you from the mechanics of what I'm doing and leave you with a purely aesthetic experience. And, surely, I get bonus paradox points for announcing that after tens of thousands of words about the mechanics of writing.

These are the risks we take in the age of DVD commentaries and making-of discs. I hope that the people who've read this far are the sort of people who appreciate a trick all the more if they know how it's done. David Copperfield once said that the difference between Vegas and London audiences was that in Vegas, they look at *him* when he starts flying overhead, but in London, they look *past him* for the wires yet end up clapping louder. I hope you're a London audience.

Anyway, I sent the book to Justin. Within a day or so, he was able to send me the cover. At first, I got a PDF file, but I soon got a nice glossy copy posted to me. I've always framed these, which means, by now, I've got enough book covers to fill up a fairly sizable wall.

The Eyeless was announced around the 25th of May. I'd spent six months knowing I was writing a tenth Doctor book without being able to shout about it! The book wasn't finished yet, though...

On June 20th, I got the comments back from Justin Richards, consulting editor and prolific author in his own right.

The note he sent was about 1700 words, and made about thirty separate points, about twenty of which were minor and easily corrected with a little bit of clarification. For example, I'd done a sequence with three people talking and it wasn't always clear who was replying to whom. Those little ones just take a minute or two to sort out, on the whole.

Justin's very good on plot logic stuff, and there were a couple of things he needed to be sure I'd thought through. Generally, there were bits that were a little confusing, and needlessly so. There were also a couple of places where I'd moved a scene around and not noticed that a character now knew something they'd only find out about later. As ever, there were a number of Hartnellesque pronoun problems (I managed to write 'They could do so much they couldn't' at one point).

A good example of the bigger things that needed fixing - in the first draft, the locals called the Fortress 'the Folly', while the Doctor called it 'the Fortress'. Gradually, some of the locals started using the Doctor's name for it. It meant I ended up with people exchanging dialogue like 'We should go to the Folly' / 'Yes, you're right, we'll head off to the Fortress in the morning'. Now, I'm sure people would have figured it out, but why not just have everyone call it 'the Fortress' from the beginning? As you can tell from the picture of it on the cover, it's a perfectly sensible thing to call something that looks like that.

Justin wanted the opening trimmed back a little. This was the only time in the whole process he invoked 'the younger readers', saying they'd want to get to the story faster. On the initial read throughs, people had made that same point: Mark Jones and Lars Pearson both suggested cutting it down; Mark Clapham wondered about it, but said he liked it the way it was.

Other than that, it was fairly straightforward. The Doctor mentions an encounter with an alien that I'd made up for the book. Justin was worried that people would think they were missing a reference to a telly episode or one of the other books. At the same time, I was meant to be avoiding continuity references, so I couldn't just change it to refer to the Daleks or whatever. I cut the Gordian Knot with a slightly meta line from the Doctor explaining that this wasn't something a reader should take as a continuity reference.

Conversely, there was a continuity reference I'd put in the first draft that I really wanted in there, if at all possible. It was smack in the middle of what *The Eyeless* is about, although I'd always known it might be a problem. Justin and I talked it through and... well, it's on page 46 of the finished book. It's a reference to Gallifrey being destroyed that's actually a direct quote from my previous novel, *The Gallifrey Chronicles*.

One thing I didn't think would be a problem: I'd broken the book into two 'parts', and there's a big cliffhanger at the end of part one. The book is a game of two halves, too - like most of the telly two-parters, there's a definite shift in emphasis for part two. This was a bone of contention for a little while - it has page count and other design implications that I hadn't realised. I did really want it broken up like that. Ideally, I'd like people to take a week off between part one and part two! It is, though, entirely artificial - going strictly on word count, the novels are more like four episodes of new *Doctor Who* (or six or seven parters in old money). In the end, Justin was able to grant my wish, and so if you're the sort of fan who insists the first story is called *100,000 BC* (it is, of course), then *The Eyeless* is actually called *The Eyes of a Child* / *Unless*. Which you can shorten to *The Eyeless*, of course.

We played around with one of the very last scenes, one where the motives of the characters and what they were really thinking wasn't clear. One of the characters was the Doctor, and - as ever - I wanted some ambiguity and mystery about his thought processes. Back in the days when Virgin published the books, it was an absolute no-no to have scenes that went too deep into what the Doctor was thinking. Here, though, what the Doctor was thinking and planning needed to be a little more explicit. It's the end of the book and he has to be resolute and strong... but not psychopathic, which is how what originally happened could read in certain lights. This was a bit where the editor was doing what a director would do if it was for TV - just making sure the motivation and movement of one scene wasn't cutting against the story.

That was, to be honest, the only tricky thing this time around, and it was tricky because - as I've said a number of times - the ending of the book was something that had to be very poised and carefully-judged. I always have a faint dread that an editor is going to want something completely removed or changed. Or, worse, that they'll ask for something they think is minor but which will mean great big structural changes. If it's in the synopsis, there's always the 'it's in the synopsis' defence. I had my new anxiety that, at some point, the fact it was a new series book would mean someone would be going through it and changing it. It still hadn't happened.

Justin is always very clear about what he wants, and open to negotiation - it's my name on the book, and I'd spent six months thinking about it and writing it. If I can make a case for something, Justin is always willing to listen. I had a list of things he wanted me to do. I'd had a month off from the book. I was now able to re-read it again with a bit of a fresh eye, and I spotted a couple of other things I could do and tricks I'd missed. With any project, it's great to be able to put it in a drawer for a few weeks then come back to it with a bit of distance. It's rarely a luxury I get, though.

The changes took a week, and I posted the second draft back to Justin on June 27th. He was happy enough with it to send it on to Cardiff for approval.

Gulp.

Once the manuscript has been delivered, a book goes through a number of different stages. This is an author's eye view of those, which is a polite way of saying that, for an author, a lot of this is pretty much invisible. You hand your book to someone, a few weeks after that you get back a list of comments and you don't do very much with your book in the meantime.

Once a book is written, it's edited. That's what Justin had done during June - he went through the manuscript looking at it artistically, making sure the story worked, suggesting ways the narrative could be improved, letting me know if there were any wider issues. With *Doctor Who*, there's the danger that you end up clashing with something that's coming up in another book or on the telly. I pretty much finished *The Eyeless* before the fourth series even started, and I had no special prior knowledge of it (less than most people reading this, probably, as I try to avoid spoilers).

The edited draft then went to Cardiff for approval. The book's going out with a *Doctor Who* logo on it, the BBC have all sorts of taste and decency standards. Obviously this is a stage most books don't have to go through. On 30th July, I got a rather anti-climatic note from Justin saying that the book had been approved by Cardiff, but that they'd asked for 'a couple of changes' and I'd see them at the proof stage. My paranoia gland started secreting whatever it is a paranoia gland secrets, but Justin assured me that there was nothing to worry about (his actual words were 'we removed all that stuff about a powerful alien fortress and replaced it with a sinister hillbilly dance routine').

It was now onto the next stage - the project editor, Steve Tribe, got in touch on 8th August to let me know that he'd got the approved manuscript and would be dealing with it from now on. Different publishers do different things at this stage, but it boils down to copy editing and proofreading stages. Steve's job was to take the completed, edited and approved manuscript and end up with typeset page proofs - a PDF file of the book that looks just like the pages of the final book (and for good reason, because the printers will use that file). A proofreader goes through the manuscript checking for spelling/typing errors, punctuation and so on. BBC Books run these two stages at the same time, but the books have separate proofreaders and copy editors. Then we all have a final read of the proofs to make sure we're happy and we sign off on them and they go to the printers.

All publishers have a house style, and one job at this stage is to make sure the book conforms to that. These can involve a set of quite idiosyncratic rules, and it's usually fairly mundane stuff about the use of dashes, the exact form that numbers and dates are expressed ('26 December 2008', not 'December 26th 2008', that kind of thing), the use of American spelling (Virgin had some quite bizarre rules about that, ones that probably made sense to someone). Consistency in place names (it's Pearl Harbor, for example - so a UK book could have a sentence that ran 'the Japanese attacked the harbour at Pearl Harbor') and titles (the rank isn't capitalised, the individual is, so the Brigadier is a brigadier).

Then there's all the grammar stuff that makes me glad I have a proofreader. Sometimes I've had fairly heated discussions about grammar. Proofreaders tend to want good grammar throughout a novel - which sounds like the sort of thing we should all want, but this has led to proofreaders in the past changing some of the dialogue I've written. Now, I want readers to be able to parse the sentences and stuff, but I think dialogue's allowed to be a little rougher ('a little more rough'?) than the narration. People don't speak grammatically. And sometimes the change of grammar can alter the sense of the sentence. A proofreader would make Mick Jagger sing 'I cannot get satisfaction'. Kate Orman has the best anecdote here - one of her proofreaders changed 'the spaceship left the planet's gravity well' to 'the spaceship left well the planet's gravity'. The way it should work is that the proofreader highlights every grammatical 'mistake', the editor and author decide whether to implement the change.

With *The Eyeless* there were no arguments.

The changes Cardiff wanted were very few and far between and almost all were incredibly minor. The thing that linked most of them was that they didn't want to pin down things the TV series hadn't pinned down - how the sonic screwdriver recharges, what the TARDIS defences can and can't do, how long the Doctor's been travelling the universe. There were notes on how they don't like referring to the person the Doctor travels with as an 'assistant' these days, and that there are some other words they're wary about. They took out a joke about shoe sizes, possibly because they didn't realise it was a joke (which is as good a reason as any for taking out a joke, of course).

In addition to those, I got a list of notes back from Steve on 4th September. Steve's developed a good ear for the tenth Doctor, and noted about a dozen places where he didn't think what I'd written sounded like something David Tennant would say. He'd altered one scene that was a flashback within a flashback within a flashback and so was hideously confusing. But there was nothing changed for being too gruesome, there was nothing major or dealbreaking at all. As with every stage, I wasn't presented with any of these things as a *fait accompli*, and we talked everything through and I persuaded Steve to change his mind about a few things, he persuaded me he was right about others.

To show how smooth this all was, we settled everything so quickly that Steve was able to go away and come back with typeset proofs on 9th September. As is the way of these things, we all noticed a few minor things that had somehow managed to elude us all up to this point, despite dozens of re-readings - an item that was described as 'featureless' on one page was 'covered in symbols' on the next, that kind of thing.

Editors have reasons for making suggestions and if a writer disagrees, his job is to work out why the editor thinks what they think. Both the writer and the editor should be able to back up their opinions, explain themselves. Often, an editor and writer agree what a scene should be trying to do, but disagree about the way to land the scene on that spot. It is possible for writers and editors to lose track of the fact they want the same thing, or for some pretty basic miscommunication to mess things up, although that's thankfully been an extraordinarily rare occurrence for me. I think the crucial thing to note here is that this stage of *The Eyeless* felt no different to the editing stage of any of my other books - it was a lot smoother than most, to be honest.

A lot of the online discussion about 'mistakes' or 'inconsistencies' or 'wrong turns' in either the books or the TV show just doesn't recognise that the writers and editors have endlessly discussed things. If a writer chooses to do something, he's almost always making a conscious choice not to do plenty of other things, things he's agonised about, talked through and so on for months, decisions that are influenced by often the weirdest things. The main influence for *Doctor Who* is, surely, time - my book came out on December 26th 2008. It had to be finished in time for that to take place. It's the same for television, only far moreso: actors have to be booked, sets built, costumes made and so on and so on.

So... 17th of September, that was it. The proofs had been corrected, the file went off to the printer. *The Eyeless* was done and out of my hands.

I received my author's copies on November 13th, hot off the press. From that first phone call to having a copy of the printed book in my hand, it had taken almost exactly a year.

It wasn't quite over, yet. On 16th of December, Michael Stevens at BBC Audio e-mailed and invited me to come up with a script for the audiobook version of *The Eyeless*. I gladly accepted. By coincidence, my *Time Hunter* novella, *The Winning Side*, was turned into an audiobook around the same time. It's unabridged, and read by Louise Jameson. (At the risk of sounding like an egomaniac, I'd like to mention that the way the lady who played Leela when I was growing up says my name, with really long As - 'Laaarrnce Paaarrkin' - makes me feel very, primally, happy.)

The Winning Side audio is about thirty thousand words, and takes up three discs. The *Doctor Who* audiobooks are two disc editions. BBC Audio needed me to abridge the book from 55,000 words to more like 22,000. We discussed readers from a fairly long list, and decided it would be one of two men - it was important, I thought, to know if a man or a woman would be reading.

Now, I thought I'd cut every last ounce of fat from the book, that not a word was wasted. So it was sobering going back into the document, intent on cutting two words out of every three. There were a couple of tricks, I realised - the reader would be doing different voices for the different characters, so I could drop all the 'the Doctor said' stuff. It soon occurred to me that the emotional stuff would be covered the same way

- so a line like " 'Really?' the Doctor said, angrily" could become "Really?" without any loss of signal.

This only carried me so far. I cut down some description, then merged and simplified a couple of incidents. After all my protestations that the beginning was paced just right, I realised I could cut great chunks of it and get to the story much faster.

That got me down to about 40,000 words.

Then it struck me that the typical script for a new series episode is about 13,000 words (it's amazing, in fact, that the writers have room to say anything at all in such a short space). I speculated that if I thought in terms of *The Eyeless* being a two-part TV story, it might help me with the pacing.

So, quite a radical reworking took place. I dramatically simplified the second half of the book. I killed Jeffip at the end of the first part, not towards the middle of the second. I cut as many subplots as I could get away with. I moved a couple of the action sequences around. I finally ended up needing to cut 150 words, and spent two hours trying to find adjectives to cull.

The final script is exactly 22,000 words long. The weird thing is that it's basically the same story. Listening to it, I wonder how many people would even realise it was cut down if it didn't say. There's a lesson for me, there: I really thought there wasn't a word wasted in the novel version.

Russell Tovey, Midshipman Frame in *Voyage of the Damned* and - more to the point - 'him out of *History Boys* and *Being Human'* was the reader. I've not heard *The Eyeless* audio at time of writing, but suspect I won't get that primal thrill when Russell Tovey says my name. Still, he's an up and coming star - so I'm hopeful that in years to come, one of my main claims to fame will be that he read one of my books.

UNMADE STORIES

I've pitched a number of *Doctor Who* stories over the years that haven't been made for various reasons. Usually, I can just tell the editor an idea I've had over the phone or in a short email. Editors know what other books they've got lined up and the direction they want to take the range, and they'll very quickly veto an idea if they don't like it. Others, they've asked to see worked up into synopses. Getting books turned down is all part of the game, and I've always had the attitude of profound gratitude whenever I'm commissioned, rather than harboured any resentment when I'm not. Besides, very often, an idea I've had can end up in another book, years down the line. More often, I've cannibalised little bits of these books to use in other books.

So... while I was writing *Just War*, I had an idea for a grim Hartnell historical called *The Gunpowder Plot*, but was told Gareth Roberts was writing *The Plotters*. Virgin didn't like the sound of the near-future story *The Last King of England* and commissioned *Cold Fusion* instead. *The Dying Days* was originally a Pertwee and UNIT story called *Cold War*. *Robot Safari* was originally a Tom and Romana Missing Adventure, which I think I may also have pitched as a Telos novella, and it eventually became the Benny novel *The Big Hunt* (although that meant there was no place for the K9 sex scene).

Iron Empire, my idea for a sequel to the *Doctor Who Weekly* comic strip *Iron Legion* has the distinction of being rejected by *DWM* (under two editors), Big Finish, Telos and BBC Books. If anyone from IDW's reading this, please get in touch.

Reprinted here are three proposals for the BBC. The first is the original pitch for what would become my first BBC Book, *The Infinity Doctors*. The second, *Warlords of Utopia*, started out as an Eighth Doctor Adventure for the "collapsing universe" arc that ran in 2002 before becoming a *Faction Paradox* novel. Finally we have *To Hold Back Death*, which was a quick and simple idea for a book in the slot after the Earth arc - when the Doctor had been stuck on Earth for a century.

I had other ideas for BBC Books. After finishing *The Infinity Doctors*, I was keen to write a Dalek novel. The BBC were a little reluctant, because the Nation estate wanted a fair amount of money for the rights to the Daleks. I was happy for that to come out of my advance - foolishly, in retrospect, I think. Anyway, my plan was that *Enemy of the Daleks* would have seen the Doctor, Fitz and Compassion fight the Daleks. Things proceeded, and I drew up a synopsis. The Nation estate then apparently approved the storyline (I had no direct contact with them), but the BBC decided they weren't so keen, and the project was dropped. A fair amount of the material including the Klade and Debbie, ended up in *Father Time*. A scene in which a woman gives birth to a Dalek wound up in my Big Finish play *I, Davros*.

Defence of the Realm was submitted after I'd finished *Father Time*, and saw the Doctor leading an army to protect a peaceful planet. I originally pitched a book called *Comeback* in 2002, and it ended up pretty much unchanged as *The Gallifrey Chronicles* in 2005.

The Infinity Doctors

Some historical notes on the version of *The Infinity Doctors* that you're about to read... as originally conceived, this was a fairly conventional Past Doctor Adventure that celebrated *Doctor Who*'s thirty-fifth anniversary. Steve Cole, the editor of the range, liked the alternative history interlude and the published book took that idea and ran with it. It owes a clear - if unconscious, at the time - debt to Alan Moore's Superman story 'For the Man Who Has Everything'. Reading it back, I'm surprised how much of this synopsis made it to the finished book.

There are a couple of ideas in this first draft storyline designed to open up the BBC Books a little bit - in their early stages (and note that I was writing this in May 1997), the books were standalone and very traditional. I came up with the Threwthicks as an English family who'd been friends of the Doctor over generations - the name's a pun on the expression 'through thick and thin'. If you've got this far into the book you're holding, the phrase 'the Robert Banks Stewart Doctor' will hold no mysteries. You'll note that the name of one of the baddies is something of a placeholder. Centro was an attempt to create a recurring big bad guy for the Doctor. His name is both an anagram of 'retcon' and, it turned out later, a bus company in Birmingham. It's a complete coincidence, but since I wrote this synopsis, the Superman baddy Brainiac has been revamped and reimagined until he's practically the same character. Centro is mentioned in one line of the published version of *The Infinity Doctors*.

*****

249

First draft storyline, May 18th 1997
by Lance Parkin

"Not even god can change the past" (Agathon, quoted by Aristotle in
The Nicomachean Ethics)

PRE-TITLES

An all-action prologue, as the Robert Banks Stewart Doctor ventures
deep under the Capitol in pursuit of his arch enemy Centro, the sentient
computer that has tried to gain access to the Matrix. The prologue features Patience.

PART ONE

We open on ancient Gallifrey, as crews - every one a hero - board a
mighty space fleet. The planet is in the depths of winter, the buildings are
in ruins. The past cannot be changed, but a glorious future can be forged.
Two captains discuss what they will soon be doing - unlike the lesser
races, Gallifreyans have no concept of 'divine intervention', they are
forced to create their own miracles.

On contemporary Earth, Badman dreams and he remembers. He
remembers his beautiful wife, he remembers their life together, their
plans for the future. He remembers the car accident in which she died.
He wakes up alongside his wife. It's all been a terrible dream.

It's 1998. The Doctor is walking along a stony beach on the Cumbrian
coast. K9 is following him. They and Romana are spending time with the
Threwthicks, a family who are among the Doctor's oldest friends. Their
youngest son is rather enamored of Romana, and the two are further up
the beach.

The Doctor confides to K9 that his dreams have been disturbed of late.
There is a black hole in his memory, and mocking laughter. Something
fearful from his past. 'You should always live in the present, K9'.

Tea with the Threwthicks is a chance to catch up with old times. The
Doctor and Romana are searching for the third segment of the Key to
Time. Threwthick is a quantum physicist working for Badman at a scientific institute based in a semi-ruined castle. Badman has dedicated his life
to his science following the death of his wife twenty years earlier. He has
won all sorts of prizes and awards for his thinking.

Romana suspects that the Segment is inside the Institute. 'A mysterious castle, surrounded by an electric fence, run by an obsessed scientist
- I'd be very disappointed if it wasn't', the Doctor replies. She wants to

go that evening, but the Doctor says it can wait until the morning. He wants to spend the evening among friends and forget about the cosmic battles.

Romana has very little time for the Doctor's angst and introspection and so she sneaks off on her own, and gets into the Institute.

She enters a room full of alien-looking machinery, clearly far beyond the capabilities of twentieth century Earth. It's a time tunnel, capable of travel into the past. As she explores, a humanoid shape detaches itself from the machine. She turns to face one of the Doctor's oldest enemies: Centro!

Centro captures Romana, and begins scanning her mind. The Doctor is telepathically aware of this - Centro dispatches a pair of androids to delay his arrival. Centro quizzes Romana about the Guardians - but this is before the Doctor has told her about them. He learns about how Gallifrey got its power - Omega's experiments.

The Doctor defeats the androids, and arrives to confront Centro.

Centro is clearly planning to go back into the past - yes: Badman wants to go back and save his wife's life. Centro has promised him this, and together they have spent ten years preparing for this moment. You can't change history, the Doctor says, his wife died. Centro cackles, and readies an experiment.

Romana is locked into a box, along with a phial containing a highly radioactive material. There is a fifty percent chance that the phial will open, killing her instantly with the radiation. The Doctor is horrified - what is Centro trying to prove?

The experiment begins.

INTERLUDE

The Gallifreyan fleet has arrived in the Ao system, Omega detonates the star.

The universe is fractured, discontinuous. Parallel universes pour out, superimposing themselves on our universe. It is chaos, with Omega at the centre.

PART TWO

The experiment concludes. The box is opened.

Romana is alive - and dead. The box contains both a living Romana and a dead one. Both quantum states have been made to co-exist.

Centro is as ecstatic as his programming allows. The Agathon Equation has been discovered. The Doctor is impressed - 'Centro is saving himself the bother of looking for the Key to Time, he's just building his own'. It explains why the Tracer has led them here.

Now Centro and Badman can go back and save Badman's wife. History won't change, not as such. His wife will die, as she always did, but she will also not die. The net effect is that history will change.

But the Doctor points out that Centro needs power. The full capacity of the Institute's nuclear reactor is needed just to duplicate one particle. Centro and Badman set the nuclear reactor to overload to delay the Doctor and Romana and travel back in time.

The Doctor sets about deactivating the reactor, while musing about where Centro has gone. To save Badman's wife, Romana replies. No - that wouldn't interest Centro. Centro has been helping Badman for twenty years, so he must have arrived on Earth back then. And if he arrived, he must have come in a spaceship. Any common or garden spaceship capable of interstellar travel has an immense power source - that's where Centro has gone.

They head to the TARDIS.

The TARDIS arrives on an oil rig in 1978, an hour before Centro and Badman. It's a base under siege - mysterious killings, unexplained power failures. The Doctor is suspected of the murders. Blah blah. The 1978 Centro is responsible. His damaged ship has come down in the North Sea, and he is attempting to recover the craft before it sinks.

Badman and Centro arrive from 1998. They corner the Doctor. If his wife survives, then history changes and Centro won't get his time tunnel. 'Perfectly logical, Doctor' Centro says. Badman and the Doctor manage to beat off Centro, who escapes into the depths of the rig. Badman corners the Doctor. 'I'm not really like this', he pleads. 'I wasn't like this before my wife died. No obsession, no killing. Please, if you can, than stop it from happening. What harm can it do?'. The Doctor saves her.

But as the Doctor is doing so, Centro from 1998 is downloading all his files to Centro 1978. All Badman's research is preserved.

Centro finds another technician that will save him, makes another pact. All is going to plan.

INTERLUDE

A rescue mission is attempted for Omega. A proto-TARDIS skims the Event Horizon, but it is pulled in. It tries to escape, but it can't. It extrudes itself, turning itself inside-out, but it can't escape. It pulls itself out, stretching until it is a tube over a light year long but only a hundred miles in diameter. All the time it is screaming, all the time the chaotic forces are spreading, the parallel universes are merging with ours.

Rassilon, wearing the Sash, stabilises the black hole. Face to face, he seals Omega into a vault.

The 'time energies' have infused the Gallifreyans with great power, the black hole will provide Gallifrey with energy, the fractures in Time are the Time Vortex, through which the new Lords of Time will travel.

PART THREE

The TARDIS lands back on the Cumbrian coast. But this is an alternative present and things have changed - the Institute isn't there, and there is a new family living where the Threwthicks did. The Thynne family have always lived here, they are old friends of the Doctor. They even have K9. The Doctor quizzes K9 about his memories.

The Foundation have a radio telescope nearby. They are the world's foremost experts in black holes and quantum wormholes.

Romana reminds the Doctor that Centro seemed fascinated by Gallifreyan history. He must be trying to locate Omega's Needle, the remains of the rescue mission. If he can harness the black hole, he would have the infinite power source that he needs to power the Agathon Equations.

Centro captures Romana, and they travel to Omega's Needle. The Doctor and K9 are close behind in the TARDIS.

Omega's Needle is an astonishing place, a place of howling winds, supporting a strip of a biosphere a hundred million miles or so from the black hole. A Gothic nightmare Rama, *Babylon 5* meets *Lungbarrow*. The ghosts of parallel universes, alternative futures and possible pasts flit around the corridors. It's a dreamlike, Lacanian space, but solid, real. The world is screaming and singing.

The TARDIS lands here. Centro is trying to locate the control room area, and is helped by an army of lionman mercenaries who have come here in their war fleet.

The Doctor is captured by the Priests, monks who have set up a monastery on the Needle, thinking that God lives here. Well, muses the Doctor, if God was going to anywhere he'd probably live somewhere like this. No, you don't understand, the Priests tell him. God is behind a specific door deep within the structure. They take the Doctor there, to the heart of their temple. A heavy ebony door, without a lock. So the door opens, and God is literally behind it? The Priests don't know. What do you mean you don't know? The Priests have never opened the door. Because what would happen to their faith if they opened the door and God *wasn't* there?

The Doctor, Romana and K9 find the control room and burst in, but it is too late. Centro is sitting in the Command Chair. It rotates to face the Time Lords:

The war fleet has vanished, wiped out of existence. Centro has contacted the 'God' in the machine, it's Omega, trapped in the antimatter universe beyond the door the Priests are guarding. Between them they've built the Agathon Engine, a device that allows paradoxes and for the past to be changed.

'I control the universe, now, Doctor!'

INTERLUDE

The Doctor wakes up on Gallifrey, where he's a tutor at the Academy. He never left. He's a widower and grandfather to Susan. The Master is still his best friend, a leader on the High Council. One of his students, Romana, is fascinated by Omega and is studying Omega's Needle. The Doctor is gradually coming to understand the Agathon equations.

He goes to steal a TARDIS to travel to Omega's Needle. Romana tries to stop him, but he kills her... if he's right, he can easily change history to fix that.

He sets off to Omega's Needle, the Master in hot pursuit...

PART FOUR

The Doctor triumphantly reasserts himself into history.

'I control the universe, now, Doctor!'

'No you don't.'

The Doctor demonstrates with Skaro, which he destroys, undestroys, destroys, undestroys, destroys (oops - it's still dead!). If you can so that to a planet on a mere whim, then what about one individual? Why shed tears when someone dies if they can be brought back, why cheer on your favourite team when if they lose they can also win? What's the point of controlling a universe without meaning, where nothing of any consequence ever happens? Centro and Omega have created a universe from the opposite of matter - doesn't matter!

Of course you *can* rewrite history, but you *shouldn't*. As long as the Agathon Engine exists, nothing is real. Omega is trapped by his omnipotence, just as he was trapped in the anti-matter universe.

Forsake your powers, the Doctor urges, become a man again, resume your place in the universe. But Omega quotes Faust: "Think'st thou that I who saw the face of God and tasted the eternal joys of heaven am not tormented with ten thousand hells in being deprived of everlasting bliss." Faking a real life would be just as much a sham. The Doctor has destroyed all Omega's hopes, condemned him to a meaningless existence. Now there is only one freedom left to him. Raging, energy crackling around him, Omega begins to destroy the entire multiverse, himself included.

The Doctor rushes to try and disconnect the Agathon machinery. The Doctor syphons off matter from the black hole, and suddenly there isn't enough to maintain gravitational collapse. It goes supernova. Omega kills the Doctor, with a massive blast of energy.

Destructive energy is building up around Omega's Needle.

Romana drags the Doctor's body back to the TARDIS, where he regenerates into Geoffrey Bayldon.

CENTRO

Centro is a machine organism, one of the oldest creatures in the universe. It is a logical creature, although it recognises the value of some emotional responses, such as curiosity and fear.

For millions of years, Centro has sought to increase its scientific knowledge. This it does either by travelling to worlds and raiding their databases, or by conducting its own experiments. It is a scientific connoisseur, often travelling halfway across the universe to observe a rare particle or element. His knowledge is vast - when resources allow, he can build spacecraft that are amongst the most advanced in the universe.

He has a full working knowledge of temporal theory, but is not capable of time travel.

Gradually, Centro has formulated the theory that there is a Supreme Observer, what we would call God. Centro has spent the last few millennia attempting to prove the existence of such a being, meeting it, possibly even usurping it.

Over the years, it has worn many robot bodies - currently it is a tall (seven foot) humanoid, sleek and lethal. He can download and duplicate his own consciousness. Centro's fingers are sharp as claws, precise as surgical instruments. He can scan organic minds, 'reading' them.

Warlords of Utopia

Warlords of Utopia was eventually published as a *Faction Paradox* novel by Mad Norwegian Press. It's one of the favourite things I've written, and I'm not saying that just because Mad Norwegian also published the book you're holding.

I'd had the original idea for the book - 'all the parallel worlds where Rome never fell versus all the parallel universes where Hitler won WWII' - years before, probably around 1998, but didn't really know what to do with it, or how to actually tell the story. It's the classic example of a story that's just too *big* to tell in any meaningful way.

When the EDAs were looking for parallel universe stories, I dusted the idea off, tried to get it to fit the *Doctor Who* format. It was originally called *The Wars to End War*, but very quickly got its final title. The synopsis reprinted here has veered away from the original idea a little. It started out as a parallel universe version of the 'Earth arc' books - a history book that covered the course of a century, in the style of *I, Claudius* - but that didn't really work as a *Doctor Who* story. The solution in the final version just took the *I, Claudius* parallel one step further, by having the history narrated by one of the central characters. I'm including this version because it's so different from the finished book.

*****

In brief: *An epic war story - imagine the opening reel of Saving Private Ryan suddenly turning into the opening reel of Gladiator. In the splintered multiverse post-Time Zero, all the parallel universes where Rome never fell are at war with all the parallel universes where the Nazis won the Second World War.*

This is part of Sabbath's plan - he's come to think that 'protecting' Earth should mean taking the opportunity the splintering of time presents to reassemble an optimised history of Earth. And, in his judgement, the perfect human society is either classical Rome or fascism.

The Sabbath character guide says that the day will come when Sabbath will realise, however reluctantly, that he has to kill the Doctor. What it doesn't say is that the Doctor could reach the same conclusion. Here, the Doctor organises a resistance against both the Nazis and the Romans, and comes to realise that he has assembled the perfect force to take the fight to Sabbath, and that with the universe actually collapsing, the stakes are too high - he has to take Sabbath down. For the good of the universe, he takes the fight to Sabbath's territory, and it's a devastating attack.

1. The TARDIS is suffering from power fluctuations and materialises in a muddy forest. The Doctor doesn't know where or when, but the crew quickly find themselves attacked by a Nazi patrol. It becomes clear that this group of soldiers is scared, and beating a retreat. They've also been affected by the power drain - their radios don't work. And then, suddenly - ancient Roman cavalry charges at them, all but massacring them. The TARDIS crew survive, as do a couple of soldiers. Together they make it back to the road, and safety. It's then they realise they are in England, 1963 - it's twenty years since the Nazis won the war.

2. At the stately home that doubles as the regional administration centre, the Doctor meets an English scientist, Julian, who has drawn up the parallel worlds theory. Together the Doctor and Julian explain it to a group of local commanders - history branches off at turning points, but there are patterns, and it's only natural that a great many universes have scenarios where Hitler won, or where Rome never fell. It would be odd to have both - and the history books here say that Rome fell in this timeline, right on schedule. The Romans are visitors to this universe ... yet barely seem more advanced from the Romans at the time of Augustus. The problems with the timelines are getting worse, the barriers between the splinters of time are breaking down.

The Doctor gets the very clear sense that some of these military commanders are already very well aware of parallel universes. He keeps his suspicions to himself.

Anji and Julian are attracted to each other.

3. There's a sense of the calm before the storm. The Nazis prepare for a new assault from the Roman army. Within hours, the stately home is attacked - but this time by technically advanced Romans in plastic armour and carrying laser guns. The Doctor, his companions and Julian double back into the woods and discover what Julian christens the T-Boat, the vehicle the Romans use to travel between universes. It's like a trireme.

The TechnoRomans return to their ship. The Doctor, Fitz, Anji and Julian are onboard as the trireme transfers between universes. They briefly glimpse TechnoRome, a timeline where Rome never fell, there was just two thousand years of uninterrupted progress and Roman supremacy. Then the T-boat lands ...

4. ... in a parallel where the asteroid that killed the dinosaurs was sixty-five million years late. It finally crashed into the Gulf of Mexico three weeks ago, destroying civilisation. Nuclear winter, sulphuric acid falling

as snow, and that's after the tidal waves and molten rock raining down has done its worst. It's hell on Earth - and the perfect place for a secret rendezvous between the TechnoRomans and their sponsor.

The Doctor sends his companions out to see what's going on, while he investigates the time machine. He discovers it's driven by the same 'frozen time' that's been cropping up in recent books.

The Doctor is discovered... by the TechnoRoman physicist, Julius, the exact double of Julian.

5. Meanwhile, Julian is getting sick. Anji is very concerned - the first hint Fitz has that she fancies him. He doesn't have much time to tease her, though, because ...

The *Jonah* is waiting for the TechnoRomans in the ruins of this London, where dinosaurs fought gladiators in a vast arena. Sabbath is here, with a robot bodyguard and his chief of staff, one of the carnivorous monkeys. Sabbath is supplying the TechnoRomans with the technology to cross between universes.

The TechnoRomans try to double-cross Sabbath, ambushing him for his shipment of frozen time. The chief of staff is killed, but Sabbath fights back. The Doctor's companions hurry back to the T-Boat. The Doctor steals it, transfers out of this universe, and maroons the TechnoRomans, who are massacred. But the Doctor has left Fitz behind, and he becomes a prisoner of Sabbath.

6. The two Julian / Juliuses meet, and are suitably astonished. The Doctor is very concerned about Julian, but as soon as they are underway, he quickly recovers. Was it something in the atmosphere there? Something to do with the proximity of his double? Neither theory adds up. Julius is also a physicist. In his universe, the T-boat technology has been understood for centuries. He explains that to travel between universes, you need to cross a 'dimensional bridge'. A person can only cross one dimension bridge. Cross two, you become sick, and die in a matter of days. Cross three and you die within minutes.

The bridges come and go, in a way the TechnoRomans don't fully understand. The Doctor nods - of course: if the TechnoRomans could freely travel across all the universes then they would have conquered the multiverse centuries ago.

Julius agrees. Ideas can be transmitted, though. TechnoRome has colonised many parallels, who in turn have colonised many parallels by using the same technology. The Emperor of TechnoRome commands a farflung empire of over a hundred Earths where Rome never fell. History falls in many patterns - but in almost all of them Germania and Rome are bitter enemies. The most savage battles happen in parallels with a bridge to Nazi timelines.

Julian notes that the Doctor and Anji crossed at least three bridges, and they're fine.

Back at the *Jonah*, Sabbath has a job for Fitz - his chief of staff was killed in the attack. He needs someone with Fitz's experience of time travel to take his place - there are very few people with the ability to travel freely across the multiverse. Even Bowman, Sabbath's robot, can only manage it by building himself a body on each new world.

7. The Doctor decides that they should go to TechnoRome. Julius guides the T-boat to his villa, and he and the Doctor quickly take the advanced technology offline to avoid detection.

The bridges are the key to this. They seem to be artificial, so someone built them, and as Sabbath can use them, he's the obvious candidate. That means Sabbath is intentionally linking up the parallel Earths.

The Doctor sets about building a device that can detect the bridges.

Sabbath briefs Fitz - they are going to an advanced parallel, where the Nazis won the war. It's a timeline where all the exotic 'wunderwaffen' were developed, and they all worked. Nazi jet bombers and guided rockets razed London to the ground, the war wheels rolled into England through the Nazi Channel Tunnel.

Sabbath has recovered the TARDIS - wherever the Doctor is now, he's not going anywhere.

8. The Doctor locates the bridge to TechnoNazi and detects the *Jonah*'s arrival there. They quickly launch the T-boat and head there.

The Nazi science council explain their achievements to Sabbath - they have built machines that can analyse DNA - racial purity will be achieved within five years, across all the timelines that TechnoNazi controls. Their experiments on prisoners are also proving successful at researching the 'sickness' that happens when you cross more than one bridge. Sabbath doesn't look happy - that area of research is strictly forbidden.

Suddenly the facility is attacked - a small group of resistance fighters has broken through the defences. There are pockets of resistance, but only a very few. The T-boat arrives in the middle of the firefight, but it's very one-sided, and the resistance members are captured. They are scheduled for execution, live, broadcast around the world.

The Doctor stages a daring rescue, flying the T-boat in and freeing the prisoners. And it's broadcast live on television ...

Sabbath is not impressed by this universe. The differences in DNA between Nazis and what they think of as the 'lesser races' is negligible. He suggests that he's capable of erasing this timeline. Fitz is horrified - how is that different from the genocide of the Nazis? Sabbath stays his hand - how indeed?

He'll think about it. In the meantime, now the Doctor's shown himself, Sabbath can track him down ...

9. At Julius' villa, the rescued resistance fighters aren't used to relaxation. The Doctor suggests that the real fight is about to begin. He's spending a lot of time in the lab. The others talk amongst themselves. War between the Nazi and Roman parallels is inevitable, and the result is uncertain.

Fitz is sneaking around, looking for clues about the dimensional bridge, and discovers that Sabbath has located the Doctor.

10. In the middle of the night, the TechnoRoman authorities attack. Anji and company are unprepared, but the resistance fighters are used to it, and put up a good fight. The authorities are just after the Doctor, though. He is dragged from his lab and taken to the Emperor.

The others escape in the T-boat.

The Doctor is brought before the Emperor. Sabbath has put out the order to find the Doctor. So why is Sabbath so interested in him? The Doctor doesn't answer. But the Emperor knows - Sabbath is scared. And the Emperor finally has some leverage over Sabbath, who controls the supplies of frozen time, so controls T-boat technology.

The Emperor shows what he and Sabbath have been working on - a fleet of T-boats. A massive armada capable of conquering any know variation in history.

But one of the Emperor's palace slaves is an agent of Sabbath. He reports back to his master.

Bowman is surprised that the Emperor is betraying them, he'd always been one of Sabbath's most loyal followers. Sabbath, though, seems to have been expecting the news.

11. The T-boat in which Anji and co escaped is being chased by a group of Roman T-boats. One manages to get alongside - a battle ensues.

The Doctor's mind is racing. The armada needn't be used for conquest ... but it can't fall into Sabbath's hands. This is clearly what Sabbath is using the various timelines for - as arms factories, supply routes for ... whatever it is he's planning. Sabbath's committed to the defence of the Earth, perhaps these are to man the barricades.

Sabbath arrives back in TechnoNazi ... and we discover that this universe has built an armada, too. He assembles a meeting of the Nazi High

Command - but instead of attending, he detonates a bomb there. He's the leader of the Nazi universes, now.

12. A Roman boarding party breaks into Anji's T-boat.
The Emperor tells the Doctor he'll spare his friends' lives if he investigates the dimensional bridges. Like the Doctor, he suspects that Sabbath controls the bridges, he doesn't just predict them. The Doctor is keen to research the bridges for his own reasons, so is happy to comply.
The Roman boarding party don't kill Anji, much to her surprise.
The Doctor sets to work examining the dimension bridges. It's very advanced technology, surely beyond the abilities of Sabbath (it is, although we don't learn this yet, Dalek technology, adapted from their time corridors). The Doctor is working away when he detects a massive breach between dimensions ...
The Nazi armada of T-boats arrives, and starts bombarding Rome, Sabbath at their head.

13. The Romans and Nazis are technically matched. As dawn breaks, the vast city of Rome is under siege, surrounded by a massive Nazi army which is digging in.
From his command post, Sabbath checks the intelligence reports - Rome is cut off. He's made his demands known, he just wants the Doctor. Fitz and Bowman survey the massed ranks of the army ... and discover a nuclear missile convoy. Sabbath's Nazi commanders have a back-up plan.
Rome is being bombarded, its citizens are panicking. The Doctor works with the Emperor to try to calm things down, get people to safety and get the defences worked out. Sabbath's forces attacked the armada first - they didn't damage the ships, but destroyed the barracks and supply lines. The pilots are dead, buried under rubble or unable to get to their ships.
Both the Roman and Nazi forces are suffering equipment failures and power cuts.
The news comes through - enemy tanks are pouring through a breach in the city walls.

14. There is mass panic in Rome, millions of citizens fleeing, jamming the roads, making it impossible for the Roman army to get to the enemy positions.
The Doctor is back in his laboratory, trying to crack the secret of the dimensional bridges. He learns that they use a vast amount of energy - which is drained from the surroundings. They are incredibly dangerous.

Staying open for a few minutes is pretty bad (it explains the power drain in chapter one). But Sabbath has kept the bridge between this universe and the TechnoNazi one open for over a day, now. The Doctor watches, horrified, as patches of his lab just start disintegrating.

Sabbath follows his army into the precincts of Rome... but the T-boats sent after Anji return, scattering the invading army, rallying the Roman army.

15. The spearhead of Sabbath's forces have reached the palace, where there is fierce fighting.

Anji, together with Julian, Julius and the resistance fighters, as well as some Roman troops cut off from their commanders, they pick their way across the city to the T-boat docks.

Sabbath plants himself on the Roman throne, kicking aside the body of the Emperor. He is the master of both the Nazi and Roman universes - hundreds of parallel timelines, all his. He opens a dimension bridge in this throne room to the Nazi command bunker, where the *Jonah* is docked. But something is wrong - objects are starting to disintegrate.

16. The Doctor is dragged in. He tells Sabbath what's happening - the dimensional bridges are draining a vast amount of energy. The whole system is unstable - thousands of timelines all trying to sustain themselves using the energy of the original, pre-*Time Zero* universe. They have to collapse the universes down to one again.

Sabbath senses a trick - the Doctor wants to stop him controlling the hundreds of Earths. He crosses back to the Nazi universe, but that's disintegrating, too. The Doctor couldn't be responsible for that - he wasn't even in the same universe. Sabbath returns to the Jonah with Fitz and Bowman.

Sabbath wrestles with the controls of the dimensional bridge. The Doctor tells him that they have to work together, and quickly. The Doctor and Sabbath team up, one on each side of the bridge. Energy from both universes is draining into the bridge. There is only enough power to sustain one timeline, the other one is going to be sacrificed.

Sabbath decides to sacrifice the timeline with the Doctor in it. Fitz attacks him, though, knocking him out. The Doctor screams at him that they need Sabbath to operate the controls.

Things are reaching a crescendo and it's too late. The universes collapse...

17. The Doctor wakes up, Sabbath is right next to him, just struggling to his feet. Everything is calm, they are in some neutral hanger area. They

think they've saved the day ... until a guard wearing a fusion of Nazi and Roman uniform gives Sabbath a fascist salute 'Heil Caesar!'.

Anji catches up with Julius... who has merged with Julian (making them 'Julianus'). They look out at the T-boat armada - one force, now, a vast merged Roman-Nazi fleet.

Fitz and the Doctor look out over the city... it's a hybrid of all the worst features of Rome with all the worst features of Nazi Germany. The ultimate dystopia... and now it's the one, true timeline.

18. Anji soon realises Julianus' mind is cracking under the strain of being two people.

Fitz and the Doctor are out in the streets, and it's clear that Julianus' pain is being mirrored by a lot of people - this universe just doesn't add up, the history is an insane patchwork. The whole thing is just... well... wrong.

Sabbath revels in 'his' universe, unaware of the problems.

The Doctor assembles an attack squad - they can storm the palace, take control of the dimensional bridge on board the Jonah.

19. Where Eagles Dare - the Doctor leads a commando raid, Anji and Fitz at his side.

They send the main group to the T-boat armada.

After much derring-do, the Doctor, Anji, Fitz and Julianus make it to the *Jonah* as Sabbath tries to make his escape.

Outside, the universe is collapsing into chaos.

The Doctor and company confront Sabbath... Sabbath says he has the upper hand, the Doctor's time has past. He's reached the conclusion that the Doctor has to die, before he does permanent harm to his plans.

The Doctor smiles, and presses the detonator in his pocket - and the explosives the commandos placed in the T-boat armada go off, utterly destroying Sabbath's fleet. The burning wreckage collapses onto Sabbath's palace.

Sabbath calls in his monkeys. An army of carnivorous apes pour through a dimensional bridge.

20. Julianus holds the monkeys off single-handedly while the Doctor, Anji and Fitz disconnect the dimensional bridge, and Fitz gets it to the TARDIS.

When they return, the bridge is closed, all the bridges are closed... but Julianus is dead.

Anji's furious, and points a gun at Sabbath's chest. Sabbath laughs - it's a Smith and Wesson, and she's had her six. Anji notes that in the timeline where this gun was made, the Smith and Wesson has seven chambers. 'Symbolise this!'

She blows a hole in Sabbath's chest, straight through the heart.

Fitz gets the dimensional bridge machine into the TARDIS.

The Doctor grabs her - how dare she? This is Sabbath's way, not theirs. They are better than him, if they win this simply because they have the better guns, then they haven't won at all.

He hurries to Sabbath. Which heart has he still got? Sabbath's coughing up blood, but manages to say 'yours'. Then they have a chance. The Doctor teaches Sabbath a Time Lordy way of controlling the flow of blood, to stem the bleeding. Sabbath has lost blood, he's weak, but he'll live.

Sabbath is defiant - he'd have let the Doctor die.

The Doctor smiles and asks him again whose heart he's got in his chest. Sabbath: 'yours'. Is this leading to some sappy remark about how as long as the Doctor's heart beats in his chest, there is hope for Sabbath? The Doctor looks him right in the eye. No, the Doctor whispers, it means the next time they meet, he'll take back what's his and nothing in the universe will stop him, because what Sabbath wants is wrong, and has to be fought.

The Doctor and Anji leave, and Sabbath lies on the floor in a pool of his own blood, acutely aware of the heart beating in his chest.

The Doctor, Anji and Fitz are in the TARDIS, monitoring the situation. The Doctor is pale. It's all gone wrong.

Fitz tries to cheer him up - Sabbath's had a setback. They've got through worse than this.

The Doctor shakes his head.

'Don't you understand? There's no way out of this. We've lost.'

TO BE CONTINUED ...

*****

TO HOLD BACK DEATH

by Lance Parkin

This Eighth Doctor Adventure would follow on directly from *Escape Velocity*.

Dumb Hollywood Pitch... Edge of Destruction meets Event Horizon - a haunted house movie, set entirely within the confines of the TARDIS.

The Doctor and his companions are trapped aboard the TARDIS, unable to fathom its mysteries, none of them trusting each other. The ship is in flight, heading to an unknown destination, with an unknown ETA. The Doctor and Anji can't believe how little Fitz knows, bearing in mind that he's travelled with the Doctor for so long - he can't even remember what 'TARDIS' stands for. Fitz, in turn, blames the Doctor and feels put upon - he might not have much knowledge, but at least he has some idea of what's going on. Anji is still mourning Davy, and just wants things to go back to the way they were. All three feel trapped and tense - as well they should.

Then it becomes clear that there is something sinister going on. The regulars blame each other - there is mounting tension as a series of incidents of sabotage start to escalate into attempts on their lives. Now, the Doctor and his companions realise they can't trust each other. One of them is responsible...

The tone is that of a haunted house movie - claustrophobia, paranoia, distrust. There are a lot of corners where evil could be lurking, and the regulars are trapped. We get to see nooks and crannies of the TARDIS, but everywhere is shadowy and sinister.

Although they come to suspect the TARDIS itself of causing the nightmares and malfunctions (Fitz knows it's sentient, he knows there are telepathic circuits), it gradually becomes clear that there's another presence on board. The Master, freed from the Eye of Harmony, trying to take control of the Doctor and his TARDIS. The Master has the answers they need: he can fly the ship, he knows who the Doctor is... he may even be able to go back to save Davy. He is Satan, offering temptations to each of the crew in turn, setting them against each other - and when that fails, just trying to kill them.

During the course of the adventure, the new regular cast get to know each other, and go from distrust to a functioning team when they join forces to defeat the Master. The story ends with the Doctor sealing the Master into the depths of the TARDIS - leaving them with a smaller TARDIS interior, like the one in the Hartnell years.

The book ends as the TARDIS lands... ready for the next adventure.

RATIONALE

A lot of SF shows have an episode early on that concentrates on the regulars - *Doctor Who* had [insert name for Serial C here], *TNG* had *The Naked Now*. It reaffirms who the characters are by seeing them in extremis, it sets up the group dynamic. At the end of *Escape Velocity*, there are still loose ends - what does the Doctor know, how is Anji affected by her boyfriend's death, what does Fitz remember? What has changed, and what remains the same?

The other SF cliché I'm, ahem, 'deconstructing' is that of the Evil Double. Let's define the new Doctor by seeing his traditional antithesis, the Master. In *The TV Movie* he was trapped in the TARDIS - he's presumably been trapped all this time - including his own century of confinement as the TARDIS regrew. Let's show how things have moved on from the Doctor we saw in *The TV Movie* by returning, in part, to the same territory. (As a side issue, this adventure also explains how the TARDIS can function with the 'real' Eye of Harmony destroyed. The answer is 'it just does'.)

It'll be quite unlike any of the other books - a cast of four, told in almost real time, in one location. It is also the only chance to do this in the EDAs before new normal service is resumed. It's the last night before a new dawn.

CONTAINS SPOILERS (FITZ'S POEM)

These are the original lyrics for Fitz's song in *The Gallifrey Chronicles*. Justin Richards, my editor, objected on the grounds it would spoil a lot of movies for a lot of people. So, be warned:

'Contains Spoilers'

I've travelled to the past, sweetheart,
And I've been to the future, too.
I'm back, you didn't wait for me,
But my darling I don't feel blue.

I'm not surprised you left me, girl:
Your future I already knew.
So have a happy time with him.
Wouldn't take that away from you.

To make you pay for what you did,
Here's what I am going to do:
I know you love the movies, girl,
So I'll spoil every one for you.

Kevin Spacey's the bad guy, love,
That's in *Suspects* and *Seven*, too.
It's Drew's bloke in *Charlie's Angels*.
And it's Scrappy in *Scooby Doo*.

That's no girl in *The Crying Game*,
You see her penis? That's the clue.
Planet of the Apes? You live there,
Oh you maniacs, (that means you).

Bruce and Nicole are really ghosts,
And J-Lo dies not halfway through
Data's killed off in *Nemesis*
Just like Spock was in *Star Trek II*.

There aren't monsters in *The Village*,
Established nineteen eighty-two.
The Bride had Bill's baby, kiddo,
And what he says just ain't true.

Darth Vader is Luke's dad, all right,
And he also kills Mace Windu.
Sirius dies in one of them,
But still does a sequel or two.

You've left me, but no hard feelings.
Hope you enjoyed this sneak preview.
You've moved on in your life, so I
Won't spoil its twist ending for you.